RANDOM SOULS

RANDOM
SOULS

DEANNA RUTLEDGE

*"Don't be surprised at the defects in good people.
God leaves weaknesses in all of us."*
- Francois de Fenelon

WestBow
PRESS
A DIVISION OF THOMAS NELSON

WestBow Press books may be ordered through booksellers or by contacting:

WestBow Press
A Division of Thomas Nelson
1663 Liberty Drive
Bloomington, IN 47403
www.westbowpress.com
1-(866) 928-1240

Because of the dynamic nature of the Internet, any Web addresses or links contained in this book may have changed since publication and may no longer be valid. The views expressed in this work are solely those of the author and do not necessarily reflect the views of the publisher, and the publisher hereby disclaims any responsibility for them.

ISBN: 978-1-4497-0535-0 (sc)
ISBN: 978-1-4497-0534-3 (e)

Library of Congress Control Number: 2010935753

Printed in the United States of America

WestBow Press rev. date: 10/28/2010

*For Jay and Emily
who, young as they are, understand
that God is always at work.*

*And for William,
the love of my life, who never, ever,
gave up hope.*

A NOTE FROM THE AUTHOR

Random Souls concerns a troubled church and how God makes Himself known in it, despite its circumstances. It is set in Honolulu, Hawaii. It is *not* about an actual church that exists or has ever existed there. All characters are entirely fictional. I chose the Hawaii setting because that's where I live, and because it allowed me to create characters I felt would appeal to a wide audience.

Sadly, struggling churches and their divisive issues are all too familiar to many of us. Over the years, my husband and I have ministered, to a greater or lesser extent, in dozens of them all across the mainland U.S. and Hawaii. For the purposes of this narrative I chose a few adverse situations I felt were common to many of these congregations.

However, there are other, much more positive factors that are also common to the body of Christ: the fact that God is an ever-present help, that His heart is always set toward restoration, that He does not treat us as we deserve but with grace and mercy quite *un*deserved. And it is this firm belief that is at the heart of the book you are about to read.

MAHALO NUI!

I would like to extend a heartfelt *malaho nui* to those who took the time to encourage me in the writing of this manuscript, especially those who made valuable suggestions: Diana Agor, Leslie Corpuz, Malia Elliot, Pastor Bill at KUC, Pastor Marv Norlien, and Jean Tsuda, And I would like to thank all the folks at WestBow Press who were so helpful in bringing this manuscript to print. A lifelong dream has come true for me

Chapter One

Jason could not figure out what was wrong. He had listened to Hazel talk non-stop for nearly two hours, but the young schoolteacher had digressed into so many side issues and repeated herself so often, he doubted if they had made any actual progress at all. His fault, of course. It wasn't like him to let people ramble on aimlessly. Yet, he had let it happen. But why?

The truth was, he sincerely loved to hear people talk about themselves. In fact, he normally became so engrossed in the problems of whoever he was counseling that he lost all track of time. But today, something had niggled insistently at the back of his mind throughout the entire session. Was there some place he was supposed to be? Something he had forgotten to do? He didn't know. At one point, he had glanced over at his appointment book. Nothing there. Then why this unusual inability to concentrate? Why was it as though red lights were flashing on and off the whole time the young woman was sitting there pouring out her desperate tale? Why did he feel so uncomfortable? Was he coming down with something? Was it those eggs, maybe, that he had cooked this morning? He hadn't checked the date on the carton and Nancy was always reminding him that if he wasn't careful…

"And then she started yelling: *I don't care. I just don't care!*" Hazel cried, interrupting his thoughts. " Oh, and Pastor Jason, that just broke my *heart*! It was like…" she furiously groped for words,

1

"...a turning point in my life. A kind of epiphany, I guess you would say."

Jason was appalled! He had totally blanked out. Who was she talking about now--the sister who had taken away her boyfriend, or the cousin who had unrepentantly totaled her car? Or, wait a minute, wasn't there a girlfriend, Jackie or something like that, a former roommate who had stolen her journal and posted excerpts on MySpace for the whole world to see?

"And then they all started making noise and I found myself shouting at them. Shouting! Imagine! Poor kids, it wasn't their fault. They didn't want to be in school any more than I did. They didn't want to study Shakespeare. They wanted to be out in the world, discovering *life!*" And here she lifted up two beautifully tanned arms as though imploring heaven to hear the cries of her heart.

And then he remembered. She was thinking of giving up teaching. Relieved, he nearly smiled, but caught himself in time. This was a crisis in Hazel's life. What on earth would she think if she caught her counselor doing anything other than listening intently? He leaned forward just a bit.

"And then it came to me. As a Christian, shouldn't I be full of kindness? Shouldn't they learn more than academics from me? Shouldn't they learn love and compassion?" She dropped her arms thoughtfully and hesitated, trying to find just the right words.

Jason said nothing. He had learned, through previous sessions, that it was best to let her talk and only interject when necessary. Otherwise, she would stop speaking and stare at him with those huge, wide hazel eyes. Which was probably why her parents named her Hazel, he reminded himself pleasantly once again. They really were very remarkable eyes. So many colors...

"So then," she continued picking up the pace, "I decided that I would be nice and give them a little break. So I said okay, you can have ten minutes' free time, but you have to keep your voices down because there's a class next door. And then, literally, in the blink of an eye it became just like *Kindergarten Cop*. Kids started throwing paper airplanes, chasing each other around the room. I used my *loudest* voice, but no one paid any attention. I even blinked the lights..."

He had already heard this story. What was wrong with him today?

He probably should stop her right here, gently of course, and let her know she was repeating herself. But why stop now? She'd been talking randomly for a long time. The problem was, there was more to it than the narrative. She was questioning her vocation, feeling as though she had failed *yet again* as she put it. So her restatements were significant. And it was a tragic situation, no doubt about that. Wasn't it curious, though, all these beautiful people, so insecure, so unhappy...

"And I said to Rebecca, 'If you don't stop, I'm going to have to take you to see Mrs. Nakano, that's the principal, and she said, '*Do it*, I don't care, and then the door flew open and...'"

He wasn't kidding himself; he knew very well that lovely young blondes like Hazel: tall, slim, well dressed, would not normally take the time to say more than hello to someone who was barely five foot eight, huge spectacles over slightly protuberant eyes, and a thin string of a mouth that drooped at both ends. And as for the rest of him, well, he had once overheard a well-meaning soul describe him as pear-shaped. Standing before a mirror later that night, Jason had gazed mournfully at the reflection before him. No, he had decided, moving his belt from up near his breastbone to an area nearer his hips (belts would never stay in the middle) he wasn't pear shaped; if the truth be told, he was much rounder. Turning sideways, he'd experienced the kind of epiphany Hazel was fond of describing. At that moment, he reconciled himself to the fact that when people looked at him, what they saw was a slightly elongated version of America's favorite breakfast food. An egg with appendages, that was Jason Price.

"And she looked so horrible and furious! And then, she started to yell at my class. *My* class! And stare at me as if to say, how *could* you allow..."

So why was his appointment calendar always full these days? Why did lissome beauties and beefy truckers alike seek him out, desiring nothing so much at times as to be closeted away with him for hours on end? His mother said it was because he knew how to listen. His wife, Nancy, said it was because he truly cared. And now that he thought about it, Professor Dansworth, at seminary, had mentioned once that Jason had the instincts of a good counselor, and he was a man who did not give compliments easily.

"And it was just as though time stopped, and in my mind I saw myself as a little girl..."

He had to admit it was all very strange. All his life people would approach him at the oddest places: a bus stop, a table at Starbucks, a car wash, a fish counter at the market. They'd just walk over and start talking about their lives as though continuing a conversation already in progress. He had never understood it. And it wasn't as if he ever had any great pearls of wisdom to...

"Always getting scoldings, no matter how hard I tried to be good, while my sister and *especially* my brother could get away with anything. Richard was always Mother's favorite, you'd have to be blind not to see that, though God knows how she put up with Sissie..."

Yet, though he felt compelled to provide understanding and comfort to the distressed, he had not pursued a counseling career per se. He had not even taken classes in the subject nor was he, strictly speaking, licensed to counsel. Instead, he had completed a master's degree in Divinity, heavy on the Greek and Latin, because deep down inside he knew his true destiny lay as a minister of the gospel. His parents agreed. When he graduated *magna cum laude* from seminary, his mother was so proud she wept. At ordination, his dad merely shook his hand, looked him in the eye, and nodded his approval. But Jason thought his heart would burst. It was the happiest day of his life.

However, marriage had required a short detour behind a desk at the denominational office doing strictly administrative tasks. Nancy, for some reason, hadn't been quite ready to be a pastor's wife "just yet." But God was at work. Eventually an Assistant Pastor/Administrator position opened up at Aloha Community Church in Honolulu and Jason had been sure this was the answer. There were some pastoral duties, enough to get him excited about beginning his ministry career at last, but the bulk of the job was administrative. An excellent compromise. Besides, look at the bonus--Honolulu! No snow, blizzards, sub-zero temperatures. Just balmy breezes and...

Wait a minute! Oh no! He'd done it again!

"And then, I thought to myself, perhaps it's all true. Maybe I've been deluding myself all along. Perhaps I just have to face up to the fact that I'm really not cut out for..."

Shaken from his momentary reverie, Jason firmly put the image of his wife and his own personal problems aside for the moment and focused on the plight of the poor soul before him. He reminded himself that what was really out of order here was her spiritual life. Hazel drifted in and out of churches as though they were shopping malls. She came to services at ACC erratically, and absolutely refused to sign up for the Exploring Christianity class that would have answered most of her theological questions. Jason was determined, before the session ended, to invite her yet again to a small group that had been meeting at his house. If she could just get to know a few church members, then perhaps…

As impossible as it seemed, he was, in fact, blanking out once more! This simply had to stop; it wasn't fair to Hazel. Jason stood slowly to his feet. A second later, Hazel did the same, wobbling on impossibly high heels. He took her by the elbow and led her to the center of the small room.

He looked up at her with his kindest expression. "Well, Hazel, a lot has surfaced today. A lot for you to think about, but we're going to have to stop now. I want to pray with you before you leave, though, because I truly believe that, if you allow Him to do so, God will…"

Sensing his empathy, she looked hard at him, gulped once or twice, and burst into tears. "But you don't understand!" she wailed, chest heaving. "You don't understand the most important thing! You see, it was the *way* she was staring at me. It took me back to that awful day in the third grade when I missed the word coffee in the spelling bee. 'How could you miss *coffee?*' my mother had demanded. 'So easy!' I just stood there, speechless. And that's *exactly* what happened on Thursday. Don't you see? I just *stood* there!" Another cascade of tears fell from her lovely eyes and soon her shoulders were shaking.

"I do understand, really," Jason mumbled, thinking frantically, "*What do I do now?*" It was unusual for people to get this upset during sessions. His fault again, he sighed, for letting things get out of hand. He ran to his desk and retrieved a few tissues. He rushed back and pressed these into her left hand while grasping her other hand tightly. It was important, at moments like this, to let the person know you felt his (or her) pain. At least that's what he had determined from his limited experience. To say to the person, "You are not alone; someone who cares is right here with you." So he held on, saying nothing, but hoping his presence would be comforting. He was gratified to notice that she clung to his hand as if it were a lifeline, which indeed it was meant to be. And eventually she seemed to calm down.

How long they stood like that, he clasping one of her hands and she sniffling, dabbing at her eyes and chin with the other, he didn't know. Time, choosing a particularly cowardly course of action, had fled. So it took a while for Jason to realize that he really had to end the session at once. This wasn't doing anybody any good. He dropped her hand and stepped back.

"The problem seems overwhelming," he said in his gentlest voice, "but I understand. And God understands, too. But more than that, in His great mercy, God is here ready to help you. He is more than able to guide you through your this situation. Now let's end with a word of prayer, and as we pray, I would like you to..."

But Hazel was a long way from closure. She looked at him through tear soaked lashes. "I *knew* you would be sympathetic," she whispered. "I *knew* you wouldn't judge me the way she always does. I *knew* that I could trust you to behave just like Jesus, with care and compassion..." And with that, she threw herself, sobbing, into his unwilling arms.

"Oh, please don't. Please!" he exclaimed, but in a somewhat muffled voice, as the top of his head only reached her chin and the arms that clasped him were strong. Eventually, he began to extricate himself, but just at that moment he sensed movement at the glass panel in the door nearby. Glancing over, he saw a wisp of gray hair and a snatch of something red hover in front of the glass for a split second, then dart away.

"Oh Lord!" he groaned as his heart sank down to the pit of his stomach like a hard, cold stone. "*Please* tell me this isn't happening."

But, unfortunately, it was.

Chapter Two

"What's wrong?" Hazel asked as Jason recoiled from her like a cork popped from a bottle of cheap champagne.

"Nothing." Jerking his tie into place as though it were the sole incriminating evidence of a gross lapse of judgment, he raced to the door and peered through the panel. Not a soul in sight. He pressed his forehead against the laminated wood, blissfully cooled by an air-conditioning duct overhead, as his future passed before his eyes. Gray hair, pinkish-red glasses. Who else could it be but the church's worst gossip, Miss Lottie? "That's it. If she saw me I'm ruined," he thought. Of course it was innocent, but would she believe that? She would not! She would read something awful into a perfectly innocent situation and tell the entire world, and what would people think! The worst, that's what. "Oh, Lord!" he prayed as his stomach soured and turned over.

He groaned softly, thinking how nice it would be to just float along the hallways invisibly until he reached the nursery at the back of the church and lie down on the nice soft couch they had there, and stay, maybe…forever.

But, wait a minute, just hold on. Let's not get carried away here. "I'm not totally positive that's who it was," he reminded himself. "It could have been somebody else with a red blouse or something. Unfortunate, but not the end of the world. And another thing, if it really was Lottie, why didn't I see her retreating? It couldn't have taken more than four or five seconds to get to the door. Miss Lottie is an old lady. She couldn't have disappeared that fast. No way.

OR, let's consider all the angles here. Let's consider that the whole thing could have been my imagination! Maybe… innocent or not, some part of my conscience felt guilty and projected Lottie's image on the glass panel for a reason. To warn me or something."

"About *what*? I didn't do anything."

"Pastor Jason?"

He turned, almost surprised to find Hazel still standing in the same place, tears trickling down her face, as though no time at all had elapsed.

"Yes?"

"Are you okay?"

"Oh, fine," he said uncertainly.

"Well, I thought…the way you rushed to the door…?"

"That? Oh that was nothing. Thought for a moment I'd, uh, missed an appointment."

"But you didn't."

"Didn't?"

"Miss an appointment."

" Oh no. No."

"Well, that's good. Pastor Jason?"

"Yes?"

"Where are the tissues?"

"Oh, tissues! Of course, let me…" Jason sprang over to the desk, opened the drawer, and returned to her, ripping open a new box.

"Thanks," she murmured. Pulling out several soft squares, she patted her face, blew her nose delicately. Even in his distracted state he couldn't help but think of how vulnerable, how very much in need she was. And all he had done was try to help!

"But if I didn't do anything wrong, why do I feel so guilty?" Ha! The obvious thought slammed into his mind like a semi into a brick wall. "Because if it really was that old busybody, whether I'm guilty or innocent won't matter. People believe what they want to believe."

"Well," he said aloud, moving around quickly, placing the chairs where they belonged, putting his note pad away, pencil in the holder. "I guess we ought to be getting along."

"I guess." Hazel glanced at her watch. "Oh, look! I can't believe how long I've been here. It seemed like only a few minutes," she laughed. She deposited all the used tissues in the nearest wastebasket, retaining only one clean square for future use. "Thanks so much. I really, *really* appreciate it."

"Not at all. My pleasure," Jason muttered while striding to the door and yanking it open. A bit startled, she nevertheless toddled unsteadily through. Jason closed the door and followed after her, barely aware of his actions as his mind tried to wrap itself around the fact that in less than two minutes he would know if his worst nightmare had come true. His throat was dry; his palms were sweaty. He felt sick. But there was no sense putting it off. He had to see Miss Lottie's expression immediately. If he waited, he might never know.

Ahead of him, Hazel chattered away following the corridor that led to the reception area near the front door. All too soon he approached the reception desk, and as he passed, he steeled himself for the dreaded encounter. Patricia, the receptionist, was out with flu. Either Lillian or Miss Lottie, maybe both, would be filling in.

But Miss Lottie wasn't there! She of the infamous strawberry framed bifocals that always seemed to be everywhere poking into everyone's business, wasn't even at her desk. Instead, as he looked over, he gazed into the cool slanted eyes of Mrs. Lillian Nakata, who came in to help out occasionally. The frosty expression he encountered was habitual with her, so he didn't read anything into it. As the wife of the chairman of elders, Mrs. Nakata always took care to exude an air of calm dignity.

Miss Lottie had not come in today! He nearly fainted with relief.

Of course he'd been hallucinating. Of course! I mean, think about it. What were the chances that at the very moment he had made the largest lapse in counseling decorum of his entire career, the biggest gossip in the church would be staring through the glass panel in his office door? Astronomical! No, things like that didn't happen in real life. He'd been watching way too much TV. A hundred pounds lifted from his shoulders.

Hazel had stopped near the front door, looking at him expectantly. He turned on his most amiable smile.

"Now Hazel," he said brightly, feeling so blessedly lightheaded he could have talked with her for another hour, "It just occurred to me that I forgot to mention, once again, that a small group meets at my house on Friday nights. Bible study, fellowship, just an informal gathering. You said you'd think it over."

"Yeah, I know, but I don't think so," she said, rummaging in her purse for her car keys. The purse, an enormous black and white leather bag, looked as though it had been stitched from the hide of a Holstein cow.

"It really is the very best way of getting to know people, developing relationships, all of that."

Hazel shrugged. "I'm not really good at groups."

"Well, let me warn you up front, the snacks are fattening," he added, forcing his smile to stay in place despite the fact that it was obvious he wasn't getting anywhere. "But the people are really great. And once you get to know everybody…"

"No, I don't think so." Hazel said firmly, closing the huge black and white cow bag with a snap. "At least not now. But…" she looked up earnestly, "could I schedule another time with you? You know, just to talk?"

Jason was disappointed and he was sure it showed on his face; everything did. The sessions were beneficial in a way, he was sure, but they were just not getting anywhere. She had said no to a very helpful Sunday school class and hit the roof when he mentioned a psychologist. Other than persuading her to join the group, he really didn't know where to go from here.

Jason's specific title was Minister of Services. During his orientation, nearly a year ago, he had been presented with a handbook outlining the menu of services available through the church. It was his job to make sure that those who ran these had everything they needed. These included the food pantry and benevolence ministry, the addiction and divorce recovery programs, the scouts, the various mid-week activities for the elderly, the referral service for Dr. Lum, a psychologist who came to the church on Saturdays, and a huge array of guest speakers, conferences and seminars. Hospital visitation was, at some point, also tagged on.

To Jason were also fielded those who had general complaints or questions (people were always complaining about the parking, for example). Often, NS's (people with non-specific problems) were sent to him for one or two counseling sessions. Hazel was an NS. She had written on her questionnaire, "I don't know how I fit into the life of this church." And that was exactly the kind of situation Jason was expected to deal with. But only in one or two sessions. After that, an NS had to be plugged into an existing class, small group, or sent to some other service. Hazel was long overdue for that.

"Another session? Well, I don't know…We've had three."

Hazel's lovely eyes flashed angrily. "But we haven't finished! We got to the part, only today, where I finally saw…Oh, I get it. You just don't want to talk with me any more. Well, that's okay. I've already taken up so much of your valuable time…" She jerked her chin upward and turned to leave.

"Wait!" Jason said in a louder voice than he had intended. "It's not that at all." He quickly lowered his voice as Dr. Martin entered the reception area and looked their way. A moment later, a family with several children exploded through the front door, all chattering loudly, and the music director burst in through a side door with a hand truck loaded with boxes. Jason wished with all his heart he didn't have to continue this particular conversation in such a public place. If only he'd brought it up earlier!

"It's just that, honestly, I don't seem to be helping very much, and…"

Her tone changed immediately. "Oh but you are! Really. I can't *tell* you how much. My school friends have all married or moved away. You know what my family's like!" she rolled her eyes. "I'm not about to go out to a bar and cry on somebody's shoulder that's for sure. There's really no one else…" she darted a quick glance over to where Dr. Martin was standing, just out of earshot.

"I understand, but …I don't know how to say this. You see, I'm only allowed to have a certain amount of sessions with one person or one family. After that, well, I have to turn it over to someone who is more qualified."

Her nostrils flared; her eyes widened. Obviously, he had touched a nerve. " But, I thought we were friends. Doesn't that count for anything!" she snapped.

"Well, yes, but here's the thing!" Suddenly Jason saw the way forward clearly and pushed resolutely ahead. "That's just what this small group is all about," he said excitedly. "Making friends, widening your circle of relationships. Honestly, you'll love it. You'll get to be friends with everybody there, not just me. A bunch of people, not just one. And I'll bet..." The smile died a sudden death on his face. At some point Hazel had tuned out. Mere politeness kept her from bolting before he finished his sentence.

At that moment, Dr. Martin, the senior pastor, moved over to introduce himself. The man positively exuded respectability. He was well over six feet tall and threads of gray ran through his thick black hair. Although his somewhat irregular features kept him from being labeled handsome in the conventional sense, he made a neat and pleasant appearance. His aloha shirts, for example, always looked fresh, his Dockers creased. Nancy remarked that he always looked as though he'd stepped out from the pages of GQ magazine--in such glowing terms that Jason was sure there was a message in that statement for him somewhere, but he wasn't quite sure what it was.

"Hi Jason, how are you?" Martin smiled. Effortlessly genial, he held out his hand to Hazel. "Hello there. I'm Jefferson Martin, and you are?"

Hazel was annoyed, that was obvious, but remembered her manners. She stated her name and shook his hand.

Even though he had absolutely nothing to feel guilty about, suddenly Jason felt terrible. His intentions had been only the best, but he had failed this woman who had come to him for help and he was afraid Dr. Martin could take one look at Hazel and read the situation all too clearly.

But the senior pastor seemed not to notice. "I saw you once, oh a couple of months ago, I think. At the traditional service," he said, leaning casually against the counter as though he had all the time in the world, "but you've been coming to our contemporary service for the last few weeks, haven't you?"

Hazel eyed him narrowly. "Yes."

"So tell me, just as a matter of interest, why do you prefer that service over the other one? The sermons are the same," his smile broadened.

Hazel hesitated for a second. "The music, I guess," she said. Then, feeling as if something more was expected of her she added, "The band is good."

" I'm glad to hear you say that," Martin beamed. "And say, the worship choir is always on the lookout for singers."

"And you're looking at me?" The thought obviously amused her. "No way. If you had been sitting close enough to actually hear me sing, you'd know why."

Jason jumped in. "I was trying to persuade Hazel to join the small group I'm leading."

"What an excellent idea!" Dr. Martin exclaimed. "Behold how they love one another!" he quoted fluidly. "That is how historians saw Christians in the early church. And that is how we want people at ACC to notice us at work in our midweek groups. I can guarantee you, Hazel, if you want to feel the heartbeat of the church, a small group is a good place to begin." He turned to Jason. "So, have you succeeded in persuading this young lady to give your group a try?"

But for once the polished older man had struck a sour note. Hazel flushed red. "No he hasn't," she said irritably. "I mean, really, how many times do I have to say it? I'm just not good at groups!" Then, as if fearing Dr. Martin would question her further, she turned and wobbled hastily out the door.

Jason sighed, looking after her. "I'm afraid that's one that got away."

"I wouldn't be so sure," the senior pastor said. "Is she a believer?"

"Yes. But she's awfully confused. She's going through a hard time. Lots of problems."

"And you've been helping her?"

"Trying to! After the first two sessions I didn't think I was actually making a whole lot of progress, but it was time to plug her in somewhere. So I suggested Exploring Christianity, but she refused, and when I mentioned Dr. Lum, she hit the roof. I didn't want to just let her disappear, so I gave her another session today, but that went nowhere and now I'm out of options."

"Still, you issued an invitation to your small group, right?"

"At least a dozen times. She said she'd think about it, but it's obvious she won't come. And now, as you can see…"Jason sighed, hunched over, looking every bit as defeated as he felt.

"Here's what I see," Martin said confidently. "I see that you listened, you cared. You gave her several options, including an invitation to your group where you felt she could learn and grow. I think you did all that could be expected. So now, let's just see what the Lord does. Give Him time."

"I really do appreciate your choosing to see it that way, Dr. Martin," Jason said sincerely. " I …"

"No choice involved. That young lady is obviously searching and, you know, I think she likes ACC. She's been coming pretty regularly for weeks. So, keep on praying, and let's see what happens. If you only knew how many times people have a change of heart. Well," he smiled, "it defies reason." A signaling figure from an open doorway caught his attention. Martin held up an index finger, as if to say *Just a moment.*

There were a few things Jason wanted to ask the older pastor, but although the family with children had left and the music director had trundled his cart down the corridor and disappeared, at least a dozen other people had congregated in the small reception area, all talking at once. The questions would have to wait.

Dr. Martin turned to leave. "See you at staff meeting then?"

"Oh yes, absolutely."

"Good. Now if you'll excuse me, I have people waiting," and with one last smile, he ambled over to the open door.

Jason stood there a moment looking after him. The more he knew Dr. Martin, the more he admired him. Such a kind person! No wonder he had pastored a series of successful churches on the mainland before coming to Aloha Community Church two years ago. He had such a generous heart. He could have easily blamed him, the inexperienced assistant pastor, for missing the mark with Hazel, but instead he had taken a truly Christian approach. For a second it felt to Jason as though the hand of God Himself had given him a little pat on the back.

True, he was still feeling sluggish, probably a touch of some bug or other, and the pulses of adrenaline that had rocketed through his veins when he thought he and Hazel had been spied upon had left him a little shaky. But, the day hadn't turned out badly, all things considered. Humming under his breath, he rummaged in his pockets for change. The only thing really missing at the moment, he decided, was the calming effect a nice cold Pepsi would have on his stomach. He headed for the vending machine.

―――

At the front desk, Lillian Nakata finished with another caller then dialed an internal number. Two minutes later, Doris Baker, who had been dusting pews in the sanctuary, walked through the side door, slipped behind the reception desk, and filled the empty chair.

"I really appreciate this. I'll only be a minute," Lillian said, rising from her seat.

"Take your time," Doris glanced at the chart on the wall to see who was in and who wasn't. "Anything I need to know?"

"Not a thing," Mrs. Nakata returned briskly. Then, she walked down the side corridor, past several offices, turned left, and eventually reached the Ladies Lounge. An older woman, dozing on a sofa, sat up quickly as the door opened.

"Lillian, is that you?" a fragile voice called.

"Yes, it's me." The chairman's wife walked over and sat down next to Miss Lottie. "How are you doing?"

"Better, thanks. " Behind the strawberry frames, the blue eyes were greatly troubled.

"Can I get you water or something?"

"No. Thank you, though."

"You're sure."

"Yes." The older lady smoothed her dress with sharp, sudden strokes.

"Okay. But...what's all this about? What happened?" The friend was concerned.

Miss Lottie stopped and turned her face away. "Oh Lillian, it was such a shock!"

"Yes, that's what I thought you meant when you called me over. What kind of shock, Miss Lottie? Something you saw, heard, what?"

"Oh I don't know. I really don't know how to …" A deep sigh escaped her trembling lips.

"Now, now. Take your time." Lillian's voice was gentle, coaxing.

"Something I saw," she said at last, casting her eyes toward the ceiling, "and something I pray to God I never see again."

Lillian leaned forward. "It was something you saw when you looked in one of the glass panels in the hallway, wasn't it? I saw you put your hand on your chest. But whose office? I couldn't tell."

Miss Lottie swallowed hard. "Jason Price."

"Oh."

"..., and a woman I didn't recognize."

"Tall? Blonde hair?"

Miss Lottie nodded silently.

" Hazel Townsend," said Lillian, who prided herself on keeping her finger on the pulse of the church. "Counseling appointment."

Miss Lottie snorted, took a wadded up Kleenex from her pocket, jabbed at her reddened nose.

"Well, if you saw something that shocking, you should talk to Pastor Martin right away. He's in for the rest of the day," Lillian suggested.

Miss Lottie turned back. "Oh for heaven sake, Lillian, not him! You know how I feel about that man. No, I'm too upset to do anything right now. I have to think…."

Lillian sat back against a worn cushion. "I'm not surprised about Jason Price," she said conversationally. "As you know, I pride myself on knowing ministers through and through; I mean, I've seen enough of them come and go around here, that's for sure. He's too young, too inexperienced. Remember that mess he got himself into last month?"

"I was amazed that Sandy's mother overlooked that," Miss Lottie nodded.

"Well that's the thing. Jason should never have called a young girl away from youth choir so that he could talk with her all by herself outside."

"That looked very bad," Miss Lottie sniffed.

"It did. Of course, turned out that Jane couldn't get Sandy on her cell phone and asked Jason to give her an important message, but…"

"But why did Jason take her out of the choir room so that he could speak with her privately? That's the question." Miss Lottie said. "And, let's face it, Sandy is a very beautiful girl."

Lillian, who thought Sandy barely one step above the nymphet

Lolita, let the comment pass. "So, I guess this was the same kind of thing?" she probed.

"Oh, a thousand times worse. A million times!" And then, a little reluctant at first, but encouraged by her friend's obvious interest, she told Lillian just exactly what she had seen.

Lillian took it in stride. She'd been around a long time and, as she was fond of saying, nothing surprised her these days. "That's a pretty serious matter," she agreed. She did not say, "That's a pretty serious accusation," because it did not occur to her that Miss Lottie would lie about what she had seen. "What are you going to do?"

"I really don't know right now," the older lady said. "But something has to be done."

"The elders…?"

"Exactly, but how? Richard Ko is out of town, and I don't want your husband giving me the third degree just because I'm doing my duty!" she sniffed. "I think I have an idea, but I'll have to think about it."

"Well let me know…"

"Of course. I'll call you in a day or two. Just let me think. Oh, and Lillian…"

"Yes?"

"Let's just keep it between ourselves for the moment. I want to handle it…" she searched for the right word, "in just the right way, if you know what I mean."

Lillian did. Both she and Lottie had learned over many years hard experience that things had to be handled very carefully in the church. Even if it was a matter of out and out sin, which this was. Even if you had the church's interest at heart. Which they most certainly did. "Don't worry. I won't say anything. But you'll let me know if I can help?"

"Of course. "

The ladies stood up.

"I suppose I should go back to work now," Miss Lottie said faintly.

"No need. It's ten to four. I can handle the desk for ten minutes."

"You're such a comfort to me, Lillian," she said, giving her friend's arm a squeeze.

"No problem. Now listen, be sure to call me if you need anything. Anything at all."

Lillian walked Miss Lottie to the back of the building and pushed open the heavy metal door. Miss Lottie stepped outside, shoved her purse under one arm, and trotted off to find her car--a lot more swiftly than one would have thought, for such an elderly lady.

Chapter Three

Thursday evening, April 29th

The three ladies, who had been friends for years, lifted their glasses for a toast.

"To Marge!" Linda grinned. And the glasses clinked.

"To Marge!" Nalani called as her glass met the others again. She then turned to her younger sister, Tiffany. "Hey, hold up your drink."

"To good friends!" Marge laughed, and the glasses clinked a third time. The ladies drank deeply.

"I didn't know you could get real ginger ale anywhere outside of a health food store. This is delicious," Linda exclaimed with pleasure. Tiffany wrinkled her nose.

"Whaat!" her sister demanded.

"Taste like medicine," the fourteen year-old replied.

Marge called over to the waiter and Tiffany happily ordered a Pepsi, extra large. Nalani reached for something that had been sitting in her lap, and looked over at Linda as if to say, "Now?"

The two women looked nothing alike. Linda was in her forties, magnolia skin, tall and athletic. Her auburn hair formed two elegant crescents around her ears. She wore designer jeans, a dark red tank top, and large silver earrings. Nalani, a decade younger, was brown as a nut. Her shiny black hair reached past her shoulders. Years ago she, like Linda and Tiffany, had worn slim jeans, but after a weight gain of forty pounds, she began wearing size 14 cotton pants from Sears, and finally, as she continued to gain, she turned to muumuus which concealed her size in billowing yards of tropical colors.

Linda nodded. Nalani pulled the package out, and placed it on the tablecloth in front of Marge.

"A present?" Marge was genuinely surprised.

"Open it up aunty," Tiffany grinned. She was tall for her age, and thin. Besides skinny jeans, she wore a magenta top, which fell off one shoulder. That, the plum lipstick, and the orange streak in her hair made her look, according to her sister, like a ten year-old dressed up for Halloween. Tiffany tried to remember to be "cool", but her constant smile was a dead giveaway. It covered half her face.

"Well, I certainly didn't expect this. I mean, it's not my birthday or anything." Marge undid the ribbon, pulled off the paper, lifted the lid, pulled out the tissue. "I don't believe it," she laughed, holding up a trophy. It was not a golden figure carrying a football or tennis racquet; it was not a silver cup inscribed with team names. It was a simple four-inch glass star, set upon a koa plinth. In the center of the star was etched the numeral five.

Tears sprang to Marge's eyes. "It's lovely. I don't know what to say."

"You like?" Nalani wanted to be sure.

"I love it." Marge clasped the trophy to her chest while her friends clapped very softly. The restaurant was crowded and they didn't want to draw attention.

Marge gathered up the paper and strands of ribbon. "Hey, I brought a bag. Can put everything in here." Nalani pulled a plastic Wal-Mart bag out of her purse.

"I don't get it." Tiffany was confused. "You came in fifth and you got a trophy?"

Marge laughed. She was in her fifties, stocky, ruddy complexion, graying carroty hair. She looked like one of those women in AARP magazines advertising the benefits of a long, brisk hike, and her voice was just as hearty. She looked at one friend, then the other. "Can I be honest?" They nodded.

"It's like this," Marge grew serious. "I'm an alcoholic."

Tiffany looked surprised. Linda charged right in, "Hey, that's AA lingo. Forget that. You're a recovered alcoholic."

"Yeah," Nalani added her support. "When's the last time you had anything to drink? Long time, right?"

"Five years," Marge said, a note of pride in her voice.

"Wow." Tiffany was uncertain just how she should react.

Marge decided she would be candid, but concise. "When my husband Danny died from a brain aneurism, I just kind of fell apart. We don't have any kids. He was all I had. We'd been married thirty-three years. I wasn't into drugs, but Longs had all the wine I needed. For a long time I just gave into it. Lost my job, nearly lost my home..."

"And then you met us!" Linda piped up, determined to keep the conversation light.

"Yeah, at the craziest place," Marge chuckled. "Cooking class at KCC."

"That's right, I remember!" Nalani's round face gleamed.

Tiffany turned to her. "You took a cooking class at the community college?"

"So I didn't pass, so what? Was fun."

"You didn't learn *anything*?"

"The important thing is," Linda said firmly, "that's where we met, and that's where we became friends.

"They saved my life," Marge was adamant.

Curious, Tiffany asked, "You didn't go to, like, a twelve-step program or any thing?"

"No need any kine program." Nalani was firm.

Marge smiled. "Your sister and Linda said to me, 'You don't need AA. You have God and you have us. We'll get you through.' And they did. It's been five years since I've had anything stronger to drink than ginger ale." Mentally, Marge added: except for two dozen times I fell off the wagon and had to get one, sometimes both of these wonderful friends to come get me. But she didn't need to say these words aloud. The friends were aware of their shared history, and Tiffany didn't need to know the details.

A figure in black and white whizzed by the table, stopping long enough to say, "Your server will be with you in a minute," and dashed off again.

Eight hands fumbled for menus and opened them.

Tiffany didn't spend much time looking. She knew what she

wanted; she slammed her menu shut and looked around. "Wow, this is such a cool place! I mean, like, it was so cool to put the tables so close to this little stream. Hey, you know I bet I could just reach over and touch those swans. But maybe not the little ducks, they move too fast." She reached over to dip her brown fingers in the water.

"Eh, don't do that." Nalani glared. "Swans bite. Get disease." Then, she looked back at the menu and gave it her entire attention. "I dunno what I like. I think maybe calamari and scallops."

"I'm going for the eggplant casserole with a side of garlic mash," Linda folded her menu. "It's so peaceful here, I think the developers did such a good job with all the many water features: streams, waterfalls, fish ponds. They made it seem like a place apart, even though it's actually in Waikiki." She looked over at Tiffany. "Maybe later we'll walk around and look at the penguins and flamingoes. Would you like that?"

"Cool. Tonight's the fireworks, right?"

"No, sorry, just on Fridays. But there's some great ice cream places."

Marge and Nalani shut their menus and looked up as the server, tall, dark and harried, arrived and rattled off the day's specials. Linda ordered, then Marge chose the mussels steamed in lemongrass, green beans and coconut rice. Nalani opted for the ginger-crusted chicken, salad and rice, and Tiffany asked for a burger with onions and fries. They sat back as the laid back sounds of Hawaiian slack key guitar filtered through the air. The songs were so familiar they could have sung along to every one of them.

"Not only is it great to see you guys," Linda said, "but it got me out of my Thursday night class. "I thought ballroom dancing would be fun, but Darren is so clumsy he takes all the joy out of it."

"I dance hula on Thursdays," Nalani smiled at Marge. "At your church."

"One of these days she might actually attend a service," Linda wiggled her eyebrows.

"Maybe. I been thinking about it."

Marge said, "I never see you on campus, but then again, I'm not around much during the week."

"Say, how's that small group you joined? Started in March, right?"

Until six months ago Linda had been a regular member of Aloha Community Church, but these days she often attended the Presbyterian Church with a friend from work. She still made it a point to keep current with the ACC news.

"No, we're the bunch that signed up late. All the area groups were full, so we got kind of lumped in together. We didn't start until after Easter. But we're all going to finish the same time. End of June."

"How's it going?"

"Really good. Everybody's still kind of new, and we've only had four meetings...but, good."

"So how do you like that young guy, Pastor Jason? Kind of nerdy, right? History buff kind of guy?"

"Yeah, but I like him. He's friendly, you know. Easy to talk to."

Linda smiled over at Tiffany. "See that guy over there?" She nodded indicating a fat man in wide shorts and slippers walking down the flagstone path on the far side of the stream. "Fly-footed. There's an epidemic of them in Hawaii." She grinned in a knowing way.

Tiffany's face lit up. "Fly what?"

"Fly-footed. See, people normally walk with one foot in front of the other, but fly-footed people stick their toes out, like this." She moved the fingers of both hands outward while keeping the wrists steady. "Half-fly people have one foot going straight, and the other canted sideways." She returned the fingers of her left hand to the forward position. "I've been watching people for a long time now, and I've made an interesting discovery. Out of a hundred people, seventy-five are either full fly or half fly-footed! "

"Wait a minute," Marge said. "You actually looked at a hundred people and counted the ones that were fly-footed?"

"Of course, I'm a physical therapist. I'm interested in the human body and how it works. "She leaned forward confidentially, "Of that seventy-five, forty-five are full fly, and thirty are half fly. Of the remaining twenty-five in the hundred, fifteen walk normally, and ten are, to some degree, pigeon-toed."

"Oh, I know what that is," Tiffany turned the fingers of both hands inward. "Like this, right?"

"Right."

"So, what causes that?" Marge was interested. Everybody else

swam, paddled, read books or watched TV. Trust Linda to spend her
free time watching people walk.

"A whole bunch of things, but let's not get into that. What I'm
trying to say is, of all the pigeon-toed people I noticed, most of them
were women with small feet. I hardly ever see men who walk that
way."

"You don't say."

"Oh, but I do! Trust me," she laughed. "I really am getting around
to tying all of this in with your group. Because, one of the few men
I've seen that walk pigeon-toed is none other than your friend, Pastor
J. Kind of a dubious distinction kind of thing."

"Marge's eyes crinkled with good humor. "Well, I guess he is kinda
unique. But not because of the way he walks. Surely you don't hold
that against him."

"Why would I?" Linda was genuinely surprised. "I just noticed,
that's all."

Marge sighed. "Of course. I know you didn't mean to be unkind,
but you know people. Some of them have been hard on him. He's short
and chubby and his clothes are always wrinkled (I think he does his
own laundry). But you know, when you talk with that young man,
it's like you are the most important person in the world. He truly
listens."

The waiter came to the table with a basket of fragrant herb rolls
and butter, then dashed off again.

"That's a good thing," Nalani reached for a roll. "Nobody listens
no more. Too busy."

"It is a good thing, and I think that's why everybody really enjoys
our small group. He tries so hard to make everyone feel comfortable."

"Hey, I didn't mean anything..." Linda was slightly embarrassed.

"Oh, don't mind me. I know you didn't. But it's a sore point with
me. It's like the whole of society wants everybody to look like a movie
star: young, handsome or pretty."

"And skinny!" Nalani interjected, taking a huge bite of her roll.

"That's for sure."

Linda folded her napkin in her lap, and redirected the conversation.
"Say, do you know Jasmine Wu?"

"Sure do. She's in the group."

"Well, she's a friend of mine. She's a chiropractor in the same business complex."

"Really! I like her. So, did she say anything about the group? How does she like it?" Marge was smiling, confident.

"Well..." Linda reached for a roll. "She really liked the first meeting. There was a college kid, blond hair? Chris something? She said he was really sweet. And there was another guy, older, sarcastic? She couldn't stand him. But she said the rest of you were nice."

"I bet I know who the older guy is, Norman Stern!" Marge turned her eyes heavenward, "I don't know about that guy. He rubs people the wrong way. And I think he's proud of it!" She paused, "You know, I haven't seen your friend for a couple of weeks. She away on vacation or something?"

"Uh, actually... she quit your group."

"What? Well she didn't tell anybody. Why did she quit?"

It was obvious from her expression that Linda was not sure how much she wanted to reveal. "You know I really shouldn't have brought it up..." she became busy buttering her roll.

But Marge said, "Please. I really want to know."

Linda sighed. "Okay, I'm just telling you what she said, remember. But she didn't go back after the second time because she said something about it being weird. Okay, I don't know if the group was weird or if somebody in the group was weird. Come to think of it, I sort of doubt it. It was more like..." Linda thought for a few seconds. "More like something weird was happening to her as a result of something having to do with the group." She laughed. "Clear as mud? I told you I shouldn't have said anything."

Suddenly, Marge looked deeply troubled.

"Hey, did I say something wrong?"

"Oh no." But it was clear Linda had hit a nerve.

"Okay, look, this is me you're talking to. Something's up. What is it? Did something happen?" Linda darted a look at Nalani who paused, concerned, in the middle of a mouthful of food.

"No, honestly. It's nothing."

"Sure?" Linda was not convinced.

"I would tell you if there was! Oh look. Here come the salads."

Nalani finished her roll, and the friends held hands while Linda said grace.

Linda was the natural choice. The daughter of missionaries, she had been a strong Christian her entire life. Marge was a lapsed Episcopalian only now finding her way back to the faith. Nalani's faith was a thin tea of pantheism and deism into which the name of Jesus had been dipped often, but not enough to change its flavor, and certainly not enough to add substance. Yet, her belief in an omniscient, caring God, had been a life raft to which Marge had clung during what she now referred to as the "dark years," when God seemed absent, and the enemy all too close.

The dinner passed quickly, everyone finally declaring they were too full to move. Yet, when the dessert menu arrived, they couldn't resist. Luscious cream cake and tropical ices were followed by coffee and soda. Then, the waiter came over again with the check. He left. Tiffany giggled.

"Whaat!" her sister frowned.

"Well, he's, like, totally hot!" Tiffany covered her grinning mouth with a napkin.

"Hot?" Marge yawned. "Oh, that's just because there aren't any trades. Wait until tomorrow. The wind is supposed to pick up." She winked at Nalani.

"Aunty!" Tiffany groaned.

"Totally hot," Linda agreed heartily. "Sizzling eyes and that gorgeous tan!"

"I know you're kidding, but he really is, *and*, " she leaned over, eyes sparkling, "I think he's French."

"So?" Nalani was not impressed.

But Linda was. "French? Oooh, how romantic." She pretended to shiver. "So, how do you figure that?"

"Did you hear him talk?"

"Yeah. He said, 'You like to order now?'" Unfazed, Nalani licked every tiny morsel of chocolate sauce from her teaspoon.

"No. He said, 'Are you ready to order?' And it was the way he said it, you know? Like, *reddee'* to *ordeur.*"

"Do that again?" Linda sat back cracking up; Nalani rolled her big brown eyes. But Tiffany stood her ground. "No, I'm totally serious.

And did you see how he looked, all tall and slim, and those bones in his face!"

"Well, he'd look a bit scary if he didn't *have* bones in his face," Linda said without cracking a smile as Nalani choked back a tidal wave of laughter.

Marge glowered at both of them. "Listen, Tiff, when he comes back with the check, why don't you just ask him where he's from?"

Tiffany was aghast. "Me! No way."

"Okay, we'll all ask him."

"Not me!" Now it was Nalani who was horrified.

In the end, Linda asked.

Turned out the waiter was from Toledo.

He didn't have an accent either; what he had were seasonal allergies.

Tiffany gave her sister stink eye, but Nalani roared with laughter. All the way home.

Chapter Four

At nine forty-five, Linda pulled her late model Lexus around the circle and stopped. "You sure you're okay?"

"Fine, really," Marge hugged her friend and climbed out of the car.

"It was fun! So don't wait six months until we do it again, okay?" Linda called. "Next time Nalani chooses, so we'll probably end up at L & L." With a wave and a smile, she drove off. Marge doubted that they would end up sitting on picnic style benches at a place known for its local style plate lunches, but then again, with Nalani you never knew.

Marge opened the gate and locked it behind her. As she stepped on the pathway leading to her townhouse she noticed again just how seedy the place was beginning to look. Debris in the small koi pond, the bench covered with graffiti and lying on its side. Bougainvillea bushes so overgrown you had to walk edgeways in places along the path; leaves everywhere. She wished, not for the first time, that she had joined the Homeowner's Association. Still, it wasn't too late. Surely everyone was interested in keeping the value of homes high.

A set of blue and pink scooters blocked her doorway when she arrived, and through the screen next-door, angry voices could be heard once again. Sometimes it ended in a screaming match, but fortunately no one ever seemed to get hurt. If that happened, Marge didn't know what she would do. She wondered how the kids could sleep through the racket. And then, she thought, they probably didn't. Poor Destiny and Teshawna. Such sweet little kids.

She gently moved the toys, collected her mail, and opened the front door.

Danny had loved this place. Eight years ago, with prices reaching the sky, a single family dwelling had been out of the question. This was the best they could afford, but to him it seemed like a real home. It had two floors, nearly 1200 square feet, three bedrooms upstairs, and a small, enclosed back yard. No lanai, but he had built a deck and pergola outside, mainly because he hated to mow grass. She could still see him sitting out there: thinning hair parted neatly on the left side, reading his newspaper over half glasses, sipping a tall glass of iced tea. Such a kind, gentle man. He had lived here exactly three years before he died.

Inside, she flipped on the lights in the living room, entered what had once been a dining area, booted up the computer, and ended up in the kitchen running water in the kettle. With no need to pretend any longer, her bright expression had long faded and the troubled look returned. She glanced over at the Dalmation on the shelf above the sideboard.

"Well, Teddy, I sure had a good time tonight. What I would do without my friends, I really don't know. But when Linda said Jasmine thought there was something weird going on, and it was maybe related in some way to the group, I nearly spilled my guts. But I'm glad I didn't. I mean…this whole thing is scary and more than a little strange, but, I didn't want to talk about it, because really, it could all just be my imagination. I mean, it only happened a few times, right? No need to get all up in arms about that."

Teddy gazed at her serenely. The shy smile stitched on his spotted face always encouraged her to talk.

"Still…" she leaned against the sink, waiting for the kettle to boil. "It kinda gets to you after a while. Sometimes I don't even want to go to bed, you know? Before I started going to the group I never had dreams like this. Never. In fact, I didn't dream much at all. But…now that I think on it, the very week after that first group meeting I had Dream Number One, and it was a doozey. Don't remember much about it except that it woke me up screaming. Not out loud, but the way you do in dreams. You know how it is."

Teddy's placid expression indicated he knew quite well.

"Yeah, well, that had to be one of the scariest moments of my life, I can tell you. But that's all I remember. Don't remember what the dream was actually about. Still can't. I think maybe something in me won't let me remember. That happens, right?"

Yes, Teddy's steady gaze confirmed, sometimes, things like that did happen.

"So it's probably a good thing, right? Yeah, I think so too." She turned back, picked up the kettle and poured out a little of the water, then set it back on the burner. She rooted around in the cupboard, found a package of mints, and popped one in her mouth.

"Now where was I?" she said after a moment. "Oh, right. So...that was Dream Number One. Now Dream Number Two? That was super scary too and I remember snatches of it. I remember it took place in a house I used to live in. Had something to do with Sebastian---haven't thought about him in years. And don't intend to waste time doing it again! But...this last one, Dream Number Three? Oooh Teddy, that was no dream; it was the worst nightmare I ever had." And here she stopped talking, and thought deeply. A few minutes later, when the kettle screeched, she jumped.

"Drat!"

The kettle, old and somewhat unreliable, boiled over. Marge snatched a faded tea towel, and mopped up the puddles. Then, she pulled a tea bag from the container and a ceramic cup from the shelf. She poured water in the cup and dipped the tea bag up and down.

"Where was I? Oh yeah, the last dream. So real I thought I was watching a movie! But it was kinda strange because it jerked forward from scene to scene and lots of stuff got left out. I don't remember everything, of course. But here's what I do remember. I remember it started with me sneaking out of a hotel room in Atlantic City. I was maybe fourteen, fifteen? My whole family had gone there for a week's vacation. And my parents had told all of us kids never to go out without them. But I did, of course. I got up early and sneaked out.

"Then, the movie jerked forward and next thing, I was standing on the beach. I don't think I'll ever forget that, Teddy, because I don't want to. It was just so wonderful. The sky was a bright shiny blue, puffy white clouds all over it, sunshine everywhere, and I was young and happy, without a care in the world. It was the most wonderful feeling you can imagine!"

She stopped for a moment, savoring the recollection. "In the dream," she continued, "I was looking at the ocean, kind of scared but excited. But then, suddenly there I was in the water up to my waist, splashing around looking at the people swimming nearby. I remember thinking to myself okay, so I can't actually swim, but look at those guys having such a good time! How hard can it be?

"Then in a flash, I was out past my waist, water nearly up to my chin and becoming kinda vaguely aware of something grabbing at my legs. I remember thinking to myself that it was probably another swimmer going past, bumping into me, and I clearly remember saying , 'Hey, watch it!' Hadn't the sense to know it was undertow. Never swam a lick in my life. I ask you, how stupid can kids be?"

Although Teddy no doubt agreed that kids often lacked intelligence, he remained mute.

Adding sugar and a squeeze of lemon to the tea, Marge leaned back on the sink again. "Now, here's where things get strange because the action started to kind of speed up. Next thing I saw in the dream was a close up of the expression on my face as something started sucking at my legs, grabbing me like some deep water creature and pulling at me. I tried to shake it off, whatever it was but I couldn't, and I started to get really scared. Then, next thing I remember was rolling over and over in deep water, not knowing which way was up. Then, I stopped, and I reached down with my legs, trying to touch bottom, but I couldn't. And then I started to panic.

"Everything got dark. Then, I started to thrash around, trying to get to the surface, which of course was wrong, because I was using up all of my oxygen. But when you're in a panic, you don't act rationally, do you? You just act on instinct."

Teddy placidly agreed. Instinct could lead to rash acts.

Marge leaned closer, as though something in his shiny black eyes would give her permission to end the story right there. But, of course, she couldn't. Having once begun, the whole dream had to be told.

"I was out of breath and my lungs were about to burst. I began sucking in water! My lungs were as heavy as leaking sand bags. And finally, mercifully, a blessed darkness overcame me, and I calmly drifted down, down, and ….

And then I died."

Tears sprang to Marge's eyes, and she jerked forward, her heart hammering away as if she had just lived through that final darkness again. *Horrible, awful, terrible dream*, she shivered. Then, she turned, and splashed cold water from the faucet over her face as though she could wash the memories away. Eventually, as her breathing returned to normal, she wiped her face with the dish towel.

She stood there a moment, then picked up her cup. With a passing glance at Teddy, she took it into the living room; sat on the sofa holding her tea, so lost in memory that she wasn't even aware of the blaring television from next door –the other side, not the one where the parents quarreled.

The problem was, the *really* weird thing about the dream was, that the ending, right from the part where she felt something pulling at her legs--wasn't real! It hadn't happened. Obviously it couldn't have. She was alive, wasn't she?

"What actually happened was that two lifeguards in a boat came and got me before I got sucked under. I remember because they were cute, like brothers with blond crew cuts. Funny how you remember that after all the years.

"The brothers rescued me! The undertow never got me at all! So why, in the dream, did I die? Experiencing your own death in a dream is beyond creepy, beyond weird, even. So, why did it happen? Is this, like, a sign or something?

"Oh Lord, look at me. Talking to myself! As if talking to a stuffed animal isn't bad enough. Am I going nuts?" She looked up at the ceiling. At least talking to God was something normal people did— sometimes.

Marge took her tea to the sink and threw it out. Suddenly, all she wanted to do was go to sleep. Maybe she should take Linda's advice and get a dog. A real one, this time. But, they were so much trouble. Was it really worth it?

She turned off her computer, pulled sheets and a blanket out of the hall closet, and took them over to the couch. She hadn't slept upstairs since Danny died. This was her bedroom now. After plumping up a pillow, she rapped loudly on the wall so that old Mrs. Kim would turn down her television (the lady was nearly deaf and would only put in her hearing aid when Marge banged on the wall), brushed her teeth, and climbed into a nightgown.

She checked the deadbolt on the back and front doors, set her alarm for 7:00 a.m., turned out the lights, and turned on the air-conditioner. It was old and clattery and blocked out enough noise that she could get to sleep. Summer and winter she slept with the air-conditioning on. She had been doing this for five years. She wondered if she would ever be able to sleep without it.

Normally, she drifted off to sleep in ten minutes, but tonight, for some reason, a picture of Danny, vivid as a snapshot, crept into her mind. If only he had been here to listen, he'd have found some way to make sense of it all, she knew. But she also knew, from bitter experience, that thoughts like that led, inevitably, to a sleepless night. It had taken many painful years to learn how to discipline her thoughts where he was concerned; she wasn't about to backslide now.

She tried to focus her thoughts on Dream Number Two, the one she *almost* remembered, but not quite. On the one hand, she didn't want to be scared out of her wits by another trip into the past. But yet she was curious. Life was like a puzzle, and to figure it out, you needed all the pieces. She closed her eyes and let herself drift back in time to see what would come of it.

But the memories eluded her, and she slept deep and long. Until Mrs. Kim's TV came on, blasting away, at 6:00 a.m.

<u>Chapter Five</u>

Friday afternoon, April 30th

Before this day ended, Chris Murray's life would change forever. But at the moment, the only thing he was really concerned about was whether or not Mei Ling would go out with him. Just the two of them this time, not a study group get-together, not a trip to the water park with the whole gang, or a freshman mixer. They had been to plenty of those.

Chris had gotten into the habit of looking around for Mei Ling at lunchtime and sitting down at her table. This was nice as it gave them a moment or two alone, but somebody always sat down and started a conversation and before you knew it there were half a dozen people there eating, all taking at once. After five months of this, Chris was ready for a real date.

Mei Ling was the most beautiful, the most feminine, the most gentle, the most appealing girl he had ever met. And, she was smart. Chris fell, and he fell hard.

It had taken a lot of courage to approach her initially. He knew that he looked normal enough now, but that was because after high school he had lost over 100 pounds, and that was a horrendous amount for somebody who was barely 5'10". Part of him still thought of himself as the fat guy.

Being grossly overweight for much of his life hadn't done much for his self-esteem. Yet, after he lost the weight, he didn't like the way people looked at him. It was though, after two years of rigid self-denial, he had changed from the Pillsbury Dough Boy into Brad Pitt, which of course was ridiculous. He was now just normal looking, nothing more. When he was fat everybody had stared at him; when he became thin, they still stared at him, only for a different reason. It got really old after a while.

And his history of dating? He couldn't look back without cringing. That's why he liked Mei Ling so much. She was so different from the girls he met after high school--in high school, most girls were just happy to pretend he didn't exist. She was not, for example, the demanding, in-your-face co-worker at his first job that he had mistakenly asked to the movies. (After that, she was there every time he turned around: acting coy, batting her clumpy eyelashes, doing everything but camping out under his desk). And she was most definitely not the grim and determined daughter of his uncle's business partner whose idea of a fun night had turned out to be sitting in her parents' living room leafing through bridal magazines. He groaned just thinking about it. He knew he had escaped just in time. He wasn't quite sure from what exactly, but whatever it was, it would not have been good. Understandably, he had decided it was time to take the money gramps had left him and head thousands of miles away to college. He chose the University of Hawaii.

During the fall semester he had kept his mind (mostly) on his studies. After all, he had to prove to Mother and his uncle that he actually did have a career plan. But he spent a lot of time girl watching, and enjoying the fact that girls actually smiled back at him when he smiled at them. In a friendly way, with no coded messages. And he had had two dates. Both nice, but not memorable.

Then, the first day of the spring semester, in French class, he took one look at this tiny Chinese student, with fine black hair, and an ivory complexion that tinged with pink when she got excited, and felt his heart turn over. It was the kind of thing you read about in books, or saw in movies. The kind of thing you laughed at with guy friends when you didn't think there was a chance in the world that it would ever happen to you. At least, not in a way that had any hope of being returned. She was shy. It had taken months to strike up a friendship, but Chris was a determined man.

That morning, he had pulled her aside and asked her to go to dinner and a movie.

"No, no," she had replied, looking troubled.

"But why not? You're not secretly married, are you?"

There was that delicious flush again. "Of course not!" She was offended that he would ask.

"Mei Ling," he said patiently. "That was a joke."

"Yes? Well, I am not married," she said sternly.

"Of course you're not. (Oh Lord). Look…"

"And I do not date. I have told you before. My family is very strict."

As a matter of fact, she had told him, several times. She lived with her mother and grandmother who had moved to Hawaii from China only last year. She never mentioned a father living or dead. He didn't know what her grandmother did; her mother was an accountant at a small firm. Mei Ling was the oldest grandchild. Much was expected of her. Once she finished her bachelor's degree, there was the master's degree to complete, and then a doctorate in clinical psychology. One day she would teach at a university just like this one. She would set the example for all the younger ones. It had all been decided. She could not be distracted.

"But you can have friends?" he had smiled, gently, keeping his face as open and unthreatening as possible.

"Of course I can have friends!" She looked at him very severely indeed, black eyes flashing. "I am not a member of repressed minority. This is 21st century. I can have friends."

"Glad to hear it," he had said, "I just want to get it out in the open that we're friends. Is that okay?" Then he quickly switched the subject before she could change her mind. He didn't want to push his luck. Today, however, after she had refused, once again, to go out with him, he said, "Okay, no date. But Mei Ling, remember, we're friends, right?"

"I suppose so, yes," she said.

"Well, that wasn't hard to admit, was it?" he laughed, and she had dropped her defenses and smiled back at him. "Listen, as a friend, I want you to do me a favor."

"What favor?" she lowered her head and looked at him warily. The long strands of her bangs nearly covered her eyes. She pushed them away impatiently.

"Well, you know, I've always wanted to go to eat dim sum. People say it's great. Would you go someplace with me? Explain all the dishes. Help me avoid anything made from fish guts or something else really gross."

"There are no fish guts in dim sum."

"Probably not, now that you mention it. But it would be so nice if you could explain everything to me. You know, like, what everything is!"

And that's how they had left it. She was to let him know where they would meet, and when. So, as Chris left the university campus and drove into the small town of Manoa early Friday afternoon, he was a bit preoccupied.

Manoa was a place you might see on a calendar. Its houses were old and quaint. There was a fire station, several churches, two gas stations, a store with a green awning that sold organic produce, a McDonalds, a Starbucks. The streets were narrow, cluttered with leafy trees, flowering plants, and cars wedged in tightly on both sides. It had a homey, comfortable feel that reminded him of the old farm his grandfather had owned in Kentucky, where Chris had spent the happiest years of his childhood. It was just as green and lush, and it seemed as though it had been around forever.

As he turned onto Orchid Drive, watching carefully for a parking place, he wondered, as he often did, what gramps would think of his adventure. Chris's father had died when he was three; gramps was the only real father he had ever known. It occurred to him that, although it opened new opportunities for his grandson, the old man probably wouldn't have liked Hawaii very much. He would have found the food too foreign for one thing. Chris couldn't imagine gramps eating tofu, for example, scooping out the black shiny seeds from a papaya, or eating sticky white rice with every meal the way they did here. He was strictly a meat and potatoes guy who thought cooking Hawaiian style meant taking pineapple out of a can and putting it on a sweet potato casserole.

Chris came to a stop as a car pulled away from the curb in front of him, and looked out the windshield. The sky was a calm, summery blue. A gentle breeze fluttered the papery green palms and rocked birds of paradise in their bushes. Over the mountains there was a layer of white milky clouds. Gramps wouldn't have liked this at all. He prided himself on being able to foretell the weather by the color of the sky, the smell in the air or a sudden dip in temperature, and he was never wrong. Trouble was, here in Hawaii, the temperature stayed pretty much the same all year. And the sky looked the same every day too. A violent storm could be gathering somewhere just over the mountains, and you'd never even know it was coming.

Chris locked the car, crossed the street, and headed for a faded pink two-story house, waving to Mrs. Fujihara, who was outside hanging her laundry. The covered lanai stretched along the entire front of the house; behind it was a perfectly good two-car garage but nobody used it, except for storage. It rained often in Manoa, and Mrs. Fujihara hung her laundry where it was sure to stay dry. The house belonged to her son, who was spending a year in Yokohama, along with his wife. The older lady kept house and lived here with her ten year-old grandson, Kevin. Chris was the only boarder.

"You like soda?" she called "I got Coke in the ice box."

"No thanks."

"Musubi too. Made fresh today," she added, popping a couple of clothespins in her mouth as she shook out a pair of boy's jeans. Mrs. Fujihara always wore one of a half dozen faded, ankle-length dresses that may once have been brightly colored muumuus. With these, she wore plastic slippers (which Chris had quickly learned not to call flip flops). When visiting neighbors, however, she put on a pair of sparkling white Nikes.

"Say hey," called Dan Marshall, elbowing his way out the front screen door, his face stuffed with food. He offered a paper plate of what looked like small black bricks, but Chris declined. A cold slice of spam between two sides of rice, wrapped in seaweed, was not his idea of a tasty snack. For Dan, however, fiftyish, husky, ex-college linebacker from Philadelphia, one of the greatest enjoyments of living in paradise was the food. He would eat anything. He had even been known to eat things still crawling on the plate.

"Seen Kevin?" he asked, chewing noisily. Dan was one of Kevin's tutors.

"No."

"Yeah, well, I guess he'll be home for dinner. Catch him then." Dan waved a half-eaten seaweed brick in the air and disappeared into the house across the street.

Chris headed for the side of the building and the ohana apartment he rented. It consisted of a small living room/ kitchen, bath--shower only, and one tiny, windowless bedroom. A small covered lanai had also been added, and it was on it that Chris found his true island paradise. He stood there now, leaning on the wooden railing, gazing over at Manoa stream. It was shallow now, but in 2004, it had flooded its banks, causing serious damage to nearby homes. But at the moment, the water was deceitfully calm, flowing peacefully over a flat bed of well-worn rocks. Trees, leafy, high up like a canopy, crowded both banks and blocked out much of the sky. At dawn and dusk, hundreds of birds flew home and nested in the branches making a sound that could wake the dead. The stream itself was crowded with dozens of ducks swimming back and forth, honking constantly to each other. He never tired of watching them.

The rent, considering the apartment was just about 400 square feet, was outrageous, but Chris felt he had been greatly blessed. It was welcoming and peaceful, a tiny place in the gigantic impersonal world where he could just be.

He leaned over the railing for a long while. Then he kicked off his slippers, opened the door and stepped inside. He deposited his backpack on the table, turned around, and opened the fridge. He poured himself a glass of water from the pitcher on the top shelf, downed it in nearly one gulp. Then, he headed for the bedroom.

He walked through the doorway, flipped on the lights, and there he stopped as suddenly as if he had been sledge hammered into a brick wall. His mouth fell open, and he took in a short breath and held it. He blinked his eyes, thinking for a split second that what he was looking at was some kind of mirage, but no—as he leaned forward and focused intently, he could see that despite the fact that his mind was registering impossible, what he was looking at was real.

Propped up against the headboard of his bed was a man he had never seen before in his entire life. Furthermore, his expression seemed to indicate that he had been waiting a long time for Chris to come home and wasn't the least bit happy about it.

<u>Chapter Six</u>

It wasn't just the fact that the man had been waiting for him in the dark that bothered Chris. Now that he looked closer, he realized that he had been mistaken. The image of the man, though three dimensional, seemed to be emerging from the headboard of the bed rather than being seated in front of it. That was really strange. A further mystery was the lack of color in the room. Everything was brown. The man was all brown: his face, clothes, hands, feet, everything that Chris could see. Brown, like the old, faded photographs gramps had in a trunk in the attic back home. Chris also noticed that the bedspread was a kind of beige as well, and there were no indentations in it. Not even a crease. The strange intruder, whoever he was, had no physical weight.

Chris's legs suddenly felt rubbery and he leaned against the wall to steady himself. He would have gladly let himself slide to the floor, but then he wouldn't have been able to see the man. So, allowing himself to breathe once again, he simply leaned back, against the cool, hard wall and waited.

The man was Asian, that was for sure. Chinese, Chris decided. Forehead shaved, or maybe it was a cap set back on his head, he couldn't tell. Cotton jacket, the kind with the funny collar that sat flat against the neck. White cotton trousers. Bare feet.

Okay, he was definitely hallucinating. Probably some weird stuff Mrs. Fujihara put in the bottled water in the fridge. Had it tasted funny? He couldn't remember. But why would he hallucinate an image of a Chinaman sitting on his bed?

Curiously, the thought of running away never entered his mind. He knew instinctively that this apparition posed no threat. There were no accompanying creepy feelings. The man didn't have half his head caved in. No worms crawling out of his eye sockets. This wasn't anything out of the X-Files.

"Why are you here?" Chris asked. "What do you want?"

The man sat up and leaned forward. "Be careful!" he said, in a high nasal voice.

"About what?" Disconcerted again, Chris hadn't been prepared for the man to speak. Suddenly his mouth was dry, his heart began pounding. His hands balled into two tight fists. Sepia photographs were old, right? So this image was old. Okay, it wasn't gruesome, but could it be, like, a message from beyond the grave, that kind of thing? Whoa! Lots of people felt the X-Files were based on things that actually happened. Maybe, this was one of them after all.

From across the room the man looked deep into Chris's eyes. There was no mistaking it now, this discarnate image had not appeared randomly. He could see it in the man's eyes. The message was meant for Chris, and it was urgent.

"Be careful!" the man repeated. "The night is coming."

Chris was stunned. The message made no sense. He took a step forward. "And…?"

Now the man's expression changed. Suddenly he was fearful. The look in his grainy eyes seemed to indicate he was afraid that he had not been understood. He sat up straighter and the shadows in his eyes deepened. "The night!" he insisted. "It is coming!"

The doorbell rang, shattering the moment. Chris glanced over his shoulder, knowing exactly who it was. Kevin had zoomed in on his bike and decided, if he wanted dinner, he'd better do his chores right away. Kevin had two chores, delivering the mail and taking out the rubbish. He was standing outside now pressing the bell and it would be just Chris's luck this was one of the days Kevin just wouldn't go away. Thinking Chris had fallen asleep on the couch, he would just keep ringing

"Look, don't go away, okay? I'll be right back," Chris said to the apparition and dashed to the door. "What is it Kevin!" he said impatiently.

The boy behind the screen looked as shocked as if someone had shouted at him. And Chris had to ask himself if he had actually shouted in a stern voice. He hadn't meant to. But maybe, in his haste, he had. The thin brown face crumpled slightly, and Kevin turned to leave.

"Hey, sorry. Look I was, uh, right in the middle of something. What is it, Kevin?"

Kevin, small, skinny, glasses, with meticulously gelled black hair, simply said, "Mail." Then, he looked closer. "Hey, Chris, you okay?"

"Yeah, fine, why?"

"You look funny. Pale. Well, paler than usual," he grinned.

"Must be the light." Chris opened the door just far enough for the boy to pass two envelopes in.

"Rubbish?" the boy sighed, as if wondering why he had to state the obvious.

"No rubbish, I'm fine."

"That's what you said yesterday," Kevin would not be moved. Gramma's gonna get mad if I don't get the rubbish."

"Tell you what. You're right. I'm not feeling so hot. How about you come back in about an hour?"

"But I'm standing right here!" Kevin pushed his glasses further up on his nose and stared at him stubbornly.

"An hour." Chris stepped backward. "I promise." He closed the door and raced to the bedroom. Somehow he knew what he would see: the apparition was gone. But that isn't what amazed him. What amazed him, now that he thought about it, was that the message the man had delivered had been spoken in Chinese, and Chris who hadn't met an Asian person in his entire life until he had moved to Hawaii a few months ago, had understood every word.

"How you know he speaking Chinese?" Mrs. Fujihara demanded.

An hour later he found himself sitting in an old stained resin chair on the lanai. The landlady had pulled up an identical chair and sat staring at him, sucking on what appeared to be a large green root. "Could be Japanese, neh? All orientals look same to you?"

"No, I'm sure it was Chinese. He was dressed like a Chinaman." Chris stopped, unsure if that was an offensive term these days, but Mrs. Fujihara didn't seem to mind.

"You know what Chinaman dress like? Here, you like edamame?" She pushed the bowl of green pods under Chris's nose. He waved it away.

"You look like you seen a ghost," Kevin repeated for the tenth time since Chris had appeared, fifteen minutes previously, wandering down the driveway, heading for his car.

"Eh! You go get one Coke," Mrs. Fujihara ordered her grandson.

"No more Cokes."

"Get tea then."

"No, really, that's fine," Chris said absently. How had he been so sure the man was Chinese? Couldn't he just as easily have been Japanese? But no, for some reason, he was sure he wasn't.

"Kevin, move it! Get one can tea."

Kevin turned to Chris. "Arizona or Itoen?"

"Nothing…"

"You drink green tea, good for you!" Mrs. Fujihara pronounced. "Here, have some edamame."

She showed him how to separate the bean pod and extract the small beans inside. "Ono. You try," she grinned. She had beautiful dentures and loved to show them off. Chris took a bean pod and opened it.

His memory of meeting the Chinaman was waning just a tad. Must have been the shock. He could recall the moment he first saw him. He could recall how the man looked and what he said. He remembered being annoyed when the doorbell rang insistently (Kevin, of course) and telling the man to stay right there he would be back in a moment. He remembered his awful disappointment when he ran back and the man had disappeared. But at the moment all of these thoughts were simply circling in his mind refusing to make any sense at all, and he was a bit embarrassed about spilling everything to his landlady. But, he had to admit, her reaction was encouraging. She hadn't looked at him like he was somebody who had escaped from the nearest mental health facility. She seemed to think that what had happened wasn't all that unusual.

"So," Mrs. Fujihara leaned over thoughtfully. "What you think message mean?"

"I honestly have no idea."

"Hmmm. No sound like end of world kine message. Sound like for you kine message."

"Yeah, I think you're, like, totally right. It was for me," Chris said. "I'm gonna have to think about it."

"No sound like scolding kine message. Sound more like warning kine message, neh?"

"Yeah. I guess."

"So, we look in da Bible. See what da Bible say, yeah?" Mrs. Fujihara was a member of the Conservative Evangelical Brethren Society of Oahu. She took her religion very seriously, and she looked to the Bible for daily guidance.

"There's something in the Bible about a guy who saw a Chinaman in his bed?" If there was, Chris didn't remember it.

Her face darkened. "I t'ink I remember a man in da Bible try see one ghost," she said pointedly.

Chris groaned. He had been avoiding the word because it was just so doggone weird. But what else could it have been. "Yeah?" he said hopefully. "What happened?"

"Didn't turn out so good."

Chapter Seven

Nancy and Jason did not live in a house. They could not afford to buy or rent one in Hawaii where prices were astronomical. They did not live in a townhouse either for the same reason. They lived in a condo, which had one exceptional advantage and several drawbacks. The perk, and it was a big one, was that during daylight hours there was a breathtaking view of the Koolau mountains out the front window: huge spires of lava rock wrapped in velvety green, so tall they pierced the clouds.

One drawback was that the condo unit was tiny and cramped. Another problem was Kimo the loud-mouthed poi dog who barked, non-stop, on the lanai next door every day until bedtime. The barking was usually, but not always, accompanied by the thumping metallic heartbeat of two excellent stereo speakers belonging to the dog's owner. Mike liked music, and he liked to party. Those were the (major) flaws. The view was excellent, balm to his soul, but Jason could understand why Nancy was anxious to move out when the lease ended. The noise was pretty bad.

When the small group was planned, Jason had hoped to have it meet in his home, but the noise made that impossible. Then, a couple of months ago, at the elevator, Mike casually mentioned that he would be taking Kimo to obedience school on Friday nights. To Jason it was a true miracle! The small group could meet here in peace. If only Nancy could change the hours she worked so that she could be here with them, everything would be perfect. He knew she wasn't crazy about group activities but he felt confident she would love these people as soon as she met them. Everyone in the group was certainly looking forward to meeting her.

At six-thirty, he turned around some chairs, added more. Then he took out the e-mail he had received from the church office earlier that day. A new person would be coming tonight. He gazed at the name with dismay: Pua Hoaeae. How on earth do you pronounce a name like that? Five vowels? He had had a hard enough time with Yumi Furubayashi and Brysen Shimabukuro. These names were killing him. But he figured, with more practice, he'd eventually get the hang of them.

At six forty-five the phone rang and he buzzed Marge and Yumi up. Twenty minutes later the rest had kicked off their slippers or shoes in the foyer and were drinking soda and chomping on snacks around the kitchen table. Marge had brought a huge tray of sushi and Pua brought a platter of sugary malasadas, the tasty Portuguese donuts Jason, unfortunately, loved. Yumi brought a delicious coconut pudding called haupia. Brysen brought a six pack of Pepsi as he did every week and so did Chris Murray. Norman brought nothing but his cantankerous self, ten minutes late as usual.

At seven-fifteen on the dot, because of those who had to leave punctually at nine, they all brought their plates and drinks to the living room area and took a seat in the circle of chairs. Jason brought the meeting to order with a short prayer.

"Amen, he said as every head looked up. "Okay, let's see now. We have two absences. Anybody know where Rhoda is, or Jasmine?" They all shook their heads no.

"Actually," Marge said apologetically, "I heard that Jasmine might have quit the group." There were murmurs from the others. Since Jasmine had only come twice, they pretty much figured she had dropped out.

"Oh? Well, I'll give her a call tomorrow." Jason scribbled a note to himself, then looked up. "And nobody's heard from Rhoda?" They all shook their heads again. "Well then," Jason said with his brightest smile, I'll introduce our newest guest! Uh, Pua, you probably know some of these people, but would you like to introduce yourself anyway?"

The woman in question was a grandmotherly type with pure white hair cut short over her ears. She wore a brightly patterned pink muumuu and the nails on her brown toes were painted a cheerful pink as well. "Aloha, I'm Pua Hoaeae," she smiled over at Marge, the only person she recognized, and several voices returned the greeting.

"Could you say that again? I didn't quite get the pronunciation," Jason admitted.

"Sure. Ho-ae-ae. Just think 'Ho!' Then two eyes." Her full lips formed a generous smile.

"Oh good," Jason was relieved. "Once you know the secret, that one's easy. " Everyone, except Norman of course, smiled. Wiping sugar crumbs from the front of his shirt and suspenders, Jason said to Pua, " Well, this is the gang and we've met four times. Each time we answered a question, so I guess you get to answer all of them. First, where were you born? Second, what do you do for a living? Third, tell us something about your family. And the fourth question never got answered because I forgot all about it last week." He laughed, and so did everyone else, except Norman, of course.

"So, I'll do it now," he continued. "This week's question is, how long have you been coming to ACC?" He looked over at Pua and nodded encouragingly.

"Me? Oh, well, I'm Pua as I said. I was born on the Big Island, Kona side." Yumi nodded; she had family there. "I'm an LPN, and see private patients. Uh, let's see… I'm a widow, with one son, two grandkids. And…" she hesitated.

"Church?" Jason smiled.

"Oh, right. Yeah, I been a member of ACC since I first become a Christian oh, maybe ten years ago now. My son and his family all come. Kids sing in da choir. And I really love Pastor Martin's sermons!" she sat back, smiling broadly.

"Very good," Jason said. "Now, who'd like to go next?"

"I will," Yumi Furubayashi spoke up. Tonight, as always, she was dressed in a dark business suit. Short, dark and compact, she seemed pressed together on the chair as though trying to take up the least amount of space. She was not exactly wary, but not overly friendly either. Still, she took her responsibility as group clerk seriously, and

Jason was thankful for her help. "I should answer all the questions, right?"

"I'm sure Pua would appreciate it," Jason said.

She hesitated, then began. "Um, some of you have heard this before, of course, but my name is Yumi Furubayashi; I was also born on the Big Island, Kona side, but my grandparents live in Hilo," she smiled briefly at Pua. "Uh, let's see, I'm an accountant with Bragg, Yamaguchi and Armenclaus, I am presently single, been coming to ACC for a long time. It's a nice church. I like the fact that Pastor Martin preaches from the Bible. Really well, I might add." Several heads nodded affirmatively.

"Very good. Thanks, Yumi," Jason crossed his short legs and looked around. "How about you, Chris?" For some reason, the young college kid had seemed distracted this evening, very unusual for him. He was sweet natured and easy-going. Normally he was right there in the middle of every conversation. Tonight he seemed lost in thought. Oh well, Jason thought. College could be tough.

"Uh, well, yeah, I'm Chris Murray, freshman at UH Manoa. Uh, let's see, family's back in Kentucky. I started coming to ACC because it's close by where I live. I like it." He thought for a moment, then something seemed to strike him funny. "Hey, you know what? In some ways this group reminds me of my home church 'cause people back home really love to eat. They have pot luck suppers, like, every time you turn around, bake sales, chili drives. Honestly, you'd think their entire theology revolved around the miracle of the loaves and fishes!" There were a few chuckles around the room. "So, thanks to whoever brought the food," he smiled, "it's really great. Oh, and by the way, I like Pastor Martin too."

"Thanks, Chris. Now who's next?" There was a long pause.

"Well, if nobody else wants to speak up, I guess I will," grouched a man in his early fifties. He was very tall and thin, Hasidic in appearance with curly black hair, thinning at the crown. The circles under his brown eyes were dark. His nose was slightly beaked, his beard and moustache an inky black.

Although Jason could hear the silent groan generated by most of the group, he looked over at the man cordially and nodded. "Go ahead, Norman."

"Well, Pua. I'm Norman Stern. Born in Baltimore and like most people from the east coast I say what I mean." He paused briefly. "Okay, now for the information. Let's just say I work in marketing, and I've been coming to ACC since Christmas." He took a deep breath. "I'm still trying to decide how I feel about the church. Unlike most of you, I'm not a Jeff Martin fan. To me the guy's like a politician or a TV evangelist. Looks good, sounds good, but when you sit back and try to decide what he actually said, it doesn't always hold water."

Pua unwisely asked him what he meant. Marge turned her eyes heavenward, Many of them were all too familiar with Norman's opinion of Pastor Martin.

"Well, let's just take two things," he said, smoothing his beard with long, thin fingers. "First, there are often holes in his logic. I've been to seminary, and I know a thing or two," he added with authority, "and the second thing is that he doesn't stick to the Bible."

This was yet another complaint in a long anti-Martin diatribe, but Marge couldn't help it, she spoke up at once, though Yumi nearly beat her to it. "Now Norman, you know that isn't true. Pastor Martin does preach from the Bible. Why," she looked from face to face, "he goes through it Book by Book."

"Well, Marge, I personally think the Bible speaks for itself. You don't need anybody reading things into it. You don't need anybody drawing things out of it. And you most certainly don't need anybody making jokes about it."

Yumi decided to make her position clear. "Pastor Martin draws principles from the Bible that we can apply to our lives. He tries to be relevant, which I, personally, appreciate."

"I like his jokes," Brysen piped up. "They're funny."

"The Bible is a very serious theological document," Norman pontificated. "I can't imagine Jesus, who as you know, often referred to the holy scriptures, telling a few..."

"Yes, yes, yes," Jason chimed in breathlessly. "The humor of Jesus is certainly an interesting topic to explore one of these days, but in the meantime, I think you left out one category, Norman. Family?"

Norman took the hint, but he didn't seem pleased about it. "Okay. Well, I already said this once. I guess I have to say it again, though

I'm not proud of it. Divorced. Twice. One child, that I will not talk about—ever. Are we all happy now?"

"Blissful," Yumi murmured under her breath.

"Thank you Norman." Jason said. "Now, let's move on…"

Moving quickly around the room, Pua learned that Marge Givens was a widow who worked for the phone company. She had been attending ACC for about a year and a half. And Brysen Shimabukuro, a young man in his twenties and new to the church, was a web developer for First Hawaiian Bank.

"Okay, now," Jason said, "in my Leader's Guide, it suggests that I ask all of you another question, and it's this: if someone could give you something really valuable right now, what would it be? All right, who wants to go first? Chris? Good."

"Somebody could give me lessons on how to talk to this girl Mei Ling. Every time I try to talk with her I just stumble all over myself." He looked down, shaking his head sadly. Pua and Marge glanced at each other and smiled.

"Just be youself," Pua said. "You one nice kid. Hang in there. What. Everybody looking at me? Okay, okay, well I like somet'ing not for me but for my son. He needs a good job."

"I pass," Yumi said, and looked at Marge. Marge thought a moment. "I guess somebody could help me put in a really well-insulated wall next to my bed. The lady next door refuses to put in her hearing aid, and her TV wakes me up every morning, way before I want to get up."

Brysen said someone could give him a better paying job so that he could move out to a place on his own. He admitted that in Hawaii kids hung around the family home longer than the national average, "But still yet," he said, "I need my space."

And finally it was Norman's turn. He pointed to his watch. "I'd like my group leader to assure me that we'll get out of here on time. I've gotta get up early."

"Point taken, Norman, I'll do my best," Jason said. "Now, tonight's lesson talks about the fact that the Holy Spirit gives us, among other things, wisdom, and…oh, what is it Pua?"

"What you like, Pastor J? If somebody could give it to you?"

That caught Jason off guard. "I guess," he said slowly, "I'd like someone to help me make this a really dynamic, life-changing group," he grinned.

Pua spoke up at once. "I tell you what I tole Chris. Be yourself. You one nice guy. Hang in there."

"I really appreciate those thoughts, Pua, but I need more than that. To make this group really life changing, I need wisdom. And for that, I need to depend on the Holy Spirit because He knows the mind of God. Just think how all of your situations would change if you could know what the Spirit of God had to say about them! Now, let's turn in our books to page 34. Chris, you did the homework, right? Good. So, what would you say is the most important thing about Point A?"

At nine o'clock on the dot, the prayer time at the end of the lesson ended. Jason stood. "Now, Pua, I'll leave it to you to review the sections you missed. Yumi will e-mail you a list of names and contact information. One thing we do ask is that each member of the group pray for the others every day. You can send special prayer requests on-line. You can call me, or anybody here for that matter, if you have questions."

"Well she can't call me," Norman growled. "Now, if there's nothing more, I've gotta get home."

Nancy came home to find Jason sitting on the red flowered couch that she personally considered to be her best furniture purchase ever. He was staring out the window.

"How'd it go?" she called, kicking off her shoes, and putting her purse where it belonged.

"I just don't know," he said morosely. "Wasn't really any...what's the word? Zip, I guess you could say, in it tonight. Maybe it's the fact that I'm still not feeling all that great, but I mean, you would think a study on the Holy Spirit would be really inspiring and encouraging. But tonight..."

"It lacked zip." She came over and felt his head. "A little warm, but I don't think you have a fever." Her uniform, a brilliant blue and green patterned muumuu, was one of the things she liked about her job, but when she was really tired she couldn't wait to trade it for her favorite island look: shorts and a tank top. "Get to bed early and take some of that green stuff I pulled out of the medicine cabinet for you this morning. I put it on the counter in the bathroom."

"Okay," he sighed. "Oh, there's sushi and malasadas in the fridge."

"Good. I'm starved." She took a paper plate from the cupboard and opened the fridge.

"How was work?" he asked.

"Exhausting. It's like check out time at the grocery store. Everybody decides to do it at once. We get some really slow days, then suddenly we're deluged with people. I never knew the muscles of my face could ache. I really wasn't made to smile for an entire eight hour shift. Oh my, this is really good," she said, biting into a crab sushi as she sank down on a kitchen chair.

Jason walked over and pulled out a chair across from her. "Well, save a smile for me," he said. "I could use it. Want some Pepsi? There's some left."

"No thanks, the caffeine will keep me awake." She finished one sushi and reached over for another. Then she glanced over at her husband. He was so despondent, his entire face sagged, and his oversized glasses made his eyes droop as well. She smiled despite herself. After a second, her smile turned into a genuine laugh, and she threw up her hands. "I can't do this. I'm telling you, my face really does ache!" Then, she stopped suddenly, eyes wide. "Hear that?"

"What?"

"Nothing, that's what. Blessed, wonderful silence."

Jason's face brightened. "Yeah, how about that? Isn't it totally amazing that Mike decided to take Kimo to obedience class on Friday nights? I'd hate to think of trying to have a class here with all the normal noise going on."

"Speaking of which…" she looked up expectantly.

"What?"

"You did talk to the rental agent, right? I told her you would call. Today!"

The woebegone look returned.

"Never mind," she sighed. "I'll take care of it. Want some of this sushi, 'cause I'm gonna finish the plate."

"No thanks."

"Well, okay, here goes." Jason watched contentedly as she ate. No one would say that Nancy was pretty by Hollywood standards, but she had beautiful brown eyes, and pale, smooth skin that needed no make-up. She had an arresting face that was always infused with a compelling energy. Usually, she won people over not by smiles and sweet words, but by the sheer force of her personality. However Jason was sorry to see that since taking the role as pastor's wife she wasn't nearly as self-confident as she had been.

"How about some malasadas?" he asked, choosing the one with the most sugar.

"Are you kidding? I'm trying to watch my weight! Hotel food is murder on the waistline." She got up, threw the paper plate in the waste basket, and put the platter of donuts back in the fridge. True, she was a bit on the pudgy side, but not nearly as round as her husband. Jason thought she looked terrific. She sat back down. Light danced in her eyes. "So, how's Norman?"

Jason's face fell. "I did a terrible thing tonight," he said, swallowing a mouthful of donut. "He was being abrasive, as usual, and I wanted to change the subject, so I reminded him that he hadn't answered one of the questions."

"So?"

"So, I already knew the answer, and it was one that brought up a lot of unpleasant information about his personal life. I'm sure he was offended."

"Now listen, from what I hear Norman has the hide of a rhinoceros. He doesn't get offended. So," she leaned closer, "Did he bring up his seminary degree tonight?"

"Made reference to being at seminary, I think," Jason finished the donut and rubbed the excess sugar from his hands.

"Well, I found out all about that," she said, with a lift of one eyebrow. "Seems as though your friend Norman did in fact attend a seminary in Texas, but dropped out after only six weeks. His main claim to fame, education-wise, is that he finished a distance learning class in wealth management, whatever that is, at a place nobody ever heard of."

"How can you make such mundane information sound so intriguing?" Jason laughed. "Now I really feel sorry for the guy. And where on earth did you find that out? I'm sure it's not information he wants made public." Jason wiped his face with a napkin and looked longingly at the fridge.

"Don't even think about it," Nancy warned. "Actually, Lillian Nakata told me, ages ago. I just haven't had a chance to tell you."

Jason shivered. "How on earth did you ever manage to make friends with that dragon?"

"Who, Lillian? She's not that bad. Why on earth you let her intimidate you I'll never know."

"Oh she doesn't intimidate me, she terrifies me! As a matter of fact, the only way I can stand in front of her without my knees shaking visibly is to do the mental image thing."

"This I've got to hear. What image?"

"Well," he hesitated. "I think of her as a sort of Asian flamenco dancer."

"Whaat?" Nancy whooped, eyes wide.

"Well, you know, she has black hair and she wears it parted in the middle and pulled back in a bun anyway. I just add the rose in her teeth and imagine her stomping on her desk to guitar music, hands over her head clicking her castanets."

Nancy sat back and roared. "That is hysterical."

"Works for me," he laughed. After a minute he said, "But seriously, how do you get information out of the old ba-- out of the chairman's wife?"

"I'm telling you, she's not nearly as fierce as she pretends. You just have to know how to approach her."

"Well I'd prefer doing that at a distance," Jason concluded. "Say listen, Nancy, as long as we're talking…"

"Oh no, please, no deep emotional dialogues. I'm beat," she pleaded, pulling off the rubber band that confined her sandy hair and shaking it out. Then she walked over to him and gave him a kiss on the forehead. "We'll talk. Only just not now, okay? Love you," she said, hurrying away. "Take some of the green stuff!" she called back over her shoulder.

"Okay," he echoed. As he took off his suspenders and striped socks, he thought to himself, "Well… things even out. The class bombed, but… my amazing wife loves me." A small balloon of happiness rose in his heart.

It very nearly eclipsed the inexplicable feeling of dread that had haunted him like a cranky ghost, clanking around on the periphery of his conscious mind all day. But he couldn't figure out why.

Unless it had something to do with Miss Lottie. Something in the way she had looked at him earlier that day had turned his blood cold. But why? Surely it had nothing to do with that incident with Hazel yesterday. Lottie hadn't even been there. So why did he feel so... apprehensive?

Well, he decided, he wasn't going to let his imagination ruin his evening. Breezing past the donut laden fridge without even a lingering glance, he headed for the bathroom and bed.

Chapter Eight

Earlier that evening.

Rhoda stared at the living room and gasped. The metamorphosis was so complete! Sarah Jensen giggled. This was a bit unusual as Sarah, who taught the older ladies Sunday school class, was usually a bit on the reserved side. However, today she resembled the sixth grader at the local talent show who, despite singing off-key, had nevertheless taken home the grand prize.

"Take your time," the gray haired lady in the rose colored muumuu grinned. "Look around."

"Does this style have a name?" Rhoda asked in awe.

"Oh honey, I don't know. I think they call it Modern Tuscan, or some such."

"Really! I just have to get the name of your decorator," she said wandering around the room. Black eyed, dark haired and eager, she looked completely at home in front of a mural of ancient Italy complete with cypress trees and a crumbling stone wall. "Who painted this?" she asked, amazed.

"Who knows? Mr. Kee got it on-line. He put it up with wallpaper paste."

"Mr. Kee? That's the name of your decorator? I have to get his number," Rhoda said, strolling lazily from the living room into the dining room.

"Stager, actually, not decorator," Sarah corrected. "The mural is new, of course, but those benches in the dining room against the wall were hand-me-downs from Milton's sister. And that fountain over there in the garden?" She led Rhoda to a window and turned on the outside lights. "A few things soldered together that we got at Ross's." The two peered outside. Turning back to the dining room, Sarah said, "Now the dining room table was in the garage for ages, holding up boxes of Christmas decorations."

"It looks gorgeous. And expensive. "

"It wasn't. Just Mr. Kee's magic again. I cannot believe how many items we had just lying around. It's always so helpful to use things you have instead of rushing around buying everything new," the former university history professor added." Now let's go into the kitchen. Would you like a glass of guava juice? I made it fresh this morning." She walked to a cabinet, pulled out a drawer. "I know I have his card somewhere."

Rhoda, an administrative assistant at the same university, sat down on a gleaming wooden chair she was sure had not been reclaimed from the garage. "Couldn't drink a thing. Couldn't eat another mouthful. Honestly, did you ever see so much food!"

"Mounds of it! But then, Josie's mother is a caterer."

"Oh, that explains it. It was one of the nicest showers I've ever been to. And I appreciate your inviting me back here to see all the changes you made."

"Here it is!" Sarah sat down in a chair opposite and reached over with the card.

Rhoda pushed her hand back. "Thanks," she said, "But now that I think about it I don't know. I can't afford to do the whole house, for one thing, just the living room. And Ed has definite ideas about what he likes, which do not include murals of the Italian countryside and fountains on the lanai. But I really am happy for you, Sarah. The house is amazing!"

"So, what does Ed like?" Sarah placed the card deliberately on the table. "Hawaiian style, right? Lots of rattan and wicker? Potted palms everywhere?"

"More like Hawaiian garage sale," Rhoda wrinkled her nose. "The room is bad, I can tell you."

"Oh it's not as bad as all that," Sarah said pleasantly. "As I remember, it was quite nice. You have that lovely rattan set."

"Well, that depends on your definition of the word nice. It's been years since you've seen the place. It's all gone down hill since then."

"I'm sure that's not true, but listen, dear," Sarah leaned close. "Milton doesn't like all of this Italian stuff, really." She waved a well-moisturized hand in the air to indicate the entire ground floor. "But upstairs the second bedroom is his own domain. He watches TV while I have my ladies Bible study down here, and one room all his own is all he needs. He's happy as a clam."

"Oh my gosh!" Rhoda's hands flew up to her mouth. "Bible study! I totally forgot!"

"What?" Sarah sat back.

"Our Friday night small group at Pastor J's house. What time is it, Sarah? I forgot my watch."

Sarah glanced behind Rhoda at the wall clock. "Eight-thirty."

"Oh no! How long does it take to get from Salt Lake to Kaneohe do you think?" She stood up, turned, and looked at the clock.

"Oh," Sarah thought for a moment. "Thirty minutes? Thirty-five?"

"Maybe I can just… No, on second thought people start leaving about nine. Some of the ladies have to get up early for work. "She sat down again, defeated. "I just knew there was some place else I had to be tonight. Problem is, I've only been to the group meetings twice, and it still isn't part of my schedule. Fridays are normally a free night."

"Well, it happens," Sarah smiled benevolently. "Everyone so busy." Ever the good hostess, Sarah got up and poured them both a small glass of pink juice. "Say, how is that group study coming along? I heard it was a rag tag bunch thrown together at the last minute. You should have signed up for mine!"

"Thanks," Rhoda cradled her fingers around the cool glass. "Well, it's my own fault," she admitted. "By the time I decided to join up, all the groups were closed." She took a sip, then another. "Mmm this is good."

"Oh but not mine, surely!"

"According to the church bulletin all the area groups were filled. But I wanted to sign up for Pastor J's group. He's a really nice guy, and I was afraid he wouldn't have enough people."

"And did he?"

"I think so," Rhoda finished her drink.

"Oh here, let me…" Sarah rinsed both glasses and wiped her hands on the tea towel. "Is Jasmine Wu in that group?"

"She is!"

"Nice girl, but rather opinionated." Sarah grimaced. "I had her in one of my classes a few years ago. Have you gotten to know her?"

"Actually, I haven't even met her. She was absent both times I went. But I'm looking forward to it. Now listen Sarah, I really do appreciate your inviting me back to see your place. It truly is amazing."

"My pleasure! Thanks for driving back here with me." They strolled toward the front door. "But let me say a final word," she turned to her guest with a twinkle. "Stagers like Mr. Kee design everything to suit your personality. He'll come in, look around, move a few things here and there, ask some questions. And according to him, the style just sort of emerges. I'm telling you, honey, get him to come and do your living room. You won't believe what he can do. The man works miracles!" And she handed the card to Rhoda once more.

"Well…okay." Rhoda put the card in her purse, hugged Sarah, and walked to the car. She adjusted her seat belt, then dialed Pastor Jason on her cell phone. He didn't answer, but she left a message apologizing. She really had been looking forward to the small group meeting. She had even made special arrangements for Ed to be home with the kids so that she could go. How on earth could she have forgotten?

Busy, busy, busy. She snapped the phone shut and put the key in the ignition. Oh well. Next week for sure.

<div align="center">~~~~~</div>

Half an hour later

Rhoda rushed in the front door, found Kristen and Travis in the den watching TV and shoo'd them off to bed. They had swimming the next day and needed to get a good night's sleep. Of course she was met with howls of protest, but in a surprisingly short time, the two headed upstairs.

Next, she walked to the front room where Ed was snoozing comfortably in his Laz-E-Boy, the newspaper folded over his lap.

Rhoda leaned over. "Ed," she called.

No answer.

"Ed." She squeezed his arm a few times. Finally, one eye opened.

"What."

She pulled up a chair so that she could look him in the eye—literally, as the other eye seemed reluctant to join the conversation. "Wake up."

"What do you mean wake up. I am awake." And eye number two popped open. Her audience was complete.

"Listen," she began with her friendliest smile. "I just came from Sarah and Milton's house and they just had their whole house staged, and honestly, Ed, you wouldn't believe the change. It was like night and day!"

"Staged? You mean redecorated." Ed, the estate planner, who also had a master's degree in English, had to have all terms made clear.

Rhoda, determined not to be ensnared in semantics, rushed on. "But the point is, their living room used to look just like ours—like one night when they were sleeping somebody sneaked in and moved all the stuff they had gotten ready for their garage sale into their living room."

"I would never sell this recliner at a garage sale," Ed pointed out, gripping the arms with both hands as if she might attempt to tear it out from under him.

"...but now that they've had it staged, it is totally Better Homes and Gardens, only better!"

"Such hyperbole. The mind boggles."

"You know what I mean."

"Yes, and I know where this is leading, too. And the answer is no. I cannot afford to have the house redecorated." And with that both eyelids slid down over his eyes as smoothly as Roman shades over casement windows.

"I'm not talking about the whole house. Of course that's out of the question," Rhoda insisted. "Just the living room."

"The living room is fine," came the somnolent voice.

"Ed!"

Ed opened his eyes and looked over. "What."

"Are you trying to tell me this living room can't use some help?"

"This, "he replied wearily, "is a living room. Notice the adjective. And we do practically live here. This room facilitates that. End of story."

"Oh Ed. Look at the place! Kristin has her gerbil zoo in one corner; Travis has his drum set in another, and the rest of the room is taken up by a big screen TV, a love seat and a recliner. What statement is that making I'd like to know!"

"We live here, Rhoda," he yawned, although he might have said, "We give deer soda." It was hard to tell because by this time he had squiggled down in his chair and pulled a pillow over his head.

"Oh Ed."

"Mmmmpf."

"And you wonder why you can't sleep at night, after you've napped for two hours," she said under her breath. She removed the pillow. "Ed, are you or are you not going to discuss staging the living room?"

"Give me my pillow," he said petulantly, "and I'll tell you."

She handed him the pillow.

"I am not," he said, and eased the pillow behind his head once more.

"Okay, so…will you sleep on it?"

"Not a chance."

"Oh Ed!"

Chapter Nine

Sunday, May 2nd

On Sunday morning, Howard Nakata was in an exceptionally good mood. Both church services had been packed. If things continued as they were, they might have to add another one. Perhaps a youth service on Saturday nights. Lots of churches were having great success with that. No reason why they couldn't do the same thing.

For several years, the church had been steadily losing people. An unrelenting series of problems and two unfortunate crises, back to back, had hit them hard, followed by a general air of dissatisfaction that simply would not go away. Then, they brought in Dr. Jefferson Martin whose reputation was so outstanding that Howard was amazed to this day that the man had considered coming to ACC. Martin was certainly doing a fine job. A large, unexpected endowment had allowed him to add a few excellent people to the staff, issuing in some well-needed changes, and now the whole atmosphere of the church was improving.

With pleasant thoughts on his mind, the chairman of the Board of Elders and, at sixty-four, its oldest member, walked over to his church mailbox and withdrew the papers and envelopes that had accumulated over the last several days. His expensive aloha shirt was soft and a little faded with careful use; his golden spectacles gleamed in the light reflected from many wall sconces, giving him the look of an aging scholar. Whether saying the morning prayer in Sunday service, or simply opening his leather briefcase and placing it on the table,

63

everything Howard did, he did with simple grace and dignity. Now, he tossed past bulletins and correspondence he'd already received through another source, in the wastebasket nearby. Bills and the mail that came to him at the church address, he put in his elegant, lovingly polished briefcase, the one with the brass clasps that Lillian had given him for Christmas ten years ago.

Ernest Cooke, another member of the board, dashed by, then stopped and backed up. "Is Pastor in his office?"

"I don't know," Howard murmured, looking critically at a monthly expense statement.

Ernest, a nervous, fidgety little man raced down the hall. In the meantime Howard folded the report and placed it in his briefcase to be scrutinized later. The last item in his box was an envelope marked "Personal and Confidential." Howard eyed the envelope with extreme displeasure. He held it between his thumb and index finger, fanning it up and down, deciding what to do. It was pink, always a bad sign. The handwriting was florid, almost a Rococo scrawl. Probably a highly emotional woman complaining about something--the music being too loud, children misbehaving on the walkways or riding skateboards, etc. It had been such a nice morning, he really didn't want to spoil it by reading a lot of complaints. Besides, the envelope wasn't even addressed to him.

Ernest came racing back. "He's here. Howard, could you come in a minute. Sorry, but it's an emergency. Please! I just found out about something really awful," he said breathlessly and darted off again.

Howard watched Ernest retreating, wishing very much that he'd just gone home after the last service and left his mail for another time. The feeling of well being he'd enjoyed earlier was rapidly fading. He took the envelope and placed it in the mailbox marked Jason Price. It occurred to him that this was exactly the kind of thing they paid the junior pastor to deal with. But then at the last minute he took it back out again, tossed it in his briefcase, and headed for Pastor Martin's office. Maybe he'd just have a quick look at it first before he passed it on.

When he arrived, the senior pastor was talking on the phone and Ernest was pacing up and down like a young husband in a delivery room. He barely glanced up as Howard pulled out a chair and sat down at one end of the long conference table. Martin looked over, nodded, and finished his call.

"Now Ernest," he said genially, walking over from his desk to take a chair next to Howard. "What's this all about?"

"What's the emergency?" Howard asked. "I have a lunch meeting, so I hope this is important." Privately, he thought the little man reminded him unpleasantly of Uriah Heep: small, slight, constantly fidgeting, wringing his hands, with a tendency to look at people sideways instead of head on. But whenever such unchristian thoughts darted through his mind, he repudiated them immediately. The man simply had poor social skills; he was to be pitied, not censured.

"It is important!" Ernest said, still pacing. His black hair was normally worn slightly longer than a buzz, but Ernest was long overdue for a trim. Wiry tufts stuck out all over his head giving him a wild, startled look. "It's a tragedy, a terrible terrible tragedy. And I wish I didn't have to tell you! But I'm the elder in charge of the Education Department, so naturally they called me, although what I'm going to do, I really don't know. And that's why I had to come to you, because I want to make sure we're all agreed as to what we ought to do."

And finally he sat down, as though he had finished delivering his message and was awaiting a reply.

The other two men looked at him blankly. Finally Howard said, "Ernest, what is the tragedy?"

Ernest looked up, as though surprised to discover that he hadn't already told them. "It's about Susan Anello of course."

Howard looked over at the senior pastor who immediately said, "Sunday school teacher, Junior Department. This is her first year, I believe. Yes, Ernest, what about Susan?"

"Well!" he began, speaking rapidly, "from the information I have, it seems that at 2 o'clock this morning Susan Anello was driving dr-- intoxicated, on the H-3. She was pulled over, failed the breathalyzer test, and has been charged with Driving Under the Influence!"

"Oh my," the pastor and elder said in unison.

"And don't ask me if somebody paid the bail or whatever term there is for paying money so that someone behind bars can get out, or if she had to stay the night. I don't know! What I do know is that all the children came in the Sunday school room this morning at a quarter to nine and sat in their seats. A couple of the parents were checking them in, so they weren't unattended. We're covered there," he added under his breath as though this were an important point of law, "and then time came for class and Susan wasn't there." Ernest stopped talking, and thought a minute.

"Yes?" Howard urged mildly.

"No, I thought I knew the names of the parents who were helping out, but it won't come to me. Anyway, usually, if a teacher is going to be out, they call the superintendent and get a replacement. But that's Gladys Hirai and she just got home from the hospital from having a hysterectomy. So these two parents—I'll think of their names in a minute—called the church office but no one answered. And of course our Education Pastor, Lawrence Sizemore, is away in Virginia fulfilling the residency requirements for his distance learning degree and won't be back for a month, so they couldn't get hold of him. And of course he hadn't thought to appoint anybody to fill in for him…" And here Ernest pursed his thin lips and shook his head as if to dispel from his mind the disagreeable information he'd just communicated.

"So, what happened then?"

"What happened, Howard, was that no one thought to contact me, which of course they should have. But, never mind, that's past. Anyway, one of the parents took over for a short while. Somebody else passed out pretzel sticks, I think. I found out about it right before service. And here I am. Although how we're going to keep it out of the papers. I just don't know." He cast his miserable eyes upward as though the ceiling tiles, glued seamlessly together in a perfect pattern, might hold the answer to his dilemma.

"I see," Pastor Martin said. "And this happened this morning, during the Sunday school hour."

"Right." Ernest shuffled around in his seat and spoke to the wall slightly to the left of Pastor Martin's ear. "As I'm the elder over the Education Department, I'll go to see her, of course. Don't worry, my wife will be with me and Florence can, you know, talk to her woman to woman and all of that. But Susan needs to be removed from her position immediately. The parents will expect it." Ernest sighed. "And where on earth I'm going to get someone to take that class this late in the church year I don't know. It's not like we have teachers standing in line."

"Removing a teacher is something for the elders to decide," Howard stated firmly. "Besides, a situation of that nature needs to be handled..." he looked over at Martin.

"Carefully," the senior pastor added. "And, there may very well be more to this story than we know. But it's true, somebody has to meet with her."

"I'll do it," Howard said, opening up his elegant briefcase and removing a pen and paper.

"Absolutely not," Ernest would not be moved. "It's up to me. And don't give me this rubbish about the elders having to approve removing a Sunday school teacher for immoral behavior, Howard. The superintendent has done it in the past. Does anybody here remember the Mary Gomez debacle?" He shuddered. "What we would have done if Gladys Hirai hadn't nipped that in the bud immediately I don't know. But since she's not here and since I'm the elder over the Education Department, the authority passes to me." He lowered his voice dramatically. "Don't worry. I'll be diplomatic. I'll tell Miss Anello it's church policy. I'm sure she'll understand."

Pastor Martin, gracious as always, cleared his throat and leaned forward. "Ernest, I appreciate your noble gesture. It's obvious that you take your responsibilities quite seriously and that is an excellent quality in an elder, but perhaps in this instance it is better if I have a talk with Susan." He looked over at Howard, "The sooner the better, I think." Howard nodded.

"Oh no, I couldn't possibly let you do that! Why, you're the senior pastor!" Ernest was outraged.

"It's such a shame I have never met Susan personally; this will give me that opportunity. I'll put it on my calendar immediately. I think I have some time on Wednesday."

"But Pastor!"

"Thank you, again, Ernest, for your concern, but I think what we should really do now is have a time of prayer together. We'll make it short because I know Howard has a lunch meeting. But I'm positive, if we ask Him, the Lord will lead us to do exactly the right thing concerning Miss Anello."

With great reluctance, Ernest Cooke bowed his head and Pastor Martin led them firmly through a prayer.

With Ernest gone, Howard turned to the senior pastor. "Are you sure you don't want me to handle that?"

"No, I can do it," Martin said.

"You're sure?"

"Absolutely. I make it a point to get to know everyone in leadership anyway."

"Well, if you're sure. Oh by the way, there's something I need to let you know about."

"All right."

"I just want to tell you before word gets around and you find out second hand."

Martin frowned. "Something wrong?"

"Well, let's just say it's something you should know. I just heard today that the Simmons family is leaving the church."

"Oh no!" Martin was extremely troubled. "Do you know why?"

"Oh, they have a perfectly good reason." Howard smiled, putting him at ease. " Charles Simmons is being deployed and Gracie is moving back home to be with her folks."

"I really appreciate your letting me know."

"Well, I didn't want you to hear about it after they'd already gone."

"How soon are they leaving?"

"Charlie goes in two weeks, and Gracie is moving at the end of the month."

"I'll be sure and see both of them before they leave, maybe send them off with a prayer in next Sunday's service," Pastor Martin said warmly.

"Excellent idea. Oh," Howard added, "Speaking of excellent, your sermon this morning was top notch." He smiled broadly. "We can never hear too much about service."

Martin thanked him again, and the two chatted easily as they left the office and strolled out to the parking lot where they said goodbye.

A few minutes later, Nancy, who had stayed late to return books to the church library, caught up with Jason as he was heading for their car.

"Something really weird just happened," she said, waving at Pastor Martin who was driving past. He returned the wave with a huge grin and sped his dove gray Audi out the gate.

"Yeah?" Jason removed his keys from his pocket and clicked to unlock the beige Toyota Camry.

"Lillian Nakata just snubbed me in the hall!"

"What?" He opened the door on the driver's side and got in.

Nancy opened the passenger's side door and eased in beside him. "Seriously! I said hi, how are you doing today, or something like that, and she jerked her head to the side so quickly I thought she would snap it off!"

"Surely you're imagining things." Jason, the voice of reason, put the key in the ignition.

"I am not!"

"But I thought the two of you were friends."

"Not friends, exactly, more like friend-ly, and every once in a while she gets all confidential. But here's a really strange thing. That old crony of hers, Lottie Waters? Did the same thing. Passed me by in the library and said not a word. In fact, I distinctly thought I heard her sniff."

"Miss Lottie snubbed you?" Jason's hand froze on the key.

"And sniffed. Like something out of a movie! What's the matter, Jason, you look white as a sheet."

"Oh nothing," he replied uncertainly, staring at the key as if he had never seen it before.

"Are you going to turn that key or rub it to death?" she snapped.

Jason started the car and eased out of the parking space. "Are you absolutely certain that both of them actually snubbed you? That makes no sense."

" I know when I'm being snubbed," Nancy said irritably. "What I don't know is why. But I intend to find out, and trust me, I will. I am so mad. Look, I'm shaking!" And she held up two hands that were indeed trembling. " What is the matter Jason? Why are you weaving all over the parking lot at five miles per hour? Do you want me to drive?"

"Of course not. Just thinking, that's all."

"Well don't try to think and drive, that's a dear. Just get us home."

Chapter Ten

"Hello?"

"Ernest, this is Dr. Ko." The voice on the line was clipped, authoritative.

"Oh. *Oh!* Yes, Dr. Ko, hello."

"Can you spare a minute?"

"Of course. What can I do for you?"

"It's my niece, Gloria. We want to put her on staff as one of the leaders in the Summer Bible Club. I've checked with Lawrence by e-mail and cleared it with him. But somebody has to meet with her, give her the packet and have her sign the W-4 forms. Can you handle that? She wants to have this nailed down before she flies out of Honolulu next week."

"Of course! As elder over the Education Department, I am always happy..."

"Fine. I'd do it myself except that I'm calling from Chicago and won't be back until well after she leaves. Thank you, Ernest. You can find all the pertinent material in my box. Goodbye."

"Oh goodbye Dr. Ko. Don't worry, I'll handle everything. You can count on me," Ernest said, but there was no one on the other end of the line to hear him.

Ernest replaced the receiver with a shaking hand. He would get on it immediately. Dr. Ko would expect no less. The man could be absolutely ruthless if crossed. The Summer Children's Program Director, who was under Lawrence, would hit the roof. Ernest was sure she had her leaders picked out and ready to go already, but if Dr. Ko had said to hire a homeless person off the street, they would do it. That's just the way it was. Dr. Ko had founded the summer program years before, and he still felt as though he had absolute control over it.

If there was a power pyramid in the church, Dr. Richard Ko, a podiatrist, well thought of in the islands, was at the top. Richard's grandfather had been ACC's pastor in the eighties. Ernest had been in college at the time, but he vividly remembered Dr. Stanley Ko, the grim, fiery preacher with hair the color of steel and a voice to match. Not only had he been an excellent speaker, forceful and persuasive, but he had been greatly admired as an administrator. "Brother Stan" was the one who wrote the church constitution, and he was also the one who, all by himself, had designed the church's organizational structure. And, Ernest reminded himself primly, this had not included an education pastor or a junior pastor.

In 2004, the elderly minister had been invited back from California where he'd retired, to preach at the church's 42nd anniversary, and the dedication of new educational facilities. A few weeks after that, he had died of a stroke. He had been well-loved; he was still greatly mourned, and it might be fair to say that many long-time church members felt that no pastor who came after him could measure up to the standard he set. These same people regretted that his grandson, who was so very much like him, had not gone into the ministry.

"Good thing I'm on excellent terms with him," Ernest congratulated himself. At lunch, he made the phone call. Gloria, all business, sounded like a chip off the old block, so it was fortunate he had been prompt. They were to meet on Saturday at church to sign all the papers.

Ernest patted himself on the back. Job well done.

Early that afternoon, across town, Helen Chang, founder and leader of the Aloha Intercessory Prayer Group, received several urgent messages. First, Pastor Martin's mother had been rushed to the hospital. No immediate details yet, but from what Helen could gather it appeared to be a stroke.

Adelle and Jeff senior had been visiting Oahu from Hilo on the Big Island when it happened. Helen would never say a word against outer island hospitals; her own mother had been treated very well at the one in Hilo, but it was convenient that if such a thing had to occur, it happened here in Oahu. Both Pastor Martin and Judi, his wife, could be there in minutes, and Jeff senior was assured of a comfortable place to stay, family at his side.

A second prayer request was from Josiah Briggs whose thirty year-old niece just learned, after repeated headaches forced her to have an operation, that she had terminal brain cancer. Five months pregnant, Cindi and her husband faced a decision that no one should ever have to make. She could continue to carry the child and hope to have the baby before she died. Or, she could receive radiation treatments to hopefully prolong her life, but if she did this, the baby's life would be forfeit. Helen shook her head. She remembered Cindi who had been a leader in the Bible Club one summer. A bright, outgoing teenager, Cindi had wanted a big family. "At least six!" Helen remembered her saying. "Oh Lord," Helen prayed. "Give us wisdom; tell us exactly how we should pray."

The final call had been from a church member whose son had overdosed on drugs and driven his car into a stone wall. He had died instantly. His wife had been taken to Kaiser Hospital with severe injuries, but in stable condition.

Always efficient, Helen made phone calls to the top two names on her prayer chain. These two saints, both of them homebound, never failed to steer urgent requests through the right channels. She then e-mailed Kathy, the office clerk, who would make sure messages were sent out to the staff. Her next call was to Howard Nakata who would no doubt rush down to the hospital immediately and inform the other elders about Pastor Martin's mother. She called Ruby Lota, a neighbor of the Briggs family, and informed her of the situation. Ruby would go right over and pray with Josiah and Amy.

Tonight, the intercessory group had its weekly meeting at the church. She called Ray Akino, leader of the men's Saturday morning prayer group, and Rebecca Hart, the co-ordinator of those who prayed around the clock for the church each week, and passed the word along. Rebecca and Ray said they would try to get to church early.

Her arrangements completed, Helen checked her e-mail once again to make sure she had received all the last minute information. Situations needing prayer were changing constantly, and even though Helen had many helpers, it was still possible for things to slip through the cracks. So, she always double-checked everything.

Helen took her position as AIPG leader very seriously. Even as a young girl she had loved hearing sermons on prayer, although at the time they mainly concerned people on the mission field in far away and desperate places. She could vividly remember listening open-mouthed to some of the first-hand accounts of astonishing miracles, attributable only to prayer, that visiting missionaries told. It came as no surprise that, in college, she had led an on-campus prayer group herself. When she returned to Oahu, aware of the mass exodus of congregants at Aloha Community Church and the crises that had precipitated it, she had founded the AIPG.

So now, like a commander rallying her troops for battle, Helen prepared the intercessors to engage the enemy. They had been trained for weeks, some of them years. They would stand in their appointed stations and they would wield the mighty weapons of prayer and worship. Helen was not naïve, nor was she inexperienced. She had long ago memorized the words of St. Peter delineating the battle: *Your adversary, the devil, as a roaring lion, walketh about, seeking whom he may devour.* And she had no doubt that this adversary had stalked the halls and sanctuary of Aloha Community Church for decades.

However, Helen was not intimidated. Every year at the Intercessors Retreat, those who assembled studied and read the passage from the Book of Ephesians that they all took to heart. In fact, it was printed on the front page of the Intercessor's Manual, handed out to every new recruit: *Finally, be strong in the Lord, and in His mighty power. Put on the full armor of God so that you may be able to stand firm against the schemes of the devil.* Well, her armor was on. And now, as always, she put her faith in the invincible strength of the greatest warrior who ever lived, Jesus Christ, who would not only lead them in battle, but assure that they were victorious.

After a short prayer of thanksgiving, Helen got in her car and headed for the church. She had to get there early; there was a lot to do.

About that same time, at Ala Moana Shopping Center, Chris stood in front of Long's Drug store, with Sears on his right, an elevator going to a lower level in front of him, and a long arm of the mall stretching out to his left. Mei Ling had refused a date, of course. However, she was helping her aunty shop for a birthday gift at the mall this afternoon and they would be finished at four. Mei Ling had to be home for dinner at five-thirty, but she could show him around the mall a little if he wanted.

"And the dim sum?"

"Not this time."

Okay, it wasn't dinner and a movie, but "not this time" sounded promising.

Four o'clock passed and then four-fifteen. Chris was getting impatient, but he had to admit if you wanted to wait somewhere, this was the place. He had heard that Ala Moana was the largest open-air mall in the world and it certainly did look impressive. Of course his home- town, Grantsville, KY, population 4,330, didn't have anything even remotely like this, only a drug store and a Ben Franklin. There were a few outlet stores in what they called a mall, forty minutes away at Crown Pointe. But if you wanted to buy anything in a fancy shop you had to travel all the way to Lexington. Or else you could shop out of catalogues, which had always suited Chris just fine.

But he had heard that Ala Moana was a place not only to shop, but for tourists to come as well. He had looked it up on-line and discovered that it had nearly 300 shops, a gazillion restaurants, Center Stage where bands and dance troupes performed, and lots of other stuff. Hard to think, when you looked around at all the new glossy storefronts, tall trees and flowering bushes, miles of paved walkways, and entertainment areas with all the fancy lighting, that it had once been a swamp.

Then, without warning, there was a gentle tap on his shoulder. He turned to find a smiling Mei Ling and decided that seeing her away from campus like this had been well worth the wait.

She was like a little China doll, petite and fragile. Today she was dressed in beige and soft tones of blue. Lots of lace and buttons with designs on them. Slim jeans and slippers with sparkles. All very feminine. Her hair was done in a ponytail and her lips were shiny with gloss.

They said hello and Mei Ling apologized. Her aunty couldn't make up her mind what she wanted so it took longer than she thought.

"Still," she said dutifully, "I promised to show you around. What do you want to see?"

"I dunno. Anything."

Her eyes narrowed. "You said you had special present to buy," Mei Ling tilted her head and looked at him curiously, trying to decide if what he had just said was another joke.

"Oh, yeah, that's right! I am looking for Christmas presents for my mom and my uncle."

"Christmas presents? In May?"

"Oh, I plan ahead."

"Hmmm. I do not know if I can help you," she said, "but here is map from the Information Desk. We can sit down and I will show you, yes?"

They took a seat on a low wall that reached all the way down one arm of the mall and formed a border for the largest koi pond he had ever imagined. Bright blue tiles stretched ahead as far as Chris could see, the fish (which looked to Chris like giant goldfish) lazily drifting along in water clear as glass.

"Hey, how 'bout something to drink?" Chris suggested. "I saw a Jamba Juice a while back."

Mei Ling did not answer at first; her attention was focused on the map. "Hmmm. This is not good map," she looked up at him, clearly unhappy. "Oh wait, this one folds out. Ah. Much better. Come close. We are here, Mall Level 2, right here, you see?" she said, pointing with one pink nail.

Chris was delighted to come close and peer over her shoulder, but then she pulled back and faced him. "What kind of presents do your mother and uncle like?"

"Hadn't thought about it," Chris smiled. "I'm open for suggestions."

Mei Ling, predictably, took the matter seriously. "We take mother first," she said. "What present you thinking to buy?"

"Wow, that is a question!" he said. "Let me think. Well, usually she gets things to wear. You know, sweaters, scarves, gloves, PJ's, perfume."

"PJ's? What is PJ's?"

"Pajamas. Uh, without the feet."

Mei Ling frowned again, and Chris had to remind himself that his sense of humor wasn't exactly winning him points here. So he decided to be serious too. "Okay, how's about perfume?" he suggested.

"Perfume is very personal," Mei Ling said, "and must match personality of the person very closely. Same with jewelry. You have sister, no?"

"No."

"Ah, too bad. She could help. Well..." she leaned back a little, thinking. Chris smelled a trace of spicy perfume which made his head spin.

"Oh I know!" He had a sudden thought. "How about something from Hawaii? But, uh, not too expensive."

Mei Ling sighed. "This is very hard for me. A son's present to his mother is very personal thing. But there are shops where you could find such things."

"Great!"

"Now for uncle. He is businessman, yes?"

"Right. How did you guess?"

"Lucky guess," she said with a slight touch of humor. "For businessman, good thing is leather or koa, like bowls or trays to keep things in. Koa is nice because you can get it only here in the islands."

"Sounds great," Chris was enthusiastic. Mei Ling returned to the map, turning it this way and that, looking for ideas. He wished that he hadn't made such a big deal out of her helping him to buy presents. But of course if he hadn't she probably wouldn't have come. Yet, it would have been so nice to just kick back and talk. About nothing really, her favorite food. His. TV shows they both liked. That sort of thing. But conversations with Mei Ling tended to be directed toward some goal. For example, she could talk for hours about American history. She knew more about the Civil War than he had ever thought of knowing, and he had been born right where part of it had actually happened! Brainy and beautiful, that was Mei Ling.

The whole issue of the Chinaman was still in the forefront of

Chris's mind, and he was trying his best to sort it out. Sometimes, he could still hear the man say, "Be careful! The night is coming!" in that fearful voice of his. Chris would have dearly loved to talk with Mei Ling about it, but cringed when he thought about what she might say. If only he could get behind the huge walls she put up, he might be brave enough to try. But that was a long ways off.

At four forty-five, Chris and Mei Ling took the elevator down to the street level and walked to the center where the shopping center stretched out its four arms, one in each direction of the compass. It took a while as the center was packed with people. To Chris they all looked as though they came from Japan, but then again he hadn't been in Hawaii long enough to tell the differences between Asian nationalities. They walked a bit, then Mei Ling stopped, motioned with a smile to a shop and put a check mark with her pencil on the map. A hula dancer was performing on the stage, and all around people were sitting on benches watching, but Mei Ling hardly noticed. They traveled briefly down another arm of the mall. She check-marked a second shop on the map, then they walked back to the center.

They took an elevator to the next level where they could still look over and see the hula dancer if they wanted to, beautifully swaying in time to the music of guitars and ukuleles. This time, Mei Ling stopped for a moment and watched.

"Do you do the hula?" Chris asked.

"No," she said simply, but there was a trace of longing in her voice. They strolled past some high-end stores to Macy's and along the way Mei Ling check-marked two more shops. There she stopped and looked up at him.

"You have to go?" Chris couldn't believe the time had passed so quickly.

"I cannot be late," she said, folding the map neatly. "But I will see you Friday. At study group."

"Aw doggone it, I can't. That's my small group night."

"Small group?"

"People from my church."

"Ah, yes, I see. And what does this small group do?"

"We study the Bible. Well, not all the whole thing. Topics, you know. I mean, like right now, we're studying about the leadership of the Holy Spirit." From the expression on Mei Ling's face he could have been talking about alien abductions or nanotechnology.

"And this meeting is more important than study group? We have test next week."

"Well, I know, but see, the thing is that right now, well…" He lifted his hands helplessly, "I don't know how to explain, I just really have to be there."

"I understand," she smiled politely. "To you, church is very important. I understand that. Now…I must go."

Chris paused, trying to think of something to capture her attention a few minutes longer. "Hey, wait. Get out your planner!"

"What?"

"Your planner, quickly."

She opened her purse and withdrew a tiny leather book. He looked over her shoulder. "Ah, there it is, just the blank date I was hoping for."

"For what?"

"The dim sum," he grinned. "You promised. One friend to another."

"Ah yes," she mused. "Well then," she put a check in the blank square, and turned to him solemnly. "We eat dim sum." And then, very politely, she shook his hand and wished him well with his shopping.

Chris just stood there watching until she disappeared from sight. He knew she had no idea why he would put the small group meeting before studying, and he was sorry about that, but even if she had stayed longer, he doubted he would have been able to explain. He'd have to tell the whole story about the Chinaman for one thing, which she was not ready to hear, and for another he'd have to admit that he needed to go on Friday because he hoped to talk with Pastor Jason about *her* and her possible involvement in all of this. And that would really freak her out.

No, he had no choice really but to let her go. It had come to him at some point, he wasn't sure when, not only that the Chinaman's message was urgent, but that it concerned Mei Ling in some way. It didn't matter how often he tried to convince himself that that was just plain nuts, he simply could not shake the notion. He had pretty much tied himself up in knots trying to figure it all out and finally he had given up. Perhaps

Pastor Jason could help. He sure seemed to be a guy you could talk to about things. Even off the wall stuff. As far as Chris was concerned, Friday group meeting couldn't come soon enough.

So, yeah, he chose the small group over study because this was really more important. Besides, he turned and headed for Subway. Mei Ling was wrong. It wasn't tests coming up next week, it was reviews. Way different. Reviews weren't graded.

He perked up a little. At long last he had a date, something actually on the calendar. Just the two of them, not a whole group of people. That was something, right? Isn't that what he'd been wanting? So she was a little disappointed in him at the moment about missing one study session. He would just have to redeem himself. He'd have to study super hard and pass the reviews with flying colors.

Yeah, right.

Chapter Eleven

Wednesday, May 5th, 7:00 p.m.

Howard Nakata unlocked the front door of his home in Mililani, took off his shoes, and placed them carefully on the mat. He picked up the mail that had been left for him on the hall table. Then, he took it and his briefcase upstairs to the bedroom that had been converted, years ago, into a small office. The son who had once occupied that room had been killed in a military training accident years ago. Even after all the personal items had been packed away and the walls repainted, Howard thought that he would feel David's presence somehow. A quiet, studious young man, like his father, the bond between them had been strong. But over the years, though grief remained, no lingering spirit had made itself known in the small 10' x 10' room. David was at peace with God.

Howard turned on two halogen lamps and sank down in a chair. It had been a hard day, emotionally draining. The inevitable decision he and the other CEO's now faced would have been unthinkable at one time. But a worsening economy gave them no choice. The parent company would remain open, but the two satellite stores would have to close. Twenty-two employees would lose jobs they had held for many years and be forced out into a declining job market. Some of these people had become close friends over time. All of them had families to support. Howard sighed deeply. All the bright hopes they'd had at the beginning. And now it had come to this.

The blinking light on the answering system caught his attention. He pressed the button; the message was from the senior pastor.

"Hi, Howard. Just want to let you know the latest about my mother. All the tests came back negative and there don't seem to be any lingering complications. As strokes go, it could have been much worse. What I want to tell you is that Mom will probably be released tomorrow or Friday at the latest, and she absolutely refuses to stay here in Oahu. She's determined to go back home as soon as they let her. So, I'm taking a short emergency leave and I'll fly back with my folks to Hilo and get them settled. I'll be back by Sunday, so no worries there, but I'm relying on you to hold down the fort until I get back. Oh, and by the way, Susan Anello cancelled my meeting with her this morning and rescheduled for Saturday. Could you handle it? And if not, I guess we could call in Ernest. You have my cell number if you need me. Thanks."

Howard opened his briefcase, withdrew his planner and a few items he had taken from his mail box at the church that he hadn't gotten around to reading, including the extended bulletin insert with all the general church news and, of course, the pink envelope. He opened the planner, took a gold pen from the holder on his desk, and was about to enter the Saturday appointment with Susan Anello when he noticed an urgent meeting already scheduled.

Before he could make a decision about what to do, a strident voice called up the stairs. "Howard! You up there? Come eat!"

Howard quickly made a notation in the margin. With another sigh, he replaced the pen in its holder. He stood, straightened his shoulders, and breathed deeply in and out several times to clear his mind and force signs of concern from his face. There was no need to let Lillian know about the problems at work. She would worry and propose well meaning, but ineffective solutions. He'd learned, through hard experience, that the best thing to do was to leave work behind when he opened the front door of his home. The Bible said each day had troubles of its own, and that was true. Many problems would be there waiting for him at work tomorrow. Worrying about them tonight would solve nothing. He washed his hands in the bathroom, and walked back downstairs.

"I didn't hear you come in," Lillian was busy pouring water in glasses and setting them on the kitchen table, "And I wouldn't have even known you were home if I hadn't come into the living room and seen your shoes in the hall!" she added irritably. "So...how long have you been upstairs?" She was wearing a pair of worn cotton pants and a baggy purple knit top that did not flatter her sallow complexion. She did not look happy.

"Only a few minutes."

"Well, you're late and the chicken's going to be tough," she sighed.

"Sorry, I had some things to do at work."

"I always have dinner ready on time," she complained, " 'cause you said you were cutting back on your hours at work, that's why. So how come you're late?"

"Things came up at the last minute."

" Things came up Monday and Tuesday too?"

Howard shook his head. "Sorry."

"And didn't I say, like a million times, call me if you're going to be late!" she muttered, under her breath, turning to the fridge, opening the door. She called over her shoulder, "What dressing do you want?" With thick and heavy hands, she withdrew a wooden bowl filled with greens and placed it on the table.

Howard sat down, drank some water. "No dressing."

Lillian snorted. "You've got to have dressing. You eat a little fat and it helps the body take in all the vitamins and minerals. You're just wasting good food eating salad with no dressing." She placed a bottle of Caesar Lite on the table along with two plates, each containing a baked chicken breast with tomato, green beans, carrots drizzled with olive oil and one small scoop of rice. After a health scare a few years ago, Howard was on a heart healthy diet. She took the chair across from her husband. The couple bowed their heads and he said grace. He put a napkin in his lap.

"So, any news about Jeff Martin's mother?" Lillian was eager for news.

"Yes." Howard nudged a few beans with his chopsticks.

Lillian rolled her eyes. It was painful dragging information out of Howard, but if she didn't ask him questions, especially about church, she would never learn a thing. If she wanted to know even the smallest little thing, she had to play reporter, that was just the way it was. "And…?" she looked at him impatiently.

"And, it seems as though she's doing well. She's going to be discharged tomorrow." He got up and headed for the fridge.

"What do you want?"

He came back with a can of green tea and popped the cap.

"Why didn't you say you wanted tea! Can let me at least put it in a glass." She jumped up, filled a plastic tumbler with ice cubes and returned it with a slight thump on the table. Then, she sat back and watched him pour the green liquid carefully over the ice cubes.

"I bet Adelle Martin is going right back to Hilo," she began. "She's never going to stay here in Oahu. Too independent. That's what everybody says. So why didn't she stay in Sacramento? That's what I want to know. They lived there for years. Nice house, too. " Lillian considered herself an expert on pastors and their wives. If one of them had asked her, she could have written them a handbook of what to do and what not to do. She had firm opinions about every facet of their lives and, as church members go, it was fair to say that she was not alone.

"And why move to Hilo!" she continued through a mouthful of salad. " Haoles never do well in an old town like that. Okay, so she didn't want to move next door to Jeff when he took the job here. But if she was going to move to Hawaii anyway, she could still live in Oahu. Buy a house across the Pali, Kaneohe, somewhere like that. But another island? Just look at all the trouble that caused. Now Jeff is going to have to go back with her to Hilo I bet. So who's going to run the church?" She continued eating thoughtfully.

Howard remained silent.

"Well?"

"What."

"How is it?" She glanced at Howard's plate.

"Good."

Lillian sighed again. This time, it was one of the deep long-suffering variety. "You know why Adelle has heart trouble, right? It's the way they eat. That whole family eats the S.A.D. You know what that means? Standard American Diet, that's what: fried food, vegetables cooked to mush and white sugar desserts. You should be thankful I fix you healthy food, Howard."

Howard crunched a blanched bean between his teeth moodily, looking anything but pleased. "The vegetables are hard," he muttered.

"No, they're not. They are cooked *al dente*. You cook vegetables too much, you lose all the vitamins."

"And if you don't cook them enough you lose all the taste," Howard thought, but instead, he said, "Why isn't the TV on?" He looked at the counter where the set was blank. They usually watched the news while they ate.

"We never talk anymore," Lillian complained, with just the tiniest whine in her voice. "And you're always working."

She said the words lightly but there was an unmistakable undertone to her voice that Howard recognized at once. Something was up. But he didn't say anything, choosing instead to cast a malevolent eye at a rigid and unsavory carrot as though by doing so it might be obliging and cook itself a bit more, add a little butter and salt.

Pleased with the conversation so far, Lillian asked Howard what was new at work.

Howard could think of nothing he wanted to share, but after a moment's reflection, he looked up and smiled. "I do have some news. Masa's Grindz moved out next door and a natural food place moved in. Opens next week. I can get healthy lunches." He sounded genuinely pleased.

"That's nice," Lillian said agreeably. "But you want to be careful. I went over to one of those natural food places Hawaii Kai side couple times and the prices were sky high. How they think they can charge that much I don't know. And I don't know why you don't let me fix you lunch."

"But I do, twice a week. Now, on the other days I can eat healthy." He finished the last of his tea and put the glass down. "So… how's everything with Dr. Kamis?" It was Howard's turn to be polite. Lillian worked as a dentist's receptionist three days a week.

"Good. Patients falling off a little bit because of the economy…" she finished the last of the beans. A bystander would not call Lillian fat, but it appeared that she definitely liked her food. Howard thought that she and her friends at work probably helped themselves to all the things he couldn't eat. But, as a dedicated wife, she never served anything at home that was not on his diet. The fact that she actually seemed to enjoy the food continually astonished him.

"That's understandable," Howard said. "Most people don't consider trips to a dentist high priority."

Lillian ran her tongue over her teeth absently. "Still yet, he's doing well enough. The prices he charges! He has plenty money saved up for sure. I always wanted Robert to be a dentist," she sighed. A small, wistful one this time.

"Robert is fine where he is."

"Ummm," They sat for a few moments in peaceable silence as Lillian ate. Howard, picking at the rice and chicken, wished his wife would turn on the TV. However, he knew that if he made a move in that direction it would be construed in a very poor light. So he chewed. One inedible mouthful after another.

"Um, Howard," Lillian said, after a bit, deliberately putting a smile into her voice. "You know on Sunday, when you went to get your mail?"

"Yes," he said, stabbing a bean with the tip of his chopstick. He popped it in his mouth, thinking *In a blind taste-test I'd have guessed this one was the Charmin*. But his face gave nothing away. Lillian was trying to keep him healthy. As disagreeable as this made his meals, he was determined to seem appreciative.

"Well, did you notice a letter? In a pink envelope?"

Howard stopped chewing immediately, looked over at his wife, and swallowed. His voice, when he spoke, had a hard edge to it. "I saw an envelope like that. What do you know about it?"

"Well...um, did you read it?"

"Why do you want to know?"

This stopped Lillian for a second, but then she plowed on. "Well, because it maybe has something important in it," she said with untroubled air of someone commenting on the weather.

Howard was not fooled. "Did you write it?"

"Me? No!" Lillian pushed the few remaining carrots around her plate with the tip of one chopstick.

"Did you read it?"

"*No.*"

"Then how do you know it has something important in it?" he asked, his eyes never leaving her face.

"Well, I just know, that's all." Lillian pushed her plate away and sat back, her mouth set in a stubborn line. Suddenly, the conversation was not going at all as she had planned.

Howard sat back as well. "And you're getting upset. Why is that? What's so important about this letter, Lillian?"

"Oh Howard," she thrust her body forward again. "You just have to read that letter. Something's happened, and you need to know about it, so that you can...do something." She put a great deal of emphasis on the last two words.

"I see, " Howard's gaze betrayed not the slightest hint of emotion. "And what exactly am I supposed to do?"

"Oh, you'll know soon as you read the letter. You'll know just what to do," she said, demurely.

That look in her eye set red lights flashing, huge banks of them. Howard was immediately on his guard. "Lillian, I don't like the sound of this. I don't like it at all," he said in a deceptively soft voice.

"What did I say?" she protested, looking around for an invisible audience that might take her side.

"You know, as chairman of the Board of Elders, I never discuss church matters at home and I've asked you repeatedly to let me handle whatever comes up without interference."

The stubborn set of her lips suggested that Lillian knew this very well and didn't like it one bit. "I just asked did you read the letter, that's all. Was that such a bad thing?"

"It might be," he said relentlessly. " Depends on why you want to know."

"Oh, forget it!" Lillian took her glass to the sink and stood there dramatically. "I'm sorry I asked. Just forget it!"

Howard said nothing for a few seconds. He was very tempted to let things end there. Fits of pique were not unusual with Lillian and there was a part of him that warned him against digging deeper. He was too tired, for one thing. Did he really need to get into all of this? Yet, he simply could not let this go. There was something quite suspicious about Lillian's interest in the contents of this letter. It brought back old and unhappy memories. It reminded him that, after previous incidents, one in particular, he had set firm parameters in place about her involvement in church matters. But it now occurred to him that she might be testing the waters again. If so, he'd soon put a stop to that.

"Do I have to remind you what happened a few years back?" he said pointedly.

That hit the mark. Several unpleasant things had happened over the last few years and she wasn't sure exactly what he was referring to. So she answered on general principle. "Why are you bringing up ancient history! I only asked a question, and now look! You're making a huge big thing out of it." She rinsed the glass noisily and banged it down on the drain board to make her point.

"Me?" Howard raised his eyebrows.

She turned back. Above the sagging neckline of her purple knit top, Lillian's cheeks flushed red. "Oh I wish I hadn't said anything!" Wiping her hands on a dishtowel, she turned her eyes to the ceiling and breathed deeply.

"But you did say something. Quite a bit, in fact."

"Oh just forget it!" Lillian threw down the towel in disgust. "Forget I ever asked you a sim-pul question."

"I don't think it is a simple question," Howard continued. "And I'll tell you why. A few years ago, you and your cohort Miss Lottie, Gladys Hirai and heaven only knows who else, began something that resulted in a terrible turn of events. And it started just like this, with a few simple questions."

Lillian's blood froze. She and Howard had gone head to head about many church situations, but there were things the chairman of elders did not, and hopefully never would know. Could one of her long buried secrets have finally wiggled its way into the light? Her heart hammered anxiously.

"And soon it became a smear campaign against Jamie Wilson."

Lillian breathed easier. He was bringing that up again, was he? Well, it could have been worse. "We didn't start that!" she snapped.

"Admit it, Lillian. You never liked him and you wanted him out. Rumors were started. Simple things at first..."

"Well, that was not me! How many times do I have to say it? "Lillian slammed her bulky frame down in the kitchen chair and glared at her husband. "We've been over this before, you know."

Howard was unperturbed. "Obviously not enough. Okay, you didn't actually start the rumors, but you did your best to get the news around. What is it you ladies call yourselves, the 'coconut wireless?' Well, you did an efficient job there. The rumors got worse."

Lillian was furious. "That is not fair, Howard, and you know it. Why do you always pick on me and my friends? Everybody complained about Jamie, not just us. Nobody liked him. He was rude to everybody. He used to work with gangs in L.A. and he tried to treat the Hawaii kids here the same way. People were so upset! Families leaving the church, and what did the elders do? Nothing!"

"I had every intention of taking him aside for a long talk…"

"Long talk. Ha! Lot of good that would do…"

"…which I have every reason to believe would have made a difference. However, before I could do that, so much pressure was put on him—from you and others—that he resigned."

"Well, good riddance," she said mulishly.

"He was a good man."

"So you say."

"I do say, and so did others. We needed him. And look what happened, we've had nothing but trouble since he left."

"That's not *my* fault! And why are you bringing all of that up anyway! What does that have to do with my simple question? Doesn't make sense."

"I have to ask myself why you are so interested in a letter that was placed in my mailbox at church. That's all, just a simple observation, because that doesn't make sense either. There's something funny about this, Lillian. I don't like it."

"Well I don't like the way you're talking to me. You should see your face. Looking at me like I'm some kind of criminal or something. How can you hurt me this way, Howard," Lillian said as her eyes filled with tears.

Howard sighed. The last thing he needed tonight was more drama and it was entirely his own fault that he had allowed himself to get drawn into one. "I will read the letter, Lillian," he said patiently, "as I read all my mail—when I have time. But I want you to know this in advance, I will not discuss its contents with you, and that is that."

"But I never asked…"

Howard got up. "Enough. Now let's just end it right there. I have a report due for an urgent Red Cross meeting at Kaena Point on Saturday, and I need to get ready."

"Oh yeah, by all means spend time doing what's really important!" Lillian mumbled under her breath.

But Howard simply took another can of tea from the fridge and headed upstairs.

Lillian, fuming, listened to him walk lightly up the steps as though he didn't have a care in the world. He had hardly touched the food on his plate and the carefully cooked vegetables stared at her reproachfully. A wave of anger swept over her and she had to restrain herself from throwing the plate, food and all, into the rubbish.

She drank some water to cool her temper. It wasn't just his disregard for all the work she put into the food she served that had made her furious. It was that doggone self-righteous attitude he had whenever anything connected with the church was mentioned. He would talk your ears off about TV, golf, or fishing. But as soon as anything relating to the church came up, he'd either clam up and look at her stink-eye as if daring her to ask questions. Or, he'd get on his high horse and give her a lecture.

She was his wife, didn't he see that! Wives were made by God to help their husbands, but whenever she tried to help Howard, this is what happened! She couldn't understand why everybody bowed to him as though he were some great oracle or something. "Sometimes," she said to her invisible audience once more, "he's just a silly old man. All that old style samurai blood in his veins makes him act crazy." Well, that was the last straw. She was sick and tired of it.

Lillian stood and cleared the table with a vengeance.

Back in his office once again, Howard's normal equanimity surfaced. Thinking back on the conversation, he wished that he had just kept his mouth shut. When the children were small they'd been such a happy family. Lillian was a wonderful mother, a little too protective, but that was her nature. But after David died and Kevin, a widower with no children, moved thousands of miles away, she had turned her attention to the church in an unhealthy way. If only she'd teach Sunday school, or join the choir! But no, she insisted on hanging around the office in her spare time and nosing around where she wasn't wanted or needed, and that had always led to trouble.

Today, he had seen the familiar signs of something brewing in her eyes when she talked about that letter. He knew in his bones it was some old biddy complaining about something--which was not even any of Lillian's business (it never was). And he knew all too well that if Lillian got into it *he* would end up as a referee in the middle of some squabble or other over something highly emotional. He didn't have the time or the energy for that. So, it was just as well he'd said what he had.

The thing was that he hated to be prodded about church responsibilities by his wife. Wasn't he a responsible elder? Didn't he do everything expected of him, including reading his mail?

He shook off his irritation, turned on the lights, and sat down at his desk, the silence punctuated at intervals by the sound of crockery being thrown around in the kitchen below. And that, despite his normally unflappable nature, irritated him once again. So he opened a desk drawer and withdrew a luscious vanilla brownie, wrapped in cellophane, from the cache he kept hidden there. He opened the package, took a whiff of the delicious aroma, and bit into the forbidden dessert, allowing the icing to melt slowly on his tongue.

After a delectable moment, his thoughts turned to the Susan Anello situation. Unfortunately, he would be unable to meet with her on Saturday. There was no way he could get out of that urgent Red Cross meeting. They were on a deadline and he absolutely had to be there. Howard took a second bite of brownie, rolled it around on his tongue, and closed his eyes as the succulent flavors mingled together on his palate. As much as he regretted it, Ernest would have to be Susan's initial contact with the official voice of the church. For a few delicious moments, Howard devoted his entire attention to finishing the brownie. Afterwards, he wrapped the cellophane in a tissue and put it in his briefcase to be disposed of later. He washed his hands in the bathroom.

When he returned, he made a note on his planner to follow up with Susan himself the following week. As he lifted the receiver to dial Ernest's number, he mentally rehearsed what he would have to say in order to walk Ernest through the meeting he and Florence would have with Susan, step by step.

As the phone rang on the other end, Howard absently tossed the pink envelope back in his briefcase, and put it, and the minor altercation with his wife, out of his mind entirely.

Chapter Twelve

"Look at all this food!" Jason exclaimed happily as the Friday night ladies wedged through the door, arms loaded with goodies. Laughing and joking among themselves, they grabbed glasses, plates, napkins and chopsticks from the cupboard and spread the food out on the table. Jason and Chris admired everything, pointing to dishes that were new, being sure to put in a word of thanks for old favorites, like malasadas. Chris whipped up tumblers full of ice in a jiffy and set out the drinks, and now all that was left was the blessing.

"Let's hold hands," Jason said, grasping the soft, cushiony hand of Pua on one side and the iron grip of Norman on the other. "Lord God in heaven, we thank you with all our hearts for bringing us together this evening. Bless this food to the nourishment of our bodies, bless the hands that prepared it, and bless our fellowship with your Presence. In Jesus' name."

"Amen," everyone echoed.

Tonight, there were no small dessert plates, but large, substantial dinnerware and Jason piled his high. He wasn't the only one. All the others, even Yumi who normally ate next to nothing, were piling it on. At one point, he looked over at Norman. "Hey there, Norman," he smiled. "Looks like you're having a three course meal."

"Yeah? Well I have no intention of leaving a tip," he said good-naturedly.

Tonight, instead of taking cookies and chips into the living area, they all hung around the kitchen table, laughing and joking easily. Marge talked about a funny card she'd received in the mail from a nephew on the mainland; Chris told a hilarious story about his landlady who, at seventy, was suddenly becoming vain about her appearance. Evidently, she refused to wear her eyeglasses and bumped into things right and left. Her grandson hid the car keys and in a fit of anger, the older lady took his bicycle and nearly ran over a neighbor out for a walk with his dog. The man had to hop a fence to avoid getting hit. The way Chris told it, you couldn't help but laugh.

Jason hadn't realized just how hungry he was until he had loaded his plate and the fragrant aromas tickled his taste buds. He ate heartily as he listened to the conversation ebb and flow around him. Evidently Pua and Yumi had gotten together to go to the farmer's market during the week and Pua was sharing a recipe she found for the avocados she had bought. Yumi, still dressed severely, but looking much more relaxed tonight, listened attentively. Getting friendly with Pua was having a positive effect.

Marge and Chris began discussing the Sunday sermon in glowing terms and Norman commented from time to time in the disparaging way everyone had come to expect. Tonight, he looked pale. His skin had a yellowish tinge. There were a few beads of perspiration on his forehead. But he was just as irascible as ever.

"I wish you'd stop talking about Jeff Martin as though he were the Pope, or Billy Graham," he said in a voice loud enough to silence Pua and Yumi. "That guy's about as genuine as a snake oil salesman, if you ask me."

Marge just shook her head. Pua started to speak, but a warning look from Yumi stopped her.

"By the way," Yumi said. "I e-mailed everyone our phone numbers as you suggested, Pastor Jason, and this week's assignment. Rhoda e-mailed me back this morning and said she was really sorry she wouldn't be here tonight. She wants everybody to know that she hasn't left the group, something just came up."

Jason asked if anybody had heard from Brysen but nobody had. Nor did they have any idea why Brysen, who had seemed such an eager group member, had suddenly dropped out. A few of them hazarded guesses, but in the end they had to admit that they just didn't know.

Jason looked at his watch. Time was hurtling by. "Sorry to say this, guys, but I'm going to have to ask you to finish up."

They finished their snacks quickly and brought drinks and study materials with them to the living area. Chris and Norman stopped for a moment, head to head in a deep discussion, and when they separated Norman spoke louder. "And, you know, I've just about had it with the church," he barked, setting his drink and Bible on an end table. "I mean, I thought the church was supposed to be welcoming, encouraging, helpful, someplace where people reached out to others." He sat down and looked around truculently. " I walk the corridors of that church like a ghost. Everybody's in their cliques and they don't even give me the time of day. I'm fed up with it."

Pua and Yumi looked at each other. It was obvious that they all were thinking the same thing. Norman was about as approachable and friendly as a porcupine, except that porcupines probably had nicer dispositions. It was Marge, of course, who spoke up, walking back into the living area.

"I think that's unfair, Norman," she said, sitting opposite him. "The church isn't just a building. And it doesn't just meet on Sundays. The church is people. We're the church."

"That's right," Chris and Pua agreed.

"And we are welcoming, encouraging and helpful."

"You always have an answer for everything," Norman complained. "You should have gone into politics with your good friend Jeff Martin.

Jason couldn't figure out if Norman really meant half the things he said or he just liked being curmudgeonly in order to get a rise out of people. Marge certainly could never resist rising to the bait. Poor Marge.

Once everyone was settled, Jason said, "I think we'll begin with a time of sharing. Anybody have anything they'd like to share?"

They looked at each other, shrugging, hesitating. Finally, Pua asked to speak. It was obvious she was bubbling over with good news. Under her cap of snow white hair, her face was radiant. "Well," she said excitedly, "Last week, after our lesson, I read in the Bible, Galations 5:16, *Walk by the Spirit and you will not carry out the desire of the flesh.* Well, maybe you remember me telling you my son was having a hard time. He had

worked for Beckler Products for about ten years. Worked himself up to
a manager position. Made a pretty good salary. Then the economy got
bad; they downsized. He lost his job. That was about, oh, eight months
ago. I tole you this last week and we all prayed for him. Remember I
said he been looking for a job? Well what I didn't say was that nobody
would hire him. Even tried the government, state. Nothing. And he was
choke angry. He had this way he saw himself, see: nice clothes, secretary,
his own office, all of that. That's the kind of job he wanted. And he just
couldn't get over it."

"Is his wife working?" Norman interrupted.

"Yeah, but it takes the two of them to pay everyt'ing. That's just
how it is here. Mortgage payment, school payment, electric, water,
insurances, food, you name it. Takes two paychecks to pay everyt'ing.
So, couple of months ago I said to him, why not try look in one other
field? He said, 'What, you like me work McDonalds!' I said you gotta
get something to pay the bills. They had gone through all their savings
by this time and was afraid they would lose the house. But he is so
stubborn that guy. Anyway, he finally got to where he said, 'Okay,
I'll take anything,' and still he couldn't get nothing. By this time he's
desperate. I didn't go into all of this last week. I just said let's pray for
him a job, 'cause. I dunno. I didn't want to go into it."

Marge and Yumi nodded. They understood completely.

"But, I dunno, Saturday I think, the day I wen read that verse from
the Bible, I went over there and I said Larry, trouble is you still thinking
of yourself as a hot shot, a big man. That's your flesh talking. That's
your flesh saying I need this or I need that. Your wife, your kids they
don't care if you one hot shot. They care if you pay the bills so they not
out on the street. Of course you neva be on the street, can always come
live with me. But you know what I mean."

He said, "Mom, no more. I don't care. I'll work anything. I'll work
two jobs if can get 'em. Just why won't nobody even look at me?" I said
son, that's God doing that. He wants to teach you something. So how
about you and me pray? And, just like when he was little, he and me
we kneeled down together on the living room carpet and we prayed.
We prayed for the Spirit of God to come and lead him so that he would
not carry out the desires of his flesh. And while we was praying I saw
this picture of a bunch of cars, all different kine. Not like a car lot or

nothing li'dat, just plenty cars and I said Larry, I see plenty cars. You know what that means?"

"Oh Mom, he said, Triple A of Hawaii wen offer me a job few days ago, I was so shamed to take it. It pays such little bit money. Thing is, Cheryl got a huge raise in her job. She'll be making so much more than me if I take it."

"Okay", I said, "Let's pray and see if this is how the Holy Spirit is leading you." So we prayed." Pua stopped and looked over at Marge and Yumi. "And after we finished he said he would take the job. So, this morning I went over there to see how they was doing 'cause he been working that job now since Monday. The kids was happy, Cheryl was happy. And Larry said he was doin' okay. Turned out he began to feel good about doing a service for people who break down on the road."

"That sounds like God working in your son's life to me," Yumi said.

"Yeah," Pua said excitedly. "And now I know why. This morning I started to read my Bible Through the Year book and the scripture verse for today was this: *Humble yourselves, therefore, under the mighty hand of God, that He may exalt you at the proper time, casting all your anxiety upon Him, because He cares for you.*"

"Wow!" said Marge. "So the Holy Spirit led you to that verse so that you could see just how God was leading your son, humbling him, for now."

"Wow, that's kinda cool," said Chris. "Like everything, I dunno, just fit together."

Jason said, "Just as we saw in this week's lesson, the Holy Spirit actively works in our lives. We may not see it at the time, but when we look back, we see that God arranged everything."

"Even the bad things," Pua said, "cause how else was he gonna find out the bad stuff in his heart if everything was going good?"

"God often uses the bad stuff," Yumi said with a sad smile. But even though Jason looked at her expectantly, she wouldn't elaborate. He paused, waiting to see if anyone had anything else to add, then he thanked Pua for sharing.

"I dunno," Norman said abruptly. "I think you guys mean well, but it seems to me you're rationalizing. I mean, what happened? The guy lost his job. He tried for eight months until he finally found something. So it was minimum wage, so what? Times are tough. End of story."

"Oh Norman, have a little faith!" Marge said.

"Oh please!" he laughed. "I have faith. I just don't try to tie things up all nice and neat with scripture. No offense," he said to Pua. "But… you know…"

It was time for Jason to jump in and steer the conversation in another direction but he hesitated because a strange thing had happened to him when Marge spoke. It was as if, when she said, "Have a little faith," the words jumped out at him and wrote themselves in neon lights. It was a strange sensation, but he had no doubt it came from God.

He was so worried these days. He had the feeling that the devil was nipping at his heels, although he really didn't know why. But at this moment he just knew that the Lord was giving him comfort. Turning to God, he whispered in his heart, "Thank you."

He looked up to find all eyes on him. Then he laughed as if to say, "Caught me," and that broke the tension. Smiling, they turned in their books to the proper page. The study flowed along easily after that with everybody, even Norman, entering into the discussions. At exactly eight fifty-five, however, Norman asked if they could finish up next week. He needed to get home. So, Jason ended with a prayer, and the ladies headed for the kitchen to clean off the table and bag up the leftovers. Norman said goodbye and headed out; Marge and Yumi followed a couple of minutes later.

After he threw out the leftover soda and emptied the ice container, Chris leaned against the sink hoping for a chance to talk with Pastor J. But just then, Pua came over and stood there with a wide smile on her face. It was obvious she wanted to talk with the pastor and might be a while, so Chris followed the others out. He was disappointed at first; it would have been so good to get some real insight about the whole incident with the Chinaman. He and Dan were certainly getting nowhere, and Chris was anxious to get the whole thing sorted out. But in the end he decided that it probably wasn't a bad thing to wait another week. For one thing, he had rehearsed several ways of telling the story to Pastor J, and still hadn't found one that didn't make him seem like a lunatic. He could use more time to get his thoughts in order.

Earlier that evening, in the kitchen of her older, detached house in Kalihi, Miss Lottie was talking on the phone to her good friend, Lillian. Lillian, as promised, was the first one she had told when she decided to write the ill-fated pink note, setting out the horrible scene she had witnessed on Thursday, and not mincing words about it either.

Although Lillian hadn't actually read the note, she knew its contents. She knew, therefore, just how important it was. And she knew that Miss Lottie had placed it in Howard's mailbox at church on Sunday morning so that he could read it at once. Both women agreed that when Howard read the note, his conscience would not let him dismiss the news it contained. He would be honor bound to bring it up before the elders and Richard Ko, when he returned from Chicago, would take it from there.

However, Lillian was now saying that she had looked in Howard's briefcase Sunday night, because he often brought work home with him. Sure enough, the letter was there and it had not been opened. But Monday and Tuesday when she tried, the briefcase was locked. So, on Wednesday, she decided to just ask him about it in a friendly, casual sort of way, which she did. And then, everything, all of a sudden, had spun out of control. She assured Lottie that she had only mentioned the letter to him, to just kind of feel out whether he had read it and maybe his reaction, but Howard had gone ballistic quite suddenly and made a *huge* issue out of her asking about it. Lillian couldn't imagine what had prompted him to act in such a mean spirit. After all, she had hardly said a word! Now, she wasn't sure he would even read the letter at all, at least not for a while. A great deal of valuable time had been lost. What could they do?

This certainly was a setback. It had never occurred to Miss Lottie that Howard would not read his mail on Sunday. He was as efficient as a machine. The fact that he put his back up with Lillian, however, wasn't surprising. She wished her friend had talked to her before going up against her husband. Lillian had never understood that a drop of honey could work a miracle where a head-on confrontation would miss by a mile.

Still, Howard was not an easy man to talk to. He had much too high an opinion of himself as far as Miss Lottie was concerned. Why, ever since Jefferson Martin and Jason Price had come on board, the three of them were thick as thieves, making changes right and left. Jason Price, that little upstart of a man, had even managed to change the times of the services, which had been in place for forty years! Who gave him that right, Lottie wanted to know. Especially considering the kind of person he was turning out to be!

Flushed with anger, the older woman fanned her face with a paper towel. It was so unfortunate that Richard Ko, who could be depended upon to at least be reasonable, could not be approached as he was still off-island. That was definitely a piece of bad luck.

Lottie turned back to her friend who was still talking. Unfortunately she had lost the thread of the conversation.

But Lillian was simply wondering what could be done. Surely there were ways to get around this setback if they acted swiftly, she said. So, the women considered and rejected several alternatives, one after the other, until Lillian had an idea which Miss Lottie claimed was "truly inspired." The only trouble was that the idea was so radical that even Lillian, whose courage was legendary, didn't seem totally sure she could go through with it. At first. However, the more they talked, the angrier Lillian became about something Howard had said or done—Miss Lottie wasn't quite sure what that was all about. But whatever it was, it ticked Lillian off big time and eventually she said that whatever she was *forced to do* to bring the Jason Price situation to light would only serve Howard right.

"Sin is sin, Miss Lottie," she said, "and whatever the cost to me personally, I have no choice but to do what my conscience tells me is right. I'll call you in a few days and let you know how it all turned out." And that ended the conversation.

Miss Lottie drank a nice cool glass of water. The phone call had been troubling and her throat was a bit dry. And while she drank she thought to herself that though they had been friends for years, Lillian *was* a bit of a drama queen. When she was on stage she would say anything. When push came to shove, however, she could very well lose her nerve and then what? Whatever problems she and Howard were having, the main thing was that at the moment the letter remained unread. No, Lottie could not wait for her friend; she had to take immediate action. In fact, she shook her head, scolding herself for not doing it sooner. She would carry on, as she had always done, by herself on the telephone.

The walls, in some churches, have built in trouble transmitters, and it wasn't a surprise that she had already received two inquiring phone calls asking her, sort of generally, about Pastor Jason. Antennas were up; noses were sniffing the air. It was time to act.

Miss Lottie had a long list in her head, and within the next twenty-four hours, she called every name on it. Lottie would have been incensed if anyone had called her a tattletale, or a gossip. How absurd! She was merely contacting people she trusted, people in whom she placed her confidence, people she knew had the church's best interest at heart. Well of course they exchanged ideas, impressions, thoughts, that sort of thing. But the main thing was that Lottie asked them to pray so that the work of God could go forward, and to a person they had signed on wholeheartedly. She could count on them, they said. And Lottie did.

When she had replaced the receiver in its cradle for the final time, Miss Lottie could confidently say that she had done her part, and the rest was up to God.

Chapter Thirteen

That evening, while the small group was meeting at Jason's condo and Lillian and Miss Lottie were talking on the phone, the doorbell rang at the house of Rhoda and Ed Thompson. Rhoda ran to answer it. She had sent Kristen and Travis over to the neighbors to do homework. Earlier that day, she had also e-mailed Yumi Furubayashi to say that she would not be at the Friday small group meeting, which was a real sacrifice. Yet, Ed was adamant. Friday was his only free evening. So, figuring she'd better grab Ed while he was feeling generous, she had agreed.

She opened the door to admit the small Asian decorator who kicked off his slippers and walked into the faux marble foyer. Ed rose from his Laz-E-Boy recliner in the living room and came over. "Hi," he said. "I'm Ed Thompson, and I guess you are Mr. Kee?"

"Collect," the man smiled, displaying a double row of unnaturally white dentures which he clicked together several times, reminding Rhoda uncomfortably of Dorothy and the ruby red shoes. Mr. Kee bowed, and the two men shook hands. That is, five tiny Asian fingers were swallowed up in the bear claw that belonged to Ed who, at 6'4" towered over nearly everyone.

Mr. Kee acted as if he hadn't noticed. "Ah yes," he murmured pleasantly, turned slightly, and bowed to Rhoda. "Now, where is loom?"

"Right over here," Rhoda stepped aside, indicating the 14' x 20' space behind her. Mr. Kee strode ahead of her walking on the balls of his feet, arms outstretched like a farmer in the Dust Bowl of the 1930's with a divining rod. Ed poked her in the ribs as if to say, "You're kidding, right?"

Rhoda could understand Ed's reaction. The little man turning in slow deliberate circles ahead of them was not the kind of person Ed would normally befriend. She could not, for example, imagine the two of them striking up a conversation around the water cooler at work, discussing the latest Dow Jones averages or comparing golf scores. As guests went, he was certainly unique.

Mr. Kee was dark, a bit rotund, and creatively dressed. He wore his graying black hair buzzed on top, pony tail in back, and thick white glasses rested on his little bud of a nose. His shirt was a crisp blue and white and glistened with sequins, a black cravat at his neck. The stockings that peeped out from under white satin slacks were a startling magenta. A bit over the top, but Rhoda didn't mind. She figured in Kee's line of work image was everything.

After a moment, their guest stopped turning, put his hands on his chest, and breathed deeply, eyes closed. Rhoda sincerely hoped he wasn't about to enter some sort of meditative state. That would be a definite turn-off for Ed. But her fears were unfounded. Mr. Kee opened his eyes, cleared his throat and stared at both of them. "Loom has no definition," he pronounced. " What you want here: music loom, living loom or animal sanctuary?"

"I've only got two things to say," Ed answered. "One, nobody touches my chair. And two, how much?"

Mr. Kee looked disdainfully at the coveted recliner and turned back to Rhoda. "You answer question. What you want loom to be?"

"Oh, a living room, definitely," Rhoda said. "For adults. You know, some place nice, where we could invite company over and sit and talk."

Mr. Kee walked the length and breadth of the room, arms outstretched again. When he returned, the expression on his face seemed to indicate that what Rhoda had asked for was not, strictly speaking, within the realm of human achievement. "Hmmmm," he intoned ominously, his face dark, his eyes opaque.

Ed looked at Rhoda. Rhoda looked at Ed. Mr. Kee looked deep inside himself.

Finally, he looked up and his expression changed. It seemed to say that he was a professional, challenges were his forte, and that he'd give it the good old college try. "Okay okay okay," he said finally. "What you budget?"

"Budget?" Rhoda was surprised. "But don't stagers usually run around the house pillaging from other rooms? Don't they do their magic just by placing things differently?" she added hopefully.

Mr. Kee pressed his lips into a firm line. "I no do magic. I need budget."

"But you haven't even seen the other rooms. There might be something you could use. Of course we intended to buy the paint, that goes without saying, but..." the stager's withering gaze stopped Rhoda cold.

"Budget," he insisted.

"How much are we talking about?" came the weary voice from Ed.

"You tell me, I work out detail," came the quick reply. " $5,000, $10,000?"

"Whaaat!" Rhoda was horrified. "But my friend, Sarah Jensen, remember her? Led me to believe you just moved things from room to room, and added some... paint." Even as she said the words Rhoda thought back and realized it was unlikely those masterful works of art Sarah so richly displayed had been hiding out in the laundry room. Evidently Sarah had been somewhat less than truthful.

"You flen had budget," Mr. Kee said doggedly.

"Hmmm, I'm beginning to see now that she probably did."

"Here what to do," Mr. Kee announced. "First, must clean everyt'ing out," He waved his tiny hands in a shooing motion at the room as though by doing so all the ratty couches, the gerbil zoo and the drum set would somehow vanish. "Then, must get feel for loom. Every loom have personality. I get to know yous after I live in it few days," he added, nodding his head as if the entire plan were already a fait accompli.

That was too much, Rhoda excused herself. In the hallway she flipped open her cell and pressed a name on her speed dial. Sarah answered on the second ring.

"Sarah, why didn't you tell me the guy had to move in for a while before he started decorating?" she whispered.

"Oh, I presume we are talking about Mr. Kee, the stager. Is he there?"

"He is, and Ed is about to pop a gasket. Now what's the deal with him moving in? Can we get around that or is it mandatory?"

"Did I forget to mention that? Don't worry. He only stays a few days. He brings his own futon and lives mainly off of rice." Her fruity laugh indicated it would be a breeze.

"Few days, are you kidding! I can't have strange men sleeping in my living room. How will Ed watch his TV? And what about the $5,000 charge? Did you have to pay that much? Personally, I don't think Ed's gonna go for it."

"$5,000, is that what he told you?" Sarah replied humorously. "Oh honey I'm afraid it's going to be more than that. But, you know, you will absolutely love it when it's done. Bring Ed over here. Let him see what the little guy did for us."

"Honestly, Sarah, I wish you'd told me. Ed isn't exactly…Uh oh, I'd better check up on them. It's ominously quiet in there."

Rhoda rushed back into the living room to find that Mr. Kee had worn out his welcome. Ed had taken the man by the wrist and at this moment was leading him, like a child who had misbehaved at a birthday party, to the foyer. There, he dropped the man's wrist and opened the front door. "And thank you so much again, Mr. Kee," he said, patting the bewildered little man on the shoulder. "We'll be in touch." And with that Mr. Kee was escorted out and the door closed firmly behind him.

Rhoda was furious. "That wasn't nice, Ed," she said, following him back into the living room.

When Ed turned to her, all traces of humor had fled from his face. "Did your good friend Sarah tell you that art work, furnishings, paint and labor would be…in this man's 'estimate', around $30,000?" he demanded.

"Gosh, and I bet that didn't even factor in the cost of rice," Rhoda said under her breath. To Ed, she said. "Of course not. I wouldn't have had him come over if I'd known." Rhoda looked around the room trying to see what the decorator had seen, trying to think how it all could be made into something livable—for what she figured was the amount of cash Ed was willing to spend. But she simply couldn't, and the thought saddened her beyond words.

Ed walked up to her and put his arm around her waist. "This means a lot to you, doesn't it."

"You know, it does. I don't know why, but...it does. Nesting instincts, I guess."

Ed gave her a big bear hug, then he stepped back and solemnly shook Rhoda by the hand. "Okay," he said, and then he walked over and turned on the TV.

"Okay what?"

Her husband, fully engrossed in finding the sports channel, did not answer. As Rhoda made her way back to the kitchen it occurred to her that something had been decided. She just wasn't sure what it was.

Chapter Fourteen

The next day, a little after 11:00 a.m., Marge hoisted her protesting body off the couch and headed for the kitchen. For some strange reason, she hadn't heard the television from Mrs. Kim on the right, nor had the neighbors on the other side erupted into violent argument last night. She had slept like the proverbial dead, and was amazed to discover how late it was when she woke up at last. Standing at the counter, she quickly devoured three whole grain pop tarts along with a glass of juice, showered and dressed, and threw some things in a gym bag.

Excel Fitness was a thirty-minute drive away and Saturday traffic was exceptionally heavy, even for Oahu where traffic was a sore trial to everybody. After paying a huge membership fee, Marge had read in a health magazine that people who lived more than twenty minutes away from a fitness center would not go on a regular basis. That had proved true. Marge drove over to Excel only about twice a month.

For one thing, even though she looked red-cheeked and healthy, she hated exercise. Absolutely hated it! Danny had always found that a brisk thirty-minute walk five or six times a week gave him boundless energy. After trying to keep up with him for half an hour, all Marge had ever wanted to do was go back to bed. Exercise wore her out.

Not only that, although she felt she ought to wear them to the gym, she felt silly in lightweight cotton workout shorts and tops (she would not wear spandex if they paid her a million dollars), and lastly, some malign force seemed to nudge her toward the scales every time she went to the showers after her workout. Being reminded that you were nearly fifty pounds over your ideal weight was not something that made anyone feel good about themselves.

Still, she had made a new year's resolution to go to the gym once a week, and now that the year was coming up on the halfway mark, she figured it wouldn't hurt to give it a try.

Marge had a routine, of sorts. First, she would hit the treadmill for twenty minutes. Then, she'd do some crunches on an exercise mat, raise a couple of five-pound weights a few times, and spend a few minutes on the stair stepper. After a final ten minutes on the treadmill at a slower speed to "cool down", she was through (and ready for a recuperative nap).

Today, all the treadmills on the window side of the great room were fully occupied. But that was okay with her. They were placed so close together, that when she used those she could often smell the ripe aroma of sweaty gym clothes from the person running next to her. As her niece would say, *gross*. However, half a dozen smaller treadmills, spaced further apart, had been tucked into a recess in the back. She headed there. On her way, to her surprise, she passed her friend Linda. She called over and waved.

This was not the first time the friends had met here. To look at her, Marge figured, Linda spent half her life on the machines. She was a poster picture for fitness: buff, toned, without an ounce of fat on her entire extremely fit body. She wore a red and white Spandex outfit, which showed every bone in her ribcage. It was a good thing they were friends, Marge thought ruefully, otherwise she would have taken one look at the red headed athlete and huffed away in the opposite direction.

Linda turned around in mid-stride. "Hey Marge! Good to see you at the gym!" Linda's face radiated happiness and good health. "Want to run a few laps outside? It's a nice cool day."

"Uh, no, not really. How's everything?"

"Doin' good. Hey, listen, I'm about ready for a break. How about you?"

"Good idea!" Marge said brightly, and the two headed for a metal bench near a vending machine. Linda bought two bottles of mineral water and returned, handing one to her friend.

"So, what's new?" Linda uncapped her bottle.

"Uh, nothing much. Thanks for the water."

"Ummm. Nice and cold."

Marge took a huge swig, eyeing the vending machine to see if they sold brownies or protein bars. They didn't. Just water. Imagine that, an entire vending machine and all they sold was water.

Linda looked at her for a long moment, then leaned back and said, "You still in that group on Fridays?"

"Yeah," Marge took a long drink, wishing it were Pepsi.

"Still going well?" Linda's smile slowly vanished.

"It's going fine. Why?"

"Been around the church lately?" Linda continued enigmatically.

"Not since Sunday, why?"

"Well, actually, I was going to call you this evening. Give you a heads up on something."

Marge lifted her eyebrows. "Something wrong?"

Linda paused again, thinking. "You like that Pastor friend of yours, Jason, right?"

"Absolutely! He's really a good leader. You know, you ought to think about coming to our group. It's not too late."

"Fridays are out for me," Linda said absently. "But, listen, there 's something I've got to tell you."

"About pastor J?"

"Yes. I got a phone call from that friend of mine. Remember Jasmine Wu?"

"Yeah. And you were right, she hasn't been back."

"I knew she wouldn't. Anyway, Jasmine is very 'well connected' I guess you could say, at church. She definitely has the inside word on all the church news, and she got a phone call late last evening that really disturbed her. She knows we're friends, knows you go to the Friday group meetings, so she called me. She thought there was something I ought to know. Said I could decide if I wanted to pass it on or not."

"Do I really want to hear this?" Marge frowned. "I mean, I try to stay away from...well, you know...gossip."

"Yeah, I know, that's why I thought I would call you personally and tell you. But since we're here…"

"Okay. I trust your instincts. But why would you want to tell me gossip about Pastor J?"

"Because I think it means big trouble for him, that's why. And because, I think he's going to need all the friends he has." Linda's green eyes clouded over, and Marge's heart turned a little flip.

"Okay," Marge said uncertainly. She sat the glass bottle on the bench beside her as though not trusting herself to drop it when she heard the news. "What's up?"

Linda took a deep breath. "Okay, now according to Jasmine, a couple of weeks ago, your pastor friend was counseling a woman. Tall blonde? Billowy hair?"

Marge shook her head. "Don't know her."

"Yeah, well, anyway, according to the word that's going around, they were doing a little more than talking in his office."

Marge's eyes opened wide. "Oh no. Please don't tell me…"

"I really hate to say this," Linda hurried on. "But according to the 'church information bureau', your friend and this woman were seen committing a sexual act."

"Whaaat!" Marge's jaw dropped. She could not believe her ears. "That's impossible."

"The thing is, I agree! And so does Jasmine. She said it didn't make a sense. After something that happened a while back—and please don't ask me to go into *that*, the church put in these big glass panels on all the doors. Just so everybody would be on their best behavior."

"That's right. You can look in and see the whole room."

"Exactly. So tell me, why would anyone commit a 'sexual act' in broad daylight for anybody to see? Doesn't make sense."

"What does that mean anyhow, sexual act?"

"I don't know. Maybe they were kissing. Maybe it went further. I honestly don't know."

"But if you knew Pastor J," Marge rushed to his defense, "you would know that's impossible. He's just not the type."

"Not an argument to sway a jury," Linda pointed out, finishing her water and tossing the bottle in the wastebasket. "I must admit, he's such a geeky little guy. Nice, but with the sex appeal of breadfruit," she shook her head. "Not the type buxom blondes fall for."

"Absolutely. And besides he's happily married."

"Have you met his wife?"

"Well, no…"

"Does she come to these Friday meetings?"

"No, but hey, I've seen them together and they look really happy!"

"Hmmm." Linda continued. "There's always the power angle. Look at all the women who threw themselves at Henry Kissinger."

"But Pastor J doesn't have any power," Marge protested. "He's just a junior pastor at a church in the middle of nowhere. And he's been here less than a year." She paused, thinking. " So…somebody actually saw them in the office? Who?"

"That's the thing," Linda stretched nimbly. "Nobody knows who started the rumor. Or if they do, nobody's talking."

"If we only knew…"

"Exactly, then we could consider the source, but we don't. Or… maybe we do. You know, you've got a bunch of old biddies in the church that absolutely thrive on gossip. That's what Jasmine says anyway."

"But we don't know for sure."

"No." Linda agreed. "But Jasmine says whoever started the rumor looked through the panel in Pastor J's door and saw them doing… whatever. Nobody just walks down that corridor randomly. You're either going someplace to meet somebody or coming from a meeting. Except the staff. So, that narrows it down."

"But surely Pastor Martin would have stopped…"

"Pastor Martin's been in and out of the office, and for the last few days he's been in Hilo."

"Oh yeah, his mom. How's she doing by the way?"

"I don't know. But evidently when he agreed to be senior pastor he asked them to bring on the secretary he had in Colorado. So, they hired Irene Baines."

"I know her. Nice. Very efficient."

"Yeah, Jasmine knows her too, and according to her, Irene would never stand for gossip. She's totally against it—which may be one of the reasons why Pastor Martin wanted her. But Irene's been on the mainland, and I guess that's why things got so out of hand. But she'll be back soon, and maybe she can figure out what started it all."

"And maybe she could put a stop to the rumors, do you think?" Marge was hopeful.

"Well, it is a big church," Linda said, thoughtfully, "but word gets around."

———

In the middle of the night, Marge woke up from a sound sleep, silently screaming.

After nights and nights of dreamless slumber, her subconscious mind had finally succeeded in connecting the dots, pulling all the shreds of memory together and generating the dream she'd been trying to remember. It was like watching a movie in high definition, every image crystal clear, on a movie screen as big as a house.

And it terrified her.

In the dream she was young, early twenties, quarreling with Sebastian at their house in Newark--the night she told him she was leaving. He was coming unglued; but that was nothing new for Sebastian.

She saw clearly how fury turned his fine-boned face a bright, angry red. She heard him yell, although she couldn't understand all the words. But the sound pummeled her body like angry blows. She watched as he drew back his hand and smacked her across the face. She felt nothing in the dream, although surely at the time it had been painful. She watched herself put up her hands to defend herself. But it was no use; he swatted them away as if they had no more substance than butterfly wings. He yelled, and punched her in the stomach.

He followed that by hitting her so hard she fell backward over a chair, onto the floor. And all the time he was yelling. Yelling. As though, if he yelled loud enough, the volume of his voice would pin her to the floor, making it impossible for her to get up, much less leave.

Then, a frame of the movie froze, leaving a still picture on the screen. It showed a young Marge, struggling to push herself up from the floor until she was in a sitting position. Sebastian was leaning over her, fist raised, spitting with rage. And then the action speeded up.

Suddenly, very quickly, without any warning at all, he ran into the kitchen. He returned a split second later and all of the color and sound drained from the film. In eerie black and white, Sebastian grabbed her by the hair with one hand and pulled her head back. With the other, he took the knife and sliced her face and neck. Twice. Three times. Huge wounds gaped from the severed flesh, and blood flowed black and plentiful. He threw her away from him as though she were something unclean, and she crumpled on the floor, blood creating a black shadow around her head and shoulders. Quietly, the black blood flowed, until at last she bled to death.

And then she woke up screaming. Without making a single sound.

Marge lurched to a sitting position and groped for the end table light with shaking fingers, still half dazed. *Oh my goodness. Oh my goodness!* Her heart was beating so fast it seemed that it would tear through the walls of her ribcage.

She pulled her legs from under the covers and planted her feet firmly on the floor. The solid feel of the carpet seemed to calm her wild heart, and bring her, second by second, back to reality.

Just be calm. Just be calm. She chanted. Two minutes passed, then three, and at last the daze cleared, and Marge said to herself, "But… that's not how it happened! It didn't happen that way at all!"

Oh yes, Sebastian had fits of rage, that was true enough. He yelled often, slapped her around, threatened to do more, and sometimes he did. But that night was the worst. When she told him she was leaving, he'd gone nuts. He'd slapped her repeatedly in the face, punched her in the stomach. She'd crumpled on the floor. That part was all true. But he didn't run into the kitchen. He didn't return with a knife.

She remembered it very clearly. After she'd sunk to the floor, doubled over in pain, he'd kicked her once, about to do it again. Then Bobby, the teenager who delivered papers in the neighborhood, had knocked on the front door. It was payday. Sebastian stopped yelling at once. It was very quiet. She could hear his ragged breathing as he took stock of the situation. Then Bobby switched from the door to the bell. He rang it half a dozen times. They both knew he wouldn't go away until somebody answered. If he knew they were home, he never did.

Sebastian dragged her into the kitchen, back near the sink, warned her not to make a sound, and walked calmly to the front door, pulling his wallet out of his pocket. Marge remembered thinking that there would be tears, remorse, recriminations later, but she hadn't waited around for that. While he was busy, she grabbed her purse and escaped out the back door.

They divorced a few months later.

That is what happened.

So why did the dreams defy reality? Why had she died, twice, in two different dreams? Was she secretly suicidal? Did she harbor self-destructive tendencies?

She got up and looked at the digital clock: 1:00 a.m.

She turned on all the lights in the living room until all the shadows were drenched in light. Then, she walked to the kitchen and turned on the lights there. She boiled water and made a cup of tea. She filled a tumbler with water and watered the cactus plants on the window sill. She returned to the living room and paced back and forth for half an hour. Nothing made any sense to her no matter how she tried to figure it out. And the more she tried to understand them, the more tangled her thoughts became.

Around three o'clock, she turned out the lights, sank down on the couch and prayed. She prayed that God would stop the dreams, or if He wouldn't, that maybe he would tell her what they meant. She then remembered that the Holy Spirit was the one who gave wisdom, and that, as an equal part of the Trinity, He could be prayed to as well. So she addressed her prayers to Him, asking for understanding. She reminded herself that the Bible talked about fruits of the Spirit, and one of them was peace. Well, worrying wouldn't solve anything. Grasping at bits and pieces of reasoning didn't help either. She asked, she begged the Holy Spirit for peace. But peace would not come.

Later, she lay back down, pulling the sheets up to her chin, but her muscles were strung tight with tension. Troubling fragments of both dreams churned around in her mind and she thought there would never be an end to them. But then, at some point in the watches of the night, a curious calm stole over her. Not like the ocean deep in the dream which had sucked the life out her and left her to drift at the mercy of its tides. No, this was something else again. A calm and a peace that came from a far deeper place.

And then, just as she was convinced that sleep would never come, a few gentle words resonated in her mind. It was not an audible voice, but an impression of words so strong that she could understand them easily. *Don't try to understand*, the voice said, *Just accept my peace.* Over and over again, like the lyrics of a gentle ballad, the comforting words harmonized in her mind, until at last, against all reason, her body relaxed and she knew, an instant before it happened, that she would indeed fall asleep.

She slept. A deep, dreamless sleep. Until Mrs. Kim's television went on at 6:00 a.m.

Chapter Fifteen

After the last service of the morning, Pastor Jefferson Patrick Martin was shuffling hurriedly through a stack of papers that had accumulated on his desk. It was a beautiful piece of furniture, graceful legs, the top carved from very expensive koa wood. On it, were framed pictures of his family, all smiling eagerly for the camera. The wall behind it was covered in framed certificates and diplomas attesting to Martin's two earned doctorates and other academic honors.

Graphic flow charts in bold color covered a side wall. On them an observer could easily trace the progress of the church in key areas. The conference table and chairs were good quality, but not luxury items. It said the church took its business seriously, but responsibly. There were three ceiling-to-floor shelving units crammed with books, many well-thumbed and highlighted. It was an office meant to inspire confidence, and it did.

There was a brisk knock on the door before it opened. "Come in, Howard," Martin called. "Take a seat."

"Excellent service this morning, pastor." The older man said, closing the door behind him. He pulled a chair around to face the desk and sat down, briefcase at his feet.

"Thanks, Howard. Your opinion is important to me."

"I mean it; it was excellent. What I like about your sermons is that they are so well organized. I can make an outline in my head as you speak," Howard smiled. "They are solidly based on scripture, and you make what you say relevant to the lives of the people in the pew."

"Thanks, Howard. I appreciate that."

The chairman sat back. Today he had on an aloha shirt in a soft pattern of blues and golds. It accentuated his gold spectacles, and the silver threads in his thick gray hair. It was one of his favorite shirts, and he wore it often. "What's the news on your mother?"

Martin had placed the papers he was looking through in three small piles. "Just a minute," he said, scribbling on an orange Post-It note and placing it on the first stack, a blue one on the second. He put the remaining papers back in his in-tray.

"There," he said, leaning back comfortably. "I just needed to get that out of the way. My mother, now there's an interesting situation," he mused. "She seemed to do really well at first, but they tell me she now has some congestion in her lungs and her heartbeat is still irregular. We don't know at the moment if this is anything to be concerned about, but the doctor says, someone her age…we need to be vigilant. Things could get tricky."

"I'm sorry to hear that," Howard said. "Are they moving her back to Oahu?"

"They think the Hilo hospital can manage well enough if need be, unless things get really bad. And Mom doesn't want to leave unless she has to. She likes being in her own home," Martin said, shaking his head. "Although I'd feel better, and so would Judi, if she and Dad came over here. But," he raised his hands helplessly, "My mother always has the last word. Thanks for asking. Now listen, I have a couple of things I'd like to run by you, is that all right? Do you have time?"

"Of course."

"Good." Martin opened a leather bound planner. " I'm looking at my calendar and I see that I have an extremely light week ahead of me, next week too. No meetings, except the usual staff meeting, but Lawrence is away and so is Irene." He flipped another page. "There was a pre-marriage counseling session with Byron and Candace, but they moved it back until the end of the month. My stewardship class is on break. The quarterly new members class just finished, but the baptisms won't be for another couple of weeks because the Stafford family is out of town.

No funerals, no weddings…" He looked over at Howard, surprise evident on his face. "In fact, Howard, I've never seen such a blank slate. So, I was wondering if I could slip in a short vacation. I could leave this afternoon for Hilo and be back on the 21st. I've spoken with Jason. He'll take over a few routine matters. Richard is due back this coming Saturday, and I was wondering if you folks could hold the fort for me for a while."

"I don't see any problem," Howard said easily. "You have three weeks coming, and I don't think you've used but two or three days."

"That's good to know. You see, although I'm an only child, my mother has three older sisters. They are all flying in." He shook his head, "It's a mixed blessing."

Howard understood. He was no stranger to older family members who demanded a great deal of attention.

"I'm thinking of leaving my lap top here, and of course my mother doesn't have such a newfangled contraption as a computer, but you can always reach me on my cell."

"I wouldn't worry about it. That's what a vacation is for. Be with your family. We'll be fine."

"Oh, I almost forgot!" Martin said suddenly. "Pastor Mitch is on furlough from the Philippines. I spoke with him yesterday and asked him to look at his schedule. He said he could switch things around with no trouble and preach next Sunday."

"Ah!" said Howard, well-satisfied, "The older people love Pastor Mitch."

"And isn't it an amazing stroke of good fortune that he's visiting his family here for just the time I need him!" Martin exclaimed. "The Lord is certainly helping me out here.

Now, one or two things before I go. Umm…meeting to plan for the graduation luncheon? That's still on, but I've asked Jason to represent me and handle all the arrangements."

"I'll be there."

"Oh, and Susan Anello? That all squared away for the moment?"

Howard looked pained. "Sorry about that, pastor. I had to ask Ernest to fill in for me. I was at Kaena Point all day yesterday and Lillian and I had to attend a function last night."

"Hmmm," Martin said. "I got a strange e-mail from Ernest

this morning, something about a new crisis? Could that mean that
something happened when they got together?"

"I certainly hope not," Howard said. "But don't worry about it.
I got an e-mail too. And a voice message. He wants to meet with me
urgently. I'll do it, but it will have to be tomorrow night. I walked
him through every step of the meeting on the phone before he met
with Susan. So, I'm reasonably hopeful that he asked her nicely to sit
out from teaching today. I told him to stress that you and I were very
anxious to hear what she had to say, and would make getting together
with her a matter of priority."

"So the urgency he was talking about probably means that she
didn't take it well?" Martin said, slightly concerned.

"That's my guess. But don't worry about it. I promise I will make it
a point to contact Susan Anello. Please, let me handle this."

"Well," Martin looked relieved. "If you say so. Now, if there is
anything else I need to know…"

"I'll call you on your cell. You take care of your family and leave the
Anello business to me. I'll see her and let you know how it goes."

"Thanks, Howard."

A few minutes later, Pastor Martin raced out the back door, and
Howard joined Lillian in the foyer. As Martin was driving away, Ernest
Cooke made a mad dash out the gate, trying to flag him down, but the
senior pastor was preoccupied with wondering what they were going
to do with Aunt Sylvia. Aunt Grace and Aunt Arlene were pretty easy
going. They could share a room at a hotel. But Aunt Sylvia…! Martin
grimaced at the thought of what lay ahead of him on that score, and
drove faster.

Wednesday evening, May 12th

It was a painful day at Howard's workplace. Notice of the closing
dates for the satellite facilities had gone out and all the CEO's of the
company met for hours, hammering out procedure, deciding on a
statement to the press, and trying as best they could to handle the whole
thing as humanely as possible.

Deciding whom to cut or eliminate was a gut-wrenching experience, and Howard dragged himself home late on Monday and Tuesday nights feeling as though he'd taken a ten hour tour through a meat grinder. The employees in the shops weren't the only ones affected. The handwriting was on the wall for him as well. Much as he had hoped to keep working, at his age he'd be among the first to feel the axe. And his retirement package had been drastically reduced.

So, as important as the Anello situation was, it was not until Wednesday that Howard found himself with Ernest in the senior pastor's office while he was away.

"All right, Ernest, you e-mailed Pastor Martin and me and said something happened?"

"That was Sunday! And I tried to get you on the phone. I said it was urgent!" Ernest said heatedly, and here it is Wednesday. "I wanted to see Pastor Martin on Sunday, right after service, but...oh what a day!" He rolled his small eyes. "I ran in here, but he had just left. So, I ran after him in the parking lot, just as he was driving away. There were several things I wanted to talk with him about, as you well know," he glanced at Howard knowingly, " but, even though I tried to flag him down, he just drove right on by."

"Pastor Martin is taking a few days vacation and..."

"What? Now! With everything going on?" Ernest wrung his hands.

"That's what we have elders for, Ernest," Howard said patiently. "I'm very sorry you and I couldn't meet sooner, but for the present I'll make every effort to get together with you if you need me, or you can talk with Richard when he gets back."

Ernest thought about it a moment, then calmed down. "Oh, I see!" he said nodding up and down as though agreeing with himself about something. "Well, that's true enough. The elders have always handled everything in the past. And Richard's coming back Saturday. Well, I suppose that's okay. A little late, but it couldn't be helped I guess. I mean no reason why the elders can't handle this, right?"

Howard had no way of knowing that Ernest's aunty was one of Miss Lottie's concerned friends, and that she had passed the rumor about Jason on to Ernest on the phone late Saturday evening. Therefore, Ernest was chomping at the bit to talk with Howard or Pastor Martin about it. However, Howard thought Ernest was talking about the Susan Anello situation. So, he agreed with Ernest that yes, the elders could and should handle the matter, but that first of all Pastor Martin had to be informed about everything that had happened in the meantime. Ernest seemed surprised that he didn't already know, but did not comment. Howard Nakata looked exhausted; the man obviously had a lot on his plate, what with rumors flying around everywhere. Still, Howard was efficient. No doubt things were under control.

"So," Howard said. "Tell me. What happened Saturday?"

"Oh, that." Ernest hung his head, looking totally miserable.

"You did meet with Susan on Saturday, didn't you? You and Florence? You remember that I asked you specifically to bring Florence along."

"Oh, I remember," Ernest's face turned red, and he addressed the wall to the left of Howard's ear. "I meant to. I had it down on my calendar, but you see, that very morning I also had to meet with Gloria Cheong, Dr. Ko's niece."

"What on earth does she have to do with Susan Anello?"

"Nothing! Except that we were also meeting here at the church. Okay, here's what happened," Ernest swallowed, and nervously picked at his shirt as he talked. "Well, turns out Florence couldn't come. But yes, that was the plan. And I had it all worked out. I would meet Gloria at nine and Susan was scheduled for ten o'clock. Except that Gloria came nearly an hour late and by the time we finished and I was walking her to the front door I saw Susan driving out of the parking space. I know it was her because she drives that yellow Fiat."

"So, what did you do?"

"Well, I, uh, looked in the church directory—the one they keep on the counter here, but her cell number wasn't there. So I checked with Directory Assistance to see if I could find her home number, but there was no listing." He shrugged his thin shoulders. "I guess these kids don't bother with land lines anymore."

"And…?"

"Yes, well don't rush me. I'll get to it!" Ernest protested. "Where was I? Oh, right," He looked down again. "About the home phone, I thought the office might have it but it was Saturday, and only Doris Baker was here to fold the bulletins, and since the number wasn't in the directory, she didn't know what to do. I suppose I could have called Lawrence Sizemore, but I didn't think about it. So, you know, short of showing up at her door--and by the way, I have no idea where she lives--I could not have done anything else." His glance jerked across Howard's face and back to the wall.

"Anyway..." he rushed on, "I had a plan to meet with her early on Sunday. I got here plenty early, but I ran into problems. The first service was running late and the parking lot was packed, so I had to park in the bank parking lot across the street. Then Florence had to go to the bathroom and I waited, but she never came out. So I went on to class, figuring she'd come when she was done. But then, just as I was turning the corner at the side of Building B, I ran into Naomi Silva who was steaming mad because she had found out (how I will never know) that Dr. Ko had put his niece on her summer staff. It took ages to get her to just stop talking! By the time I got to the class, all h---, uh, all heck had broken loose." And here he stopped totally.

Howard shook his head. "Tell me," he said with resignation.

"Listen," Ernest wheezed. "You're just going to have to wait a minute. I have to get some water. This air-conditioning is very drying and if I'm going to talk this much, I simply have to keep my throat moist. Pastor Martin probably has some water in his fridge here. I'm sure he won't mind." Ernest walked to the back wall where a stainless steel sink was located. Under that was a tiny fridge. He returned with a six oz. plastic water bottle. "Last one!" he said triumphantly.

"All right," Howard said, "You got to the classroom and there was pandemonium."

"Yes, but before that..." Ernest unscrewed the cap and drank deeply. "Oh, that's good. My throat was really parched," he explained, after which he belched discretely. "Oops, drank that way too fast." He screwed the top firmly on the bottle and looked up to find Howard's eyes burning into him.

"Okay okay okay, I'll tell you!" And he chose the wall again for his audience. " Now listen, all this is second hand. It happened before I got there. Okay, early in the week I did manage to get Jennie Pearson to sub, and believe me that was a miracle. So anyway Jennie was there on Sunday, getting her things out, that was about fifteen or twenty minutes before class. The mothers were bringing in their children, and then Susan shows up."

"Got it."

"Right. So Susan asks Jennie what's going on and Jennie says she doesn't know, just that Ernest Cooke, that's me, told her to come and teach the class this morning. And Susan says what do you mean teach the class, I'm the teacher of this class. Or something like that."

Ernest hurried on. "And then, Takeisha's mother, Arlene Swale? She spoke up. Do you know Arlene?" Ernest rolled his eyes again. "Let me tell you, there is a woman you never want to cross. So Arlene says to Susan you are not teaching this class because if you are teaching the class I and my child are leaving. And Susan says why is that and Arlene tells her straight out that she is not going to have somebody with Susan's reputation teach her child the Bible. And evidently the other mothers agreed with her, although nobody said anything except Arlene.

"And Susan went ballistic! I know because by that time Naomi finally stopped talking and I had just put my head in the door. She, Susan that is, not Naomi, said she was going to sue the church for defamation of character. Arlene says how can it be defamation of character when it's the truth? And Susan says get out of my way because I am going to take care of this, you just watch! And she just ran out of the class, and that's it.

"Except," Ernest looked at Howard with pleading eyes, "Suppose it isn't the end of it? Suppose she *does* sue the church? I mean, we all remember what happened a few years ago, right? And, okay, we settled out of court, but it cost us…"

Howard groaned, feeling very guilty. He should have known that, well meaning as Ernest was, this sort of thing was beyond his skill.

"What can I say?" Ernest felt his mouth go dry again which was unfortunate as there was no more water in the small plastic bottle. "So, what do we do?" he squeaked at last.

"I don't know, but I'll do something. Just let me pray about it."

"Okay," Ernest said, still troubled. "And…about that other matter?" Ernest brought that up mainly to take the attention off of himself, but Howard, putting notepad and pen in his briefcase, pushing in his chair, and heading for the door, was not listening. He was trying to figure out just how to diffuse the situation before it got worse.

Ernest switched off the light and followed Howard into the hall. He could see that the older man was gravely concerned. "Never mind," he thought to himself, "A little late, but the elders will take care of it. They always do."

And with that, he shuffled on down the hallway, leaving Howard to lock up.

Chapter Sixteen

Friday, May 14th

The group that sat around the kitchen table that Friday was smaller than usual. Norman had the flu; Yumi left word that she had finally gotten in touch with Brysen, but he had refused to comment, and Yumi herself was at a meeting she couldn't get out of. Still, it seemed to Jason that Pua, handing around steaming dishes of noodles, looked very happy tonight, confident that God was working in her son's life. Chris and Marge appeared to be a bit subdued at first, but then Rhoda came in, full of high octane energy. After a few laughs, they lightened up.

As they enjoyed all the delicious dishes everyone had brought, Rhoda finished up the story of why she'd been absent for two weeks:

"And so I asked Ed if we could get somebody to decorate our living room, or stage it, since that would be cheaper, and I talked him into letting Sarah's stager come in and look around. But, well, let's not get into *that* story, we'll be here all night," she laughed. "Anyway, the guy was super-expensive. So Ed says he'll do the whole interior decoration thing for me."

"Your husband is an interior decorator?" Marge asked, reaching for the rice.

"My husband is an estate planner. He is a no nonsense person whose favorite home decorating style is nouveaux drab. So you can imagine how excited I was when he said he'd do the whole thing: design the room, paint it, buy new furniture, everything," she said without enthusiasm.

"Hey, wait a minute," Chris grinned, trying unsuccessfully to capture a piece of chicken katsu with chopsticks, "Us guys can surprise you, you know."

"That's what I'm afraid of," Rhoda said dryly. "Anyway, I'm concerned, but I have to go along with it."

"Why?" Chris asked.

"Because he roped the kids in! He said it would be like one of those shows on TV. He picked a weekend and I have to stay with my sister. In the meantime, he and the kids go to all the showrooms and look at the stuff."

"Oh, that's nice!" Marge exclaimed.

"You obviously don't know Ed," Rhoda groaned. "He'll look at the show rooms for inspiration and then see if he can find something similar on the cheap. I'm lucky if I don't get a sofa made out of cardboard."

"Yeah, but the kids gonna love it, right?" Pua smiled. "Is he gonna let them paint?"

"Paint, *and* choose the colors. My daughter's favorite color is electric yellow, and my son, who intends to join the military one day, likes colors that resemble soiled fatigues."

"Well, at least the kids are excited," Marge looked on the bright side.

"Are you kidding? They are over the moon--unfortunately," Rhoda laughed.

"Okay now, folks, let's get started," Jason pushed back his chair. Chris gave up on the chopsticks and finished the chicken with his fingers. Pua cleared the table, shoving the leftovers in the fridge. Marge washed her hands in the sink, then headed for the living room. She sat next to Rhoda. "Be sure to let us know what happens," she said.

"Don't worry, I'll need a shoulder to cry on," Rhoda joked as she pulled her books out of a canvas bag. Chris sat on the sofa next to Pua and Jason opened with a prayer after which he asked if anyone had anything to share.

The group was silent for a while. Jason looked around and settled on Chris, who looked troubled tonight. He was a good-looking boy, blond hair, cheeks red from the sun. The All American Kid, and a nicer person you'd have a hard time finding. So Jason went with his instincts. Chris evidently had something on his mind.

"Chris?" he asked. "Something you'd like to share?

Chris looked startled, began to say there was nothing, then stopped. He looked at Jason, long and hard, then over at Pua, Rhoda and Marge in that order. Only then did he make a decision. "Oh man, this is so hard," he said, a pink blush creeping over his entire face. "So I'm glad its only you guys tonight, because I really wouldn't want to share what I'm going to say with, uh, everybody, if you get my meaning."

"Loud and clear," Marge assured him.

"It's just that I know you guys will listen and not think I've gone off my rocker or something."

"Chris," Jason said, "We're your friends here."

"Absolutely!" Marge agreed.

"Thanks," Chris hung his head for a minute. "Gee, I don't know where to start…"

Jason looked at the others. Pua bowed her head. Marge and Rhoda leaned over, gentleness and compassion in their eyes. They obviously were prepared to hear the worst. But none of them was prepared for what Chris finally said.

"Okay, you guys know where I live, right?" He looked around. Everyone nodded. "Right, well, okay. Last Friday, I was driving home from school and I was kind of, I don't know, daydreaming, I guess. There's this girl, right? I think maybe I mentioned her once. I've been trying to get her to go out with me, but…well, that's another story. Anyway, that day I just thought it was, like, an ordinary day. Finished school, drove home thinking about Mei Ling mainly, said hi to my landlady and then I walked into my bedroom and there was this Chinaman on my bed."

"What!" Marge said.

The whole group looked at him, wide-eyed.

"I know it sounds weird, but just kind of bear with me, okay?" Chris took a deep breath. " I came home, walked from the kitchen where everything was normal: fluorescent lamps, sun shining in the windows and all, went into the bedroom where there is no window, and there everything was kind of all brown, like those really old timey photographs, you know? On the bed was this guy who looked to me like a Chinaman. Don't ask me how I knew; I just did. He was brown too: clothes, face, arms, everything. And he didn't have any..." Chris thought for a moment. "He didn't have any weight. I mean, he didn't sink down on the bed or anything. But I'm telling you, he was just as real to me then as you guys are to me now. If you could have seen the expression in his eyes, well..."

Chris stopped, wondering what to say next, but Jason smiled reassuringly. "Just take your time. We're in no hurry tonight."

"Yeah, okay. Well, thing is, this guy was trying to say something, but you could see he was afraid. I dunno why. Maybe he thought I wouldn't understand because..." Chris hesitated. "Because...to be honest, he spoke in Chinese."

Pua, Marge and Rhoda exchanged surprised looks, but didn't say anything.

"And of course," Chris rushed right along. "I don't speak Chinese. Never even heard the language before. But...thing is, when this guy spoke, I understood every word. Weird, huh."

"What did he say?" Jason was anxious to hear.

"Oh, that. He said *Be careful. The night is coming.* But it was in this really—I don't know how to describe it, profound maybe. Profound voice. Like it was something really super important. Like it was life and death maybe!"

"It was a warning?" this from Jason.

"Yeah, definitely."

"Did he say anything else?" Rhoda wanted to know

"No, just that."

"And then what happened?" Marge asked

"Uh, nothing. That's it. Kevin—my landlady's grandson—knocked on the door and I had to go talk to him, and when I got back..."

"The man was gone." The words came from three voices.

"Right. But if you had just heard him speak. Just looked into those eyes. I mean, it stays with you, know what I mean?"

The ladies had questions. They wanted to get the picture clearly in their minds, and Jason was happy to answer because they were all such nice people, so caring, and they all believed him totally. Even Rhoda who had only known him a short while.

Marge asked if Chris knew the man, but Chris said he had never seen him before in his entire life. All of them agreed that his appearance was a portent, a sign. Of what, they didn't know.

"I feel as though…I don't know how to describe it." Chris hunched his shoulders, looking up, waiting for the words to come. Finally he said, " Have you ever found yourself somewhere you never intended to be? Maybe somebody who passes by hands you a slip of paper, maybe you choose a class you never meant to sign up for, or you attend a church you never meant to go to," here he grinned." And you think to yourself, at first, man what's this? But then, you realize somewhere along the line, without you being aware of it, this was, like, a life-changing event. There was something written on that paper, something happened at the class or that church that turned your life around a hundred and eighty degrees and you will never be the same. I can't get that guy's message out of my mind. I think about it *all the time*. I think it's going to change my life. But I don't know how."

What was it he said again?" Marge asked. "The night is coming?"

"His exact words were: 'Be careful. The night is coming.'"

"I hate to say it, but it's kind of scary," Rhoda said.

"What do you think night means?" Everyone turned to Jason.

He brushed a few limp strands of hair out of his eyes. "I guess we all think of night, juxtaposed with day, as something negative. Things hide in the dark. Things are covered up by the dark. Night restricts you from doing the things you do in the day. I guess, taken to its logical conclusion, you could say night is a metaphor for a kind of death."

Auwe! I getting chicken skin," Pua said, rubbing her arms.

Jason smiled. "Let me look something up." He opened his Bible, found the passage, and read: *As long as it is day we must do the work of him who sent me. Night is coming when no one can work.*" He closed the Bible and looked at Chris. "Jesus said this after he had healed a blind man. So, many people think that He was referring to the fact that, as His death was imminent, Jesus still had much work to do."

Rhoda interrupted, "Yes, but it said *we*."

Jason looked back in the Bible. "Yes, you're right. *We must do the work of Him who sent me.*"

"So," Chris thought aloud, "I guess we all have to do the work God gives us as long as we can?"

"Well, at first blush, that would seem to be it," Jason nodded. "What that work would be in this case…?" he shrugged.

Chris looked at Jason a long time, inviting him to say more. When he didn't, Chris added, "Oh, yeah, one other thing. I think this has something to do with Mei Ling. Do you…think…I mean, does that seem…right?"

Jason shrugged again. "There's no way to actually know, since none of us was there. This seems to be a personal message, just for you, and only you would know if Mei Ling would be involved somehow"

"But it could be, right?"

"Could be what?"

"It could be that it wouldn't apply to me at all but maybe to Mei Ling? Or, no, that's not right. I know it applies to me…" Chris frowned. "But somehow Mei Ling is in there. I just know it."

"Then I would go with that," Jason said, looking around from face to face. "Anybody else have another insight on this?"

" I agree with you when you say this message is going to turn your life around," Rhoda said thoughtfully. "Somehow, I don't know. That just seems right to me."

Chris sighed, "I am, like, so totally confused. Me and Dan, that's my neighbor, we talk about it a lot, but so far we've come up with zip. I was hoping that Pastor Jason…or you guys, could help."

"We can't give you an answer, but I know one thing we can do," Marge said brightly. "We can pray…"

"That the Holy Spirit will give you the wisdom you looking for, yeah? That was what you was gonna say, right Marge?" Pua beamed.

"Took the words right out of my mouth," Marge smiled, then looked at Chris. "I know it doesn't make sense now, but it will all become clear," said Marge. "Have a little faith."

And just at that moment, in Jason's heart those very words, once again, lifted themselves up and clothed themselves in neon light. "Have a little faith." That was a message for him, too.

"Thanks, guys," Chris said. "I really appreciate the prayer."

"You can count on it," Jason said. "But first… anybody else?"

Pua shook her head, Rhoda had nothing. Then Marge cleared her throat. "Well, since Chris has been so honest about everything, I'm going to trust you guys with something, too. Because, just like Chris,

I don't think you guys will get a butterfly net and haul me off to the funny farm. Still, things like this are hard to talk about."

"Take your time," Pua said.

"Okay. Well, here goes…I've been having these dreams. Well, not dreams exactly, more like nightmares…" Marge took them through the first dream that she remembered, trying to keep it short, but at the same time trying to tell them just how frightening it was. When she came to the part where she died in the ocean, everyone was startled, especially when she said, "But you see, that didn't actually happen. Okay, the first part did: leaving the hotel room, going to the beach, going deep in the water even though I couldn't swim. But I was rescued. Obviously I didn't die!" she looked around at several puzzled faces.

"This was the only nightmare, or there were more?" Pua asked.

"Yes, you said nightmares, plural," Rhoda added.

"Right. There were two more. One of them I can't remember at all, and the other was just terrifying. And she briefly recounted the scene long ago in the living room with Sebastian. When she got to the part where he slashed her face and neck, the women gasped. Chris and Jason looked horrified. Then she explained that that dream also ended with her dying, which could not be true as she was very much alive.

What she didn't understand, she told them, was why the dreams were so real, and why they didn't stick to what really happened. Like Chris, she felt as though there was something here, some secret, some sign, something that, if she only knew what it was, would change her life or the way she looked at her life. But she couldn't figure it out.

"So, what was it like, to die in your dream?'" Pua wanted to know.

"You mean, did I feel drawn to a big light, or see God, or anything?"

Just then, the landline phone rang. Jason left the others talking and answered it. He came back a minute later. "It's Yumi," he said. "She says she has to come up. It's an emergency. I buzzed her. She'll be here any minute."

True enough, two or three minutes later, an extremely agitated Yumi Furubayashi rushed into the room. No one had ever seen her look other than calm, businesslike, and a little reserved. They were all alarmed.

"A terrible thing happened," she gasped.

"What?"

"It's about Miss Lottie. I think somebody wants her dead!" Yumi said, and collapsed in a chair.

Chapter Seventeen

A stunned silence lasted for what seemed like ten minutes but was probably only a second or two, then everyone yelled "What!" and started talking at once. The din was so loud Jason couldn't hear a word Yumi was saying. He called for order.

"Quiet down everybody. I can't hear. Now Yumi, this is just shocking…"

"You like water?" Pua asked. "You look like you gonna faint."

However, Yumi was regaining her composure by the minute. She sat upright and waved them all away in the businesslike manner everyone expected.

"No water, I'm fine. Please." She shook her head, annoyed. Then, she leaned forward and spoke to Jason. "But I just came from the church. That's where I was tonight. The missions committee meets there every month. I just got put on it and had to be brought up to speed. So I was there when somebody ran in and turned on the six o'clock news, and after that the whole place went nuts. People were saying…lots of things, and I, um, I thought…" she looked down and pursed her lips.

"Yes?" Jason said.

"Well, Pastor J, you're a nice person," she said as though defying anyone to disagree. "I don't believe for a second that you would ever do anything…wrong. It just doesn't make sense to me. It never has. So, I thought that…under the circumstances, you know. That I ought to come over here and tell you exactly what happened."

The ladies exchanged looks. They knew perfectly well what Yumi was referring to. Pua had had no fewer than three friends call her with the "hot rumor." Linda had told Marge, of course, and Sarah had called Rhoda. Only Chris looked puzzled.

Jason felt the blood drain from his face. "Thank you," he whispered. "But...what did happen?"

"According to the news report, something or someone was slaughtered on Miss Lottie's front steps! Blood everywhere. It was a short newscast--just a few seconds. They showed still photos. The lights were high, and it was easy to see that blood had been sprayed all over the place. There was a huge smear of it on the front door, the top step had the most. Some blood had spilled on the bushes on either side and ran down the walkway."

"Oh Lord," Pua said. Marge grabbed her hand. They were speechless.

"Was it blood?" Chris asked. "I mean, couldn't it have been paint? Kids doing pranks, that sort of thing."

"Oh no. The police have definitely released the fact that it was blood. But there's a suspicious amount of it, which leads them to think that it might not be human. Still, no one can say for certain right now."

"And Miss Lottie?" Jason asked.

"She wouldn't open the door, naturally. And the policeman who gave the statement didn't reveal her name. Of course in the newscast they gave the address, and everybody at the church put two and two together at lightning speed, you can count on that. I think in the news report they said that the owner could not be reached for comment. Anyway, even though the newscast was short, lots of people like Joe Moore and listen to the Channel Two news in their cars. I know I do. So, word got around fast, you can be sure of it."

"That certainly is shocking," Rhoda said, "but at least...I mean, when you started, I thought..."

"Sorry, Yumi said. "But really, if you'd been around the church. Well, it's a three-ring circus I can tell you. Anyway, you may or may not see it on the ten o'clock news. Depends on whether they think it's a hot story or not."

"So the police don't think it's human blood, right?" Chris asked.

"They won't say, and the newscast left it up in the air. But who knows what people think? A lot of people feel that Miss Lottie's life is in danger, that's for sure. I think she's going to stay with a cousin in Ewa Beach."

There wasn't much conversation after that. Jason asked them all to hold hands while he led them in a prayer time, but everyone's prayer concerned only Miss Lottie. After that, feeling as though there was nothing they could do, one by one, the group members gathered their things, said goodnight and left. Yumi, however, lingered near the door. When they were alone, she said.

"Sorry, Pastor, I forgot about the group. With all the excitement it just didn't enter my mind."

"That's okay. It was probably good for them to hear it before it got out."

"But I came over because there's something else. Something I wanted to tell only you. I guess I could have called, but I wanted to say it in person." The hard angles of her face softened with concern.

"Do you want to sit down?"

"No, this will just take a second. Um, I have a cousin who's a reporter, part-time. She got a call about the bloody step story because she lives just a few houses down from Miss Lottie. She said that once the police got there, they cordoned off the area and wouldn't let the press through. However, she arrived at the scene early. In fact, when she got there, the blood on the front door wasn't just a smear. The blood spelled out a word. It was a message. But just as she was reading it, an old lady came out and wiped it away, then went back inside again. I don't think she saw my cousin standing there.

"I wanted to tell you so that you could be prepared. My cousin called me immediately when she found out the owner of the house worked at the church. She knew I attended there, and she wanted some background information. She told me what she had seen on the door, and I begged her not to tell anyone. She said they weren't sure it was human blood anyway. And, since the word was erased, there was no hard evidence it had ever been there. So, unless it was human blood after all, the networks will probably drop the story. Then again… maybe not. It may be considered a warning after all. You never know how things will work out," Yumi shrugged.

"But your cousin is sure she read exactly what it said…?"

" There's a street light right in front of Miss Lottie's house. She read it clearly while she was just yards away. The letters, evidently, were large."

"So…what was the message that was spelled out in blood?"

"Just one word: LIAR."

———

How Jason managed the rest of the conversation he didn't know. He sincerely hoped he had been polite to Yumi who had been kind enough to drive over to tell him the news in person. All he could really remember was, one minute she was there, the next minute he was alone.

He sank down on a chair, thinking furiously. What an idiot he had been! That awful day, standing there with Hazel Townsend draped around him like a dripping fountain, he had seen a snatch of gray at the window, a touch of red. And his gut told him exactly who it was. Why had he deluded himself! If he had taken action, he might have avoided all of this heartache, although what action that might have been still eluded him. This was his worst fear come to life. Miss Lottie had leaked what she thought she knew all over the church. Why else would Yumi have rushed to his defense proclaiming openly that she believed he had done nothing wrong!

Lottie spreading the word was bad enough, but this new development made it ten times worse. If people ever learned what the message said, then they would wonder who would want it blazoned on her door for the world to see. Who stood to gain from making such a statement? Why Jason Price, of course. That's what they would say.

But wait. Miss Lottie had wiped the message away. Obviously she didn't want anyone to know that somebody thought she was a liar. So, without the message, would people be able to connect the dots? Surely not. Perhaps he was letting his imagination run away with him. But still, when this kind of thing happened, people did not think rationally; they let their imaginations go wild. And suppose they did find human blood! Surely, that would open up all even more speculation! Where would it all lead? Jason groaned. He was beginning feel sick at his stomach.

His cell phone beeped the hour. Oh Lord. Nancy would be home in fifteen minutes. He couldn't possibly face her. Not tonight. Not until he had a chance to think and pray. He'd just have to pretend to be asleep when she got home, and get up early and leave before she woke up in the morning. He felt like a fugitive, but there was no helping it.

He hurried around in the kitchen putting everything away. Then he jumped into bed and pulled the covers up to his chin and closed his eyes. He heard Nancy come in a few minutes later, heard her open the fridge and close it again. Heard her use the lavatory. Heard her come in the bedroom, quietly so as not to disturb him. Felt her ease into bed. Heard her sigh and turn over. Not once, as far as he could tell, did she look over to see if he was awake.

Chapter Eighteen

Saturday, May 15th

The next morning, Saturday, Jason overslept. He awakened to discover two things. First, Nancy had turned off his alarm, and secondly, she had gotten up early and sneaked out of the apartment without even leaving him a note as to which (frozen) lunch he should take with him to work. Jason left work at three o'clock on Tuesdays but worked half days on Saturday twice a month. And on those days he always took a lunch. Nancy going off without leaving him a note as to which microwave meal to take was unprecedented. He didn't even want to think about what it might mean. The thought would simply be too depressing.

The clock said eight o'clock. If he hurried, he could get to church in an hour, but his body would not co-operate. He dragged himself listlessly into the shower, toweled off, then forced himself to glance in the mirror. He decided he really couldn't go without a shave if he didn't want to look dissolute, which was something, under the circumstances, to be greatly avoided. So he shaved, and nicked himself twice. He wandered into the bedroom and stared into the closet. Somehow, trying to decide what to wear today was just too much effort. Finally, he put on his navy trousers, a white short-sleeved shirt and blue suspenders. The suspenders were bright and new, but they gave him no joy today.

He was standing in the kitchen trying to decide what to have for breakfast when the door opened and Nancy walked in. She carried a bag from Starbucks. She wasn't smiling, but she wasn't frowning either.

"Good," she said with satisfaction, "I thought I would time it just about right. Is there any reason you can't go in later?"

Jason took a minute to think over his schedule. No, he decided. Today was the day of the month he did vouchers, checked inventories, prepared his monthly report. Only one clerk worked on those Saturday mornings and she spent most of her time in the duplication room. "I think I should call Kathy. Ask her to put a note on my door," he said.

"Okay. Just say you'll be late. Don't give a time. We have to talk, and I don't know how long it will take."

The lack of warmth in her voice chilled Jason to the bone. He made the call, then sat down in a kitchen chair. He watched as his wife opened the bag and handed him a cup which no doubt contained a decaf latte with 1% milk, took the lid off the second cup for herself, and set it down on the table. Then, still without saying a word, she put the lid in the bag, walked across the room, and put it in the rubbish.

Jason looked around, hoping for another container of some sort that might hold an oat cake or a Danish. "That's it?" he asked. "No pastry?"

Nancy pulled out a chair and sat down across the table from him. "Jason, you're lucky your coffee isn't laced with arsenic," she said.

He grimaced; it was an attempt at humor, but dark. Nancy stirred an envelope of sugar into her cup with the wooden stick, took a sip, and wiped the foam from her mouth with a napkin. Jason didn't know what to do, so he sat and stared at his coffee. He didn't even take the lid off.

"I don't know what to say," she said at last and looked up at the ceiling for a moment. I'm probably the last person in the church to hear about you and whats-her-name."

"Oh please," Jason groaned.

"But I told you I'd find out why I was snubbed, and now I know."

Jason looked over at his wife. Her brown eyes were clear, devoid of all emotion. In the second or two that he waited while she gathered her thoughts, he counted every freckle on her face, every tiny hair in her full, curved eyebrows. He felt as though his heart had stopped beating.

"I want to hear what you have to say," she said at last, "but first I want to know why you didn't tell me about this yourself."

Jason shook his head miserably.

"Surely you didn't think I'd believe such a lie!"

"No."

"Then…?"

"I really don't know what to say." Jason slouched over in his chair. "I kept hoping against hope that I'd made a mistake."

"Mistake?"

The words started slowly, then rushed out all at once. "That I was mistaken. That nobody could have seen anything. That Miss Lottie really had been absent that day. I nearly had a heart attack when you said she'd snubbed you, and Lillian had too. And, to be honest, there were other…clues. But I just couldn't bring myself to face what they might mean. It was just too overwhelming, so I blotted them out, all of them. And that's the truth. And then, last night Yumi came over, and I couldn't deny it any longer. I mean I wanted to. I hoped desperately, but after a thing like that…"

"Now you are totally losing me," Nancy interrupted. "So, why don't you just start at the beginning and tell me what happened." She sat back and crossed her legs.

Jason paused to get his thoughts in order. "Okay, here goes," he said at last. "Okay. Two weeks ago, Thursday, I had a counseling session with a young woman named Hazel Townsend. She is a schoolteacher, new to the church, and she's been having some problems. I think most of it involves her relationship with her mother, but it all blended into her job. Evidently she's trying to decide whether to continue teaching or just give it up. The important thing is that she feels like a failure. Now, I don't think she is, but she feels that way because.…"

"Jason! Cut to the chase."

"Uh…" Jason was disconcerted. He didn't know how far ahead to move. "Well, I guess the main thing is, she was upset."

"How upset?"

"Crying. She was crying. And I got her some tissues. I ran to the desk and opened the middle drawer and took out a fresh box of Northern…"

"Jason!"

"I, uh, handed her some tissues."

"Tell me exactly where you were standing," Nancy took another sip of her coffee.

"About four feet from the door!"

"In front of the glass panel." She wanted to picture the scene exactly.

"There isn't room to stand anywhere else! It's a small office."

"Okay." She summarized: "A young woman you were counseling was upset. In fact, she was crying. The two of you were standing about four feet from the door. You handed her tissues. Now you can get specific. Tell me exactly what happened next."

"We were standing in front of the door. She took the tissues in her… " Jason moved his hands around as if to picture the scene exactly, "left hand. Yes, that's it. Her left hand. And I reached over and grabbed her right hand."

"I think I can picture that," said Nancy

"Right. Now, I held on to her hand because I firmly believe that when a person is upset, really upset, it's always good to establish contact and let them know that they are not alone, that someone…"

"I've heard this a million times. Will you just get on with it?"

"All right. So, I was holding her hand, then I said something. I honestly don't remember what. And before I knew it, she threw herself into my arms, sobbing.

"Sobbing. Hmm. Okay, but let's go back to when you were grasping her hands."

"One hand."

"How long did that last. A minute, two minutes?"

"I don't know," Jason looked totally helpless.

"Let's be generous and say three minutes."

"No! Couldn't have been that long."

"And then, she threw herself into your arms, sobbing. Anything else?"

"Well, now that you mention it," Jason said with difficulty. "There was. Obviously I didn't let her stand there with her arms around me for long…"

"Of course not," Nancy said dryly.

"And I was trying to pull back, when I looked over and I saw some… uh, movement at the glass panel."

"Movement."

"Yes. I thought I saw a little snatch of something red and something gray."

"A red and gray shirt perhaps?"

"No, not like that. In fact," Jason's entire body sagged. He struggled for words. At last he said, "It popped into my mind that it was maybe gray hair and reddish glasses."

"The kind that Miss Lottie wears."

"Right," he added dejectedly. "But then, I walked out in the reception area a few minutes later and she wasn't there! I was so relieved! I figured she hadn't been in that day. Figured it was just my imagination or something. So, I pushed it out of my mind."

"You pushed out of your mind the fact that Miss Lottie just might have seen you through the panel in your door, in the arms of a blonde woman who was not your wife."

"Well, when you put it like that!" Jason was exasperated. "What should I have done?"

"It doesn't matter now, does it?" Nancy retorted sharply.

"No, I suppose not. " Jason looked down and inspected his coffee cup at great length. Finally, he said. "But there is something that matters, and matters very very much." Behind his thick glasses, his eyes grew damp. "Nancy, please. I know when I say how it was, it sounds awful, but you do believe me, don't you? " he paused.

Nancy sighed. "Of course I believe you, " she said. "You're foolish but you're not stupid. Sorry, that didn't come out the way I meant."

"That's okay," he said, wiping at his eyes.

"What I meant was, if you *had* been carrying on with whats-her-name…"

"Hazel."

"…which of course you never would do," she smiled at him briefly, " you'd hardly do it four feet from a glass panel with people passing by. So…" Nancy thought, "gray hair and reddish glasses. I should have known." Then, she sat and stirred her coffee.

Jason put three envelopes of sugar in his, and took a huge gulp. Then he pushed it away. Even Starbucks tasted bad today. "I'm sorry," he said at last. "I didn't think…"

"That's for sure," she said, still staring at the coffee. "So, let me have it. What does all of this mean for you?"

"I honestly don't know," Jason said at once. "All of this is new to me. They didn't teach us about this kind of stuff in seminary. And although the church I grew up in was huge, this kind of thing didn't happen there. Or if it did, we didn't know about it. My folks didn't get involved. Just went to Sunday service and Sunday school. Period. So, I didn't grow up knowing the shadow side of churches."

"Well I did," Nancy said, taking the stirrer out of her cup and throwing it angrily in the trash. "You led a sheltered life."

"Okay, to be scrupulously honest, I'd have to say that I heard things from time to time, when I was working in the denominational office. But, you know how it is, it's kind of like the scary stories kids tell each other late at night at summer camp. It didn't seem real."

"Well, this is real enough," his wife said moodily.

"It's a nightmare."

Nancy drank the last of her coffee as though it had suddenly turned bitter. She pushed the cup away but continued to stare at it, deliberately not looking at her husband when she asked the next question. "So, tell me the worst," she said, in a flat voice. "Could you get fired over this?"

"Fired? Good Lord, I hope not!"

"Don't think it's not a possibility, Jason. Stranger things than that have happened in churches that I've heard about," she said darkly.

"I'm out of my depth here. I really don't know."

"Well I can tell you one thing," she said irritably, standing up and shoving the chair under the table with such force that Jason's cup nearly spilled over. "All of this is not helping me with my opinion of the church. Not by a long shot." She threw the cup in the trashcan and washed her hands in the sink.

When she had finished, Jason cleared his throat. "That's not all of it," he said softly. "Maybe you'd better sit down again."

Puzzled, she did. And he proceeded to tell her everything that Yumi had told him the previous night. Nancy had not watched TV, nor had she heard the news on the radio. It was all new to her. And it was definitely not good.

After Jason stopped speaking, she nodded her head slowly. "Okay," she said at last. "Now tell me what we should do."

"Other than pray?" he said. "I honestly don't know."

Chapter Nineteen

O n Saturday evening, Howard Nakata found himself, once again on his way to church. This time, he was to attend a planning meeting for the high school graduation banquet. For the last decade he, Gerald McMullen, and Rosa Cheong had overseen this activity, and Howard had come expecting things to move along rapidly so that he could get home at a reasonable hour. It had been another tiring day and he was looking forward to getting to bed early.

At six fifty-five he arrived, along with Gerald, Rosa, and Mike Dunn, a new recruit on the Elder Board. Jason Price was also punctual. He was representing Dr Martin as, for reasons lost to history, the senior pastor was always the chairman of this committee. Four new people had been added this year, and they were all late arriving. There had been a pileup on the H-1.

Despite that fact, once everyone gathered in the meeting room and Howard opened with a prayer, the meeting did not begin at once. After all the excitement about the TV broadcast the previous evening, all anyone seemed to want to talk about was Miss Lottie. Rosa, an attorney for the local teacher's union, had heard that a policeman had showed up at church earlier that day looking to speak with someone, but at that moment all the pastors were out. Evidently Kathy had been attempting to contact Howard by phone when the policeman was called away urgently, but he said he'd be back.

A policeman showing up at church? Half a dozen voices were

impatient to share their own ideas about what he might have wanted, and they speculated loudly. After that, a good half hour elapsed with everyone trying to find out how Miss Lottie was doing only to discover that nobody knew a thing. The sister in Ewa Beach wouldn't answer the phone and Miss Lottie didn't have a cell phone. But, again, everyone wanted to voice what they thought she might be feeling after all the excitement. "I mean, blood on her steps!" Rosa shook her head, speaking the words everyone was thinking. "Poor Miss Lottie, she must be sick with fear."

Leo Nakamura chimed in saying that acts of malicious mischief weren't new to Miss Lottie. Hadn't there been a spate of them around her house a few years ago? Didn't somebody throw a rock through her back window way back when? He was sure he remembered that. Various voices joined in as everyone tried to remember, and then another ten minutes were given over to a discussion of whether or not Miss Lottie should sell the house and go live with her sister. Everyone agreed it would be a shame if she did because the market was so soft. But blood on her steps! Surely safety was more important.

Mike Dunn and Howard looked over at Jason Price more than once, but Jason seemed content to let the conversation bounce back and forth until finally it was decided that Gerald McMullen would drive to Ewa Beach the next day to see if he could find out how Miss Lottie was doing, and the matter was settled at last.

And so, it was nearly eight-thirty before all of this discussion wound down and Jason Price called for order and got the group to focus on the matter at hand. It was getting late, he knew, but they really had to settle down and address a few really crucial points about the banquet. According to the minutes of last month's meeting, the date had been settled, and the place, but a few more details had to be nailed down tonight. This time of year there was a lot going on and if they didn't get it done right now, he just didn't know when they could. It wouldn't be possible to schedule another committee meeting in May even if they wanted to.

The first item of business was the caterer. Josie and Bert, loyal ACC members, had gone out of business, so an alternative had to be agreed on. Everyone obediently took up the discussion. While this was going on, Mike Dunn nudged Howard and whispered, "Stick around a minute after the meeting."

It was not a request. Dunn, a retired military professional, whose body language and crisp speech indicated a person accustomed to meetings conducted by the clock, hadn't been pleased with the laid back way in which the meeting had been run. He had been especially unhappy at the fact that it started over half an hour late, during which time people just sat around and gabbed. And he was furious that the person in charge had let things get so out of hand.

The caterer agreed upon at long last, Jason announced the next items of business: a speaker for the program, the entertainment, publicity, and gifts. These important elements invited further vigorous discussion and it was quarter to ten before Howard was asked to dismiss the group with prayer, which he quickly did.

Most of the group filed out of the room on their way to the parking lot, but two or three lingered in the hallway. Dunn approached Howard, "Let's talk in private. " He nodded toward a room far down the hall.

And so, once again, Howard found himself in Pastor Martin's office while he was away. He turned on the lights and air-conditioner, and settled himself in a chair. Mike Dunn, his back straight as a ruler, sat across from him.

"What's all this about? Couldn't it wait for another time?" Howard asked, suppressing a yawn.

"Absolutely not," Mike was adamant. "In fact I'm surprised you didn't call a meeting long before this. I've been expecting to hear from you."

Howard looked at him quizzically.

"And surely you agree that Price should not have been here representing the pastor tonight. I mean, not only did he do a poor job, but under the circumstances, he shouldn't have been here at all," he said bluntly. "As chairman of elders, I had expected you to take action, Howard. Frankly, I'd like to know why you didn't. If you didn't want to make the call yourself, you could have called us. We would have found the time to meet."

The older man was confused. "Wait a minute, you expected me to call the elders together to discuss Jason Price sitting in for Pastor Martin at this meeting?"

"Among other things, yes. If you didn't want to take action yourself, that is. Now listen, I didn't know about this mess myself until I got the memo, and then I asked around. My wife had heard the rumor, but usually she tends to turn a deaf ear to that sort of thing..."

"The rumor..."

"Yeah, but after what happened to Miss Lottie, this news will go through the church like wildfire. You know how it is, the two names are linked now. People are putting two and two together and probably getting six..."

"Miss Lottie's name is linked to Jason's...?" Howard was confused.

"Of course! Especially since what happened yesterday. And until all of this is sorted out, the last thing we want is Price chairing meetings, counseling people and well, that sort of thing."

"Why *shouldn't* he?" To Howard this was making no sense.

"Why shouldn't he! Look, I know I haven't been an elder very long, but even I know that you don't let people continue in their position with this kind of thing going on."

"What kind of thing?"

"You know doggone well what kind of thing, Howard! Now listen, I don't want to exceed my authority, but I've got to let you know where I stand on this. Price should be suspended and that's all there is to it. At once."

"I don't know what you're talking about," Howard said with a trace of annoyance. " But if you're considering suspending a minister of this church, I'd appreciate it if you'd let me know why."

"But you *know* why." Now it was Mike's turn to be annoyed.

"If I knew, I would hardly pretend that I didn't," Howard pursed his lips.

Mike looked closely at Howard again as if not believing his eyes. "Okay, I'll take you at your word." He leaned back and thought a second. "Now, I'm just repeating what I heard, you understand. And... the thing is, there seems to be some confusion as to what actually happened, I mean it changes according to who you talk with," he said carefully, "but the crux of it is that Pastor Jason was seen *by several people*, not just one, in a compromising situation. I can't believe you didn't know!" He threw up his hands. "That just does not make sense."

"Jason?" Howard couldn't believe it. "When did this happen?"

"From what I hear, nearly two weeks ago. All this time and nobody has done a thing as far as I can see!" Mike thundered, "And here Price is, big as life, chairing meetings for goodness sake. I'm telling you, something has to be done, and now!"

"Humor me," Howard said in a level voice. "What compromising situation? What do those words mean?"

"Howard! Eye witnesses saw him groping some woman!"

"Where?"

"In his office."

"At night?"

"No, during regular office hours."

"*Groping* a woman?"

" It's worse than that," Mike continued heatedly, "And, if you want the whole truth, what I actually heard was that they were caught performing a sexual act."

Suddenly, Howard was angry. "O come on! Never! The insinuation is ludicrous. Gossip, that's all it is. Mean and spiteful." Howard ran his hands through his hair and shook his head. He still could not believe it. "Does Pastor Martin know?"

"How would I know? I figured you would've told him," Mike shrugged, frowning.

"I got a call from Jeff earlier today," Howard said. "He was very worried about Miss Lottie. And he asked me if everything else was okay. His mother has taken a turn for the worse, and I didn't want him to worry. So, I said yes. Because... I thought everything *was* okay!"

"Now that's what I don't understand," Mike said, his face dark. "I'm sorry, I don't get it. You, of all people, how could you not have known!"

" Mike, I'm at a loss here. Would you please connect the dots for me? Why, would I of all people, have known?"

"Because of the memo."

"What memo!" Howard demanded, getting a little pink in the cheeks.

"The memo from your wife!" Mike said, and threw up his hands as if to say, "Duh!"

"My wife!" Howard sat back dazed. "What does my *wife* have to do with this? She doesn't write memos. " A confident half smile crossed his face. "She has nothing to do with church business--and we should all thank God for small blessings," he added under his breath.

Mike looked at him, incredulity written all over his face.

"Do you have a copy of this memo?" Howard demanded.

"No. It was an e-mail."

"Sent to you?" Howard's eyes betrayed his absolute amazement.

"To me, and all the elders. And probably the pastor, too."

"My wife sent a memo to the *elders of the church*?" Howard looked as if he were about to have a stroke.

Suddenly, Mike knew that Howard really was clueless. His accusatory tone changed. "Wait a minute, I'll bring it up." He walked to Martin's desk and booted up the computer. There was a universal password so it didn't take long. Finally, he got up from the chair, motioned for Howard to sit. "Have a look," he said.

Howard gazed with unbelieving eyes at the following:

To: The Sr. Pastor and the Elders of Aloha Community Church
From: Lillian Nakata
Date: May 11th
Re: Indecent Actions on Church Property

Gentlemen:
This memo is a testament by me to the fact that someone (not me, myself) did witness, on April 29th, a highly indecent situation in Pastor Jason Price's office. This witness wrote a letter and put it in the mailbox of the chairman of the Elder Board who, I am sure, will take the proper action once he is aware of the contents of the letter. I am simply testifying to the fact that I was there when the incident occurred, and that I know for a fact that this person did witness said incident. I know also that this was a traumatic event for her, she was horrified, and she has

been upset ever since, as of course anybody would be. I am writing this testament so that you will know that an incident did, in fact, take place and that you need to take this witness's statement seriously. I am confident you will do the right thing.

Sincerely,
Lillian Nakata

Howard stared mutely at the screen for a very long moment, not trusting himself to speak. His blood was pounding in his ears and he could feel the red flush creeping up his neck into his face. She had written this e-mail to deliberately provoke him into doing what she wanted. How dare Lillian go behind his back this way! It was unthinkable! Had the woman gone mad?

"What letter is she talking about?" Mike wanted to know. "And why didn't you tell the rest of us about it?"

"Give me a minute," Howard said. He shut down the computer, got up, and returned to his original seat, taking his time. Finally, when he and Mike were sitting down together again, he looked over at the soldier. "I do apologize," Howard said with as much dignity as he could muster. "A letter was put in my box about two weeks ago, or thereabouts. It was on pink stationery, in a florid hand, and I assumed it was from a woman in the church complaining about something. We get lots of those. So, I put it aside. Someone reminded me about it a few days later, but…for reasons I won't go into here, I simply didn't think it was that important. I intended to look at it, of course, but …" he shrugged. "I didn't. So, let me do it now. If you'll just give me a moment…"

Howard took his fine old briefcase from under the table and opened it. He rummaged around for a moment or two, came up with a pink envelope, and tore it open.

The room was totally quiet for the brief time it took Howard to read the missive. Then, he looked up and handed it to Mike who read through it quickly. The note was short and it did use the unfortunate phrase Mike had mentioned earlier.

Finally Mike said, "You see why we need to take action, and do it quickly. Although it will take the entire Elder Board to take any permanent action, you could put Price on suspension yourself."

Howard looked troubled. "As volatile as this note is, I think we need to put it in perspective. Yes, it appears to be damaging, but the problem is, the note was signed *Anonymous.* It has never been our policy to act on information given anonymously."

"But everyone agrees that it was Miss Lottie!" Mike's tone was urgent. "She was working here that day. She is the person referred to in the memo! She was the one who looked in the glass panel and saw Jason committing a sexual act. It says it right there in the note. And then, on top of that," Mike continued before Howard could interrupt, "last night she was the victim of a nasty act of vandalism."

"Which has nothing at all to do with this accusation!" Howard protested.

"But the problem is, nobody knows *what* happened. Howard, my own wife, who really doesn't get involved in church matters at all, got a phone call this afternoon from somebody suggesting that there *was* a connection. That Jason is somehow involved. You know, trying to scare the old lady so that…"

"Come now! No disrespect to your wife, but I simply will not listen to any of this conjecture. You know as well as I do that's all it is, and where it can lead. Now, you want me to do something? Very well, I will, but I'm certainly not going to put Jason on suspension on the basis of any wild rumors."

"Okay, I will admit the whole idea of Jason being involved in the vandalism is a huge stretch. But, the problem is, like I said earlier, all over the church some people are adding up two and two and getting six and making a big noise about it, so *something* has to be done, and now! Besides," Mike tapped the letter with a heavy finger. "This is more than speculation. This is a documented fact."

"Signed *anonymous!* Okay, here's what I'm going to do. I will call an elder's meeting as soon as possible and we'll all sit down and discuss this. It's the weekend. Jason has no responsibilities in the Sunday services. Richard will be back when?"

"Tomorrow."

"All right, we'll meet then."

"You're not going to do anything before that!"

Howard looked at the soldier for a few seconds before replying. "Yes, Mike, I am. I am going to pray, and I suggest you join me. If we need anything right now, it is the wisdom of God."

Chapter Twenty

Today was a banner day. Chris and Mei Ling were to eat dim sum at the food court, Ala Moana Center, and there would not be a cousin, aunty, or UH student in sight. She said that she had about an hour to spend with him before heading off to Barnes and Noble to pick up the book she had ordered, and then home for dinner.

He showed up an hour early, nervously pacing the floor, and drank three Jamba Juices while waiting. Normally he watched every single calorie that passed his lips, but not today. Today he just wanted to get through this meal without making a fool of himself. If he needed to start with a few liquid appetizers, so be it.

Mei Ling was punctual. Dressed in beige cotton Capri pants with a gray top, lots of lace again, and accents of pink. He thought she looked like a million dollars.

For a moment, when they first entered, Chris stood like Alice in Wonderland looking around at what he thought must be the largest food court in the world. Okay, maybe a slight exaggeration, but not much. It had to be at least half the size of a football field, jam packed with people, all of them hungry.

The court offered an amazing variety of menu items especially designed to tempt the palates of visitors from the U.S. mainland, Asia, and those who lived locally. This wasn't the best place to eat dim sum, Mei Ling cautioned him. If you wanted genuine dim sum, the best thing would be to eat home made from someone's kitchen. Her grandmother, for example, made excellent chicken feet in black bean sauce, and you could not find a restaurant anywhere that made it nearly as good.

However, she directed him to the Tastie China Kitchen, where she said the food was probably okay, Chris stood in line for several minutes until a space opened in front of him. He stepped forward, perplexed by an assortment of food he couldn't identify. The server, unsmiling in yellow and black, pointed abruptly to several items.

"Lup Chong," she barked, tapping a tray with a chopstick.

Mei Ling whispered in Chris's ear, *Chinese sausage*. Chris nodded and the sausage was thrown on a plastic plate.

"Char Siu Bao," the server crowed.

"You remember char siu," Mei Ling said. "Red-colored barbeque pork? You eat this at the manapua shop in Manoa all the time."

"Oh, right!" Chris said he'd take one, and after that he just went along, pretty much, with what the server pointed to: pork hash, chop suey chicken, Kalua pork and some shrimp dumplings out of the bamboo steamer because Mei Ling said that these, made from flour wonton wrappers, were much better than the rice paper ones they served at the Thai counter. He nodded to several egg custard tarts, and soon the plate was overflowing.

Mei Ling had three small items on a plate half the size.

Finding a place to eat took some time. There were countless rows of pedestal tables in long lines in the center part of the mammoth court, and metal chairs to sit in. After walking around the entire perimeter, they found a table at the end of a line and sat down.

He looked around, and for a second he had a little nip of culture shock. There were hundreds of people here, mostly families with lots of children, all with hair dark brown to black, nearly all of them dressed in monochromatic shades of brown, black, white or gray. Every once in a while he'd see a small pod of tourists edge in. They all looked to Chris as though they came from the mainland: big men in striped polo shirts, shorts, baseball caps with logos, tennis shoes with white socks pulled halfway up the calf, and very pale complexions. Blonde headed women came with them dressed in brightly colored slacks and patterned tops. He thought of his own choice of clothes: jeans, red shirt, tennis shoes, and it occurred to him that these people would think he also had just gotten off the plane.

Thank goodness the server had handed him a fork. Chris had fumbled with chopsticks on a few occasions but he never handled them well. He figured it was an acquired habit, one best begun, if possible, at birth. He watched Mei Ling manipulate the wooden sticks easily, picking up dainty morsels of food, her pale hands small and quick. It was definitely a science.

Chris hesitated. He usually prayed before meals, but felt it would be impolite to do so now. A yawning chasm of uncertainty stretched between him and Mei Ling, not only due to ethnicity, but because of a basic belief system he embraced and couldn't share with her. Even simple things, like a prayer before meals. He said a short, silent prayer and dug in.

Mei Ling said, "Did you choose present for your mother and uncle?"

"I couldn't decide," he shrugged. "But I still have time."

"I told you. It is only May."

"Well, you know how it is. One day it's only May and then before you know it there are five shopping days left to Christmas," he smiled.

After that, conversation lagged. Chris kept eating. Mei Ling finished and placed her chopsticks across the edge of the plate.

Chris's mind churned over several possible topics of conversation, but so quickly that they all became a blur. Then, inspiration hit as a small voice inside of him urged him to start with something easy and familiar, like food. "Let's talk about food!" he said brightly. "'cause they sure have everything here. You like food, right?"

A smile hung uncertainly around her lips as Mei Ling tried to decide what part of that statement was meant to be a joke. Finally, she said, "Of course."

"Great. Italian? You like Italian food? Calzones, pizza, spaghetti?"

Her nose wrinkled delightfully. "Not really."

"Yeah, didn't figure you for an Italian food person. How about Japanese? You like sushi?"

"Sometimes."

He thought a second. "Hawaiian? Filipino?"

She shrugged her delicate shoulders as though wondering where this conversation was heading. "I eat local food, like everybody else. Little of this, little of that."

Local food, he didn't know what that meant. "I like Italian," he said with more conviction than he felt. "It's my favorite."

She simply looked at him. "I had meatballs once," she said politely. "With spaghetti."

"Did you like it?"

"It was..." she thought. "Different."

"Yeah, like me and this dim sum."

"You don't like dim sum?"

"Well...honestly? It's, uh...different," he laughed. "The tarts are good."

"Only the tarts?" She smiled, a lovely, gentle smile.

"I like desserts. I used to like them a lot! Too much. How about you?"

"Hmmm..." She thought for several seconds. "I like ice cream."

"I love ice cream!" he grinned. "Let's get some after this!" At last, a point of agreement. Chris was beginning to hope that things were easing up. But it sure was a lot of hard work. He felt like the two of them were on a quiz show and he was asking all the questions. She sure didn't help him out much.

But then, gradually, the conversation took a more natural turn. He asked about her favorite movie, but Mei Ling didn't go to movies very often. When pressed, she admitted the last time she had been to the movies was a year ago and she didn't remember what she saw. She didn't watch TV at all. Her grandmother thought it was a waste of time. She read a lot. Chris steered the conversation away from that subject at once. As brainy as she was, talking about books was bound to make him look silly.

He decided on sports since, back home, he had played tennis. Mei Ling didn't play. She had tried it once, a few years back, but had sprained a wrist. During a short vacation in England she had attended football matches but only because everyone there was mad about the sport. She was good at volleyball, but with so much schoolwork she didn't get much chance to play anymore.

"You know, my church has a volleyball team. They're always looking for players. I was thinking of joining up. Would you be interested?"

She said she was too busy, but the thought crossed Chris's mind that maybe it was the fact that it was at the church that put the damper on the idea. He didn't know a thing about her religion. Many oriental people, so he had heard back home, did not want to come to Christian churches for anything.

The conversation dragged to a halt. Mei Ling repositioned the chopsticks on her plate then looked up at him politely with a glance that suggested to Chris that she might just be waiting for him to finish eating so that she could make a dash to the bookstore, and maybe get home a little early. After all, she had only agreed to bring him someplace where they could eat dim sum.

So Chris toyed with his food, determined to make the small meal last as long as possible, and doubly determined not to fall back on that old standby, schoolwork. Not during the few priceless moments he had her to himself. So much to say, and yet the words stuck in his throat. If he kept on acting like this, she'd never meet him again.

He just didn't understand her. He had always thought that girls kind of let you know whether they were interested or not. His mother had called that flirting. Evidently she had flirted with his dad a lot before they were married. And around the holidays--Christmas, anniversaries, birthdays--she often talked of those early days. Places they went, fun times they had. The girls back home had let him know how they felt when he was fat. No way were they interested. And then he had lost the weight and all of a sudden, especially here in Hawaii, there were special smiles, a light in a girl's eye that said go ahead ask me out. But with Mei Ling he just couldn't figure it out. Okay, she was polite. That was a cultural thing, even he knew that. He'd watched the movies. But would she meet him alone, twice, just out of politeness? Surely there had to be *some* kind of attraction. Just a little? He looked long and hard into her beautiful black eyes, but could read nothing.

Then he realized the conversation had stopped yet again. On impulse, he asked the first question that popped into his head. "So, what's the most important thing in your life?" He was pleased with that. It sounded at least halfway intelligent.

She had a quick answer: "My family first, of course. And school."

"Hmm. Yeah, family is important. Although for me it's only my mother and my uncle, some cousins, but nobody close. My dad died when I was little and my grandpa took his place, but, well, he died a while back."

"Ah, very sad," Mei Ling replied and her concern showed in her eyes. However, it didn't look as though she was going to venture anything further about her own family other than the information she'd already given him.

Subject closed. Chris sighed. Okay, they had covered all the important things: food, sports, entertainment, family and school, all the basic stuff. What was left? Cars? Nah, she wouldn't be interested in cars. Clothes? He shuddered. "How about your religion? Is that important to you?" The words jumped out.

"It has its place," she said, her eyes darkening a little.

"I don't know what you mean by that," he smiled. "Do you have a specific religion? I mean are you, like, Buddhist or something?"

"Out of respect for my family, I follow sometimes the old ways," she said, but there was not a speck of warmth in her eyes.

Religion, was he crazy! Had he really been so desperate for a topic of conversation he turned to *religion*? Wasn't that the subject everybody said you absolutely had to avoid! Okay, he should change the subject.

Instead he found himself saying, "But…I get the feeling, just from the way you answered me, that it's really not important, right? I mean, deep down. I mean, that's just how it seemed," he finished lamely. Mentally, he kicked himself in the shins once again. Why on earth had he gone and said *that!*

"You have strong belief." It was a statement, not a question.

"Well…yeah, I do."

"And it means much to you."

"It's the foundation of my life," he said honestly. No use pretending. He'd stuck his foot in his mouth and there it would stay, but he wasn't about to apologize for it, or pretend he didn't believe when he did.

"Foundation of your life?" She was slightly amused.

"I guess that kind of just jumped out. But…" Chris shrugged. "Oh man, to try to explain that could take a while. But I'll make it short…"

"No, please," Mei Ling hastened to stop him. "I did not mean you should…"

"But, really, I want to. I don't know why, but I feel this is something you ought to know about me," he said earnestly.

Mei Ling was not convinced. Still, always polite, she let him speak.

"Okay, here it is," he began, and the words rushed out. " I grew up going to church on Sundays. Nobody in my family was particularly religious; it was just something my grandfather and I did. My mom didn't go." He stopped, groping for words. He had started this conversation, and he had to go on with it. But how much should he say?

"But then, my grandfather died, and I had a lot of questions and I stopped going. Life got…tough. I had problems, you know? And then, at some point, I decided I couldn't be the only thing in the world. There had to be something greater than me. So, when I was old enough to drive, I started going to church again. And it seemed to, I don't know, kind of put things in order. I needed God in my life, I don't know how else to put it. And now I'm here in this really great church, and all of a sudden I really want to know more about God, and faith, and all of that."

"And so, because religion is so important to you, you think must be same for me." She sat back as if satisfied about something.

"Well, I didn't mean that. I was just interested is all," he said sincerely, wishing with all his heart he could go back in time and restart the conversation as of five minutes ago.

She looked at him with a glance both speculative and appraising. "You are curious."

"Yeah! That's it, I'm just curious, that's all."

"But *honestly*, as you say so often, I do not think I can satisfy your curiosity."

"Okay, then let me just back off here. I didn't mean…" Chris shook his head, embarrassed.

"You did, I think." Sadness and resignation flitted across her delicate features. She leaned forward a little. "So here is what I say. Because you must know something, I say something. I say that I believe in cosmos, yes? Cosmos? And my place in it. I believe in order and harmony of all things." She tilted her head again, as if trying to read his reaction but Chris kept his expression neutral.

" I believe in cycles of life," she continued, carefully choosing her words. " Birth and death and rebirth, so that things stay in balance. I believe partly my grandmother's belief system though belief systems evolve, even ancient ones. But," she hesitated briefly before saying the next words. "I think, maybe, if we compare values and traditions, we find some things in common."

"You think so?" Happiness lit up Chris's voice.

"Could be," she cautioned.

"That is, like, totally cool!" Encouraged to think there might be some connection, Chris leaned forward, elbows on the table. "So, Mei Ling, what do you believe? I mean, if you died tonight, what would happen to you? Where would you go?"

"Agh!" She jerked back suddenly, stung by his words. He felt her shut down, close off from him immediately. "I know that question," she said in a brittle voice. "It is what Christians ask when they want to make others believe as they do."

"Well, I don't know about that, it's just that we happen to think that, as religions go, ours is pretty good," he joked.

"No." she glared at him. "I take back what I said. We have nothing in common because you are sure that yours--Baptist, Presbyterian, Orthodox, whatever-- is best."

"But…"

"And why? This is what I do not know." Passion infused her cheeks with a delicate blush, her eyes flashed, bright with emotion. "Look around you, look at life. Everything in life is…" She sought for a word. "Diverse? Yes? Diverse. Yet you Christians see things only through single lens. You think I should accept you for that, but you cannot accept me for the way I see things."

"That's not true. Besides, I don't even really understand how you do see things. But I'm trying," he said earnestly.

She looked at him hard and long as though she were not pleased at all with what she saw. "You never understand," she said flatly. "It is how your religion works for you. There is no room for anything else but how Christian doctrine…Doctrine, yes? How that is superior. I have come to know this very well before."

"But maybe I'm different," Chris tried his most winning smile. "Maybe if you really got to know me..."

"I thought so, yes," she admitted ruefully. "I hoped because you were here in Hawaii, in this place where so many different cultures exist, because you were in university seeking knowledge, your heart was open. But no. I know now this cannot be true. Please, no more!"

The door slammed shut. Just like that. Brilliant, Chris. An A-Number-One job. Your first time up at bat and you strike out.

Mei Ling stood up and thanked him politely for a delicious meal. But after that, she refused to see him alone again.

In the days that followed, Chris tried to see her alone, but she hid from him in groups. He had such deep feelings for her! He prayed so hard! Surely, if there wasn't something there, God would change the way he was feeling.

She had admitted that she only followed the "old ways" out of respect, and then just sometimes. And the rest of what she said didn't sound like much of a religion at all, so Chris had to wonder how much of it she actually believed. Seemed to him, although it could just be wishful thinking, that she was still experimenting. And okay, it seemed like she had had some bad experiences before with Christians. But surely if he could talk with her again, really talk, she might come to trust him, just a little. And if she did that, who knew what God could do? Wasn't He in the miracle business after all? It couldn't be hopeless. He wouldn't *let* it be.

On her birthday, and once shortly after that, he gave her a worship CD, all instrumental, with a card inside. He thought that God might just use music, the universal language, to open Mei Ling's heart and let him, Chris, inside. She accepted the presents graciously. But with every day she slipped further and further away from him, into a world he didn't understand and into which he was no longer invited.

Chapter Twenty-one

Tuesday, May 18th

B ecause of conflicting schedules, and despite his promise to Mike Dunn, Howard was unable to assemble all of the elders on Sunday or Monday. He had debated long and hard about whether or not to call Jeff Martin in Hilo, but decided against it. Jeff's mother was still doing very poorly. Howard felt that even if tempers ran high at tonight's meeting, he could make sure that nothing would be passed before the senior pastor got back in a few day's time, so there was really no need to bring him into the situation just now. In the meantime, it was a good idea for everyone else to get together and clear the air a bit.

So, it was not until seven o'clock on Tuesday evening that all of the elders filed into Pastor Martin's office and took a seat around the conference table. Howard Nakata, as chairman, assumed the place traditionally reserved for the pastor. Present also were Dr. Richard Ko, Mike Dunn, Ernest Cooke, and Clayton Kobata. A systems analyst in his late twenties, Clayton was the only one wearing cargo shorts and a golf shirt with a Blue Tooth headset clamped to one ear. And he was the only one fingering his iTouch as the others talked. Don Webber, substitute clerk, was also present to take notes. But Richard Ko dismissed him immediately.

"This is not our normal meeting," he said to the college student, "And before we decide what should be officially recorded, we need to talk. So, we'll just have Mr. Cooke take a few notes tonight."

Don, had come up through the ranks of the ACC Sunday School

and youth department and had been excited to be a part of this elite meeting. Still, he said, "Sure. No problem. You've got my cell number if you need me to come back." He gathered his pencils and pad and left the room.

Dr. Ko turned severely to Ernest. "Why did you ask him to come?"

Ernest was immediately defensive. "We normally have somebody take minutes; Kevin moved to California and…"

"Oh yes, yes," Dr. Ko said irritably, "But Kevin was church clerk for twelve years, and he knew exactly what to put down. I don't want some kid listening in on tonight's discussion and recording everything we say. You can take a few notes if necessary. Now could we please get on with the meeting?" After that scolding, he leaned back and drew his lips into a tight, determined seam.

Nancy Price had once whispered to her husband that Richard Ko used too much starch. Indeed, everything about Ko looked recently laundered and pressed: his crisp shirt, trousers, socks, and probably (as Nancy had once imagined) his underwear. Looking closely, it might almost appear that the wrinkles and creases on his face and bald head, brown as a paper bag, had been smoothed away with spray starch and a steam iron. Even his movements were stiff.

Howard brought the meeting to order. Richard gave a concise prayer and shuffled through his notes. But before he could begin, Clayton, still playing with his iTouch, raised his hand. Richard frowned. "Mr. Kobata! This is not a classroom. Say what you have to say."

"Okay. Before we get started, can I ask a question?" Clayton looked up from trendy half glasses. "I've been on Maui for a couple of days. Just got back this afternoon. What's the news about Miss Lottie?"

Mike looked at Howard. "Is it true that it was cat's blood that was sprayed around her front step?"

"Yes," Howard said with obvious relief. "I met with the police chief myself. And that's what he said, unofficially, of course."

Ernest jumped in. "I heard the police found two dead cats in the neighbor's yard. Decapitated!"

"Malicious mischief," Clayton mumbled, looking back at his iTouch.

"It was not!" Ernest flushed. "I think it was a warning of some kind. Some people say it was a death threat!"

"Why on earth would anybody say a thing like that?" Howard wondered. "No, don't tell me, I don't want to know. The thing is that Chief Warner thinks it is just a particularly nasty act of random violence. But here's another thing. Evidently, the chief got in touch with Miss Lottie and she said that she wasn't going to press charges even if they found out who it was. So, I guess that's that."

"I'm sure we all agree that what happened to Miss Lottie was a shame," Dr. Ko said impatiently, "but could we please get on with the matter at hand?"

"Susan Anello!" Ernest piped up. He turned to Howard. "Don't worry about it, Howard. Richard said he'd take over the entire matter and deal with it."

"Yes," Ko agreed. "Ernest brought me up to speed on what happened. I'm going to meet with Miss Anello on Saturday."

"No need for that." Howad glanced sternly at Ernest. "I'm taking care of it."

Ko, however, was not to be brushed aside. "Well, yes, Howard, but be that as it may, I happen to think that this kind of a situation calls for a certain, how shall I say…decisiveness. Firmness, you know. And although we all agree that you have great skills as a diplomat, this is not the time for tact."

"I'm just going to sit down and talk with the woman reasonably before any decisions are made," Howard argued. "After all, we are not her enemy."

"But she seems to be ours," Richard corrected. "There was talk, if I heard right, about a suit," he looked around the table for confirmation. Ernest, however, was the only one nodding his head.

"People often say that when they're angry," Howard dismissed the idea.

"And some of them follow through. So, make a note Ernest, the vice chairman will meet with Miss Anello on Saturday."

"What are you going to say?" Clayton looked over at Richard with interest.

The question startled Ko at first, but then he remembered that over the past couple of years, four elders of long-standing had retired for one reason or another. Clayton, Howard's appointee, and Mike, whom Richard had brought in, were new and unfamiliar with how things worked.

"I'm going to explain the facts to her," he said, managing to sound condescending and accommodating at the same time. "And they are the following. Fact: this church does not now allow, nor has it ever allowed the consumption of alcoholic beverages. Fact: we have a no-tolerance law against that, and we always have."

"And if this had just been added to the church constitution..." Ernest interrupted.

"Fact three," Ko raised his voice slightly, "Pastors, staff and church workers of all types are held to the highest standards of decorum. No exceptions. And Fact four: any breach of this decorum shall be met with decisive action by those in authority."

"So," Clayton said, returning to his iTouch, "You're going to sack her, just like that."

"The parents wouldn't settle for anything else," Ernest piped up, red-faced with repressed energy.

"I can understand the parents being concerned," Clayton looked up. "But just laying down the law, isn't that a little mean? She got pulled in by the police so she for sure knows that she did something wrong. But, people make mistakes, don't they?"

"Ah, I see where you're going with this," Ko sat back, amused. "You think we should institute a three times and you're out rule? Three felonies, three drunk driving arrests, three..."

"Of course not." Clayton was offended. "I didn't mean that at all! I just meant that, you know, what Howard said, "somebody ought to just sit down and talk with her before....well, sacking her."

"I'm going to talk with her! " Dr. Ko scowled. "I'm not going to march in and read her Miranda rights. But I am not going to change my decision on the matter. Drunk driving is inexcusable."

"I think what Clayton means," Howard explained, "is that now days we have so many fine programs in place, excellent vehicles for helping people who...make unfortunate decisions which they no doubt later regret. Then, there is always Dr. Lum who is kindness and gentleness itself. After a few sessions with her, there is no reason why we couldn't reinstate her in the classroom."

"Sounds good to me," Clayton interjected.

Dr. Ko pressed his lips together again, exercising almost superhuman forbearance, "I'm sure we are all relieved to know that it meets with your approval, but let's keep in mind, as I said before, she has threatened to sue. Offering options is not the way to deal with litigious people."

"Yeah! Remember what happened a few years ago," Ernest shook his head.

Mike Dunn, who hadn't said a word until now, joined in. "Clayton," he said looking across the table at the young man kindly. "We are not drumming Miss Anello out of the church! But we do have to take action with regard to her position as a Sunday school teacher. Richard is totally correct. The woman was completely out of line. That's what we have rules for. We can't make exceptions."

Howard spoke up. "Suspending her temporarily makes sense, of course. But before final actions are taken, I really think we ought to wait and see what Lawrence Sizemore has to say. He is over the Sunday school, as you know."

"And we elders make policy!" Richard Ko shot back. "But, anticipating your concern, I talked long distance with Lawrence this morning. And he is in complete agreement with me. Susan cannot remain as Sunday school teacher and that is that!"

Clayton returned to fingering his iTouch and did not reply.

Richard continued, "Now, I think we have exhausted that particular...Mr. Kobata!"

Clayton looked up.

"Would it be too much to ask for your *complete* attention!"

Clayton put the iTouch in his pocket but he took his time closing it down, turning it off, snapping it shut.

"Thank you," Ko said in clipped tones. "As I was saying, I think we've discussed this enough. I will see Miss Anello. I will give her the facts, and I'll report back to you at our regular meeting. Next item of business," he said briskly. "Jason Price." He looked from face to face. "We need to do something, and do it tonight!"

"Before we get into all of this, I have something to say," Howard spoke up.

Ko looked at him wearily. "What is it."

"About Pastor Price's ostensible indiscretion…" Howard began.

"My my my," Ko interrupted, favoring the group with a well-pressed smile, "such language. You should have been a lawyer, Howard."

"I'm using this language advisedly, Richard."

"So am I," Ko shot back. He leaned stiffly forward for emphasis. "And there's nothing ostensible about it."

"Ah," said Howard, "that is where we disagree. The man's guilt—which I take it, is what we've all gathered to discuss--rests on one letter, which is easily discredited, and one actual testimony, which I have here." He reached in his briefcase and came up with several Xeroxed pages which he passed around. "I took it upon myself to talk with Jim Apapa, and I have a statement."

"No one told me there was a second witness!" Dr. Ko said, alarmed.

"Are you kidding?" Ernest said, "There were five or six."

"There were two, perhaps three, from what I was told," Mike Dunn corrected, "but at least now we have something concrete." He looked meaningfully at Howard.

"We have indeed," Howard replied. "On Sunday, since all of this was new to me, I did some canvassing. Fortunately, all of the office workers who were in that day are also church members. I talked to each of them except for Patricia who was out with the flu. They hadn't seen a thing except that Kathy said she that when she passed Miss Lottie in the hall she thought she looked sick. I talked to the youth leader, the music director, and to the ladies who come to clean the sanctuary on that day. I also talked to the janitor. No one saw anything unusual.

"But then, I talked with Jim Apapa, the maintenance man. That day, he had been coming down the hall, checking the ceiling lights. Several had burned out and he was replacing them. There is a socket right next to Jason Price's office, so naturally Jim stopped and checked it out. It was working fine. Then, by chance, he looked through the glass panel in Jason's door, and this is what he saw. Perhaps you'd like to read for yourselves."

The men read:

TESTIMONY OF JIM APAPA

I was coming down the hallway, looking to see which lights needed changing, and I happened to look in Pastor Price's office. I saw him standing right there in the middle of the room with a blonde woman I didn't recognize. He was holding one of her hands and she was crying. Looked to me like she was really upset about something.

Did it seem to me like it was a romantic situation? No, I didn't give it a second thought. Doesn't Pastor Price counsel people? I guess some of them are pretty unhappy. The woman looked pretty unhappy to me.

Signed: Jim Apapa   Date: May 16th

"My my," Dr. Ko observed wryly, " Jim's command of the English language has certainly improved," Everyone laughed. Jim Apapa spoke pidgin with such a heavy accent that even the locals had a hard time understanding him at times.

"This is inconclusive," Mike Dunn shrugged. "So the maintenance guy didn't think it was romantic. Doesn't mean it wasn't."

"Doesn't mean it was either," Clayton said at once.

"My point exactly," Howard agreed. "There is nothing here that can in any way be construed to convince me that what Jim saw was indecent, as accused."

"Holding hands with someone who isn't your wife may not be indecent, but it is inappropriate." Ko raised his well washed eyebrows.

"Not necessarily." Howard insisted. "As Jim said, Jason counsels people. Some of them get upset. I'm sure a lot of people would appreciate having their hand held, under the circumstances."

"Especially by a buxom blonde," Ko uttered the easy riposte. "But those of us in leadership know the type. We are expected to avoid those situations like the plague. Besides, nothing so far has convinced me that, as Mike pointed out, it wasn't romantic."

"And you have to take into consideration the letter," Mike jumped in. "That, on its own, is pretty doggone explicit."

"No it isn't." Howard raised his voice.

"Whaat?" The confusion on Mike's face soon gave way to irritation.

"It is not explicit at all, that's the thing. The letter said that Jason and Hazel were seen committing a sexual act."

"Well…!" Mike lifted his hands as if to say *What more do you need?*

"A sexual act could mean anything," Howard said.

"And usually does," Ko laughed darkly.

"You know some people think kissing is a sexual act," Clayton mused. "Were they kissing?"

"We will never know," Howard pressed his opinion home. "Because the person who wrote this letter signed it Anonymous. So we can't question this person, and we don't know exactly what did go on. We only have this person's interpretation of what went on."

"Come on Howard, you know as well as I do who wrote that letter," Ko laughed under his breath. "And so does everybody else in the church."

"Of course I know. And I also know that she won't talk with any of us. I know that because I've tried to set her up with an appointment to talk to any of the elders, but she won't hear of it. And there's no way I'm going to sit back and see a perfectly good young minister convicted of anything over an anonymous note."

"I think there's plenty of information in that letter to cast grave doubts," Ko thundered." And that's enough for me."

Howard knew he was going to have a hard time getting past Ko. The doctor's antipathy toward Jason Price was well known. He had never been quoted as saying anything blatant, he was far too smart for that, but Ko and Howard were on the finance committee. For the last six months, at every monthly meeting, Richard hauled Price in and grilled him mercilessly. He questioned every expenditure. He examined every time sheet. He tallied every expense sheet and matched it to budget. And, unfortunately, on many occasions Price was unable to justify himself. Ko had an uncanny knack of tripping people up so that they contradicted themselves. At times, Jason didn't know what had hit him, and the result was pathetic. It had gotten so that Howard, and two or three others on the committee, dreaded the meetings. So Howard knew exactly where Ko planned to take this issue with the young junior pastor, and he was determined to stall any final action.

"Not for me," he said quietly. "If Miss Lottie wrote a note, and if we give its contents credence enough to cast a man's integrity into question, then I think she should have the courage of her convictions."

"What do you mean?" Mike asked.

"She should come in here, talk to us, tell us exactly what she saw."

"She'll never do that. That's why she sent the letter anonymously," Ko pointed out.

"My point exactly. She wants all the sensationalism that accusations bring, but she won't stand behind them herself. Therefore, we are not required to take the note seriously. And don't even think of saying where there's smoke there's fire, because a man's reputation is at stake here."

"Well, I'm convinced there was a certain element of fire," said Ko with conviction.

"So am I," Mike Dunn agreed. "I mean, let's think about it. What are we going to do, wait for the two of them to get caught by somebody else? If a person is seen with a gun in his hand, even by an anonymous witness, do we wait for him to shoot somebody? Maybe this Apapa guy just doesn't want to say what he really saw because he'd have to get in the middle of a bunch of long drawn out discussions."

"Besides," said Ko, looking from one to another. "We've had more than our share of these kinds of problems in the past, and if we're not careful we'll become a church known in the community for sexual misconduct."

"The sex church! That's what they'll call us, you know," Ernest squeaked. "The sex church, imagine!"

Ignoring this outburst entirely, Richard continued. "We have to act now about Jason Price, and decisively, before things get out of hand."

"Seconded," Ernest shouted before the words were out of Ko's mouth.

"We can't." Howard spoke up.

"And why not, I'd like to know," Ko turned on him angrily.

"Because, Price is the senior pastor's assistant. Martin brought him on and oversees everything he does. Pastor Martin made it crystal clear when we hired him that he was a hands-on pastor, and that he wanted to be consulted personally on every issue concerning any pastors who would be hired under him before any action was taken, positive or negative."

"Well did he now," Ko said in tones so sarcastic, they reduced the room to an uncomfortable silence. "I don't remember agreeing to that."

"You did, Richard, it's right there in the man's contract."

"Don't think we can't override that little technicality..."

"Wait a minute," said Clayton, alarmed. "Where are we going with this?"

Ernest, who had remained silent so long that he was about to pop, blurted it, "What do you think! We're going to fire him of course."

"What!" Clayton's jaw dropped.

"Not like it hasn't happened before," Ernest mumbled.

"We are not doing anything until Pastor Martin has his say," Howard insisted.

"If Jeff Martin wanted to have a say in this, then why hasn't he? Why didn't he call a meeting earlier? Why hasn't he communicated with us all? There is such a thing as long distance calls and speakerphone, you know. Hilo isn't the end of the world."

"It's my fault," Howard apologized. "Evidently the others thought I had kept Pastor Martin current with events, and rightly so, but as it turned out I was probably one of the last to even hear the rumor. I guess I dropped the ball."

"You certainly did," Ko said with asperity.

"I ran after him in the parking lot the very day after I heard the news," Ernest was red-cheeked with indignation. "He just drove right past me!"

"Look, don't forget, Pastor Martin's hardly been here since his mother got sent to the hospital..." Clayton rushed to Howard's defense. He'd always liked Howard Nakata, ever since the days when Howard had been his Sunday school teacher.

"Now listen," Mike Dunn chimed in. "I'm sorry if his mother's sick, but the fact of the matter is that we can't wait for his say so before we take some action, because, as I said to Howard, after Miss Lottie was threatened..."

"We don't know what happened to her was a threat!" Howard interrupted.

"What else could it be!" Ernest shrilled. "I'm telling you some people think whoever did this wants Miss Lottie dead!"

"Calm down Ernest," Ko commanded.

"The thing is," Mike continued, "As I keep saying, after the incident with the blood on her steps, the rumor about what Miss Lottie saw through Jason's window swept right through the church, and everybody will expect us to take action. In fact, I'm sure a lot of people will wonder why we haven't acted before."

"I don't get it," Clayton said. "They are two completely different things. Just because they both involve Miss Lottie doesn't mean they are connected."

"That's where you are wrong!" Ernest was nearly out of his chair, determined to be heard. "People aren't dumb. They see what's going on."

"Well I don't!" Clayton turned in his seat and glared at the nervous little man beside him. He could hardly believe his ears. "There is no connection. A bunch of kids threw cat's blood on an old woman's steps. There is no way to connect that with Jason Price!"

"I'm not saying it," Ernest squeaked. "It's not me, it's other people."

"I may be a new elder," Clayton said, shaking his head, "but I'm not new to the church. I grew up here. We kids used to be scared of Miss Lottie 'cause she was mean to us. If I had a nickel for everybody she has offended over the years, I'd buy a nice thick juicy steak. Heck, I'd buy a nice new car. Who hasn't the old witch offended? Any one of them could have done the thing with the cat's blood."

"Clayton, I will *not* have you talking about one of the pillars of our church in that appalling language!" Dr. Ko's watery eyes suddenly shone clear.

"I could have used worse," Clayton murmured under his breath.

Fortunately Ko did not hear as he was preparing his next statement. "I think we've talked long enough," he announced.

"I agree. We need to close this up," Mike said, looking at his watch. "What are our options?"

Howard recited, "One, we do nothing and wait until Pastor Martin gets back."

"Unacceptable," Richard Ko stated blatantly.

"Two, we put Jason on suspension."

"Or we just fire him outright," Ernest said. "We're the elders. We can do that."

"You don't need, like, a congregational vote?" Clayton asked.

"We would only if it were the senior pastor," Howard sat tall in his seat. "And let me say this again. We can't do anything final until we meet with Pastor Martin. Now you might as well know where I stand on this." He looked around the table. " I'm all for setting Jason aside for the moment. I think that's sensible, but...."

"Setting him aside? More diplomatic language, Howard?" Ko's voice was strained, his patience wearing thin.

"It will get him out of sight. With Miss Lottie away as well, perhaps some of this will diffuse."

"I disagree. I say we nip this in the bud. Our reputation in the community is at stake here." Ko was adamant; Mike listened closely and nodded.

The men debated heatedly for another twenty minutes. In the end, Mike Dunn had a question. " I need to get one thing straight. The pastor does not have a vote in this, right?"

"He does not," Ko said curtly. "Only the elders will decide."

"But the elders, out of courtesy, can't actually vote until Pastor Martin has his say."

"Correct," Howard emphasized.

"Well then," Mike looked around. He had reached a decision. "Here's what I think.

I think Jason Price should be suspended immediately. Whatever he's doing, counseling, small groups, whatever, he doesn't get to do it. I think a letter should be placed in his file putting all of our concerns in writing, and I think we should get together the moment Pastor Martin gets back to make a final decision."

"I'm not happy about that," Ko's lips formed a taut seam once more.

"Truthfully, neither am I," Mike admitted. "If it were up to me, I'd say let's vote and get it over with. I mean, a firm decision causes less pain in the end, right? But I think our hands are tied."

"For the moment," Ko said. "All right, I'll write the letter. Howard, you be sure that Jason knows about this. He is under no circumstances to counsel anyone or to preside over that small group of his. Or to do hospital visitation, or to represent the senior pastor in any way. And for heaven's sake get in touch with Jeff Martin. Can't he fly over tomorrow or Friday just for a couple of hours?"

"Wait a minute," Mike Dunn consulted his calendar. "I can't meet then. In fact, I'll be off island until the weekend. Probably late Sunday."

"Monday, then," Ko gritted his teeth and glared at Howard. "Make it happen."

No one was completely happy with the meeting. Ernest was charged with putting the decision in writing. And, with very little conversation, everyone gathered up his papers and things and headed out.

Howard caught up with Clayton in the parking lot. The young man looked troubled, and Howard could understand why. Normally, Richard was simply dismissive when it came to anything Clayton said, but tonight he had been downright rude. Two years ago, when Howard had put the young man's name forward as a prospective elder, Richard had a fit. He said he wasn't about to "elevate kids to positions that should be reserved for men of maturity and experience." But Clayton's family had been prominent ACC members for decades and he was easily voted in. Richard quickly reverted to treating Clayton in such a demeaning way that Howard was afraid he would give up and resign.

"How are you doing?" he asked.

Clayton shook his head. "Man, it was like a boxing match in there tonight. And I got knocked down several times."

"Don't let it get to you. Richard can be abrasive at times, but he has the good of the church at heart."

Clayton looked at him. "That's one way of looking at it," he said at carefully. "But the thing is, my grandmother told me it was going to be like this. And what happened tonight just proves her right. She wants me to quit. She says if I stay, sooner or later I'll speak my mind, and if I do, I'll make enemies."

"I'm not sure that's true," Howard said. To his knowledge, Clayton had never been other than respectful to those older than he was. "But I have to ask. Are you thinking of quitting?"

"To be honest, I don't know. No offense Mr. Nakata, but I've gotta go."

"Well, any time you want to talk, just call my cell. You have the number," Howard said.

But Clayton didn't reply. He simply waved, got in his Mini Cooper and drove away.

Howard stood there a moment thinking what a shame it was that these youngsters, the future of the church, weren't welcomed and mentored into responsible positions. What was going to happen when all the old timers retired? Clayton wasn't *that* young. He was twenty-eight. Howard had been a father at that age. Besides, he was a thoroughly nice young man: smart, eager to learn, and always happy to help, and he'd been through the ranks of the ACC Sunday school since cradle role. Being part of the Elder Board was changing him, and not in a good way. Howard decided right then that somehow he would find the time to invest in Clayton Kobata. True, his schedule was busy, but a person can always make time for things that are important.

Although it was late when he arrived home, Howard left a lengthy voice message for his old friend Helen Chang. One person whose help he could really do with right now was the head of the prayer department, and Helen was sure to know just what to do. He asked her to call him urgently tomorrow at work. It was very late. Lillian was asleep. Howard reached in the drawer for another forbidden dessert. The brownie was delicious.

Chapter Twenty-two

S usan Anello clamped her cell phone shut and stood rigidly still. She counted to ten. That didn't work so she counted to twenty, but no luck. Susan was about as mad as she ever remembered being. Over the past few weeks she'd had plenty of occasions to get mad: steaming mad, shouting mad, even raging mad. She'd been furious, enraged, even ready to spit bullets, a phrase her mother was fond of using. But this phone call was the last straw.

True, the other incidents had involved a very personal situation with Mike but nothing there had really come as a surprise. The whole sad course of their relationship seemed inevitable, looking back. True also, she had never met the man who had just called, and she did not intend to. Not on his timetable anyway. She could tell from his voice just the kind of person he was: smug, conceited, vain, self-important, condescending, oh she could go on and on. But the worst thing was that he actually thought that she couldn't see through what he was doing, using well-oiled phrases as a thin veneer over what was essentially an order: get your butt in here on Saturday morning or else.

She didn't know a whole lot about churches. She'd been coming to ACC for about a year. She'd gone through the three obligatory classes before becoming a member, and she had felt good about the decision. It seemed like a nice enough place. The pastor's sermons were interesting, and sometimes they really hit home. More than anything, she had felt a great deal of comfort just sitting there as people all around her sang and prayed, as though she were in an atmosphere where hope was possible. Where problems actually did have solutions. Where pain, even extreme pain, didn't have to be the end of the world.

The pastor was an up-beat kind of guy, but he didn't sugar coat reality. She liked that about him. He was honest. Stuff happened, and it wasn't always good. She liked the way he would tackle true-life situations and bring insight into them. Sometimes he would go to great lengths to tell the congregation how circumstances could be...what was the word he used? Redeemed, that's it. He pointed to the cross. Jesus knew pain. He overcame his circumstances. We could too.

She had been feeling very positive about her church experiences. And then she had made a mistake. Things were going from bad to worse in her marriage. Her job was stressful beyond imagining. Their bank balance was zero. Their three credit cards were maxed out. Mike lost his job. And then, the worst happened. And then, she made the mistake.

She had been strongly thinking about taking one of many helpful programs the church offered. One in particular, Cleansing Stream, sounded especially welcoming. She had been carrying around so much junk, she knew that. It was weighing her down, killing her little by little. Oh, to bathe in that cleansing stream the brochure talked about, and come out whole and new again! She tried to sign up immediately only the class was full and the next one didn't start until fall. Okay, fair enough, lots of hurting people out there. She could wait.

Then, two Sunday school teachers left the church at once. One left on maternity leave; the other was deployed unexpectedly. Stuff happens. Gladys Hirai, a smarmy creature not unlike the one that had just called her, approached. Would Susan take a Sunday school class in the junior division? Susan was about to say no. But then, she sat in for one class and she was hooked. Here was all the innocence, the joy, the hope of the future that was missing in her own life. Perhaps it could be something of a trade-off. She'd help the kids learn Bible verses and stories; they would bring a little sunshine into her life. It seemed a fair exchange.

It wasn't. That was her mistake.

And then, the worst happened, with Mike. After that, she found herself at a friend's house, literally crying in her beer. Two beers. Then, who knew how many after that. She didn't remember getting into the car to drive home. She barely remembered being pulled over by the police. By the time a friend came to post bail and she got home, it was very very late. She woke up at noon. Long after Sunday school had started. So, there was a reason. Not an excuse, but a reason.

However, the church didn't know; they didn't ask. They just wanted her out, simple as that. Funny thing was, she could understand that. Driving drunk on the highway? What kind of a role model was that for a kid? No, Susan had been prepared to step down for a while. She had expected a phone call from someone at the church when she hadn't showed up for class. She figured it wouldn't take long for everyone to learn about the D.U.I. She had even come to the church to meet one of the elders on a Saturday morning to talk with him about it, but after half an hour's wait, no one showed. Since no one had called her to tell her that she shouldn't teach the class the next day, she figured she had the situation all wrong. Evidently it wasn't such a big deal after all. Eventually somebody would talk with her. But in the meantime she could go ahead and teach the class. Susan really didn't know; she hadn't had a lot of experience with churches.

And that's when it happened. It wasn't as bad as what happened with Mike, but it was bad. Really bad.

She showed up early on Sunday, half expecting that someone would be waiting. Half expecting to have to explain why she hadn't been there the preceding week. She expected, if people actually did know about the D.U.I., that some parents would be a little upset, and maybe take her aside and talk with her. She had no problem with that. After all, that's what this elder guy was going to do. Of course why he didn't show she had no idea. But still, somebody taking her aside and talking to her was entirely reasonable. She'd expected that.

What she had not anticipated, however, was to be scolded by a parent one step away from frothing at the mouth in front of God and everybody. She had not expected that people would just stand there mutely with judgment in their eyes. She had hoped that someone would ask why she had been out driving drunk. But no one did. Perhaps, in their carefully sequestered universe, people didn't do drugs, or drink alcohol, or anything else that was against the Christian code. Perhaps this was so far beyond their experience they could conceive of no excuse. Perhaps what she had to offer in her defense was not an excuse they would accept.

But they could have asked.

They had no right to humiliate her, vilify her in front of the kids (that was so bad). And that sanctimonious old man, Richard Ko, had no right to demand that she drop everything and show up at his convenience because he "had something he had to say to her." No way would that happen. Not in her lifetime! When she threatened to sue for defamation of character in the classroom that day, she had been only half serious. But now she wondered if that might not be a good idea. She called a friend whose aunty worked for a legal firm downtown. The aunty told her there was no doubt about it, she had a case, and made an appointment for Susan to see one of the lawyers in the firm. Susan was satisfied. Richard Ko would come to see her at her lawyer's convenience, not the other way 'round.

She was not normally a vindictive person, but doggone that felt good!

———

Friday, May 21st

It had been a dismal few days for Jason. He had to hand it to him, Howard had been nice enough. On Wednesday morning, he had knocked on Jason's door pleasantly. He didn't seem edgy or furtive. He didn't seem to have an agenda he was carrying out. He was just an older, concerned elder of the church, and he wanted to talk.

He had been candid about the Tuesday night elders' meeting. Without naming names, he had indicated that accusations had been made and were being taken seriously. He further stated that the elders had decided that for now, until Pastor Martin returned and they had a chance to meet with him, it was probably best that Jason be relieved of his responsibilities. That's the way he put it, "relieved of his responsibilities." Had Jason been a cop, he imagined he would have been asked for his badge and gun until Internal Affairs had had a chance to look into his conduct. (At least that was the way everything happened in movies, and Jason dearly loved movies).

As he was only a junior pastor, however, no physical emblems of his vocation were confiscated; he was asked merely to clear his calendar for the next week. And this was said in such an understated, reasonable manner, that Jason could have easily felt his calendar was being cleared because they needed to paint the room, fumigate the building, something like that. But of course, that was not the case. Gently or not, Jason had been suspended.

Howard said that he would be talking to Pastor Martin soon and more than likely the senior pastor would want to set aside some time to talk with Jason himself at his earliest opportunity. He added that no definite action would be taken on the matter until Pastor Martin was updated thoroughly and the two of them had met. He added that it was probably best that everyone concerned take the time to consider the matter at length and pray about it. He and Jason had a short prayer, and Howard left.

Jason had taken the rest of the morning to reschedule his counseling appointments and itemize some concerns about the business end of his job that might need attention. And finally, he had called each of the group members on their cell numbers and told them that the group meeting had been cancelled on Friday. He gave no explanation; he simply said that he was sorry, and that he wasn't sure if or when the group would meet in the future. A bit dramatic, but Jason was aching so hard inside he didn't have time to phrase things diplomatically. He wasn't in Howard's league, not by a long shot.

He left the church around three o'clock. There was nothing more for him to do. He went home, fixed the microwave dinner Nancy had left for him along with a note. Evidently, there was a huge convention in town, and she would have to work lots of overtime hours. She promised to try to be home in time for milk and cookies and the ten o'clock news. But it was much later than that when she got home. Jason was already in bed and, to her surprise, sound asleep.

For the next few days, Nancy woke up early, dressed rapidly and headed out even before Jason was out of bed. Jason had debated as to whether to tell her he had been suspended, but decided against it. This wasn't the kind of thing you could say in passing. She would have questions, understandably, and he decided to wait until there was time to talk everything through. So, he wrote her a note saying he'd be going

in late to work but working late as well for a few days and would explain
later. To his knowledge, Jason had never before lied to his wife, but for
the life of him, he couldn't figure a way not to this time.

Jason stayed home, eating canned food from the pantry for lunch,
and taking the guilty remains of his meals to the trash chute promptly
after eating so that Nancy wouldn't see. He could have gone out to
a nearby fast food place, restaurant even, but he just didn't have the
energy. One evening he went out to do a short errand, but other than
that he stayed home. He pretended to be asleep when Nancy got home,
although how long he could keep this up he didn't know. She was tired
and overworked, but sooner or later she would figure things out.

He screened his calls, of course. There were several from group
members, but he just didn't have the heart to talk with them. He stayed
away from e-mail for the same reason. He watched more daytime TV
in three days than he'd watched in his entire life. Friday was especially
hard. The morning felt as though it lasted an entire day, and then he
had the afternoon to get through. Hours of introspection led him to a
pretty good perspective on what he had done wrong, and some things
he might have done better. However, the future was a huge question
mark, and he had no idea what to do in the meantime. Around the time
the small group usually assembled, Jason decided he'd watch the news,
eat a peanut butter and jelly sandwich, turn in early. Doing nothing
was exhausting.

He was sitting around in board shorts and a polo shirt channel
surfing when, at six forty-five, the landline rang. For a second, he forgot
that group had been cancelled and he nearly picked up the receiver to
buzz the up the first arrivals. But of course that couldn't be. He'd called
everyone and told them specifically not to come. He looked at caller ID,
but didn't recognize the number, so he figured it was a wrong number
and sat back down in front of the TV.

Ten minutes later there was a loud banging at the front door.
Obviously he couldn't ignore that. He shuffled over, looked through the
peep hole , and could not believe his eyes. There stood Marge and Pua.
He opened the door while conflicting emotions raced through his mind.
He genuinely loved these people, but tonight he really wasn't sure if he
wanted to see them or not. He was feeling pretty bad.

However, the ladies were full of smiles and chatter. "Pastor Jason,"

Pua said. "Why you neva buzz us up? Lucky 'ting people believed us when we said we forgot our key."

"But," Marge said brightly, moving past Jason who stood like a statue in the doorway, "when the phone rings again you better answer it. The others may not be so lucky." Evidently, the group had met in the parking lot and decided that all of them couldn't get through security, so they sent Pua and Marge, like spies into the Promised Land. They figured those two could talk their way past anybody and they were right.

The phone rang again. Jason pushed number 9 which activated the buzzer. A few minutes later, in walked Chris, Yumi, Rhoda and Norman, punctual for the first time ever! "We told him he'd better come on time tonight," Pua said merrily, clearing the table so that food could be set out. "Or else he might not get in."

"I didn't believe them," he grouched, "but I came early anyway." Norman had brought a loaf pound cake (another first), and he handed it to Pua. "All I could find at the last minute," he complained.

"Perfect!" she smiled busily, taking it from him. She rummaged in a drawer for a cake knife.

Jason managed to say, "Didn't you guys get the message? Group was cancelled."

"Oh yeah, we heard that," Marge said, putting napkins, plastic forks and spoons on one side of the table, "but we came anyway."

Pua stopped what she was doing, searching for words. Finally, she said, "You know, Pastor Jason, we didn't come as group members tonight. We just came 'cause we your friends."

Jason couldn't believe it. He watched in amazement as the entire group worked as a team to put the leaf in the table, and filled the entire surface with food. There were desserts, casseroles, plates of meat, cheese, bread, bowls of chips. Nobody had brought a study book and only Yumi carried a Bible. Evidently tonight they would just sit around the table and talk. No lesson. That was fine with him. He was still in shock.

"But how did you know I'd be home?" he wondered.

"We didn't," Rhoda said. "Until we got here."

"Your car is here. The guard told Pua," Chris said, cracking open an ice cube tray. "And we walked around back before coming up the elevator. Your lights are on."

How Pua had managed to get information out of the crusty old security guard was one for the books, Jason thought.

When they were seated, Marge passed him an enormous platter of malasadas, crunchy with sugar. He took two. Marge said. "It's like this, Pastor. My friend Linda has a friend Jasmine. Remember, she came two times to the group?" Jason nodded. "And Jasmine is kind of on the inside track, you could say, at church. She learned that you had been told to cancel everything, pack your things and get out. She told Linda, and Linda told me. I called Yumi."

"And I did my duty as group clerk," Yumi smiled.

"We decided you could use a friend or two," Pua said resolutely.

"So here we are," Norman said. He didn't seem nearly as pale as usual. His face, surrounded by a forest of unruly black hair and beard, seemed almost normal in hue, and he sat up straighter, as though for the first time he was actually happy to be here. "Now where's the mayo? You have to have mayo with roast beef," he groused as though this were a restaurant and he a paying customer.

Marge found the mayo in the fridge. Chris took charge of filling the drinks to order. Pua passed around the napkins and put spoons in all of the bowls.

"Would you bless the food, Pastor?" Marge asked.

After the blessing, everyone talked for a long time. Chris had another story about his landlady who evidently was a pretty funny character. Pua was bursting with news. "I can't wait to tell you," she said excitedly. "Okay okay. Now, you know the bulletin board beside the ladies bathroom in the church?" Everyone nodded. "Okay, that one always has employment information: who's looking for a job, who's looking to hire. Since the economy got so bad, there are plenty people up there looking for work, not so many hiring.

"Anyway, " Pua continued brightly, "I filled out one card for my son long time ago, but he got the Triple A job. I was going to take it down, but then I thought no, I'll keep it up just in case somebody offers him a better one. Then, on Sunday, Melvin Berry came up to me. He's the president of the Christian Businessman's League. Did you know they are the guys who do the bulletin board? They keep it up and everything."

Everyone was mildly surprised. It was a largish church. Lots going on that people didn't know. Pua continued.

"Anyway, Melvin said they put the cards up for ninety days. What I didn't know was, these men keep a list of these names for their own selves, and they pray over them all the time. Melvin said that early on Sunday, that's the day I was talking with him, he had been praying for my son. He said he had such a sure knowledge—that's the words he used—sure knowledge-- when he prayed for him, that he knew that God was working in Larry's life. He was going to give him not only a great job but a great future too."

When Pua stopped talking her eyes were wet with tears. The ladies smiled and hugged her and everyone looked both happy and encouraged. Pua looked at Jason, "Pastor, I telling you. God is not through doing miracles."

After that excellent news, and more excellent food, the talk wound down. The atmosphere around the room gradually changed, and people were, so it seemed to Jason, trying to put words to questions they were struggling with. Finally, it was Yumi who spoke. Jason and Yumi had not talked together since she had stayed behind the previous week to tell him about Miss Lottie erasing the message on her front door. Once the blood was known to be from a cat and not a human being, the press had backed off. This was ordinary news for people living in a changing neighborhood. The message had never been revealed; Yumi's cousin had kept her word.

"We came here as your friends to support you, Pastor," she said. "We're not sure what you're up against, but we want you to know that we are on your side. We want you to know that we'll be here for you. No matter what."

For a moment, Jason didn't know what to say. He looked around the group at all the faces he'd come to know so well in just a few short weeks. Support, that was what the small group was all about. Growing together in the Lord, in trust, in sharing. Reaching out, closing the barriers that kept people isolated from each other. He was touched beyond words, but there was something he had to make clear.

"I can't tell you how much I appreciate your being here," he said.

"Or what your support means to me, but some of you are just here on faith. You've heard some rumors and decided not to believe them, and for that you have my eternal gratitude. But I think there's something you need to know."

<u>Chapter Twenty-three</u>

There was not a sound in the room. Jason took a minute to gather his thoughts. Finally, he said, "I think you deserve to know what happened." No doubt there was a pastor's manual out there somewhere that said pastors must always show a brave face and pretend they always have everything under control so they could inspire the confidence of others. But these people had come over tonight as friends. And friendship was based on honesty. What good would it do to pretend when it was obvious to anyone who had a brain that he was in an awkward position?

So, he told them the same thing he told Nancy. He started from the beginning, from where Hazel had come for a counseling session. Without going into detail about her problems, he admitted that he had allowed her to ramble on entirely too long without guidance. Because of this, she had become very emotional. In fact, at one point Hazel got so upset she burst into tears and rushed into his arms for comfort.

He told them all about the conflicting thoughts in his mind when he looked over at the glass panel and saw, or thought he saw, someone looking in at that very moment. On the one hand, he admitted, he was terrified. If someone had been there, it would be a pastor's worst nightmare. But then, when nothing happened right away, he allowed himself to think that it had been his imagination.

However, he made it clear that soon there were clues: looks, feelings, indications that things weren't quite right, but that he had chosen to ignore them. But then it all came out. Someone, maybe more than one person, had in fact looked through the glass, just at that time.

After that, Jason said that he had learned that the matter had made its way around the whole church, and from what he had heard, that the facts had been greatly exaggerated. People were upset. He said that it was entirely reasonable that leadership would ask him to step down for a while. After all, they could hardly go on pretending nothing had happened. But he was sure that in time all the elders would get together with Pastor Martin and discuss everything. And at that time, he was sure, the truth would come out and everything would be set right.

No one asked any questions. Not even Norman. They were all quiet, digesting the information.

Finally Norman spoke up, "So what you're saying is that somebody looked through the glass panel in your door, saw this woman crying on your shoulder, made a big deal out of it, spread it around the church, and because of that, your reputation is in question," he said angrily.

"To be scrupulously fair," Jason said, pulling his shirt down firmly, it was an old one and tended to ride up, "I'm short, Hazel is tall, and she was wearing these really huge heels. I don't know what it looked like, but obviously it looked pretty bad."

"Do we know who this was?" Norman demanded.

Yumi had sat thoughtfully through Jason's entire narrative. "Yes, we do. Well, we know the main person. Her name is Miss Lottie, and she has something of a reputation for, uh, getting information around, I guess you'd say."

"In other words, she's the church gossip," Norman nailed it down.

Yumi smiled. "True, but she didn't spread it around the whole church herself. Lottie has a group of friends who gossip among themselves; they've been doing that for years, and well, things get around."

"This is the first I've heard of it. I don't talk to people at church much, only you guys," Chris said unhappily. "I didn't know anything about it at all until Marge filled me in."

"Well nobody filled me in!" Norman barked, "And I still don't know what somebody vandalizing an old lady has to do with Pastor J!" he thundered.

"Nothing, das the problem," Pua explained.

"So, a rumor got started that…what? Pastor J spilled cat's blood on Miss Lottie's steps?" Chris could hardly believe it. "Nobody could think *that!*"

"Ha!" interjected Norman darkly.

"Here's what I think happened," Yumi said. " Miss Lottie peeked into Pastor J's window, spread around what she thought she saw. Then, somebody threw cat's blood on her steps, who knows why. Problem was, it got on TV. Everybody knew about it. After that, there was a bit of mass hysteria. People tried to connect two incidents that were totally unconnected." She glanced at Jason, "There was absolutely no reason to connect Pastor Jason with the incident," then she looked at the others, "But then, it only takes one or two to say the unthinkable, and then people pass it on just because it is so bizarre. I think in time, cooler heads will prevail. People will see reason because people like me will speak up."

"My friend Linda says that Miss Lottie has ruined the reputation of a lot of people in the past," Marge said. "She thinks it was one of them who did the thing with the cat's blood."

"Taking advantage of the rumor concerning Pastor Jason," Yumi added. "Well, that makes sense. 'cause even if people leave the church, they still keep in touch with others who stay."

"That's what I been hearing, too," Pua agreed. "If so, she's done damage to her own self. Nobody to blame but her."

"Then why does the church allow people like that around? Doesn't she work in the office?" Norman was incensed that a known culprit could go on passing around gossip and nobody would stop her. Of course he said that he knew all along that churches were like this but he'd never been actually confronted with this kind of thing. "And now that I am, well…it just defies reason," he sputtered. "I mean, it's not like we're in the Middle Ages or something. The church is supposed to be run by reasonable people!"

Chris was greatly worried. "Pastor J, what about your job?" He looked from face to face, hardly able to say the words. "I mean, you don't think…"

"I don't think we should be alarmed. I'm only being asked to step aside temporarily. And, as I said before, from what they tell me, when

Pastor Martin gets back, everybody will get together and sort the whole thing out. So, although I would appreciate your prayers, I think everything will turn out right in the end. It's just that in the meantime, well…" he allowed his voice to trail off.

"Pastor Martin will take care of everything," Pua said confidently.

"And then you'll get your job back, right?" Chris looked hopeful.

"I don't know why not," Jason said carefully. Of course, having only been at the church less than a year, he did not really know church policy all that well. He actually had no idea *what* they would do when the dust settled. He wanted to be honest with the group members, but there was nothing to be gained by looking on the negative side. And that's what he told them. Everyone seemed to feel better. Except Norman.

"Well, if you want to know what I think about it, I think there's something wrong with the church. I mean, it just doesn't feel like a church. I never feel that God is there at ACC on Sundays for one thing," he grumbled.

"Norman, we are the church. I've told you this before. Weren't you listening? The building is just where we meet. The presence of God is in us, and people like us. Wherever we are, we bring the presence of God with us. And we're there on Sundays."

Norman was not to be pacified. "No, no. This time you are not going to talk me around, Marge," he said waving his hands animatedly as he spoke. "And I'll tell you another thing, this is more than I bargained for. When I joined this group it was because people said to me Norman you don't really know the church. You should get in a small group and get to know people. So I did, and now look. Here's Jason, a really nice guy—and I mean that, you are—" he glanced at the group leader, "being railroaded because of circumstantial evidence. It's really disappointing. I'm going to another church."

Marge looked at him for a few seconds and said, "Where would you go, Norman? God is everywhere."

Norman snorted.

"No, really, what is that verse about not being able to run away from God?" she turned to Jason.

He answered promptly, "*Where can I go from your Spirit? Where can I flee from your presence? If I go up to the heavens, You are there. If I make my bed in the depths, You are there.* Psalm 139. Is that the passage you were thinking of?"

"The exact one," Marge said. "You see, Norman, all churches have problems. If you're looking for the perfect one, it doesn't exist. I should know; I hopped around to plenty. And, besides, if God wants you to find him, He can make Himself known to you anywhere. Why do you think changing churches is going to make a difference?"

Norman threw up his hands in mock surrender. "Always an answer," he said and rolled his eyes. "What are you, lady, a spiritual Mary Poppins?"

Everyone laughed, and it broke the tension. Then Norman got up to refill his soda, and Chris followed him and helped himself to more chips and dip. Yumi washed her hands. Pua brought out more food from the fridge and Marge got up and stretched. Before she sat back down, Pua went up to Norman and gave him a grandmotherly hug. "No need worry," she said. "It's gonna be all right. God's in control." Even Norman could not be ungracious to such a sweet lady. He nodded and sat back down.

When everyone was seated, Jason said that as long as they were together, they might as well check in on what was happening with everybody. He turned to Chris who was about to chow down on a truly magnificent sandwich. "So Chris," Jason said, "Any more clarity on your Chinaman?"

Norman jerked his head up and looked at Chris as if to say, "Chinaman?"

"Oh yeah! A really strange thing just happened. Just last week I went with Dan Marshall, a friend of mine who lives across the street, to a natural foods store. It was one that Dan goes to a lot, over in Pearl Ridge. Anyway, we got there and Dan wanted to find the water fountain and somebody said you have to go in the back of the building and go down the hallway to the elevators. So we did. And we found the fountain. And then, okay get this, I'm facing away from the elevator looking at Dan, right? Well, behind him I see these huge pictures on the wall, so I go over and take a look. They were photos, in shades of brown, blown up really big, maybe 3' x 5'. One was of an old train and I didn't pay much attention to that. But the other one was a picture of a bunch of migrant workers resting in a field. All of them Chinese. And guess what…?"

"Your Chinaman was one of them!" Marge gasped.

"I couldn't believe my eyes. He was right there in the front row!"

"Wow," Marge exclaimed. "What are the chances of that happening?"

"Auwe, I got chicken skin," said Pua, rubbing her arms. "The exact same guy?"

"Yep. Honestly, scouts honor, and I do not ever remember coming to that market before."

Everyone sat still and digested this amazing information. Then Yumi said, "But couldn't you have maybe seen the picture somewhere else? Lots of businesses use old Hawaiiana photos for decoration, so maybe that's where the image came from."

"So maybe the Chinaman was just the memory of a man in a picture that my mind stuffed away somewhere? Could be. But then what about the message? Was that just my subconscious mind talking? Was I actually just giving a message to myself?" Chris grimaced. "Man, that is totally weird."

"A little strange, maybe," Rhoda added. "But it doesn't matter. I think wherever that message came from, it's important, don't you?"

"Yeah, don't throw it out," Pua agreed. "I personally t'ink it makes it even more like a mystery. You sure you neva went to that market?"

"99.9%"

"Okay, I have to ask. What's this about a Chinaman?" Norman didn't like being left out of the loop, and because Chris had been brought up to be polite, he gave Norman a three minute synopsis of events concerning the Chinaman in his bedroom.

"Chinaman," Norman said in a voice without inflection. "Kind of like the Indian in the Cupboard? My kid used to have that book. Very, uh, what's the word, imaginative."

"Look, I've told you all I know," Chris shrugged. "But, like Pua says, I could have maybe dredged up that picture from my own mind, but even if I did, the message is still important. Although it might just mean I've been working w-a-y too hard on my schoolwork. Nah, just kidding," he grinned. "You know what, the thing is that ever since I saw the photo on the wall, the opposite has been true. What I mean is, instead of just thinking oh I made the whole thing up, I've been getting these really strange feelings. Like seeing that picture on the wall means I'm getting a lot closer."

"Close to what?" Norman asked, "Another Chinaman?"

Chris smiled, "Close to understanding."

"Oh well," Norman said "You be sure and let us know how that works out for you."

"You think this still might have something to do with your little friend, what was her name?" Marge asked.

"Mei Ling?" Chris blushed. "Well, I don't think I'm her favorite person right now." He shook his head sorrowfully, "But yeah, I do. Somehow, Mei Ling is part of this whole thing. And I just can't give up on her. I pray for her every day, and I gave her a couple of worship CD's."

"Is she a Christian?"

"No."

"But she's open to hearing about it?" Marge asked.

"At first she was, well, I thought she was, but now she hardly even speaks to me, so I don't know," he shook his head again.

"We'll all pray for her," said Pua. Heads nodded around the circle.

"Thanks, I really appreciate that," Chris said, "So...uh, I don't have anything else to say. Just a lot of stuff to figure out."

Jason gave Chris a moment or two to see if he would change his mind, then he said, "Anybody else? I know we're not an official group tonight, but it's always nice to touch base."

"Oh," Rhoda spoke up. "I have something!" Marge and Pua smiled expectantly and she wiggled her eyebrows as if to say, Listen to this. "Ed and the kids have been going around to different furniture stores, making the rounds! And even more amazing, Ed has been watching the H&G station sometimes instead of the golf channel! Anyway, he passed me in the garage yesterday and wanted to know if purple and orange actually did go together, and if so, would a good accent color be yellow."

Marge laughed, "What did you tell him?"

"I said that no husband alive would put those three colors together if he wanted his meals cooked on time and his shirts washed. Oh, and Kristen? She walked by me this morning and said, "I hate pink. I absolutely hate pink, and if I have to paint with it I will throw up."

"Oh dear," Pua smiled. "Sounds like you're in for a colorful redecoration."

"I dare not think about it too long," Rhoda said. "I've got to keep reminding myself that my family really does love me." She said that with such a woebegone face that everyone laughed again.

Pua looked at Rhoda as if to say, "Anything more?" Rhoda shook her head. "Well," Pua looked around, you've heard my big news. Marge?"

"I'm not sure I have any news," Marge said slowly " but, like Chris, I'm getting the feeling that things are coming into focus. I think it has a lot to do with prayer, but why I don't know. Just a feeling." She shrugged. "I'll let you know more when I do."

"Well that told me nothing," Norman mumbled under his breath.

Rhoda spoke up. "Oh, I nearly forgot. I do have something to share. I mean, it may be nothing, but..." she shrugged. "Well, okay, it was, like, a couple of weeks ago, the night the decorator came over? And he left suddenly, as I told you. The kids were staying at a neighbor's house and they called and asked if they could stay overnight. Ed fell asleep in his Laz-E-Boy during the first fifteen minutes of a rerun of Moonraker, and I thought I might as well have a prayer time. It isn't often I get the house this quiet.

So I did, have a prayer time, that is, and I don't remember much about it. I read from our study guide, of course, and another book I'm trying to get through, and then I just sat there listening. A house with active kids in it doesn't always get still, and it seems really strange when it happens. Even the gerbils packed it up for the night, and they're nocturnal creatures! And then, this picture came into my mind. Now, please stay with me here. I am NOT, make that n-o-t, a person with a huge imagination. My job at the university is pretty down to earth. As a matter of fact, it's the kind of job that if you did use your imagination, you'd get in trouble."

Everyone nodded; they knew exactly what she meant.

"So, when I saw this picture in my mind, I didn't think much about it, but then, during the last couple of weeks, it popped up at the strangest times. Like it did just now. I was thinking about something else entirely and the picture popped in my head again."

"So, what's the picture?" Yumi, who had been up since five and was starting to fade, was suddenly wide-awake.

"It's a man with a flashlight." Rhoda. said.

Everyone's face was blank. "That's it?" Chris said.

"Yeah, except it's a very bright flash light. Okay, here's what I see, and it's always the same. I see a dark room, not like a cellar or anything, more like a room without windows, and it's night." She stopped again to gather her thoughts, "Oh, and it's a big room."

"Well that definitely helps," Norman grumbled.

"Norman please," Marge said as though she were his mother. "Go on Rhoda."

"A big room, no windows, lots of dark. But the dark moves, see. As the man walks along, the dark moves, but everywhere he shines the flashlight, the darkness kind of like peels back, as though it's afraid."

"So this is a creature?" Norman asked with a disgusted sigh. "Gotta love that science fiction."

"It's not a creature, that's the thing. It's just darkness. But the light is very bright, much brighter than you would think it could be coming from a mere flashlight, and the dark recedes, like the ocean on a beach when the tide goes out."

"The dark moves away from the light," Yumi wanted to be sure she understood.

"Right. That's it. I've seen it dozens of times. It never changes. I don't have a scripture verse or anything to go with it. So….? Interpretations?" She looked around.

"Okay," Norman said grumpily. "Even I know Jesus is the Light of the World. End of story."

"True," Jason agreed, "And there is a lot in the Bible about light and dark."

Yumi turned quickly to her Bible concordance. "Here's a verse. Psalm 18 *My God turns my darkness into light.*"

"Well, that would be a kind of mental thing, wouldn't it?" Pua said, "Like you have bad thoughts or something?"

"Psalm 119," Yumi continued, "*…and a light unto my path.*"

"I don't think it was any of those," Rhoda said. "It wasn't like the man was going on a journey. He was just moving forward."

"*I will make you a light for the Gentiles,*" Yumi read, "*Let your light shine before men.* "*The light shines in the darkness,*" she looked up. " Oh, and here's lst John, *If we walk in the light...*"

"Wait a second," Jason interrupted, "Could I see that please?" Yumi handed him her Bible and he looked something up quickly. "Here it is," he said, finding his place. Psalm 43:3 "*Send forth your light and your truth, let them guide me. Let them bring me to your holy mountain, to the place where you dwell.*"

"Isn't that what we're doing here? Searching for the truth? Well, according to this verse, the light and the truth work together," Rhoda said slowly.

"And they are leading us straight to God," Jason finished.

"Amen," Marge said, as though Rhoda and Jason had uttered a prayer. Then she smacked Norman lightly on his knee. "I told you so," she said.

Norman didn't say a thing.

After a prayer time, the group departed. The nine o'clock curfew was still necessary for those early risers. But Jason was surprised to find that Nancy came home just a few minutes later. She looked totally drained.

"I don't have a muscle in my body that doesn't ache," she said, pulling the rubber band from her hair with what looked like her last ounce of strength. She looked around, "You have a party tonight?"

"The whole group came," he said, and the happiness in his face was a wonderful thing to see.

Nancy smiled, patted his cheek and said, "Don't eat too many malasadas, okay? I'm off to shower and bed. But we have to talk. I have a comp. day tomorrow, so we'll talk in the morning. This time you do Starbucks." And off she headed for the bathroom.

Chapter Twenty-four

Saturday, May 22nd

Jason was up and out early, anxious to buy out Starbucks if that what it took to set the stage for his talk with Nancy. He ordered two venti 1% lattes, and two different kinds of pastry. Then, on impulse, he added a pound of House Blend beans. The place was crowded, so he leaned against the wall to wait.

Next Saturday they would celebrate their fourth wedding anniversary. Where had the time gone? The first two years he'd worked in the denomination office, a fifteen minute drive from their home. His hours were a standard 8:00 to 5:00; she had worked part-time while she finished school. There had always been so much time, now that he looked back on it. Time in the evenings for him to do lots of reading while Nancy studied. Time on Saturdays for long walks and hikes in the nearby woods. Time on Sundays for long, leisurely meals after church with his parents who lived nearby, or even, on holidays, to drive three hours to visit her folks. Time to talk, plan, and dream, though those talks always stopped abruptly when he mentioned the possibility of taking a pastoral job in a local church one day.

He knew that Nancy was a strong believer, but had grave reservations about "getting involved" in church. She had made vague references to churches being full of hypocrites and people who believed they had "the inside track" to God, people who were nice enough as long as you didn't ask too many questions. People who would turn on you in a second if you didn't agree with every single thing they said or if you

197

stepped out of the box in some way. That, according to her, was a huge turn off and pastors and their wives were right in the middle of it. They lived in a glass fish bowl. She didn't want any part of that! So, early on, they decided on a compromise. Jason would work a regular job at the denominational office and they would attend Our Savior together. It worked like a dream.

Then, the job at ACC popped up out of the blue, and something inside of Jason just jumped at the chance. It was only a junior pastor position, he pleaded to his wife. One step up from the denominational office. It was mostly administration, some counseling. Preaching from the pulpit only twice a year, when the senior pastor was away. Weddings and funerals. And look at the location-- Hawaii! Was that or was that not a dream come true!

Nancy, surprisingly, had been ambivalent about the location. She admitted it looked like paradise, but then she went on line and discovered it cost "the moon and the earth," as she put it, to live there. Jason's salary would not be large; no way could they live on it alone. She would have to supplement with a job of her own. That was fine in the short term, but what would happen, she wanted to know, if children entered the picture?

And as for his job, she had never liked the idea, not from the beginning, and hadn't been shy about making that clear. However, because she loved her husband, and because she knew he'd never be happy if he didn't give it a try, she'd gone along with the adventure of it all, with one caveat. "Don't make me get involved, Jason," she'd said with those big expressive eyes trained on his. "Don't make me join committees, teams, groups or anything like that. I'll do the social bit, attend all the functions, have people over for dinner, but that is positively the extent of it." As Jason, who had been chomping at the bit to get to his first real ministerial job, figured her restrictions seemed entirely reasonable.

Big mistake.

There were absolutely no problems for the first three or four months, the "honeymoon period," everyone always talked about. Nancy was true to her word. She attended second service every Sunday. She attended large functions: conferences, for example, banquets, that sort of thing.

When people in the church invited them to picnics at the beach or dinner in a nice restaurant, she gladly went along. But nothing else.

Lawrence Sizemore, the minister of education, was dead set on getting the bulk of the congregation involved in some part of his Christian education program on an ongoing basis. He figured anyone in the church leadership (including spouses) were the obvious choices to head up each its facets. And he was extremely successful in getting them involved. His own wife taught Sunday school in the high school division. Even Jeff and Judi Martin hosted conferences and workshops several times a year. And Judi led a weekly ladies Bible study!

Sunday school and small groups were his pets, but there were plenty of other activities in which wives could get involved. The youth club for teens, Wellspring, for middle school age, or the summer children's Bible program. And, if all of that failed to entice, there were numerous teams and committees concerned with missions, outreach or worship. Nancy, however, declined to serve on any of them.

Lawrence had approached her several times, as had Gladys Hirai and several others, but she told Jason she was sticking to her guns. She would not be pushed into doing something she didn't want to do, and that was that. However, as she had phrased her refusals with exquisite tact, the people who had approached her seemed content to wait.

But now that their first year's anniversary with the church was coming up, hints were being dropped again. It was all a bit awkward. Of course, if worse came to worse, Jason thought morosely, it would all be moot. He'd have to find another job, and she would never be pressured into doing anything she disliked ever again. And God only knew what this experience would do to his wife's opinion of the church, which was already poor. With all of that flooding back into his mind, all of a sudden, the conversation he'd been looking forward to lost its appeal. It wasn't a matter of choosing among a smorgasbord of options anymore; it would be a matter of seeing if they could survive.

The coffees were ready. He walked home with his cardboard tray and paper bag filled with goodies as though he were bringing refreshments to a wake.

But Nancy surprised him. When he walked in, she was just coming out of the bedroom. She was freshly showered and dressed in a very nice frilly garment that looked like something between a top and a dress, with jeans underneath. The rainbow of colors made her look youthful and alive, but the most amazing thing was her hairstyle. She had it kind of puffed up and it looked wonderful.

"How do you like it?" she beamed, turning around for his inspection.

The hundred pound weight fell from his shoulders at once. "You look gorgeous," he said, his thin string of a mouth turned up at both ends in a satisfied smile.

"I was ready for a make-over," Nancy said, taking the cardboard tray and the paper bag from him. "And I want you to see what I've done." She put the coffee and pastries out on the table and looked over at him. "Four pastries?"

"Didn't know which you'd like," he shrugged.

"Well, choose one, but not now. First, come on over here and sit. Right in that chair. Good. Now take a good look at me, Jason. Don't I look as though I've lost ten pounds?"

Jason hesitated. She looked great, that he would have to say, no problem there. But how was he to assess the specific amount of pounds she had lost? He was out of his depth there. "You look great!" he said with a great deal of genuine enthusiasm. Fortunately, that was enough.

"And I'll tell you how I did it," she said. "First, I got this new hairdo which gives me height, see that?" And she pointed to the hair puffed up in all kinds of interesting ways that did indeed make her look a bit taller.

"I got some streaks put in, which draw the eye upward," she continued knowledgeably.

Jason walked over and peered at her head. Doggone if she wasn't right. Blonde streaks in her sandy hair. Subtle, but nice. He smiled and sat back down.

"And I am wearing a vertical pattern in my top which is also longer than usual so that you have the impression of greater length, not width. And, I wear taller heels, but of course I'll put them on later." Nancy was extremely happy with herself and Jason was totally amazed. He would have never thought of such things. To him she looked like a model on a magazine cover and he told her so. She favored him with a luscious kiss.

"Once I got myself figured out," she said, light dancing in her eyes, "I started to think about you. Now go ahead and fix your coffee and then I have something to show you."

Jason was all for the coffee, which got fixed in a jiffy, but he felt a tiny bit apprehensive about where all of this clothes business was going. He had adopted a "look" ten years ago that he felt suited him pretty well: short sleeved shirt (plain), suspenders (to give a vertical look), shiny belt, really shiny shoes. He figured people always looked at your shoes sooner or later. And this is what he wore pretty much all the time. He hoped all this emphasis on clothes didn't mean that she was proposing a change.

Nancy fixed her own coffee and motioned for him to sit down. "Let's get some caffeine in us first," she said. Jason agreed and poured cream and sugar into his cup and stirred it well. He took a sip. Excellent. Then, he reached for a pastry.

As he revived himself with caffeine and sugar, Nancy asked if he had remembered that their anniversary was coming up, and Jason hastened to assure her that he had. No worries there; he knew full well it was just around the corner!

But, she also wanted to know, did he realize it was a fruits and flowers anniversary? Jason had a dim memory of gemstones associated with wedding anniversaries, but flowers? No, he admitted, he did not. As she talked about it, he wondered what you could do with flowers and fruits, and how much of each you were supposed to supply. Nancy would hate the ordinary things, fruit baskets, that kind of thing, flowers in a vase. Maybe some flowery soap? He didn't know at the moment, that was for sure, but when he tuned in again he discovered that she had proceeded to the next topic: choosing a restaurant for the big night. She had several suggestions, and Jason knew from experience that he was expected to do more than say that whatever she wanted was fine with him. She always wanted him to be involved, take ownership of things, so he listened closely.

Nancy had the dining section of Sunday's paper ready. They discussed several choices at great length, each sounding better than the last, until finally Jason implored his wife to please just choose something that she really wanted. Much to his relief, she softened and said okay, if he really had no preference, she would.

Pastries eaten, and half the coffee drunk, Nancy handed Jason a napkin, told him to wipe his mouth, and motioned him into the back bedroom. "Bring your coffee," she called. She walked ahead of him, carrying a cup of her own.

On the bed, several items of clothing were laid out, some of which he had never seen before. Nancy sat him down in a chair facing a mirror. "Okay," she said, "I've given this a lot of thought, and I'm not the only one needing a makeover. You do too."

Jason was not absolutely certain that she was right about this, but the pastry had been delicious and the coffee was good and, well, Nancy had that look on her face that said you'd better pay attention to this, so he did.

"Now," she said brightly. "We're going to start with your hair. I found out where Pastor Martin gets his done and I've made an appointment for you late this afternoon." She sprayed something on her hands and moved them through his hair. "You have fine, limp hair," she commented, "and that bowl cut is just not flattering. See how your bangs just hang down in your eyes?" She turned his face toward the mirror. "Now see how it looks with a little height!" And she lifted up handfuls of hair for him to observe. Jason thought this made him look slightly demented but he kept a smile plastered firmly in place anyway.

"Well, you get the idea," Nancy said, patting the hair down again. Next thing, the glasses. They have absolutely got to go! Nobody wears those oversize froggie glasses anymore."

"Froggie?" he gazed in the mirror. Okay, they were kind of large, but he had to see.

"Contacts," she ordered sternly. "It will bring out the green in your eyes."

"Contacts," Jason mumbled unhappily. He had never liked the idea of pasting small plastic discs on his eyeballs, but as Nancy seemed to think it was so important...

"Now turn around," she ordered, and he swiveled the chair around. She drew his attention to the two outfits she had laid out on one half of the bed. These were the staples of his wardrobe: the khaki polyester trousers, lime green shirt with the red suspenders (Jason's favorite), and the navy blue trousers, white shirt and blue suspenders.

"These have got to go," she said, tossing the shirts aside. "The navy trousers will do for Sundays, but forget suspenders and belts. They section you off, and for you that's not good."

No suspenders? No belts? How was he going to hold up his trousers?

"I want you to try on these Dockers that I found." She pointed to the other side of the bed where a buttery tan pair of Dockers lay next to a pair of Levy jeans. Jason nearly choked. He had always hated jeans, and refused to wear them even as a teen, opting for easy care polyester trousers and shirts. He felt it suited his studious look. He had added the suspenders to give the look some style. But jeans! He had always felt silly in jeans and he saw no reason to change that view now.

"Don't look like that, Jason," Nancy commanded. "Wait until you see the entire ensemble. " She handed him two Macy's boxes. "Merry Christmas, happy birthday, and happy anniversary," she said. "These were expensive."

Jason took the covers off of the boxes and pulled apart the tissue paper. His wife had bought him four absolutely beautiful aloha shirts. Her eyes danced happily as she prepared to tell him how to pull the ensembles all together.

"Okay, these three are good enough to wear on Sundays, but casual enough to wear to work. This one here I bought to go with the jeans, but I'll get you some other casual stuff later. That's easy. Now just go ahead and put on the Dockers."

He did, knowing full well that, as short-legged as he was, they would have to be altered. But they fit perfectly. He looked slightly dazed.

"I measured, and had them altered," Nancy said. "It's not rocket science, Jason." She helped him into one of the aloha shirts and turned him to face the mirror. "See? Those big shiny belts you used to wear always cut you right under your belly. And the suspenders sectioned off the top half. These aloha shirts are worn with the tail out. See how everything flows in one vertical pattern all the way down? It makes you look twenty pounds slimmer! We'll get you some boat shoes or loafers or something to go with the outfit. Slippers, maybe."

"No slippers!" Jason felt he had to draw the line somewhere.

Jason was actually impressed as he turned to view himself from side to side. He had never paused for a second to consider how he would look in aloha wear, but actually it was very nice. He didn't look nearly so egg-shaped, he had to admit. How clever of Nancy to figure all of this out!

The jeans were not as spectacular, but he couldn't convince Nancy. She was sold on the entire "ensemble," and imagined all sorts of checks and plaids that she would go out and buy the following week.

"I saw some Polo shirts at Sears," Jason offered.

"No!" she returned violently. "Just let me do this, Jason. I know where I'm going."

Jason was jubilant. This was the best time, bar none, he and Nancy had had together since they arrived in the islands. Right from the beginning he had hit the ground running: in addition to his normal office hours there were committee meetings, mid-week prayer meetings, small group meetings on Fridays, half-day Saturdays twice a month, and all sorts of special conferences and events that were his responsibility. And then Nancy started working at the hotel. There was never any time. Until today. Jason felt as though he'd been given a wonderful gift. He kissed his wife gently and thanked her with all of his heart. It wasn't about the clothes. He didn't care much one way or another about those. It was what the clothes represented. For that, he was very grateful.

Later, with everything hung up in the closet, and Jason back in his board shorts and T-shirt, his hair hanging limp in his eyes again, "froggie" glasses newly polished, they sat with their backs against the headboard of their bed and drank their lukewarm coffee. Kimo, the poi dog, was barking non-stop again, so talking in the living room was out of the question.

The clothes, coffee and pastries had been a wonderful idea. They made the morning special, something to look back on and remember. But there was something uneasy in Nancy's posture, the way she kept looking away from him, as though she had something to say, but couldn't quite find the words. A knot formed in the pit of Jason's stomach. Obviously, he had not heard all the bad news there was. Nancy had been sweetening something terrible with all this talk about makeovers. Sure enough, she turned to him with troubled eyes. He sighed deeply. What now?

"I have news," she began, looking down. "I was supposed to keep this a secret, but…considering everything, I thought I'd better tell you."

"What?" His voice faltered.

"Your mom and dad are coming over to celebrate his sixtieth birthday."

Jason sat forward at once. "Wow! That's great. June 16th, right? How long are they staying?" he asked excitedly.

"Oh, they want to stay a while. See two or three islands."

"Great news! Thanks for telling me," he rushed on happily. "I knew they would, eventually, so it's not much of a surprise, really. But we will need time to plan, and…" Then, as truth dawned, the excitement drained from every fiber of his face. "Oh no," he groaned.

"Well, we don't know, do we? That's the thing," Nancy said. "Could be that everything will go as planned."

"Could also be that they come over to discover their only son disgraced and out of a job."

Nancy patted his arm gently. "I just thought you needed to be prepared either way."

Jason said it could be worse. Some people had parents that would get all hostile and everything, play the disappointed parent card, that kind of thing, make everyone miserable. The only trouble with his parents was that they would be too kind. Too anxious to make everything okay, even though it wasn't.

Nancy agreed that was true, his parents were wonderful people. Then she searched his eyes again. "But that's not the bad news," she said.

Jason had lifted his cup halfway to his lips but now he stopped. "So…what is?"

"Hilary is coming with them."

"Oh Lord!" Jason shouted, as the cup slipped from his hand, spilling drops of coffee everywhere.

Chapter Twenty-five

The coffee had dripped on Jason's old shirt, yet Nancy rushed to the kitchen for a damp cloth just in case an errant drop or two had fallen on the bedspread. But Jason hardly noticed. As he made his way to the bathroom to change into a clean shirt, the only thing he thought about was Hilary.

Rats! So he was back in town, was he? A picture, clear as a Kodak snapshot, popped into Jason's mind of a teenager with a slightly oversized head, tight blond curls, pasty skin, pudgy arms, pudgy legs, and pudgy fingers splayed on the keyboard of a sparkly red accordion.

Jason had never thought himself capable of despising anything so blameless as a musical instrument, especially one usually associated with the streets of Paris and the lilting music of Edith Piaf (one of his grandmother's favorite singers). But in the fat little hands of his cousin, the accordion had become a weapon of torture. How many hundreds of hours, Jason wondered, had he sat over his homework and endured Hilary in the converted attic practicing the same arpeggio over and over again.

"Stop! You've played that thing a hundred times!" he had pleaded.

"Gotta get it right," the quasi-musician had shot back, mischief swimming in his fishbowl eyes. "Everything is founded on chords, you know," he'd chuckled. Most people laughed; Hilary chuckled. Sometimes he chortled. But never a giggle, never a belly laugh or a guffaw. Just that horrible chuckle. Jason had had nightmares about it.

Poor Hilary was fifteen when he had arrived on their doorstep. His father, Uncle Rick, had died, leaving his only son without a dollar to his name. But the teen had been welcomed warmly by Jason's dad, mother, and grammom who had been living with them at the time. Their hearts were touched, and they called the teen "Poor" Hilary, so often, that Jason thought his name should be changed legally to P. Hilary Price.

Life was not easy for Poor Hilary. He had now lost both parents. He had to change schools and had no friends. Surely Jason could introduce him around? The fact that Jason was only eleven at the time and attended a completely different school hadn't seemed to pose any difficulty to his parents. He was expected to do his best.

Poor Hilary ate only white bread. So, the family ate white bread. He ate no meat, so the family diet was restricted. He was allergic to dust and had to have special sheets. He snored. Loudly. But worse, although to Jason he had the personality of a boiled potato, Poor Hilary was referred to by every female member of the family as "sweet." Jason did not agree. Bland, pale, and seemingly innocuous as Hilary might appear, he knew right from the beginning that this potato had a dark side, and he was right.

On an evening which would be etched on Jason's mind forever, Mr. Price had arrived home bearing with him a prize which he had won by means of a Four H raffle ticket sold to him by his friend and co-worker Jeff Golden. The prize was a sparkly red accordion. Mr. Price had lifted it triumphantly from the battered black case as the family looked on. "Now, who will play the accordion?" he asked, looking from face to face.

Jason had grimaced; his mother had laughed and said she didn't have a musical bone in her body. Grammom couldn't even lift the instrument, she was so frail, so that left only Poor Hilary. A red flush crept upon his pallid face. "I'll take it," he'd chuckled, and the rest was, as they say, history.

Hilary took to the accordion as though it were his personal key to immortality. He took on a newspaper route to make the money for lessons, and of course he had to go to school and sometimes to church, but every other spare hour was spent practicing. Unfortunately, Poor

Hilary had not been gifted with musical talent; he was, however, gifted with a ruthless tenacity.

Jason's wonderful parents gritted their teeth and spent an inordinate amount of time in the den, the room farthest from the attic room Hilary occupied. Jason gritted his own teeth and complained unceasingly until his father took him aside one day and reminded him that the accordion was the only thing Poor Hilary had and wouldn't it be nice if, instead of complaining, Jason took a page out of his cousin's book and developed a little persistence of his own--in his studies, for example.

But the worst thing that happened was that Poor Hilary discovered Lawrence Welk. To be precise, he discovered about a dozen tapes that Grammom had that featured the accordionist Myron Floren. Grammom and Hilary listened to music together for hours. The music of that era formed the entire repertoire of the budding musician. Jason thought that if he ever heard *Lady of Spain* again, he would literally throttle whoever was unlucky enough to be playing it.

And then, a few years later, Hilary took his accordion with him to the state teacher's college. That same year Grammom died and of course Poor Hilary played at her funeral. Not *Lady of Spain*, thank God. But *What a Friend We Have in Jesus* had been ruined for Jason forever. Fortunately, after college, Hilary moved out of town and, Jason thought, except for the exchange of seasonal cards, out of their lives forever. When had he crept back? Had he infiltrated the family home again? Was he, even now, serenading Jason's vacant bedroom with the cheery musical sounds of a bygone era?

Ridiculous, of course, to think disparagingly of a Poor orphan who really hadn't done much harm to Jason except for expunging whole grain bread from the family menu. But the thing Jason could never adequately explain was, that for eleven years he had been the only child in the family, the focus of everyone's attention. When he won a merit badge in boy scouts, it was a big deal. Likewise, when he got all A's on his report card. It was not so much that Hilary eclipsed all that, which he did, it was more that after Poor Hilary came, their lives became like a movie with a really bad sound track that played all the time.

His parents arriving in the islands just after what might be the worst thing that ever happened to Jason Price in his entire life, was unfortunate, but allowing Hilary to tag along would be unbearable.

He was bound to chuckle at some point, and then...well, Jason could not be responsible for what happened then.

Nancy came back with the damp cloth; Jason returned with a clean shirt, and they explored the whole enigma of Poor Hilary and his return to Springfield together. But Nancy knew no more than Jason, and eventually the conversation turned toward the church.

"I've been meaning to tell you something, but of course I've been so busy. I've made a friend at church!" Nancy announced.

"Who? Wait a minute, I know. Lillian Nakata!"

"Very funny. No, that blossoming friendship ended quite abruptly. I'm talking about Helen Chang."

"The lady who leads the Intercessors?"

"You know," Nancy hesitated. She wanted to choose just the right words. "I usually hate bossy women, - control freaks, I call them, the *my way or the highway* kind of people. And Helen is bossy. Helen is opinionated. But she's not like the grade school teacher who can take one look at you and tell you didn't do your homework. Helen actually likes my questions."

"See? You were afraid to open your mouth before, and now you've found somebody to talk with."

"You didn't hear me, Jason. I said she likes my questions! You know how hard it's been for me to even *ask* questions? I mean, I don't have a seminary degree, you know? And Judi Martin and Lawrence Sizemore's wife do, both of them. And I'm always, like, walking on eggshells in case I say something dumb, you know? So, I don't get involved in anything. But you should see Helen, I ask some outrageous question, and she laughs!" Nancy grinned. "I mean, really. She does! And then, of course, she gives me an answer."

"That's great."

"It's more than great, honey. It's, I don't know, kind of a miracle, I guess. I don't know why, but I never really thought people in church would accept me the way I am. I thought I couldn't, you know, qualify for membership in the "insider's club." But Helen honestly does accept me, and I think she likes me too."

"I am at a loss for words," Jason said, marveling. "It's better than great. It's...wonderful! So, when did this start?"

"Couple months ago. I met her downtown at Borders on my lunch hour. She has some kind of Bible study at the Starbucks nearby on Wednesdays. So, we kind of started talking. And I really liked her right off. Twice, we got together for a long lunch and, I don't know how it happened, but I just started talking and she seemed so interested."

"Well, you're an interesting person," Jason said loyally.

Nancy laughed, a rich, deep, happy laugh. "I don't know about that. But anyway, as I said we met for lunch a couple of times, talked a bit here at church in the prayer room, but never about you, or the church for that matter. Mainly I asked kind of general religious questions and she answered them. And then...one day, I overheard people talking. Your name was mentioned..."

"Oh no." He hung his head.

"Jason, it was awful. I was embarrassed. Not because I didn't believe in you. I did. But because there were things going on I didn't understand. One day everybody's all nice and everything and the next day I'm overhearing people say that you might be out on your ear."

Jason shrugged miserably. "That may be all too true," he admitted.

"I didn't talk with Helen about it, not at first. But, one day when I had to come to church for something, I saw her standing at the door to the prayer room. She was just looking at me, and there was just so much compassion in her eyes! It was like she was saying I know all about this, and you shouldn't worry about it.

"So I walked in, and because we were alone, I said, without any explanation or anything, "Jason is innocent." And she said, "I'm absolutely sure that he is. And you must believe, that whatever happens, God is bigger than this." And gave me such a hug! It was just like Jesus himself holding me in His arms and saying, don't worry, I'm here." At the memory, two fat tears fell down Nancy's cheeks and Jason teared up a little himself, because he was so grateful that someone had reached out to his wife.

"I told you, I had some bad church experiences when I was young," she admitted. "And I never really trusted Christians, deep down, after that. I think I expected her to be just like everybody else once the rumors started. Oh, but honey, she was just the opposite! She's just the way Christians ought to be."

"But, see..." he began excitedly. "That's the local church at its best, being just like Jesus. And that's why, all those years at the denominational office, I couldn't get it out of my mind that I wanted to be a pastor. Because when I was young I met somebody like Helen Chang myself. My Sunday school teacher, Mr. Hardesty, was incredible. It was like he knew Jesus. And, it was like when he read the Bible to us, he could take us back there with him. We felt like we were walking down the very streets of Galilee. We could see Jesus moving among the people, listening, caring, healing. Mr. Hardesty brought the Bible alive. Actually, he is why I went to seminary.

"And you remember when I was working at the denominational office and we went to Our Savior?" he continued, eyes bright, "It was never a matter of oh no we have to go to church. We were always excited to go. Remember?"

"Excited may be stretching it," Nancy said. "But I'll admit Dr. Cooper was an interesting speaker."

"He was. But that's not what got to me." Jason edged up on his seat eagerly. "What I really remember were the once a month all church prayer meetings. Remember how the place was always packed because people just knew something really exciting was going to happen?"

"Yeah, now that you mention it."

"I can still remember so many amazing, wonderful testimonies! Remember that old guy who had prayed for his nephew for, I don't know, twenty years or something. But the nephew wouldn't let anybody talk to him about Jesus. And the pastor went up to the hospital one day and the man not only let him talk about Jesus, he accepted the Lord. And then he died, two days after. Remember that?"

"How could I forget it," Nancy said. "When the old man told everybody about what happened with his nephew, there wasn't a dry eye in the church."

"And remember that college guy, Reese, Rance, something or other. He was in the choir, but also into drinking big time, running around on his wife. But after that choir retreat he gave it up, entered a rehab program, and the last we heard of him, he was doing great."

"I don't remember that one," Helen admitted.

"And that homeless guy Fred?" Jason continued. "Because of him, the church started having food drives. And that unmarried mother, Alissa? She said she left the doper guy she had been living with because, instead of turning their backs on her, people had reached out to her with kindness." And I thought to myself, "This is it! This is the real church, the church in action, and I want to minister in it! And when this job opened, it was like God saying it was time. A fresh start, a new place. Paradise. Nancy could be happy and I would be happy too."

"I can see why you felt that way," Nancy smiled. "I don't think I really got into Our Savior the way you did. I was doing my usual thing, holding back. But you sure were excited. And, looking back, the church did have its moments."

"Hey, remember Theresa?" Jason said, laughing.

"Who could forget Theresa?" Nancy smiled. "If her mom and dad didn't get up in time to get her to children's church she ran across the street and pounded on our door—with three or four of her neighborhood friends. Who knew children's church could be such a draw?"

"And who knew we could fit so many ten year-olds in our car!" Jason replied. "But what I remember about Theresa, and Our Savior in general, was that there was so much excitement, so much anticipation. And, believe it or not, I sometimes sense that here at ACC. I truthfully think that an effective church depends on the leadership of its head pastor. And I think Pastor Martin here is a lot like Pastor Cooper at Our Savior. Those men remind me of the Jesus I met in my Sunday school class, the Jesus who walks among the people, listening, caring, who hears from the Father, who endures a lot of negative stuff because there is a whole world to save." He sighed. "If I could one day be just a fraction of what they are!"

Nancy looked down, thinking hard.

"I know this is all new to you, Nance, but the crazy thing about all the negative stuff that's going on right now is that, right in the middle of it, I am just realizing myself how much I believe in the local church."

"Okay, but what if the worst scenario happens? What if this church turns out to be the kind that would just kick you out because they're embarrassed about the gossip or something?

Don't look at me like that, Jason. Things like that happen. And I know Pastor Martin is a great guy, but from what I've heard the elders make all the decisions. And who knows what they will do? So...worst scenario. What then?"

"I'll go back to Springfield. Back to the denominational office, and ease the pressure off of you for one thing. We were happy there once; we can be happy there again. But I'd also like to volunteer at Our Savior. Really get involved. I am absolutely certain that Dr. Cooper will understand. What do you think?"

"I think you've given this some thought."

"I have."

"Well, I need some time to think about it too. All of this is coming so fast. Will there be any options for you, do you think, or if it goes against you will you have to just leave?"

Jason shrugged. "Who knows? This is a foreign country to me. But I do know one thing. I'm really glad you made a friend like Helen Chang."

"Me too. I think I'm going to need her."

Chapter Twenty-six

Nancy wasn't sure it was a good idea for Jason to go in to church. She didn't know if being suspended included Sunday services. But Jason said that nobody could be excluded from church services. That would be unthinkable. Besides he had talked with Pastor Martin on the phone the night before and although they hadn't gone into the nitty gritty details of the matter, Martin assured Jason, just as Howard had, that the elders could not take further steps until he had met with them and with Jason. He didn't promise anything, of course, but Jason was certain that if Jeff Martin had anything to do with it, he would get a fair hearing. They had set a time to meet on Monday.

So he got up early, showered, and dressed in one of his new aloha shirts. Nancy helped him blow dry his hair so that it looked nearly as good as it had when it was cut and styled the previous afternoon. Then, turning her back to him so that he could zip up her dress, she confided that he looked so good, as soon as he got contacts, people would have to look twice to make sure it was really him. Jason was absurdly flattered. All this attention from his wife made all of the other problems less traumatic. In fact, whole minutes went by when he didn't even think of them. He took his wife in his arms and kissed her tenderly.

By the time they arrived at church, service was just beginning, so they sat in the back. That didn't stop a few heads from turning around, but the looks were merely curious. Some people smiled and nodded;

others looked through Jason as if he didn't exist. Jason tried hard not to attribute any significance to this.

The worship choir, small but still growing, sang especially well this morning. Then, a quartet of musicians walked center stage. Keonaona Tom, on guitar, and three others on ukulele, led the congregation in *How Great Thou Art* in Hawaiian and English and it was absolutely beautiful. Jason stumbled over the words on the giant screen ahead, but just hearing the mellifluous sounds of a language not his own brought back to him all the romance and excitement he had felt when he first discovered they would be moving to Hawaii! But then a pang of fear smote his heart as it occurred to him that all of this, the entire house of cards, might come crashing down on him at any moment.

Dr. Martin walked confidently to the podium and all over the congregation people settled back in their cushioned pews, opened bulletins, and took out pens and pencils. The pastor was an excellent speaker, but he moved right along. Nancy handed Jason a bulletin insert which included the fill-in-the-blanks section so people could easily take notes, and a pen. Jason pushed away the multitude of conflicting thoughts that were crowding his mind, each screaming for attention, and placed his focus firmly on the speaker.

The senior pastor was in fine form this morning, moving smoothly along from point to point, supporting everything, of course, with scripture, interjecting a few stories here and there, making a reference to local and national news items when appropriate, and adding small bits of humor. The entire effect was a powerful, memorable message. Afterwards, Jason and Nancy would compare notes and inevitably they would discover that Dr. Martin had sensed their individual needs and it would be as though he had spoken a separate message to each of them. Jason didn't know how he managed to do this. But it was amazing.

All too soon, the senior pastor was ending with a prayer, the choir rising for one final number, and then the service was over. As they filed out of the pew, Nancy said she had to stop in the prayer room for a minute so she hurried on ahead. Jason took his time. Big mistake. It could have been his imagination, but it seemed to Jason that once he reached the foyer, people smiled, but kept their distance and hurried off. Others, like Marge and Pua, ran up to him and greeted him so effusively, that it was a bit embarrassing. As Jason turned a corner, Dr. Richard Ko was waiting. He didn't look happy.

"Morning Jason," he said sternly.

"Morning Dr. Ko."

"You came to service I see."

"Yes." Jason wasn't too sure where this was heading.

"Do you think that was a wise idea?" Dr. Ko asked making it all too clear that it had been a very poor idea at best.

Are you saying I should have stayed home from church! Those were the words that Jason thought, but he was too startled to speak. Instead, he simply stumbled all over himself and said, "Well, I, uh, don't know."

"Think about it," Dr. Ko ordered and walked off.

You think I should have stayed home!! Again, the words reverberated in Jason's mind, but it would have been impossible to say them. Too many people were nearby.

Jason stood rooted to the ground undecided as to where he should go. Nancy waved to him from the prayer room across the hall and he rushed over. The multi-purpose room was small, windowless, and square. A casual visitor would probably not identify it as a prayer room at all. There was no altar, no prie-dieu, or upholstered chairs to sit on. A simple cross was the only adornment on one entire wall. There was a portable table with metal chairs around it, and a coat rack in the corner. Here, the prayer band met on Sundays to pray through the services, and here the Intercessors met many times a week.

Helen Chang came over to Jason, arms outstretched, and enveloped him in a warm hug. Helen was in her forties, heavyset, black hair cut short, with a smile that could melt stone. "Have a seat, Jason," she said pleasantly. "If you have a moment, that is. Something I'd like to say to you."

Shaken from his brief encounter with Richard Ko, Jason sat down as though he hardly knew what he was doing. As if intuiting his thoughts, Helen said, "Saw you over there with Richard." Jason said nothing. "He didn't look happy."

"He wasn't," Jason sighed. "I guess I should have stayed home."

"Stayed home? Why? Just so Richard Ko could feel comfortable?"

"It's not just him, a lot of people…Was it just my imagination, or were they avoiding me?" he frowned at Nancy

"Think about it this way," Helen said. "They've heard rumors, or snatches of rumors, or they just have a general impression that something's up. They know it concerns you, but they don't know how concerned they should be. So, they take the line of least resistance and avoid you like the plague. Don't worry, once everything is sorted out, they'll be friendly again. Try to feel sorry for them. Most of the old timers have been through this before, some of them several times. They didn't like it then; they don't like it now. They're just waiting."

"I see," Jason mused. "That puts things in a different perspective."

"Now, I do have something to say to you, but before that, let's have a word of prayer, all right?" They grasped hands and prayed that God would come and help Nancy and Jason in their time of need and help the church as well, as people struggled to live a good decent Christian life.

When they finished, they settled themselves on the metal chairs and Helen said, "If you don't mind, Jason, I'm going to be honest with you. I know pretty much what you're going through. I've already talked with Nancy about it and we prayed together. I prayed about it myself all week long, and I think I have something for you to consider." There was a note of hope in her voice and Jason seized it like a lifeline.

"All right. Here's how things stand. You were seen in a compromising situation. Someone spread the word around. It didn't get too far for a while, why we don't know. Just one of those things, I guess. Then, after that incident with Miss Lottie, rumors spread like wildfire through the church. Why do things like that happen? Who knows? Somebody swears he spotted a space ship hovering in the sky late one night, and before long the whole town is seeing aliens. You hear that sort of thing on the news all the time. Or in the tabloids. It happens. So now, I would imagine that you're waiting to see what the elders will do. Does that about sum it up?"

Jason nodded. He fidgeted in his chair, but he didn't say anything. There wasn't anything to say.

"But here's what I want to say to you today. No doubt, a lot of your thoughts are concerned with the possible consequences of all of this. What it will mean for you and Nancy. You imagine one outcome after another, and not one of them is good. That is entirely understandable, given your situation. But, I want to ask you to do something different.

I want to ask you to take your attention off all of those worst-case scenarios that have been running around in your mind, and look at the problem in a different way. Try to step back and look at it as you would imagine God would, not you. You're too emotionally involved."

Jason looked at her blankly. It had never occurred to him to do that.

"First, let's consider some aspects of the situation objectively. Think to yourself, why did things fall into place just the way they did?" Helen smiled as though inviting him to consider an absorbing problem in logic. "First of all, this happened during the crucial few days when Irene Baines was on the mainland. Let me tell you something about Pastor Martin's assistant. She hates gossip. She doesn't stand for it. And if she hears something, you can be sure she traces it to its source in double quick time.

"So, if Irene had been here, she would have traced the rumor back to Miss Lottie immediately and confronted her. However, she was not here. And now we ask ourselves another interesting question. Why? Because she attended her grandson's high school graduation on the mainland.

"But why? Mainland people don't celebrate high school graduations the way we do here in the islands. Her entire family is coming next month to Oahu for a vacation. So why didn't she just wait for them to come over? Interesting, right?"

Jason nodded. He didn't quite know where this was headed, but it had its interesting points.

"Next question. Why wasn't Pastor Martin here? Answer: his mother became ill. However, we now know that, although it was severe, it was never really a matter of life and death. Actually, when the aunties flew over to Hilo from the mainland, that's what kept Pastor Martin hopping. He didn't have a minute to himself. So, he didn't even know about your situation for a long time. Another question to ask: why?

"Think about it. If Jeff Martin had been here, even with Irene away, he would have jumped on this at once. He and Howard would have confronted Miss Lottie, no doubt about it and then she would have been in a pickle. She wouldn't have been able to hide behind an anonymous signature. Oh yes, I know all about that! She would need to stand up for her convictions. And, I think she would have backed down.

She and Lillian didn't want to go through a reprise of what happened a few years ago. No, Lottie wanted to stir up trouble but stay safely in the background.

"So, from what I understand, she handed the matter over to the elders thinking that Richard Ko, who as you have probably guessed by now isn't exactly a fan of yours, would fly off the handle as he usually does and take some kind of action. That way, he'd be branded the troublemaker. However, Richard was out of town. And then there came the incident with the cat's blood; she hadn't counted on that either. After the initial shock wore off, she discovered that was pure gold because it made her such sympathetic figure. Poor Miss Lottie! Who on earth would do such an awful thing to an old lady? So, it's my guess that she's probably thrown caution to the winds and has told everyone she knows what she thinks in order to play the sympathy card to the max. So, emotions are running high.

"But the thing to remember is, neither Pastor Martin nor Irene were here. And now, let me tell you another little tidbit of information I have just heard. Howard Nakata, himself, didn't hear about the rumor until just a few days ago. Why, I don't know. You would have thought he would have, as chairman of elders, but he didn't. And I do know that Richard Ko was furious about it when he came back from Chicago. Howard is a meticulous man. Why didn't he know about it and act on the situation immediately?"

She threw up her hands. "There are probably other elements in this grand scheme that I don't know about, but here's what I think you ought to do. Think of the situation from God's perspective. Why did He allow things to happen just this way? What is His purpose in all of this? Things don't happen just by accident. God controls everything. He brought the entire universe into being! And He is at work here to achieve His own purposes." She leaned over and patted him on the knee. " Have a little faith."

The familiar words ran through him like an electric current! Suddenly, all out of proportion to the circumstances, he was flooded with hope. Everything Helen said had put matters in a different perspective. He hadn't actually thought about it before, but he also didn't believe in coincidence. Things did, as Helen said, happen for a reason. And for reasons only God knew, the events of his life and those he touched around him, were unfolding in this peculiar way. Looking at it this way was immensely comforting. He hugged Helen Chang fiercely and on the drive home, he actually smiled.

⌒

Sunday evening

Later that evening, in Ewa Beach, Miss Lottie was talking on the phone to her good friend Lillian. She had just returned from visiting the house in Kalihi, grateful to discover that a few dear friends had come over to wash the worst of the mess away on her steps and front yard while she was away. Except that there were still some disturbing red patches remaining. Lottie had still not returned to church, but many people had called to see how she was doing and that was very gratifying indeed. They wanted to know, if she moved back, whether she would be worried, living all alone, after what had happened. Wouldn't it be better to stay with her sister?

Of course she was worried, she told them. Who could know when some maniac would take it into his head to kill more innocent animals, or worse! Her sister wanted her to sell the house immediately and move in with her. But Lottie didn't know what to do. She was thinking about it carefully, and that was exactly what she was talking about at this moment with Lillian.

"Everyone has been so kind, but really, I don't know what to do," Miss Lottie said. Tears sprang to her aged eyes. Lillian knew because she could hear her sniffling on the other end of the line.

"I'm sure you'll make the right decision." Lillian tried to be consoling.

"But *why* did Jason put that awful message on my door? Just how vindictive is he going to be?"

"Message?" Lillian had heard of no message.

"I mean," Miss Lottie quickly recovered, "What message was Jason sending with blood on my step?"

"You really think he did it?" Lillian asked. "You think he came down to Kalihi?"

"Of course not," Miss Lottie snorted. "But he was behind it somehow. You mark my words."

But the strange thing was, Lillian Nakata was not sure about that at all. She prided herself on knowing pastors and their wives through and through. Jason had acted foolishly with that blonde (she knew as soon as she had seen her that Hazel would be trouble) but she wasn't surprised about that. Things like that happened from time to time and had to be dealt with. But the whole thing with the cat's blood, that was something else again. No matter how she turned it around in her mind, Lillian could not figure out what Jason had to gain from getting someone to put blood on Lottie's step. Nothing. In fact, all this whole thing did was to turn the attention back on him! And…wouldn't that be the last thing he wanted? And who would he have gotten to do it anyway? He lived at church; the only people he knew were the people on staff. And nobody on staff would do something like that. No way.

As Lottie chattered on and on about her terrible experience, (*She could still smell the blood on the step when she went in to get a few things*, etc. etc.), Lillian thought about a new and disturbing rumor that she had just heard. Word was going around that one of Lottie's own neighbors right there in Kalihi had been behind the cat's blood incident. Evidently, a long time ago, a younger Lottie had fingered the man's father (incorrectly as it turned out) when a lawnmower went missing on campus. The father left the church, of course, but relatives still attended. They had heard the gossip. And now the son was heard by those who went over to clean up the mess on Lottie's steps to say that as far as he was concerned the only bad thing about the mess on the old lady's property was that it hadn't been done more often. According to witnesses, he had called Miss Lottie a variety of very bad names.

This caused a little niggle of doubt to raise its head in Lillian's mind. Oh, she was positive that Lottie had looked in Jason's office and seen something bad. She agreed that Lottie did the correct thing in writing that letter. If it was a matter of sin, the elders were honor bound to do something about it. But the whole thing about the cat's blood, that was truly over the top. No matter how she looked at it, Lillian could not connect the two incidents, and the fact that Lottie kept dragging Jason's name into her suspicions was annoying. It was all a plea for attention now, Lillian could see that. Lottie was lapping this whole thing up like gravy!

Irritated beyond control, Lillian quickly ended the conversation and sat brooding for a long while. There was something that was bothering her even more at the moment than Lottie acting like a prima donna. She had known, once Howard read the letter, that he wouldn't rest until he discovered the truth. That was just the kind of person he was. Sometimes things happened fast, like the Jamie Wilson situation, before he had time to try and do something about it, and on occasion Richard Ko outvoted him, but Howard tried to be fair and honest. Oh there were times when living with him drove her crazy, but deep down he was a good, honest man. And admitting that made it even harder for Lillian to look back on what she had done a few days ago.

Like Lottie, over the years she had worked behind the scenes from time to time. Discreetly, of course. That was because no woman had any influence in any really important decision that was made at church. What the elders (all men) decided was law. Except that they didn't always have the facts. They didn't have their fingers on the pulse of the church like she and Lottie, Gladys Hirai and others did. There had to be *some* way to bring really important information to the attention of the men in charge who would otherwise be too blind to notice! Working behind the scenes wasn't ideal, but there were times when you just had to do it. And if you got caught, well, you tried not to think about that.

When the Jeanette Harkins affair (which still made Lillian shudder to think about) dragged on and on through a civil suit that was finally settled out of court for an astronomical amount of money, Howard was angry. When Jamie Wilson left, and his entire large family, he had been furious. In both situations Lottie had been involved and had not been smart enough to cover her tracks. Lillian had been branded guilty by association. Which of course she was, but still it was unfair that it gave Howard such leverage.

So, after that, she and her husband had called a truce. Howard laid down the law and Lillian had learned to be extremely careful in everything she did that concerned the church. It wasn't the best way, by a long shot, but it had worked. Until this matter with Jason Price which Lillian regretted with her whole *heart* ever getting involved in. For one thing, whether Jason was guilty or not guilty rested entirely on what

Lottie, and Lottie alone, said that she saw. Lillian groaned aloud. Why oh *why* had she ever gotten involved in that mess! Okay, so that day in the office she saw that the older woman was upset about something, and because they were friends, she wanted to help. Still yet, she could have offered a little sympathy and then left Lottie to deal with it by herself. Why, oh why hadn't she done just that!

Because, when Lottie was all upset and emotional, she called upon her good friend Lillian for help, that's why. She called her on the phone, over and over again, and told her every single little thing and asked her advice about what she should do about it! As a good friend, of course Lillian listened. What else could she do? But this time Lottie had gone too far. This time, Miss Lottie had goaded, absolutely *goaded* Lillian into sending that fatal memo. Just thinking about it made her feel faint. Looking back, she had to admit, that sending that e-mail was idiotic. How could she ever have allowed Lottie to push her into doing something so totally stupid!

Howard's face, when he found out, had been a mask of anger, but Lillian was used to that. However, this time there was more to it than just that. This time he had been deeply hurt. He felt he had been betrayed at some deep level; she could see it in his eyes. And this feeling ran so deep that, for the first time ever, he hadn't even said anything about it. He remained polite as ever, but distant. He came home for dinner four times a week as usual, but insisted that the TV was on as they ate. The rest of the time he was busy with some crisis at work. Which may or may not have been true. Something deep and wide had opened between them, and this time she didn't know if she could make it right.

Besides that, there were other consequences she was going to have to deal with, and these made her so angry she could spit. She knew in her heart that this one foolish mistake would cause the movers and shakers of the church, read that *men*, to brand her as the worst elder's wife ever. In the future, they would probably avoid her like the plague and take to hiding their valuable secrets from her as though, if she knew them, she could bring down the entire church all by herself! While Lottie, who was busy hiding behind the role of poor crime victim, was looked at with nothing but sympathy.

It just wasn't fair.

Chapter Twenty-seven

Monday afternoon, May 24ᵗʰ

At 1:00 p.m., Helen Chang and Nancy Price pulled into a condominium guest parking slot on Wilder Avenue. They had already prayed a good deal the previous evening on the phone, and right before they made the drive. Nancy was nervous and excited at the same time. She had asked Helen repeatedly if she was sure she didn't want a more experienced person to go along with her. Helen had assured her that Nancy was the exact person she wanted.

"You want to know what the church is all about?" she said. "Well, now you'll see."

So, they locked their car, checked in with the security desk, and rode the elevator to the 22ⁿᵈ floor. Then they walked down a short hallway and knocked on door 2201. Nancy was so nervous that part of her wished no one would answer. Helen had given her all of the information Pastor Martin had passed along, and she knew that what the two of them were doing was the right thing, but confrontation wasn't Nancy's idea of a good way to meet anyone. She already knew the person she'd be facing in a few seconds was angry, furious even, and on impulse she decided to leave it to Helen to make the first move. Slowly and carefully, she stepped back and eased over until she was halfway behind Helen, who just looked around and smiled. "It'll be fine," she said.

Just then, the door opened revealing a woman in her mid-thirties, sandy hair pulled back tight, and beautifully sun bleached. She was thin, but not skinny. Her eyes were a clear shade of blue. Ice blue, Nancy thought uncomfortably, and everything about her from her severe white shirt and black Capri pants to the plain gold watchband on her wrist said *I won't put up with any nonsense; say what you have to say, and leave.*

Obviously Helen smiled when she introduced herself. Nancy could tell because the effect on the younger woman was immediate. No one could resist Helen's smile. It was honest, inviting, and immediately accepting. It seemed to say, *you may not know me, but I know you and I like you very much.* This was not what Susan Anello had expected. The muscles in her face relaxed a little; she invited them in.

"I hope we came at a good time," Helen said, kicking her slippers off in the foyer.

"I told you when you called I'm taking a week's vacation, so it's fine."

Helen and Nancy walked around the living room, admiring everything. The room was modern in color and design, the furniture an expensive Scan Design set, but the personal items, the framed pictures on the walls, the flowers and potted plants, all softened the effect. It was someone's home, that was certain, and a lovely one. The city views out the windows with Diamond Head in the distance were spectacular.

Helen seemed especially drawn to the pictures. They were of a little boy of about five or six years old. They were more the kind of pictures you enlarge from snapshots than the school pictures taken of kids at the beginning of every year. The child had an olive complexion, wavy black hair and big brown eyes.

Helen turned to the woman standing just behind them. "Is this your son?" she asked pleasantly. To Nancy's surprise, tears welled up in Susan's eyes at once.

"No, ...that is...." It's hard to explain," she said, fighting to keep her voice level.

"It's a great photo. Captures his personality, I think. Did you take it?"

"Yeah. Few months ago."

"He's a beautiful little boy," Helen said kindly.

"Yes, yes he is." A tear flowed silently down the woman's cheek.

Nancy watched in amazement as Helen went up to Susan, as

though it were the most natural thing in the world, as though they had known each other for years, and gave her a warm hug. Susan tried to hold back the flood of tears, but unsuccessfully, and Nancy went in search of the Kleenex. After a moment or two, the three of them sat down, Susan clutching the tissues and patting at her face. "Sorry, this is kind of an emotional time for me." She seemed embarrassed.

Helen rushed to put her at ease. "Oh don't worry about it. Obviously we barged in at the wrong time. We should be the ones to apologize."

"I don't usually burst into tears the moment I meet somebody," Susan said in a weak attempt at humor. "I don't usually cry much period. But these days…"

Helen and Nancy said they understood completely. Some days you could just go along and take things in your stride, and put on a happy face and nobody would know that anything was up, but sometimes no matter how hard you tried, life just got the best of you and you were a wreck.

"Well…you've come on a day when the wreck is at home, obviously."

"Would you rather we come back some other time?" Helen wondered.

But Susan said no, she hadn't planned much for today. Vacations were like that with her. If you planned them, then they weren't really vacations, were they? That was the beauty of time off, you could just relax and do whatever. So, really, this was as good a time as any. "Anyway, you wanted to see me about something?" she added.

"I do, but you know it occurred to me that you don't know us at all, so I'm thinking maybe it would be good if we told you a little something about ourselves first," Helen sat back, relaxed, as though Susan had invited them over to do a bit of scrapbooking and they had all afternoon to chat.

"I'm Helen Chang, and I'm a nurse at Queens Hospital." She talked about how she grew up here in Hawaii, and how her husband who was a really nice guy couldn't seem to hold down a job. She talked about her two daughters, one in high school, one in college, and their hopes for the future. On and on she talked, a seamless strand of conversation that was so calm and comforting that it felt to Nancy as though Helen was patting Susan gently on the back, squeezing her hand and wrapping her in love and care that was very real and deeply felt. She did not mention the church once. Susan nodded her head, wiped a few stubborn tears from her face. When Helen stopped talking it was as though someone had turned off a shower of sunbeams.

Nancy went next. She knew she lacked Helen's skills. She was such a blunt kind of person. Yet, as she talked, Susan sat up a little, like a sick person in bed after you've fluffed the pillows, and listened. Nancy looked out the window toward the beautiful view and talked about all she'd expected when they moved to Hawaii. How she thought they'd have lots of time to see sights, swim, surf. "We drove around the island, went swimming once, and spent one day at the Polynesian Cultural Center. That's pretty much it," she said flatly.

" After that my husband's job took over, and then mine kicked in." And then she talked about her job: it was chaotic, the hours were terrible. And finally, she alluded to the fact that she was finding it hard to fit into her husband's professional life. It was like everyone knew a language she had yet to learn, and it was a bit embarrassing.

"You're the young guy's wife, right? Jason something or other?" Susan asked.

"Price. Jason Price."

"Yeah, I know who that is. And you guys are new to the church?"

"Yep. We came July 4th last year."

"I'm kind of new too," Susan said. And then, as though it had just occurred to her that these ladies were her guests, she invited them into the kitchen where she put a kettle on to make coffee, and excused herself for a moment. When she came back, the tears were washed away, fresh lipstick applied.

"How about something to eat?" she said briskly, and Helen and Nancy agreed that it had been a long time since lunch and a snack would be just the thing.

Susan opened the fridge and pulled out a bowl of strawberries and a loaf cake. Helen found a knife and began slicing it, just as if they had all known each other for years. They chatted about the weather, debated whether or not organic groceries were really worth the cost, and whether the proposed high rail system was really a good idea for Oahu. And when the coffee was brewed, the snacks set on paper plates, and they were sitting around the island on stools, Helen looked at Susan as if to say, "Okay, Susan, now it's your turn."

"I know what you've come about," Susan said to Helen. "When you called you sounded so nice on the phone that I said sure, come on over. But then, I thought to myself: 'What have I done? I mean, do I really want to talk about this? Shouldn't I just put it all behind me and get on with things?' But now that you're here..." She looked from Helen to Nancy. "Well, it's okay. More coffee?"

"I'm just fine," Helen assured her, so did Nancy.

"Well then," Susan took a breath, trying to decide where to begin. She chose to start from when she met Mike Anello four years ago, in L.A. He was a single dad; she had just been through a terrible break-up with a man she'd been dating for eight years. Jim was a nerdy guy, but nice. Computers were his life. "He meant to make time for me, but a real person can't compete with a virtual world these days," she shrugged. "Anyway, he couldn't commit. Then, I met Mike and he introduced me to things I had never experienced. Get this, bowling! Baseball, football, all the real jock stuff, you know? It was a whole new world to me. I grew up in D.C. My parents are mathematicians whose idea of a good night's fun is a game of contract bridge.

"Anyway, Mike swept me off my feet as they say. We got married three months later. He hated L.A. We had both been to Hawaii on vacation a few times, and so we thought hey let's start over in a completely new place. Turns out it was more that he was looking for a mother for his son than a wife, but I didn't mind. I loved little Joey. I loved him from the first time I saw him."

Helen asked if that was the lovely child whose pictures she had seen, and Susan nodded as fresh tears rolled down her cheeks again. She told them that Joey was just as sweet as he looked in the pictures. A nicer kid you could never find.

"And did you have children of your own?" Helen asked gently.

"No. I had two miscarriages and ectopic pregnancy, all in three years. Doctors say there's no reason I can't carry a child to term, and they didn't give me much helpful information about preventing further problems. But to Mike, it was, like, an insult to his manhood. And Mike had lots of issues with his manhood."

She stopped talking for a moment and looked out the window as if deciding just what to say. Then she turned back. "Okay, I might as well be truthful. He turned out to be a real jerk. We fought. Constantly. I tried not to, but arguing was a way of life with Mike. If you didn't argue, there was nothing to say. And he didn't just argue, he screamed and hollered and threw things. He seemed to think that was normal, and when I met his mother and father I knew why. They were just like him. Their house was like living in a war zone. I knew that some Italians were hot blooded, but this was crazy. And to make matters worse, his parents didn't believe in divorce. To them, Mike and I were just shacking up."

Susan told them that she and Mike fought mostly about Joey. Now that he was growing up a little, Mike wanted him to be a chip off the ole cement block. But Joey was a happy kid. When his dad tried to argue or fight with him, he got upset. He cried. And of course Mike blamed her. Things got pretty bad, with all the miscarriages and everything and then Mike started staying out. Lots. It didn't take her long to find out that there were other women. So, Joey became her world, and then, a few months ago, she thought she was pregnant again. She told Mike, and he seemed happy about it. Happy enough to stay around at night more often. But it turned out that she had just miscalculated, that was all.

"Mike refused to come near me after that," Susan admitted sadly. "It was like it was my fault! Then, two things happened. I got a big raise (I'm a civil engineer) and Mike lost his job. For him, that was the last straw. A few weeks ago, he left. Went back to L.A. with Missy, his latest, and Joey."

Helen and Nancy sat in sympathetic silence and waited. There really wasn't much they could say.

" That's what broke my heart. I could do without Mike, I mean, who needs a guy like that? But I loved that little boy. I couldn't have loved him more if he'd been my very own," and here Susan wept again. "Sorry," she said. "I thought I'd be over it by now, but I'm not. I still have his voice on my answer machine and when I'm lonely I listen to it. Is that dumb or what!" She shook her head and gave them a wry smile.

Helen said that her actions were quite understandable. She still carried a picture of her daughters when they were in preschool. That was just how women were wired.

A moment later, Susan threw her shoulders back, pasted a smile on her face and said. "Okay, enough about that. You came here to talk about the church. What do you want to know?"

Helen shrugged. "Whatever you want to tell us." She thought for a second. "Have you been coming to ACC long?

"Not long. Actually, I don't have much experience at church at all. I didn't grow up religious. But over the years I knew a lot of people that felt as though church really helped them. And somebody here mentioned ACC. So, when things started getting really bad with Mike and me, I decided to give it a try. Mike was staying out on Saturday nights, so Joey and I got up and went to church on Sundays. Joey was in the primary division of Sunday school and I, in a moment of sheer insanity, said I'd teach a class in the junior division. And, well, you know all about what happened next." She hung her head.

"But Susan, we don't," Helen said. "We don't know at all."

So, Susan told the story that no one had wanted to hear. Mike had left. He took Joey. He took all of their money, cleared out everything. He smashed up all of the furniture in the apartment. What Helen and Nancy saw was a rented living room set. He smashed up her car. She was driving a rental the night she went to see Kristine, a really good friend from work. She had too much to drink. Kristine told her later that she had begged Susan not to drive home.

"But I don't remember," she said honestly. "I barely remember getting arrested." Kristine bailed me out and fortunately my folks sent the money to pay her back. I don't know what's going to happen with that. But the liquor got to me because, you see, I don't normally drink! Mike did, and I figured both parents shouldn't when there was a small child around. And I had no idea about the church's no alcohol policy that idiot Ko kept ranting on and on about when he called me. It's not like I make a habit of getting drunk. My world collapsed, and I caved. And then, because nobody told me not to, I showed up the next Sunday at church, ready to teach." And she told Nancy and Helen what had happened in the classroom.

After listening to everything attentively, Helen said. "I think it's very unfortunate that Howard Nakata was not able to meet with you. Everything would have turned out differently if he had. The same goes for Pastor Martin."

"I really like Pastor Martin," Susan admitted.

"But that isn't what happened. What happened is that somebody dropped the ball in a big way, and the result was extremely unfortunate. Now, I can talk with those parents, and I intend to," Helen began.

"Oh, don't bother. I'm not going to teach again!" Susan said, horrified.

"I agree," Helen said, "But only because you need to be ministered to, you don't need to try to minister to others right now. Still, we need to wipe the slate clean, so to speak with the parents."

"I won't talk with them," Susan said simply. "I just...please. I can't."

"That's fine, but I want you to know that I will," Helen said firmly, "for their sake as much as yours. Now," she paused and looked a Susan closely, "There was talk of a civil suit?"

"Oh no," Susan shook her head. "I was just mad. You should have heard the way that nincompoop Ko talked to me on the phone! I wanted to throw a pie in his face. And the suit was my way of doing that."

"I see," Helen smiled, "Richard often has that effect on people. But you leave him to me. Now, here's the next question. I presume Mike will seek a divorce?"

Susan nodded.

"So, are you staying here or moving back to the mainland?"

Susan hesitated a long time. "You probably guessed that May's an unusual time for a vacation," she admitted. "Actually, my lease is up at the end of the month, and I'm moving out this weekend. This place has too many memories. But Kristine, the friend I told you about? She found me a nice studio in her building that I can afford. So, I'm thinking of taking it. I like my job," she said as though thinking aloud, "and I really don't have anywhere to go. Even if I moved back to L.A., Mike wouldn't let me see Joey. He made that clear." Tears threatened again. Nancy handed her another Kleenex.

"So you've made one decision," Helen smiled encouragingly. "And that can't have been easy. Now, tell me this. How do you feel about ACC? After everything that happened?"

Susan looked at Nancy, then at Helen. "I don't know," she said slowly.

"I think you have an idea. Go ahead, be honest," Helen prompted.

"Well," Susan was slightly embarrassed. "I don't want to go back. I mean, who needs it, right?"

Helen seemed satisfied with the answer. "It's perfectly reasonable that you should feel that way," she assured her, " and you certainly don't need all the stress in the Sunday school, but...what you do need is Jesus Christ. And your best chance of getting to know him at the moment , believe it or not, is right at ACC."

Susan looked unconvinced.

"Stay with me just a moment," Helen said gently. "Now, I want you to think, just for a moment, of the church as a family. Like all families, they have their good moments and their not so good moments. And then, they have their really awful moments. Even the best parents in the world would get upset if they had triplets with colic that kept them pacing the floor for a few nights in a row!"

Susan smiled. "Wait a minute. I'm, like, a case of colic?"

"You came into their lives out of the blue and handed them a situation they didn't know how to handle, and they did poorly. Remember, you only actually heard from one mother. The rest stood by and said nothing. True, no one asked to hear your side of the story. But then, in cases like that, people don't. They might do it privately, but they won't do it in a group. Now, I know it was painful for you, especially at a time in your life when you were going through so much. But, if you could find it in your heart to put all of that aside...just for the moment," Helen said kindly, "Perhaps this is the time to do what you wanted to do. Take the Cleansing Stream class. It's life changing. Come with Nancy and me to Intercessors; we're a great bunch. We do lots of stuff in addition to prayer. Join us. Just take what the church has to offer and don't try to give anything for a while. Does that sound like anything you'd possibly consider?"

"Cleansing Stream doesn't start until September," Susan reminded her.

"True, but there's another, very similar class, that has a summer session starting soon, and I happen to know the teacher very well." She laughed. "It's me!" Susan smiled broadly.

"I'll think about it," Susan promised. "I really will. But I can't say, right now. I'm just too…emotional, I guess. But thank you for coming over. Really, you've been super kind and I appreciate it."

"I'm glad we came," Helen smiled. "But I want to leave you with something to consider. I think, Susan, that things are going very badly for you right now, and you could use someone to come along side of you and help. I'd like to be that person, if you'd let me. I'll leave you my cell number and e-mail address. Call me. Any time, really. It's what I'm here for."

Fresh tears flowed down Susan's face, and Helen reached over and hugged her again. Really hard.

Chapter Twenty-eight

Monday began excellently for Pastor Martin. He and Judi were happy to be back home. It was always wonderful to sleep in your own bed, he thought, even though the spare room in his parents' condo had been comfortable enough. On the good side, quite suddenly Friday morning, Martin's mother had taken a huge turn for the better. Right now, all things considered, she was actually doing well. All the relatives were greatly relieved. If this continued, they would fly back to the mainland in a few days.

On Saturday, when Jeff stopped by the hospital on his way to the airport to say goodbye, Aunt Sylvia's parting salvo had been, "Next time invite me to come when somebody's not sick." So, of course, all the aunts were invited for Christmas. Martin had no doubt that, of the three, Aunt Sylvia would be the one to show up.

On the negative side, Howard Nakata's phone call on Thursday had been a shock. The chairman had filled him in on the highlights of everything that happened in Martin's absence, including a précis of the elders' meeting and his subsequent conversation with Jason Price. Jeff had wanted to jump on the next plane to Honolulu, or at least arrange a conference call, but Howard had been quick to explain that it would not be necessary. At the time of that phone call, Adelle Martin's condition had been uncertain. Jeff and his father were still debating whether to fly her over to Oahu early Friday morning to seek further medical attention. Howard told Martin point blank to concentrate on his mother. Jason hadn't done anything criminal; he wasn't in jail. In fact, as far as Howard could see, Jason hadn't done anything wrong at all. Rumors were flying around; the elders had blown off a lot of steam, but no one would take any action until Martin was back. And the Anello situation could wait. Besides, it might just be a good thing to let tempers cool down a bit.

That was good advice. Until Friday morning's sudden turnaround, Jeff had needed to be at his father's side. The older man kept a smile pasted on his face when confronting hospital personnel or the formidable aunts, and they were a handful! It was only with his son that he could let down his guard. Martin was thankful that, with Howard's help, he could remain with his family during this critical time.

However, after Adelle's spectacular recovery, Martin got back on the phone again and made two calls: one to Jason and one to the chairman. He wanted, among other things, to call Miss Lottie himself and asked Howard for the number, but Howard said that was impossible; the sister was screening all calls from the church and Martin wouldn't be able to get through. Martin gave Howard a short version of the phone conversation he'd just had with Jason Price. Then, deciding that there really wasn't much more Martin could do long distance, the two men had settled back for a long talk, going back into the far reaches of church history that hadn't seemed necessary before.

When Martin appeared as a candidate for senior pastor, nearly two years previously, Richard Ko, with an indulgent smile, had openly admitted that ACC had had its problems, like any other older church. The elders were quick to reference a few of the most glaring, but only the problem ending in a lawsuit was discussed in detail.

However, when Martin agreed to take the job, he knew full well that with a church as old as ACC, there was a lot of negative history he hadn't heard about. He knew also that people in congregations had long memories, not all of them good. And he was aware that before he could begin to build the church, he would have to pray earnestly for the Lord to lead them in a process of restoration, which would not be easy. So, the first thing that he did was to make sure that the church was bathed in prayer as often as possible. Twenty-four seven if they could work it out. He and Helen Chang spent many profitable hours setting this in place.

And then, that summer, the second thing he did was to institute a series of three "town meetings" to try to clear the air. During these gatherings, church members were invited to express their concerns about anything at all. The floor was wide open.

The crowd that gathered on these occasions was not large, but the meetings themselves were significant. At the final meeting, after a great deal of hesitation, Martin was gratified to see that a few long time members did open up—some with tears in their eyes—about concerns they had and long buried feelings. He had learned since that at that particular meeting one friendship that had been fractured by an unfortunate occurrence years past had been healed.

Still, despite this excellent progress, Martin felt that more needed to be done. And so, he had arranged for a speaker to come from the mainland. In June, ACC would host a conference on peacemaking which would help, he hoped, not only to target a few areas that still needed resolution, but with conflicts in the future. In a church of any size conflict was inevitable. Therefore, Martin strongly felt that an introduction to peacemaking skills would be one of the most beneficial things he could do for the church and he was anxious to get started.

"And look what happened," he said to Howard on the phone on Friday, "A month before the conference is to begin, the Susan Anello problem has blown up in our faces, there is all this trouble with Miss Lottie, and the Jason Price situation is threatening to charge through the church like a runaway train. And in the middle of everything, my mother gets rushed to the hospital. You would think someone had an agenda against the church!" Martin laughed darkly and Howard agreed, adding "The battle never ceases." The two men ended with a prayer.

But bright and early on this Monday morning, the senior pastor had entered his office whistling a hymn tune, turned on the AC, booted up his computer and listened to his phone messages. He rummaged through a neat stack of mail left for him by his assistant, and then he buzzed her in. Irene knocked on the door a moment later bringing with her two notebooks and another stack of papers.

Martin was glad to see her and asked about her trip to the mainland. Irene told him briefly about the event, made a few jokes about the bad flights going and coming, then asked about his mother. She had heard that things were not as bad as they had seemed a few days ago. Martin agreed. In fact, he told her, all things considered, she was doing well. That being said, they got down to work.

For the next two hours they sorted through the pile of messages and Irene made copious notes; then, they tackled the mail. It took another forty-five minutes to do calendar and handle a few miscellaneous items. One of them was especially important to Martin. "Before we send that honorarium to Pastor Mitch," he said, "I want to add a personal note. I want him to know how much we appreciate him filling in for me at the last minute." And he took a moment to write a note on personal stationery.

Miscellaneous items taken care of, they turned their attention to the Jason Price situation. Irene had been with Martin for years. He had discovered in her a loyal and wise confidant, and had benefitted often from her insight. "The problem is," he said, bringing their long conversation to a close, "no one has talked with Miss Lottie. But, although the note was signed anonymous, emotions are running so high at the moment, and tapes of previous scandals being played back so often, that it's going to be difficult persuading these people not to take an action they might one day regret."

"And you're meeting with the elders when?"

"Tonight." Martin sat back. "And it's not something I'm looking forward to."

"I'll pray for you," Irene promised.

"Thanks. I count on that," he smiled. "Now, what's next?"

"Jason's workload will need to be passed around."

"Right. Who can we get to fill in for him?"

"I can take care of some of it myself," Irene assured him. "And I'm sure I can pass along other responsibilities. The main thing is getting someone to handle the seminars he has scheduled for later this month."

"Who are the speakers? Run those names by me again…" Martin began, but just then there was a knock at the door and Kathy poked her head in, welcomed him warmly back, and invited him and Irene into the kitchen where some of the women volunteers had prepared a small lunch for everybody.

"I'm starved!" Martin said enthusiastically. "Come on, Irene. Work can wait for half an hour."

At five o'clock, Jeff dashed through the front door of his home. He called to his wife and told her that he had had a huge lunch, could she just make a snack for dinner? He had to leave in about an hour for a meeting at church. "Evidently they all have multiple meetings tonight, so they wanted an early start. Hopefully, the meeting will be short."

In the bedroom he took off his shirt and trousers, walked to the bathroom and splashed himself with cold water in all the appropriate places, and twenty minutes later, having changed into something a bit more appropriate, he joined Judi in the kitchen.

Over apples, sliced cheese, and poached egg on toast (his favorite) Martin filled his wife in on the latest happenings at church. He seemed especially concerned that because he hadn't been there, poor decisions had been made, not only about Jason, but the Anello situation as well. Emotions were running high, and he seemed to be fighting a battle on two fronts at once.

"Poor Jason," Judi sympathized.

"I'm glad we set up an appointment to meet tomorrow."

"How did he sound on the phone?"

"As though he was gathering strength to meet a firing squad."

"He is, that's the problem." Judi, rising to clear the table, was frank.

"Not if I have any say about it."

She paused. "Yes, but having a say is one thing, having a vote is another. I know you can be persuasive, darling, but it sounds as though some of these people have their minds made up."

"Which is why I need people like you and Helen doing double time in the prayer room." Martin stood up and enfolded his wife in his arms. He wondered how anyone could possibly pastor a church without able and loving people supporting him all the way. He was blessed and he knew it. He gave his wife a firm squeeze.

Then the phone rang. It was Helen Chang.

The call took ten minutes after which Martin turned to his wife and grinned.

"Good news?"

"The best!"

After she heard all about it, Judi's eyes twinkled. "Things are looking up," she pronounced.

"A tad," he admitted, "but we still have a ways to go. Keep praying! Now, I really must go." He ran upstairs, brushed his teeth, carefully combed his hair, and rushed out the door.

Martin met Howard outside his office at six-twenty. They shook hands, then walked inside to find that Richard had preceded them. The lights were all on, the air-conditioning going full blast, and Richard was sitting in his accustomed seat, looking through his mail. Ernest was rinsing his hands in the small sink.

Clayton Kobata was unable to attend, a fact that displeased Richard to no end. What was the use having new elders, he wanted to know, if they didn't have the decency to turn up at meetings? I mean, really. What was the point! Mike Dunn rushed in at precisely six-thirty, dressed in uniform, reminding them he couldn't stay long; he had to shuffle two meetings tonight.

So the men were seated right away and Richard Ko gave a perfunctory prayer, after which he said, "I had a talk with that Anello woman." His well-ironed face was dark with ill-humor. "A troublemaker, that's for sure. However, I've called our attorney and he said not to worry, he'd make her sorry she had ever uttered the word 'suit.' " He looked at the others. "As for me, I'm beginning to feel sorry I ever heard the name Susan." It was a wry attempt at humor.

"Then I have some news that will come as a relief to you," Martin said congenially. "Miss Anello has withdrawn her intention to sue. She has stepped down, voluntarily, from any position of responsibility in the Sunday school, and she has joined a prayer group."

"Excellent!" Howard's smile was broad. "That news couldn't be better! Prayer group? Did Helen have anything to do with this change of mind by any chance?"

"She did, and she made an excellent job of it too," Martin sat back, well-pleased.

"Oh, let's be sure to call a nurse the next time someone threatens to sue," Ko said with a sour expression. "Evidently she has the right prescription."

"She does indeed," Martin beamed.

"All right," Mike Dunn spoke up. "That's one problem taken care of, but you know pastor, we have another. " He glared at Howard, "And it's one that should have been dealt with by now."

"And by problem, you euphemistically refer to Jason Price?"

Mike nodded. "Now, Richard and I have given this a lot of thought, and we have an idea."

"Yes?"

Ernest looked from face to face. "We're going to let him go, right?"

Mike looked at Richard as if to say *do you want to say this or shall I?* Richard nodded. Mike continued, "As we all know, Price was seen by a witness in a compromising situation. But the testimony accusing him was brought to us by an anonymous source. That seems to be the defense's case at any rate. And we want everyone to know that we seriously considered it." He pursed his lips in Howard's direction, and looked at every face in the group. "But still, whether or not it could be proved in a court of law that Jason Price did, in fact, commit a sexual act with this woman in his office, the fact remains that his conduct was gravely questionable."

"The Bible says," Ko intoned somberly, "that we must avoid even the appearance of evil!"

"Which he did not!" Ernest chimed in.

"And, there have been other incidents brought to light that I didn't know of until just recently." Mike looked at Richard as if to say, should we go on with this?

But Ernest jumped right in. "That would be the thing with Sandy Miyamoto, right? He pulled her out of choir practice, *enticed* her into the parking lot, and talked with her privately!" Beneath the wild hair that stretched unbecomingly in all directions, thin eyebrows rose. "He has also been seen with women at the missionary cottage."

"Oh please, enough!" Howard was exasperated. "Everyone here knows the whole thing about Sandy was blown way out of proportion, and what's this about the missionary cottage? I guess he has to go inspect it from time to time, and the ladies that clean it probably go with him."

"The appearance of evil," Ernest said knowingly. "And that's not all!

He and Dr. Lum have looked *pretty* cozy during those long meetings at…"

Howard stopped him in mid-sentence and looked at Mike, Richard and Ernest angrily. "For reasons I don't understand, you three seem determined to get rid of this young man, and I for one…"

Pastor Martin interrupted gently. "It's all right, Howard. Let them speak."

"I think, all things considered, some action should be taken. The people will expect nothing less," Mike stated.

"All right. Now Mike, Richard, you had a long time to pray about this matter, tell me what you decided."

Mike spoke up. "Well, under the circumstances, taking into account appearances and everything, which Richard here thinks is pretty important, and so do I, we decided that a letter should be put in his file outlining the accusation against him."

"Mike, there's *already* a letter in his file; Richard wrote it," Howard protested.

"Right, I'm just saying the letter should remain there. And then, we recommend a demotion."

"What!" Howard looked as if he hadn't quite heard the last part of the sentence.

"Demotion," Martin repeated with no inflection whatsoever. "To what?"

"Some quasi-administrative position. Maybe a clerical position of some type," Richard said with the insouciance of one changing a lunch menu.

"But then," Mike spoke up, eager to explain, "he can go through some of those *excellent* programs Howard is always talking about, and in a year or so we can look at his progress, and in time…"

"If a higher position opens up, he can apply along with everyone else," Richard stated, as if to say, "Problem solved."

"Let me understand this, you're pulling him out of a pastoral position and asking him to take a job as a clerk." Howard's expression was grim.

"We will create a job for him in a quasi-administrative capacity. Something he can do without getting into trouble. But the important thing is, we aren't going to fire him. And the job switch will be temporary!" Mike explained as though having to summon deep reserves of strength in order to clarify what was obvious.

"Right. Only for a year or two. And in the meantime his job will be filled by someone else." Disgust was written all over Howard's face.

"Oh for heaven's sake," Mike's flushed red. "We thought long and hard about a way to save face for the guy. Okay, he's got to go, but a demotion does not carry with it the stigma of being fired. I think we're being pretty humane, if you want to know the truth."

Pastor Martin cleared his throat. "Mike and Richard, you too Ernest, I want you to know I appreciate the amount of time and prayer you have devoted to this matter." Richard looked pained, but the senior pastor continued. "I know this has not been easy. There have been many elements to consider. But the thing is, I have not had the time that you have had to consider all of the facts. Most importantly, I haven't had a chance to meet face to face with Jason myself, and it is very necessary that I do that. Surely we have an obligation to him. After all, we hired him." He looked searchingly from one face to another.

"Wait a minute," Mike was brusque. "You have to spend time considering all the facts. Then you have to talk with Jason. Then you have to call another meeting with us, and *then* we get to vote? That could take forever!"

"Oh no. I'll just talk with you briefly for a few minutes before you vote," Martin said with a disarming smile.

Ko was not to be mollified. "Have you even set a date to meet with Price!" he demanded.

"I have. Tomorrow."

"Okay, that's Tuesday. If you can have your meeting sometime in the day, we can get together around six. Is that all right with everyone here?" He jerked his eyes from face to face.

"I'll be here," Ernest squeaked.

Mike pulled out his calendar. "Hmm," he frowned. "It will have to be Friday for me."

Ko was clearly disappointed. "All right then. Friday it is!"

"Saturday," came a soft voice.

Ko swiveled his glance to rest on Howard. "And just why can't you make it on Friday?" he wanted to know.

"Saturday," Howard repeated.

"Saturday sounds good to me," Martin said brightly. "We'll meet here early, say eight o'clock? I'll have a little chat with you beforehand, and then you gentlemen can cast your votes. So, is Saturday all right with everyone?" Martin smiled around the group.

"It's not all right, but it will have to do," Ko growled. "Just as long as it's before Sunday. We can't have Price parading around the church after services making a scene again. This has gone on far too long as it is."

Mike looked at his watch. "Sorry," he said. "I told you I could only stay a few minutes."

"And I have an ad hoc in the library at seven-fifteen," Richard added. "So, Pastor, will you dismiss us with prayer?"

Martin prayed briefly. As the men filed out, he nodded to Howard who walked Mike, Ernest, and Richard to the front door, locked it behind them, and backtracked to the senior pastor's office.

"Have a seat," Pastor Martin suggested, and Howard sank gratefully into a chair nearby.

"That was a close call," Howard breathed deeply.

"I take it you couldn't have arranged things before Saturday?"

"Not a chance. And I still don't have anything nailed down. But I put a couple of things in motion."

"Then I'm sure you did all that you could do. So, how is that looking?"

The chairman hesitated. "At the moment? Fifty-fifty."

"Well, that will have to be good enough. You know, Howard, as ideas go, I think yours was pretty amazing."

"A bit radical for sure," he smiled.

"Look back. In times of crisis Christians were often radical."

"That's true, but…" the light faded from the chairman's face. "The problem is, it's a gamble. I can put the players in place, but who knows what they will do? It's just an unknown."

"I expected that. At least this gives us a chance. I mean, you agree with me don't you that if the vote were taken now it would go against Price?"

'In the worst possible way. And that whole face saving exercise? Even though the words came from Mike Dunn, that was quintessential Richard. You probably guessed he's pulled that one before."

"Yes," Martin admitted. "And of course, no matter what, the demotion won't fly. Price will resign first."

"They always do," Howard said, sorrowfully. "But you know, Pastor, I must be fair. There is a lot about Richard that is solid and good. It's just that…well, he feels as though a lot is expected of him. As a leader, you know. Even if he's not sure he's right… even if he knows he's *wrong*, he'll fight to get his way. When that works positively, it's a good thing."

"I understand. People have issues," Martin said. " But Howard, God is on His throne. He loves this church; this is His bride. And He loves Jason Price. He won't abandon either one. His ways may not be our ways, and He does, as the Bible says, work in a manner that baffles us at times, but one thing I guarantee: this situation has not escaped His notice. He's doing something mighty in the midst of it all."

"I believe that," Howard nodded.

" So" Martin said brightly, "shall we go to Him in prayer?.

Slowly and reverently, the two men got up from their chairs and knelt down. Then, they bowed their heads and prayed fervently for a very long time.

Chapter Twenty-nine

Tuesday evening, May 25th 10:30 p.m.

Chris Murray turned off the lights in his tiny kitchen and slipped out the door. Mrs. Fujihara and Kevin were usually fast asleep by this time, so he was very quiet as he eased on his slippers, made his way down the wooden stairs and down the driveway. He looked across the street to see if Dan Marshall was home. It looked as though he just might be in luck. He could barely discern his friend sitting in a rocking chair on his lanai.

As Chris walked up, Dan jerked the earbuds out of his ears.

"Hey," Chris called "Got a minute? Something's come up."

"Got all night," Dan took a swig of his beer. "Want a brewski? Got some on ice."

"Nah. Just finished a nice cool green tea."

"Man, are you getting local or what," Dan laughed softly. "Come on in. Voices carry out here at night."

He opened the door and padded into the living room; Chris followed, blinking to adjust his eyes to the light. There were books everywhere, just as he had remembered. Not just on the sofa and armchair. Stacks of books covered the mantle, crowded the coffee table and both end tables, and piled themselves against the facing walls. Dan hadn't gotten around to bookcases.

"Just move something onto the floor," Dan eased a stack of magazines to the side with one arm and sat on the sofa. His graying hair was much too long, and his sideburns were so wide they looked as though they had been painted on. His T-shirt stretched tight across his belly, the knees of his jeans sagged. His outlook on life was just as easygoing. Dan was the kind of guy you wanted to talk with when crazy things happened. Just exactly the kind of person Chris needed tonight.

Chris moved a pile of books from the armchair to the floor and sat down. "If you were doing something important I could come back."

"I was listening to an audio of *The Iliad*. Reviewing my notes. As if Kevin would care one way or another."

"Tutoring still not going good?"

"A total waste of time. They should put that kid in school. He's got lotsa smarts and they're all being wasted. I can't get him to do anything that isn't on-line, preferably with a game attached to it. Anyway..." he leaned back, and looked at the beer in his hand as though it were an old and trusted friend. Then he finished it in two long swallows. "You didn't come over here to talk about Kevin. What gives? Seen any more Chinamen?"

"Nah, just the one. But that was enough."

"Still workin' on that message?"

"That's what I came to talk with you about. I think I may have just gotten a clue because of what happened earlier tonight."

"Cool! Give me a minute. Gotta get me another cold one. I allow myself two a night, you know. Sure you don't want one?" Dan picked up the empty and shuffled into the kitchen.

"No, thanks." Chris listened to the fridge open and the pop of a cap on a new bottle. When he returned, Dan eased his well-padded frame against a comfortable cushion. "Shoot."

"Okay. I had this phone call from Mei Ling."

"Mei Ling Leong!" Dan's eyes brightened. "She of the mellifluous name." Dan had two graduate degrees, and though he was never pretentious, sometimes the sheer beauty of words carried him away."

"The same. The China doll who hardly says a word to me these days, if you'll remember."

"Since you decided to put the squeeze on her, theologically speaking," Dan nodded, and took a long swallow out of beer.

"Don't remind me," Chris groaned.

"Sorry."

"Yeah, it's been over a week, but since then I've been good. Trying to respect her feelings and all."

"You are a true gentleman," Dan nodded agreeably.

"Yeah well I try, but she's still kind of keeping her distance. Okay, so tonight we go to the study group as usual, but I left right away 'cause, like, I was really starved. I drove by Taco Bell and got some food to go, brought it home and ate. Watched a little TV. Took about forty minutes, I guess. Hour tops. Anyway, right then I get this absolutely frantic phone call from Mei Ling. She is, like, totally over the edge. She was so hyper she wasn't making any sense."

"Something happened," Dan guessed, taking another swig.

"Bingo. Okay, here's what it was. She's driving home, see, and, from what I can tell, she stopped at a stop sign and was about to turn left onto an overpass. She looks right, left, doesn't see anything and eases out to make the turn. Then, according to her, some car comes streaking out of nowhere, grazes her bumper; he goes barreling past and, get this, piles into a guard rail."

"Was she hurt?"

"Mei Ling? No. Her car got turned around a little, but she's fine. But the other guy is, like, dead! "

"Whoa! No kiddin'"

"Yeah. And she freaks out like you wouldn't believe. I mean, I guess it was pretty much of a circus: medics, cops, maybe even media, I don't know. She had to give a statement and all. So, she calls me. Me!"

"Ah! She wants you to come over and hold her hand. You have anguished in vain. True love triumphs!" Dan finished the beer cheerfully and put the empty on the table. Then, he burped.

"You couldn't be wronger."

"That's not a word."

"It says what I need it to say. Which is that you are, like, totally wrong, because after she told me what happened she says she wants me to stay away from her totally. Do not send her any more presents; do not pass her any more notes. Do not even speak to her."

"What!"

"It gets better. She says she's changing study groups and I am not to follow her. If I continue to harass her—that's the word she used—she'll change schools!"

Dan cocked his head. "Okay, let me get this straight. She's in an accident. She's knocked around a little but is otherwise unhurt. However, the guy who hits her dies, and her reaction is to call you, a person who wasn't even there, and tell you to stay away from her."

"That's about it."

"Did she give a reason?"

"Well, she was pretty upset, like I said. And she didn't make much sense. Something about how everything had gone wrong since we talked that day at Ala Moana--which I told you about before. And then she said something about me putting a curse on her!"

"Hold on there. That's a new wrinkle. But first, let's get back to the part where you passed her notes. What kind of notes?"

Chris hung his head. "Two notes and it's embarrassing. I'll be honest with you. I groveled. Practically begged her to see me again. Give me another chance."

"Ouch. And, then you said you sent her some presents?"

"Two CD's. Christian music. No words. Just instrumental." Chris lifted his hands in frustration. "Honest truth, that was it. And after that, I tried to give her some space. So where did this whole thing about a curse come in? I don't know what she's talking about."

"Well…" Dan thought a moment, "You know, some cultures think that spirits attach themselves to things, objects, stuff like that. So…the connection *could* be made that somehow or other something you passed on to her is responsible for what happened tonight."

"Oh come on!"

"A real stretch if you ask me."

"That's the understatement of the year. But I told you before, she has issues with Christians."

"Yeah, that's probably true. But you know what I think?"

"What?"

"Personally? I think she really likes you—in a truly messed up kind of way." Dan grinned and looked longingly at the fridge. There were always lots of snacks in the fridge.

"No, I told you, she doesn't like me any more, if she ever did."

"So, how crazy is this girl? Crazy enough to take some kind of legal action against you?"

"I doubt it. I told her I wouldn't come within ten feet of her if that's what she wanted, and after that she said okay and hung up."

Dan shrugged. "You're right, as strange things go, that's right up there. But hey, I thought you said you came over to talk to me because you had a new clue about your Chinaman?"

"I do!" Chris sat forward eagerly. "And ever since Mei Ling called I've been trying to figure it out. I'm convinced that everything that happened tonight has some deeper meaning, you know? In fact, I think this whole accident thing is about God giving me a message."

"Wait a minute. A guy dies so that *you* can have some kind of revelation? Are you serious?" Dan, a nominal Christian, was nothing if not liberal in this thinking but this was too wild even for him.

"Of course not! I don't mean the accident happened so that I could have a revelation. But it happened and there is something to it. Just listen, okay? Okay this might seem like a bit of a stretch, but here's the thing. The Chinaman says the *night is coming*, right? Remember that?"

"Can't forget it."

"And you and I talk about how maybe it's the Apocalypse and the end of all things, remember?"

"Yeah, made sense to me. It's in the Bible."

"Or we think maybe it's just a personal message: *Be careful, there are things out there that go bump in the night.*"

"Literal, but entirely possible."

"Okay, now stay with me here. Mei Ling is not a Christian. I mean, I really wish she *was* one. I really wanted to help her understand so that maybe she could be at some point, but she cut me off when we talked. And now, she's shut me out entirely."

"Okay."

"But here's the thing. The accident happened, right out of the blue. Just like accidents do. The guy was going too fast, cut Mei Ling off, crashed. He died; she didn't. But, a few inches closer, it could have just as easily been her too."

"Yeah, and...?"

"And, I suddenly realized, the night isn't, like, an apocalypse, like we were talking last time. It isn't the end of all things. It is the end of one thing—a person's life."

"Night, as a metaphor for death."

"Right! That's just what Pastor J said. But the thing is, the night comes and no one can "work" – no one can change that person's mind one bit. He's dead or she's dead. And, it's coming for everybody!" Chris said excitedly.

"Whoa, calm down there buckaroo," Dan smiled. "So, what is the message?"

"The Chinaman's message was backwards—which, in itself is not surprising. It isn't: *Be careful. The night is coming.* It is: *The night is coming, and you've got to really care about that!*" Chris sat straight up, his eyes wide.

"Huh?"

"Okay, I admit, I can be pretty dense, and it took me, like, a couple of hours to figure this thing out tonight, but I finally did. 'cause it was like God pulled back a curtain and showed me something."

"And that is…?"

"Dan, there's a whole world out there dying and going to hell!"

Chapter Thirty

I rene Baines, Pastor Martin's assistant, pulled her blue Nissan into the parking lot behind Zippy's restaurant on Mokaukea St. Inside, she purchased a dozen cream filled Long John pastries. Fresh and fragrant, she knew these would be sure to please. After that, it was only a short drive to the house she sought, but before getting out and walking up the sidewalk, she took a moment to catch her breath and get her thoughts in order.

She had been back in Hawaii less than a week, but each day had been jammed full of things to do. With Pastor Jason out of the picture for a while, responsibilities had piled up, but Irene called John Salas, a retired ACC administrator and pleaded with him to come help out. John was nearing eighty now, and hadn't attended ACC for a while, but he said he could spare a few hours. Sure enough, once he started nosing around, things came back to him. Except for the fact that he only worked four hours at a time, he was a big help.

John dealt with the vendors, room reservations, and the benevolence ministry which was having a food drive this coming Sunday. Irene also prevailed upon Glenn, the Treasurer, to take care of preparations for the two seminars, one of which was finance related. The other was a women's seminar on healthy eating, but she figured Glenn could handle that, and with his growing waistline, might learn something valuable as well.

Irene also checked in with Dot McKinney, and was happy to see that the recovery group was doing well. Dot said they had run out of paper goods, so she went to Safeway and bought some herself but they were expensive. Could she get reimbursed? Irene gladly took the sales slip and promised a check in the mail. Dot went away happy.

Next, Irene approached Dr. Lum who said her calendar was full to bursting and would it be possible not to schedule any new patients for a while? She had stretched her Saturday hours to the limit because she felt there was a need here at ACC, but everyone must realize she also had a full time practice. In addition to that, since her sister's death last Christmas, she was taking care of her nephew, and the child needed a lot of attention. In fact, she had been thinking of pulling back just a little. She wondered if Irene thought the church would be disappointed if she did, just for a few months.

Irene assured her that everything she did for the church was appreciated. Overextending her commitments so that she could not do her job or take care of her nephew was hardly a way to give glory to Him. They tackled the calendar with a new eye, and both women came away satisfied.

The ministry to the elderly was planning an outing to Barbers Point in June, but Joe Silva was upset. No one had stepped forward to co-ordinate it. He had done his part by calling everybody and reminding them about it but, as he was legally blind and confined to a wheelchair, there was only so much he could do. Irene said not to worry, she had just the person in mind, and went in search of Florence Hayes, a former elementary school principal who had just retired. Florence said she was accustomed to planning events and, as her own mother was part of this ministry, she'd be happy to help.

That left the NS counseling, the Friday small group and hospital visitation. Irene spent an entire afternoon trying to find someone to take the NS people, but struck out. So, that was on hold. The Friday small group was on hiatus, nothing to do there. Pastor Martin said he would take hospital visitation but that was not fair, really, since the man's calendar was already full to bursting. So, it took another afternoon and another dozen calls to find a few temporary volunteers for that ministry. And other miscellaneous items surfaced every day, some of them urgent.

At one point, with her phone ringing off the hook, and pages on her to do list, Irene decided it would be a real shame, in more ways than one, if Jason Price were not allowed to return to his job soon. Obviously, no one had any idea what the man actually did!

Then, after another session with the senior pastor, it had suddenly struck her, once again, that one absolutely crucial area had been overlooked (or avoided) entirely in her absence. No matter how busy she was filling in for Jason Price, it had to be done. Therefore, with Dr. Martin's blessing, she had taken it upon herself to spend her lunch hour today making a visit. There was quite a bit of information that needed to be gathered from the person she was going to see and some difficult things that needed to be said. Fainter hearts than Irene Baines had failed in the past to elicit usable information from this source, but Irene was determined. The pastor was counting on her and she would not let him down.

So, here she was today, carrying a pink box of pastries down a sidewalk cracked and overgrown with weeds. The grass had not been mowed in a long time, giving the place a seedy look. When she got to the steps she noticed patches of red here and there on the bushes and the top step. There was a small smear on the front door as well. The place did not look inviting. However, Irene knocked resolutely and waited quite a while until she heard the chain latch being undone on the other side. The door opened a foot or so, and an older lady stood in the shadows. Her gray hair was neatly combed and the dark eyes that peered out from behind the strawberry colored bifocals were sharp and none too friendly.

"Why hello there, Miss Lottie," Irene said brightly. "I heard that you had returned home, and I just came over to welcome you back. Could I please come in? I think we need to talk."

Marge had not suffered with nightmares for several nights, but she had been doing a lot of thinking. Right now she was home getting over the last of a nasty bout of flu. The coffee table in the living room was piled with books, papers, and two Bibles. Several DVD's lay out ready to watch. Since there was no group meeting, Marge had read on to the end in their study book.

One of the things she learned that was most helpful was that

she should pray to the Holy Spirit as part of the Trinity. She had
never thought of doing that, and it intrigued her. It did not come as
a complete surprise to her that the Holy Spirit dwelled within her;
she had heard that somewhere before. But each lesson in the book
talked about what the Holy Spirit does. Evidently, He convicts, gives
"illumination", teaches, guides, directs and warns. Marge had looked
up all the accompanying scriptures, and she had come away feeling as
though she had learned something very valuable.

It occurred to her also that her dreams were trying to tell her
something valuable as well. There was some message there that she
could not figure out. And, helpful as her friends wanted to be, no one
had enough knowledge to figure it out for her. So, putting aside their
disturbing properties, Marge had decided to seek the Holy Spirit and
ask Him to "illuminate" this situation, as the book phrased it. To give
her some insight into what was happening.

It might have been the fever, the coughing, the aches, whatever, but
she hadn't gotten a whole lot of illumination during the past couple of
days. She looked at her notes:

1. *Dreams concerned traumatic things that happened long ago.*
2. *Dreams were partly true. Endings different.*
3. *But, each situation could have ended that way.*
4. *Only it didn't.*
5. *Why?*

Then she thought to herself, what is it that prevents bad things
from happening? Couldn't be fate because Christians don't believe in
that. They believe God controls all things, and rightly so. So, if God
controls all things, He obviously intervened so that her life had turned
out differently from the way it turned out in the dreams, right? Maybe
the dreams were telling her she could have died, but didn't. If so, why
not? And then, the answer came to her in a flash: prayer. Prayer changes
things. Prayer invites God into a situation. Had people prayed for her
during those years?

She thought back. Yes, certainly. Her grandmother had been a
devout Christian. In fact, Gram prayed every single night, knees on

the floor. As a child, Marge had seen her do it often, and thought it was odd, but "sweet." She, like her parents, didn't think for a minute it did any good, but they had said nothing, deciding to humor the older woman they all loved. Were the dreams trying to show her what might have happened if her grandmother had not prayed?

And when she had been married to Sebastian, her next door neighbor was a prayer giant! Joyce prayed all the time and she was always popping over inviting Marge to church. Marge even went a couple of times but stopped when Sebastian objected. Joyce prayed for her constantly. So, just how effective had those prayers been? Is that what the dreams were about?

But wait a minute, on the other side of the equation, people had prayed for Danny and he had died anyway. So, what did it all mean?

That was the problem with trying to figure things out, she sighed. You no sooner thought you had something all worked out, when another set of facts or memories turned them all around.

But, now here was something else. One day, while she had been home sick, Marge had switched on the TV to find a woman preacher really going to town. Marge was fascinated because the woman was so animated! She obviously had some strong beliefs. Marge liked that. And she liked the fact that the woman never asked for money. So, today, around about the same time, Marge had turned on the TV, and there was the woman again, in different clothes, talking just as passionately. And today she had said something that really stuck with Marge. She said, "God will go to a lot of trouble to get your attention If He wants it." She said that more often than not, when people depended on themselves, God would allow their finances to dry up, or they would become ill, or something like that. Something to get them away from thinking they ruled the world as little gods themselves. Marge was quite impressed by that phrase: little gods. It sounded awful.

So, was that what all of this was about? Was God just getting her attention? And why did the word *redemption* keep going over and over in her mind?

She didn't know. She just couldn't figure it out. She prayed and prayed for illumination, and as she did, she remembered Rhoda's man with the flashlight of truth. God was shining a light on something, but what? By mid-afternoon she figured that this was about as clear as things were going to get for a while. So, she added the following to her list.

6. *"Prayer?"*
7. *"Flash light of truth?"*
8. *"Redemption?"*

Then, she fixed herself some soup, and went back to sleep. If illumination was going to come, it would come in God's own time.

Chapter Thirty-one

The condo that Nancy and Jason Price rented had another perk: a fairly large common room with potted plants, comfortable blue striped chairs, and small tables, where tenants and owners could entertain guests. The room was air-conditioned and quiet; it's ceiling to floor windows overlooked a sparkling pool with deck chairs and umbrellas. Later in the afternoon, the after school crowd would swarm over that area, and teens would use this room to play games and hang out, but at this hour hardly anyone was around.

So, at 1:00 p.m., Jason met his visitor in the guest parking area, and walked him inside. Pastor Martin, perfectly groomed as usual, this time in shades of rose, mauve and tan, seemed at home in these beautiful surroundings. He admired the marble lobby, the faux Hawaiian crafts on the walls and comfortable sofas. And he seemed especially thankful that the room was cool. There were no trade winds today and it was scorching hot outside. Jason had thought ahead, and tumblers of ice and bottles of water were waiting.

The senior pastor took a seat, leaned back comfortably, and looked around. "Thanks for suggesting we meet here, Jason. This is perfect," he smiled.

Jason nodded. At first, when Pastor Martin called and wanted to set up a meeting outside of the church, Jason had inferred that he might have done this to emphasize the fact that Jason was no longer a pastor in the church; he was *outside* the church. But now, looking at his wide,

open smile, it suddenly occurred to Jason that he had been unfair to
Dr. Martin. The man probably wanted to meet somewhere away from
prying eyes, and where others, like Richard Ko, couldn't just drop in.

"How long have you lived here?"

"We moved here as soon as we got to Oahu. Nancy found the place
on-line. Which turned out to be mistake."

"Really?" Pastor Martin's expression said *looks nice to me.*

"Yes, well, this room is nice, but the reason they have this recreation
area is because the condo units are so small and noisy you really don't
want to entertain there."

"But you had your small group…?"

Past tense. But Jason forged ahead anyway. "Now here's the thing,"
he said eagerly, and he told Pastor Martin all about Mike and Kimo
and the Friday night obedience training that kept the unit quiet for
just as long as the group met. Pastor Martin smiled through the whole
narrative. He had a knack of making people feel at ease, and despite
the fact that his entire professional life was hanging in the balance, not
to mention his reputation, Jason was not feeling nearly as nervous as
he had feared.

One thing that helped was that he had set aside the "new look"
(aloha shirt and Dockers) in favor of his old favorites, the navy trousers,
the short sleeved lime shirt (rescued from the waste paper basket,
washed and ironed) and of course the red suspenders. He figured Pastor
Martin wouldn't care if his clothes accentuated his egg shape, and Jason
needed the comfort of feeling like himself. After days of fighting with
his new contact lenses, he had also given up on those, and was now
happily adjusting his old "froggie" frames to just the right place on the
bridge of his nose.

Finally, after a few minutes of small talk, Pastor Martin suggested
they start with a word of prayer. Then, he got right to the point. "I am
awfully sorry that I wasn't here when you needed me, Jason, I'm sure
the situation has been painful for you."

"I appreciated the e-mails and phone call," Jason said.

"The least I could do under the circumstances. But before we go
any further, why don't you just explain the whole thing to me once
again. Take your time and tell me in your own words everything that
happened. Start at the beginning."

Jason had prepared a lengthy, beautifully phrased speech just in case Pastor Martin had said those exact words, but the text of it suddenly disappeared from his memory. Instead, in the simplest terms possible, he told the senior pastor exactly what had occurred in his office the day he met with Hazel, and then gave a précis of all that happened after that.

Martin listened attentively, a slight frown creasing his brow at times. Then, he said, "I see." He leaned over, twisted the cap off of the bottle of water, and took a sip. "I've checked all the information available to me," he continued, "and I see absolutely no reason to disagree with anything you said. It appears to me that everything happened just as you described—unfortunately."

"Thanks," Jason said simply, although the phrase came from deep in his heart.

" Now, next question. How do you feel?" Pastor Martin took another sip and put the bottle down on the table.

"Honestly?" Jason thought a second. "Depends on when you ask me. Sometimes I feel okay, even positive. But that's when I'm being strong for my wife. Nancy's a strong believer, but not a great fan of the local church. I think she saw a lot of negative things growing up. So I've got to keep things positive for her. The last time we talked, I gave her this huge sermon on the value of the local church. I told her no matter what happened I was still determined to serve in a local body. And I meant every word. I always want to serve the local church because I believe in it."

"Very commendable," Martin said. "I do too. "And how does Nancy feel?"

"Pretty well, considering," Jason said, "But I have Helen Chang to thank for that!"

Pastor Martin beamed. "Thank God for saints like Helen."

"Amen," Jason shook his head. "It would have been a lot different if Helen hadn't been there to walk Nancy through the whole thing. And Helen's been trying to help me too. Encouraging me to look at the situation to see what God might be doing."

"Always a positive thing to do," Martin agreed.

"And the small group people have been just wonderful Even when I was suspended, they came over and rallied around me and gave me great support. Funny, we've only been together a couple of months but I've grown to really care for each one of them. But the thing is, when I'm all by myself, it's hard not to give into, I don't know, doubts, fear."

"You mentioned the word suspended. How do you feel about that?"

"Embarrassed. Confused. Humiliated." Jason thought for a moment. "I mean, Howard came to see me and he was extremely polite..."

"Howard always is," Martin conceded.

"But it was as if he wasn't actually putting me on suspension. It was as if he was asking me if I'd mind staying out of my office for a while as a favor to him. Does that make sense?" Jason withdrew a Kleenex from his pocket and wiped his brow. Air-conditioning or not, he was burning up.

"That sounds just like Howard."

"But the thing is. Doggone it, no matter how politely it was done, I was suspended. Booted out. Maybe that was right and maybe not, under the circumstances, but I guess it was awkward having me around, so I reconciled myself to it. But now that I'm out, I realize every day that I might really be out permanently. They could actually decide to fire me altogether. But the thing is, I don't know why they would. I didn't do anything."

Pastor Martin said nothing.

"Okay, that's not true," Jason rushed on. "I was foolish. I was naïve. That much I admit. But I will deny to my dying day that I committed any immoral act. But here's the clincher. I don't think they believe me. And do you know why?" Jason leaned over, his face flushed a sudden red. "Because nobody, even Howard, as polite as he was, ever asked to hear my side of the story!" Jason opened the bottle of water and dashed it over the ice cubes. He held the tumbler in his hands as though the coldness could reduce the heat of his anger. "Until now," he amended.

"Go on."

Jason looked up, reluctant to reveal more of his personal feelings. He'd already said more than he had intended. Then he decided, what the heck, might as well be honest. "You know, nobody told me what the board is actually voting on, and they're meeting about me! Except

I pretty well figured out that it was to determine if I had committed an impropriety bad enough to cost me my job."

"I don't have the exact wording either, but that would be the gist of it. So, suppose that happens. What would be the worst thing about all of that for you? What do you fear most?"

"Being treated as a pariah. People mumbling *unclean, unclean*, as I pass by. Losing my very first job under suspicious circumstances. Disappointing my wife, my friends. Not to mention my parents who are coming over in a couple of weeks to celebrate a special event."

"And you think that might happen?"

"Don't you?" Jason's thin string of a mouth trembled.

"I don't know. But if the worst happens, what will you do?"

Jason spoke quickly, as though he were delivering a prepared statement. "Go back to the denominational office in Springfield. Volunteer at the local church. As I told you, no matter what, I'm devoting my life to the local church."

"Yes, very commendable," Martin agreed. "So you've obviously given that some thought. Now, what happens in the best case scenario?"

"You mean, if I'm exonerated?"

Martin's smile was kind. "You won't be completely exonerated, I'm afraid. Some of the elders will insist upon having their pound of flesh. But you may not lose your job."

"But if I'm *not* completely exonerated, I'll still be under a haze of suspicion, right?" Jason fidgeted uncomfortably in his seat.

"No matter what I say, and I intend to defend you to the best of my ability," Martin was straightforward and honest, "there will be one or two of the old die hards who will cling to their prejudices for a while. Then what?"

Jason shook his head. "I don't know," he shrugged. "I haven't been able to think that through. God will know the truth, of course, and that's supposed to be enough for us as Christians, isn't it?"

"Supposed to be," Martin admitted. "But is it?" He poured the remainder of his water over the melting ice cubes. "How will you feel if you have to encounter these people on a daily basis who have treated you in such an… unchristian, shall we say, manner?"

Jason hung his head. "I honestly don't know."

"I'm not surprised you feel that way," Martin said, then thought for a second. "As I was driving over here I prayed about what I could do for you today that would be of real value. First, of course, I wanted to listen to you in detail. I wanted to hear everything you had to say, and I wanted to know how you are feeling about what you're going through. But more than that, I thought that I should try to help you prepare for what might happen, either way. And I think the best way to go about that would be to tell you a story."

Jason looked up, surprised.

"Not the usual drill, I'll agree," Martin said with a wry smile, "but this story is about something that happened to me, and it changed my life, and I think...I hope," Pastor Martin's eyes sparkled, "that it will be a great help to you." He drank the rest of the water, sat back comfortably and took a deep breath.

"Okay, this goes back to my student days. I had finished my masters, I was going for my doctorate and looking around for some fieldwork in youth ministry that would give me both information for my dissertation and help with expenses. I was on scholarship, so that paid tuition and books, but Judi and I were expecting our first child, so this job would have to pay all of our bills.

"Luckily, a growing mid-sized church hired me at a good salary, to replace a youth worker who was graduating. Evidently Thom Stark had plenty on the ball. He had begun with only a handful, and now there were over a hundred young people in the youth program. Dr. Waring, the senior pastor, had explained that I need only keep the ball rolling: invite newcomers, continue discipleship, plan activities, and when they were ready, take them on short missions trips. There were proven leaders in the group and that would make my job easier. The hours were whatever it took to get the job done.

"I went to work at once and created a schedule. A very generous schedule, I thought, that would allow me to get everything done in record time, and still be with Judi when she needed me. But I ran into problems immediately. Despite the fact that I thought of myself as a friendly, approachable person, the kids didn't respond to me. That was, to my thinking, because they had absolutely adored Thom Stark. Evidently he had spent an incredible amount of hours hanging out with them. They expected me to do the same, but I couldn't. My schedule was too tightly packed. So, I decided that even if I didn't have an infinite amount of hours to just hang around with them, I could use the hours that I did have to give the kids a far superior quality of services. The old quality vs. quantity argument. I'd just finished a course in youth education. I felt well up to the task.

"My pride ruined me. It was as if I had a sign on my chest saying, *I know all there is to know. Listen and learn!* The kids hated it. The leaders seemed unimpressed with any of my revolutionary ideas and often refused to cooperate. In an amount of time so short as to be nearly impossible, I had lost two thirds of the kids, including the leaders. They simply weren't coming around. I didn't know what to do. I didn't have a lot of time to spend chasing after them. I tried to focus on the remaining ones in order to build the group back up. I put in mega hours. But it was a losing battle.

"To make matters worse, my 90-day review was looming perilously near and Judi's delivery date was two weeks away. Tensions were high. Fieldwork was required for every grad student, so there were people standing in line to take my place. In order to keep the job and the raise that automatically followed the probation period, I needed to receive an excellent evaluation. I was a 4.0 student on a full scholarship. I had never flunked anything, ever. But there was no way my evaluation could be anything but a dismal reflection of my poor performance.

"Three days before my appointment, I found out that Dr. Waring had already met with the youth committee: a group of pastors, volunteer workers and parents. I was pretty sure I knew what they had decided. I had failed. I was out. I had exactly $273 in the bank, a sick car, and a wife about to give birth. I tried to prepare myself for the interview, but it was no use. I was a nervous wreck. My studies were falling behind, and Judi was worried.

"Inexorably, the day arrived. I walked into Dr. Waring's office and sat down. His look was grave. I knew the worst was coming. And then he said to me, 'Jeff, we're all very worried about you.'"

I hadn't expected that. "Why?" I asked.

"Because you're running yourself ragged. Aren't you a doctoral student, and isn't your wife expecting?" he said In a kindly voice. I nodded.

"I thought so. So I met with the committee, and here's what we decided. First, we feel that you have great strengths. Your vision, organization, and education do you credit. Your flow charts and organizational tables are truly exemplary. However, the implementation…" he left the sentence hanging.

"I apologized profusely, but he wasn't listening. Looking back I confess that I was very annoyed by the fact that the kindly clergyman seemed to be waiting for me to finish so he could end it all. At last I did stop talking, and he proceeded."

"Jeff," he said, "here's what we want to do. There's another student, Harry Bates, maybe you know him?" I didn't. "Lots of personality. Tons of it. Never met a stranger, you know the type." I did, and my stomach clenched into a knot. I knew exactly where this was heading, but Dr. Waring surprised me.

"What we would like," he said, "is to split the job in two. If you consider the generous raise given after the 90-day period, your share of the salary will be only slightly less than it is now. However, the committee wanted to take into account your personal situation, so they voted to give you an extra $200 per month, and that will bring you over your present stipend." I couldn't believe my ears. Their generosity was overwhelming.

"You see," Dr. Waring chattered on happily, "we think that both you and Harry can help each other. Harry can help you bring the kids on board, and then you can give them the excellent Biblical education and direction that is your specialty. What do you think about that?"

"I was stunned," Pastor Martin said. "They hadn't needed to do that. They could have hired another wunderkind from the masses milling at the gates—excuse me if I get poetic," he laughed. "But they didn't. They chose to back me, a proven failure. Now here's the lesson. After I got over my surprise, I said to Dr. Waring, 'I don't deserve it. I failed. I should be fired.' And he said, very simply,' Jeff, do you know the meaning of grace?'

"I stumbled over a few words because I couldn't quite remember the exact Bible quote, but here is the definition he gave. *Grace is being given something you didn't earn and don't deserve.* He went on to talk about the grace that Jesus extended to the woman at the well when he said, 'Go and sin no more.' He pointed to the most amazing example of grace in history-- Christ on the cross begging his Father to be merciful to the very people who had crucified him. He explained that grace was God taking our worst moments and bringing redemption out of them and ultimate glory to Himself. He said, 'Grace not only blesses us beyond measure, but puts us on display to a disbelieving and ridiculing world.'

"And then he said the most important thing of all. He said, 'But grace does us no good if we hug it to ourselves thinking of it as a prize we were awarded by some divine accident. No, we must accept that grace is the unconditional outpouring of God's love, and it is given to us so that we, in turn, can give it to others.'" And there, Dr. Martin stopped speaking and waited.

Jason looked at him blankly for a moment, then said, "So...you received grace, and the job...?"

"Was life changing. I learned more in my time there than I did in ten university courses. But more than that, in the years to come, when I myself was tempted to lay down the law, I remembered the grace that had been given to me and acted accordingly."

"So...despite my foolishness and naivete, you want to give me grace? Or God's going to give me grace in this situation?" The story Pastor Martin had told was inspiring, but Jason still wondered how it applied to him.

"Oh, I think you're receiving lots of grace from many people at the moment," Martin said amiably. " You've mentioned your loyal wife Nancy, Helen Chang. You've talked about the support you've received from the people in your small group. You could count me in, I'm not blaming you for anything, neither is Howard. So, in your case, Jason, I don't think it's a matter of receiving grace." He paused and waited a second for the next words to sink in. " I think, in your case, it's a matter of extending it."

Jason was so startled he just sat there with his mouth hanging open. And then, very kindly and patiently, Pastor Martin explained to him the spiritual principle of forgiveness.

Chapter Thirty-two

The women who gathered at ACC that night had expected to hold their meeting in the open-air courtyard. However, it began to rain and they found themselves inside the administration building, shaking their umbrellas and getting their bearings. Irene Baines, who had been heading home, had seen them and brought them inside.

"Our small group is not meeting tonight, so we decided to come here and pray. Is that all right?" asked Marge.

"Absolutely. How about if I open a room for you?" Irene was happy to help.

"Oh, wherever is fine with us."

"What time do you think you will be finished?"

"Let's see. It's seven-fifteen now. I guess in about an hour. Is that okay?"

"Perfectly fine," Irene assured them. "Don't worry about locking up. There are several meetings on campus tonight, a couple right here in this building, and they'll last quite a bit longer than yours. Just pull the door to when you leave and turn off the lights. The security man will lock up. Oh, and there's always a pot of coffee on in the kitchen. Help yourselves." She unlocked a door to the duplication room, smiled at everyone, and left.

The room contained a huge Xerox machine, a long table on which staplers, hole punchers, tape holders, pens and pencils, and neatly folded bulletins rested. There were also three huge metal closets holding paper goods, and a table and chairs by the window. Pua, Marge, Yumi and Roda each pulled out a chair and sat down.

"I think this was an inspiration!" said Rhoda, looking around.

"When Marge called I thought to myself why pray by ourselves at home? We should go to the church," Pua said.

"The sanctuary's locked, of course. But I never thought we'd get inside the administration building either," Marge said, surprised. "It's always locked too. I thought we'd have to meet outside. But here we are."

"Okay, remind me again. What's actually happening?" Yumi asked.

"Well," Marge began, "as I said on the phone, Jasmine Wu called my friend Linda and told her that the elders are meeting tomorrow morning to talk about Pastor Jason. Of course we already knew that from his voice message. But she was concerned. Some people told her they thought the elders were taking a vote whether or not to fire him. Other people said they were just going to talk about all the gossip and stuff. But still, I think we need to pray."

"You're absolutely right, Marge. We have to pray about it." Rhoda said. "He sounded so forlorn on the phone."

Jason Price had left voice messages for each of the group members telling them that he would have to cancel tonight's get together. "That meeting that we talked about last week with Dr. Martin and the elders?" he had said, "Well, that took place on Monday, and tomorrow I'm going to talk with the elders myself. I have every hope that things will go well. But if you don't mind, I need to be alone with the Lord tonight. I need to make sure my heart is totally right with Him before the meeting tomorrow. Thanks for your prayers. I'll let you know how everything turns out. Don't forget to pray for each other, and read the lessons in your course book. God bless."

"Yeah, well, as soon as Marge told me what was going to happen, this thought popped into my head *Go to the church. Pray at the church.*" Pua said.

"That makes sense," Rhoda said. "So, where is the meeting going to take place?"

"Yeah, we need to know so that we can pray specifically. I read somewhere you need to be specific in your prayers," Marge said.

"Let's look on the wall," Yumi suggested. "Then we can see exactly where."

The four women left their umbrellas, Bibles and sweaters in the room and headed out into the maze of hallways. Eventually they came to the bulletin board outside the ladies lounge. On it were posted an assortment of items: things for sale, services, employment information, flyers about coming events, and calendars showing room allocations for all the events on campus. Yumi looked closely, "Here," she said at last. "It's penciled in. Elders' meeting, Pastor Martin's office." She turned to the others, "That's right here in this building."

"Well now we know," Marge said.

"Okay okay, now this is gonna sound weird, but how 'bout if we pray outside the actual office where it's all going to take place?" Pua suggested.

"You mean stand in the hall outside Dr. Martin's office? Suppose somebody sees us?" Yumi frowned. "And suppose Dr. Martin is in there! Working late or something."

"We can look through the panel!" Pua beamed. "And if he's there we'll go down the hall a little bit. No need worry; it's way in the back of the building. Not many people over there."

"Which is exactly my point!" Yumi exclaimed. "We'll stick out a mile!"

"Hey, wait a minute," Marge said. "We're not planning to set fire to the place. What are we doing anyways? Praying. So what if people see us?"

"I don't know," she was reluctant, but Rhoda hooked her arm around Yumi's and coaxed her down the main hallway, where they passed several people, across the breezeway, where they passed one more, and down another hall where there was no one at all. At last all four women stood before a door with Dr. Martin's name on it.

The panel was dark. No one was inside. "Okay," Marge whispered. "How are we going to do this?"

The women clasped hands, bowed their heads, then hesitated. They didn't know.

Pua said, "I think we just pretend we're in our usual circle praying. Just start..." Everyone looked at her. "Okay okay, I will. Uh, Lord, we thank you 'cause we know You are with us always, everywheres. You are with us tonight, right here, and we want to pray for our friend, Pastor J. We don't know how, so Holy Spirit, would you lead us? That's what we been learning in our books. You can do that! So please, could you?"

Eventually, what started as a trickle of prayer turned into a stream of praise and the women soon began to pray from deep in their hearts, heedless of whether anyone saw them or not.

On the way out, they passed the mailroom. "Try wait," said Pua, noticing the message pad and pencil laid out on the counter. "Let's write Pastor J a little note and put it in his box," she suggested. "He gonna see it tomorrow and it will make him feel better." And they did.

Chapter Thirty-three

Saturday was a busy day at ACC. There were many events going on at the same time and the church campus was swarming with people. The Foreign Missions Committee was holding its World Challenge Conference in the gym, and it was packed. Helpful volunteers ran back and forth from the kitchen to the fellowship hall, preparing for the large buffet lunch. Break out groups were planned in most of the Sunday school rooms and people were rushing in early to set up. In the sanctuary, a training class was being given by the sound engineers and a surprising thirty people had already arrived for that.

The meeting room over the Sunday school classrooms was packed with boy scouts getting last minute instructions for an overnight event that would begin later that day. Their parents crowded the stairwells and sidewalks filling the two-hour time slot on lap tops, iPods, or just talking story with friends.

The elders' meeting was scheduled in Pastor Martin's office, away from the hubbub. Richard Ko was not too pleased that although he had arrived early, he couldn't get a parking space in the church lot but had to park across the street at the bank. It wasn't the walk that bothered him, it was the fact that several cars had been vandalized in that area in weeks past. The scouts usually patrolled parked cars on big event weekends, but they were not available today or tomorrow. Ko felt that his sparkling new Lexus looked particularly vulnerable as a result, and the thought did not make him happy.

At five minutes to eight, the elders had assembled in the hallway outside of Martin's office and were talking softly among themselves, even Clayton Kobata who, in deference to the gravity of the situation, had showed up in long pants and an aloha shirt, no headset. At precisely eight o'clock the door opened and they filed in. Pastor Martin, perfectly dressed in gray linen slacks and white on white Tori Richard shirt, greeted them warmly.

Pastor Martin took his seat at the short end of the rectangular table. Richard chose the space nearest the senior pastor and Mike sat next to him, edging out Ernest who had dashed over, hoping for that spot. Howard, across the table from Richard, reached in his elegant briefcase for pen and paper, and Clayton, next to him, turned off his iTouch and put it in his pocket. Don Webber stood there uncertainly, face scrubbed, hair gelled, with his pencil and pad, until Dr. Ko motioned him to a metal chair, a discreet distance from the others.

As chairman, Howard would bring the meeting to order. Richard hoped very much that he wouldn't drag it all out. Really, it was all a fait accompli. He, Mike and Ernest had the votes between them to pass the measure; it was simply a matter of fine-tuning it. Today, he had other pressing matters on his mind. For one thing, he had agreed to meet with his eldest daughter this afternoon and he was anxious to get going. An attorney of some standing in the community, she was considering running for public office. Richard had some definite thoughts about that which he was anxious to share. She wouldn't like what he had to say, but that had never stopped Richard Ko from stating his opinion in the past, and it wouldn't now.

Howard and Martin conferred briefly about something and then Howard sat back and cleared his throat. All eyes turned his way. However, before he could begin, Ko spoke up, addressing Don Webber who looked totally confused about what he should be doing. "Before we begin, " Ko looked briefly from face to face, "let me say a few words to our church clerk. Today, Don, the Elder Board will vote on an action regarding the allegations against Pastor Jason Price. We'll try to go slowly so that you can get the important points down. But first, we'll read the motion. The motion before the board today is… hold on."

As he was speaking, the door opened and two elderly gentlemen walked in.

Howard looked over at them and smiled; Richard's eyes opened wide. He had not expected this. However, as the others stood up and greeted the men politely, he followed suit, shaking their hands, and showing them to vacant chairs. "Elliot, Raymond, what a surprise," he said without a trace of warmth. "We're glad to see you, but we are having an official meeting here."

"Oh I know that," said Elliot Kam, former CEO of a very large electronics company in the islands. He and Raymond Sato, who had entered with him, were past elders who had served ACC for quite some time. A few years previously, when they stepped down, they had been given the courtesy title of advising elders. Evidently, today they had come to give some advice.

"The official meeting is what we're here for," Elliot said in a hearty voice. Somewhat on the heavy side, his friendly face was distinguished by round cheeks as brown and toasty as muffin tops. "Hello Pastor, Howard, Ernest. And this is Mike Dunn? Did I get the name right?" he said, shaking Mike's hand enthusiastically. After that he smiled at the others, exclaiming happily when he reached Clayton, a cousin of his sister-in-law. "And of course our newest elder, Mr. Kobata!" He shook his hand, and thumped him on the shoulder.

"I saw your grandmother last week," Raymond said to Clayton, in a weak voice. At nearly eighty, he was stooped over and somewhat frail. Two heart attacks had forced him into a more leisurely lifestyle than he would have liked, but he enjoyed visiting the homebound and those in hospitals once in a while, as his health allowed. He seemed to have trouble pulling the heavy chair out from under the table. Elliot stood up to help.

Clayton grinned. "She said you were there. You brought her chocolates."

"Not just any chocolates, Sees Chocolates, her favorite," the elderly man boasted. "You didn't eat them all did you?" he joked. "Oh thanks Elliot," he gripped the arms of the chair with purple veined hands and sat down.

"Oh, I had a few," Clayton assured him, laughing.

"I think the peppermint creams are her favorite," Raymond continued.

By this time everyone was seated. Dr. Ko cleared his throat. "Yes

yes yes. As pleasant as it is to see you both, we don't have time to talk story," he said briskly. "Actually, "we're about to vote on an important matter. So, is there something we can do for you?" His eyes indicated that he had an uncomfortable feeling he knew what they had come for but was holding out hope that he might be wrong.

"It's what we can do for you!" Elliot assured him jovially. "We know all about the situation and we're here to add our votes."

"But," Ko looked at Howard, "only presiding elders can actually vote."

"Come on, Richard. You know better than that," Elliot laughed. "Of course we can vote. It's just that up until this year you've had the required nine elders. And the rules do say that no more than nine elders can vote on any issue. We weren't needed." He exchanged a smile with Raymond. "But I hear that now you're down to the minimum of five."

"We had seven until three months ago," Ko reminded him stubbornly.

"Well, yes, but you don't have seven now! Poor James died, and... Harry Fong moved over to Molokai, right?"

"Say, he didn't fly back here for the vote, did he?" Raymond looked around as if trying to see if Harry was hiding behind a potted plant." Everyone laughed, except Richard. "Didn't think so," Raymond smiled. "Oh hold on." His cell phone buzzed. He took it out very carefully, as though it might slip from his grasp, opened it up, and pulled the screen close to his nose, then he put it back in his pocket. "My daughter," he grinned. "Calls me five times a day. I tell her no need, but she worries. I don't know why," he said, "I'm healthier than she is." Howard and Clayton smiled at this untruth.

During the brief interlude, Richard began assessing the situation. Raymond had no way of knowing this, but Richard actually had tried very hard to get Harry Fong to fly back from the outer island to vote on this issue. Harry was a person who could usually be counted on to see reason. But, he wouldn't budge. And, after it seemed that Mike Dunn and Ernest, of course, were in agreement with him on the matter at hand, Ko didn't see the need.

He wasn't totally surprised at Jeff Martin's strategy to bring in the older men at the last minute. Martin was shrewd and Ko would have been surprised if he had not had some kind of ace in the hole. But he would bet a year's salary that it was Howard Nakata who had put him up to it. It was a complete surprise seeing Raymond Sato here today; Richard had heard that he was practically on his deathbed. And it was bad news, as he would surely vote in favor of Price. Howard had made a smart move there, no doubt about that.

Elliot Kam, on the other hand, who hadn't even set foot in the church since he moved back to Oahu last month, did not always vote as expected. Fat and friendly as he was, he had a mind of his own. It was obvious that Howard didn't know Elliot the way Richard did. He had no doubt counted on a vote for Jason that very well might not materialize. But it was hard to tell; where Elliot was concerned, anything was possible..

Elliot smiled. "So, all right with you folks if we join you?" He had a gold front tooth that made him seem, to Richard, like a wily old pirate.

Everyone nodded, but Richard made a sound that was somewhere between the gnashing of teeth and a cough, or so it seemed to Mr. Sato, and that appeared to gratify him immensely. Raymond didn't like Richard much. He hadn't liked his grandfather much either. He thought the man had been a tyrant of the first order, but in this instance the detailed structure that Stanley Ko had drawn up for the running of church business, was turning out to be extremely useful.

"Let me explain something to you," Elliot looked at Clayton and Mike. "'cause you're new and you might not know. I don't think it's telling any secrets to say that when Brother Stan, Richard's grandfather, was pastor, he wrote the by-laws of the church, and those laws said that nine elders had to be present to vote on any major issue. No absentee ballots, of course, which is still the case. Changing the minimum to five came later, with Pastor Cox," he added. "'cause by then we didn't have as many people. But anyways, when Brother Ko was pastor and there was something important on the table, but not enough elders for a vote, he would just call back one or two who had retired, or who had rotated off that year. But the by-laws made it clear that the pastor could bring on no more than two. Because, just like shares in a company, a pastor can't just purchase himself a controlling vote."

"Not that we've been purchased," Raymond laughed weakly. He

thought the joke was extremely funny. If he'd been sitting closer to Clayton, he would have poked him in the ribs with a bony elbow.

Pastor Martin spoke up, "And I, as pastor, having no vote of my own, asked these gentlemen to climb back on board. I'm happy to announce that, although Raymond will be with us for this session only, now that Elliot has moved back from North Carolina with his family, he's agreed to stay with us for a while."

A few of the men smiled and nodded their heads appreciatively. Richard Ko was not among them.

"Glad to do it. I've really missed Hawaii, I can tell you. Okay, now let's hear the motion that is before this board," Elliot said in an authoritative voice, pulling himself up ramrod straight in his chair. Suddenly, he was all business and Richard remembered the days when Mr. Kam had pretty much been the driving force behind the ACC Elder Board. He wasn't a man to be intimidated, or influenced when he didn't have a mind to be, that was for sure. And, Richard reminded himself with a smile, he was never a man to let sentiment sway his vote.

Ko crossed his well-pressed trousers. Watching Mr. Kam sitting there stone faced, eyes dark and appraising, he suddenly sensed hope. If all went well, it was entirely possible that Elliot would use his head in this matter and vote sensibly. It could turn out positively after all. He glanced at his watch. They were running a little behind, but if things moved quickly from here on out, he could still make his next appointment. Richard's shoulders relaxed; he was beginning to enjoy himself.

As there was nothing more that needed to be said, Howard Nakata brought the meeting to order officially. "Pastor, would you bring the prayer?" he asked. Martin prayed, and took his time about it. Finally, it was time for Richard to speak.

He pulled several typewritten sheets from a manila folder, chose one, and said, "The motion before us is as follows:

One: That Jason Price be removed from his duties as pastor at Aloha Community Church, due to impropriety, and that he be offered in return the opportunity to take a clerical/quasi-administrative position at

the church. If one is not open, one will be created
for him. After a suitable time, and the appropriate
sessions with Dr. Lum, Mr. Price will be invited to
candidate for higher positions as they fall open.

Two: That a letter of censure be placed in his permanent
file.

Richard looked from one face to another. "Anybody need to see
that in writing before we proceed?"

"I second the motion!" Ernest chimed in enthusiastically.

Richard lifted a few sheets of paper and asked again if anyone
needed to see the motion in writing. No one did. He handed a page to
Don. "Record the motion and that it has been seconded," he said. "And
do it precisely as it reads on this sheet!"

Don nodded, hoping fervently that his notes would be up to Dr.
Ko's exacting standards.

Very well," Richard turned to the others. "As stated in his
employment contract which, contrary to popular opinion, was not
signed by me," Richard purposely cast his eyes away from Howard, "
but approved by the necessary committee, nevertheless. Pastor Martin
is allowed to say something." He folded his papers in a neat pile, sat
back, and waited.

Martin glanced around the table at each face with a warm smile.
"I realize this is somewhat of a departure from the norm," he began
smoothly, "but I do appreciate the chance to talk with you."

"Not at too great a length, I hope," Richard said. "I'm sure I'm not
the only one who has to rush from here to another extremely urgent
appointment."

"I'll keep that in mind, Richard," Martin said easily, turning to the
others. "I just want to begin by saying that Jason Price is my assistant
pastor, as you know. I interviewed him, I made sure his references and
credentials were scrupulously checked, and I hired him. He has an
excellent degree from a first rate school. In other words, he's smart. And,
he's eager to learn. True, he's new to the pastorate, but I felt he had all
the necessary qualifications to be a first class pastor when I hired him.
I still feel that way.

"With regard to the current situation, I'll tell you up front that

Jason does not deny the fact that in one sense he acted foolishly. In fact, in a minute, I'll let him tell you himself." This caused a stir among Ernest, Mike and Richard, who had not been briefed about this ahead of time. "But I want to reiterate again, as I have told each of you recently, that based on no more than an anonymous source, I cannot condone relieving that young man of his pastoral position.

"Now," he hurried on, "about that source. My office assistant--you all know Irene Baines--talked with Miss Lottie yesterday at great length. However, Miss Lottie absolutely refused to state in so many words what she actually saw. That would have left us to conclude that she had the impression of impropriety, but we would not have known the exact and specific nature of it."

"I told you she wouldn't say anything..." Richard interrupted, impatient to get on with the vote.

"We took that into consideration when we decided not to fire him outright," Mike added sharply.

"True, however, Irene was well aware that we needed to know specifics, so when she talked with Miss Lottie, she did not accept that refusal. Representing me, she pressed further. And, in time, Miss Lottie did, in fact, articulate to Irene what she actually saw."

That got everyone's attention. Richard sat up, pressing his lips together. Ernest twitched nervously and glanced from face to face. Everyone else stared silently at the senior pastor as he carefully withdrew a page of notes from the stack in front of him. His eyes scrolled down the page until he came to the information he wanted. "Ah, here it is," he said.

"Now, Miss Lottie says here that she saw Hazel and Jason standing in the middle of his office, and the date and approximate time. She says she saw Jason pressed closely to Miss Townsend and held there because the young lady's arms were, to use her words, 'locked around him like a vise.'"

Clayton chuckled.

"Do you think this is humorous!" Dr. Ko demanded, turning furious eyes on the young man.

"Well...in a way," Clayton would not back down. "I mean he's a little guy; she's tall. It's a funny picture."

"Like a vise!" Raymond giggled, "Ha, that's funny." He smiled widely and despite themselves, several of the men found themselves smiling back at him.

"Well, I don't think there is a single humorous..." Richard began, but Martin interrupted and asked if he could continue, which he did when Raymond stopped smiling.

"Now, in answer to specific questions, Miss Lottie states that they were not kissing, they were not fondling each other inappropriately, nor..."

"Oh *please*! Do we have to hear this!" Ko thundered.

"I think we should have heard this a long time ago," Martin said reasonably. He returned to his notes. "...nor," he continued. "was the physical position of the two in any way inconsistent with what Joe Apapa testified or Pastor Price alleged, i.e. that Miss Townsend was greatly upset, and simply wanted to have her hand held or to cry on his shoulder."

Mike spoke up, "Your friend Irene obviously led the witness there."

Martin smiled in a disarmingly friendly way. "My assistant gave us the specific details which we needed to get a clear idea of what was happening. He turned to Raymond and Elliot. "Did you get a chance to read Jim's statement?"

They nodded. Howard had brought them up-to-date with all the information that had been discussed before the meeting today.

"Good." Martin sat back and looked around the group. "Now, I think you will agree that, at last, we know what the accusing witness actually saw. But, there is another element in all of this that I want to address because I think it's germane."

"Is this necessary?" Richard grumbled.

"It is, and if you will bear with me, it will only take a few minutes. I learned from the police that, contrary to the rumor that was widely circulated concerning the source of the blood on Miss Lottie's steps, there were no cats decapitated..."

"There were too!" Ernest squealed.

"There were not," Martin stated emphatically. "In fact, there were no incidences of domestic animal abuse in this case at all. What was sprayed around Miss Lottie's property was a mixture of blood that could be obtained from any butcher, a thickening agent, and paint."

"Paint!" Ernest said, incensed. "There was no paint."

"I think, if you'll visit Miss Lottie sometime soon, you'll see that splotches of oil based house paint still remain on her property. And," he looked from one face to another, "we are close to knowing who actually committed this vandalism."

"What does all this have to do with the accusation!" Mike wanted to know, exchanging an exasperated look with Richard.

"A great deal," Martin said sternly, "because it was the combination of a highly inflamed eye witness account and vicious gossip connecting an entirely unrelated matter to this one that has brought us to where we are today."

"Amen," Howard agreed.

"Gossip aside, there is the actual fact that both witnesses saw Jason Price in a situation that could have been construed in the worst possible way," Mike persisted, "And, for all we know, there might have been others who saw it as well. No, It's a matter of appearances. When we hire people, we assume they have the sense not to let that sort of thing happen. The ripple effect through the congregation from the incident at Miss Lottie's would not have occurred if this situation had not preceded it. As far as I'm concerned, Price exercised a gross lapse of judgment and that is a punishable act." He sat back, grim faced, ever the military man executing a difficult but necessary decision.

"And we absolutely must consider the negative publicity this generates for the church," Richard ordered. "How it makes us look. I think our people are fed up with leaders who appear to be one thing and turn out to be something else entirely."

"Ah, now we come to the crux of the case," Martin agreed. "Appearances. Well, Richard, you can't fire a man because of how things appear. "

Richard raised his chin stiffly as if to say, "Oh can't we!"

"In the case of the leader to whom I presume you are referring, an incident that happened not too long ago here in this church, there was actual evidence of wrongdoing and, if I'm correct, a confession. We don't have those elements here. But I will agree with you about one thing, it is entirely possible that an innocent situation can be made to appear in the worst possible light simply because of how it looks. Now, specifically because all the hoopla that was generated by this incident has brought us to the unfortunate reason for this meeting today, I propose we bring someone in to help all of us understand just what we're up against in today's society, specifically with regard to the problems an appearance of impropriety can cause."

"You must have read my mind!" Howard said, relieved. "I have already thought of contacting Donald Blake. His law firm, if you will remember, represented us a few years ago in a very unpleasant civil suit in which there was no clear evidence, only hearsay on all sides. Donald is well qualified to talk with the pastors and staff about these issues. We all need to be careful about propriety. Now more than ever."

Ernest jumped to his feet. "Has anyone thought about how this woman will react to having her name smeared all over the church? She is the innocent party in all of this. Suppose *she* sues! Huh! Think about that!"

Mike spoke up as if Ernest had not said a word. "Well, we could do that, I suppose, but we have a vote on the table today. And I still say, a pastor is a unique person in a church. He represents no less than Jesus Christ Himself to the congregation. He must be above reproach, or suffer the consequences!" He would not be budged.

"Well said," Richard agreed. "People have had their trust betrayed, and now we must—at long last—decide the penalty!"

Elliot looked at him and nodded, "Well I've heard enough. We could talk all day about civil suits and harassment issues and the like, but let's not get sidetracked and forget the motion at hand. I'm ready to vote. And for heaven's sake, Ernest, sit down."

Martin smiled. "Fine, I'll leave you to it. But don't you think, before I go, that we owe Jason Price the courtesy of hearing what he has to say? I'm sure he would welcome the opportunity to talk with you."

"Now that's a good idea!" Raymond's pale face brightened.

"I don't see any reason for that," Richard countered. "We have all the information we need. We should get on with it!

"I could not agree more," Mike spoke up. "This is simply a waste of time."

"Well, I want to hear what the young fellow has to say," wheezed Raymond. His nose had started to run and he searched in his pockets for a Kleenex. "But before we ask him in, could we take a short break?"

He looked sheepishly from one to the other. "My bladder isn't as young as it used to be, you know."

Howard announced a ten-minute recess. Richard was not happy about it, not one bit.

Chapter Thirty-four

A few minutes later, Raymond Kam washed his hands and walked out of the men's room. He had chosen the one farthest from Martin's office. In fact, it was across the courtyard and in another building entirely. Raymond persuaded himself that his motives were pure: his back was acting up and he had been sitting too long. He needed to stretch his legs. But if he were honest, he'd have to admit that he insisted on the break in part to irritate Richard. A huge grin appeared on Raymond's face as he remembered Ko's outraged expression when he had suggested the interval.

"And what are you so happy about today, Mr. Sato?" Janella Chu, on her way back from the kitchen, walked up to him with a tray of freshly made snacks. She put the tray down and hugged the older man warmly. "Good to see you! How have you been?"

Raymond was extremely pleased to see how this awkward young teen with the unattractive overbite had blossomed into a lovely young woman. It was amazing what dentistry could do these days. When he was growing up there was no such thing as getting braces. As if anyone could afford it! But this was a new and amazing era. He chatted with Janella for several minutes sending his aloha to her mother and grandmother, and left with two cone sushi, each wrapped in a napkin.

The older man took his time getting back. No doubt Richard would be frothing at the mouth by this time, he thought cheerfully. Well, age didn't have many privileges, but not being bossed around by somebody with an agenda was definitely one of them. He'd been nettled by the fact that Richard and his friend the military man had showed up this morning determined to rush the motion through because they were sure they had the majority. No doubt Richard had already crossed off this matter and was anxious to get to the next item on his list of things to do today.

Well, he'd just have to wait. If he kept going like that, stress would kill him before he turned sixty. So, really, Raymond was doing him a favor. Besides, the older man was reluctant to hurry a decision that could affect the life of a young pastor he didn't even know. True, Howard had brought him and Elliot up to speed on the important data, being careful not to slant the evidence in favor of Jason, (though his opinion was crystal clear by his body language). Still, it was important to hear everything in a case that could have such serious consequences.

It was just like Richard and his pals to push through a vote and not even ask the person in question to speak for himself. He remembered with great remorse being a party to such unfortunate actions himself back in the day. Stanley Ko had often pushed him into a corner. Which was no reason Raymond should allow his grandson to do the same thing.

It was a shame, really. Richard hadn't been a bad kid. Always saw things black and white, of course, he had that in his genes, but when he was younger he was pleasant enough. Back then, he'd had his mother's influence to balance out the negatives.

Raymond stopped for a moment by a wooden bench at the end of the courtyard remembering Laura Ko sitting there, smiling to the crowds of people that always seemed to surround her. A lovely and beloved woman, her husband and children adored her, as had the church. When she died, a light went out in the whole community; the family had never been the same since.

After his wife's death, Richard's father moved to Kauai, leaving the children to the care of his own father, Stanley. It had ruined them. It had brought to the fore all the negative characteristics young Richard had possessed as he strived to imitate his grandfather, and it had driven the sister to an early and unhappy marriage. Stanley's dominating personality controlled Richard in his early adolescence, but when he came of age, the young man chose medical school rather than seminary.

"Brother Stan" refused to speak to his grandson after that and remained aloof even to his death. A shame really. But still, Richard was now as he was, and it did him no good to think that he could have everything his way all the time.

Entering the administration building, Raymond noticed the young man he had seen earlier still in the same position, sitting in a dark corner, all alone, waiting. Raymond shuffled over and sat down beside him. He introduced himself and handed Jason a cone sushi. He could tell this item wasn't on the youngster's normal menu and was amused to see that he eyed it suspiciously. But Raymond was also pleased to see that the young man had good manners. He unwrapped the snack and ate it as though he really enjoyed it.

Midway through, Jason had asked if it was really okay for them to be having this conversation. It wasn't unethical or anything, was it? He wanted to make sure. But Raymond, old enough to be his grandfather, assured him that they would not talk business. And they didn't. They talked about Nancy, because a man's wife was important to know about. (You could tell a lot about a man by the way he talked about his wife). They also talked about the seemingly infinite varieties of See's Candy, which Raymond Sato maintained was the best in the world.

Twenty-five minutes had passed by the time Jason Price opened the door and followed Mr. Sato inside Pastor Martin's office. To judge by Richard's expression, you would have thought it had been an hour. The soldier didn't seem too happy either, but Clayton, Howard and Jeff Martin were talking comfortably as if enjoying the opportunity for a long chat.

"I brought this young fellow in with me," Raymond explained as Elliot helped him to his seat.

"About time," Ko muttered under his breath as he would never be overtly disrespectful to the older man.

There was not a vacant chair, and it looked as though Jason would have to speak standing, but Howard found another collapsible one and opened it. Jason sat down.

"I think you know everyone here," Pastor Martin began.

"He probably doesn't know me," Elliot Kam said and introduced himself.

Then Martin continued, "Now Jason, perhaps you'd like to tell these gentlemen, just exactly what happened in your office a couple of weeks ago that has caused such a stir."

"Make it short," Ko barked.

"Oh take your time," Raymond laughed. "I'm in no hurry now. But speak up, will you? I'm a little hard of hearing," he pointed to his left ear and grimaced. "Too much wax."

Clayton laughed. The others smiled. Except for Richard who gritted his teeth.

The junior pastor looked very well this morning. His hair was combed nicely, his aloha shirt and Dockers matched, and behind the froggie glasses, his eyes were clear. More than that, he seemed at ease, given the circumstances, and when he spoke, it was with disarming honesty and complete openness.

He began by thanking everyone for allowing him to come and talk with them. And then he did exactly as Pastor Martin had advised: he started with the date and the approximate time, and he told his narrative as thoroughly and succinctly as he could.

"I want to admit, right up front," he said, after his summary, "that I got carried away with Hazel's problems. It just didn't enter my head to think about the possible ramifications of meeting an emotional young woman in my office, alone. After all, there was a glass panel in the wall, and I honestly never thought things could get out of hand—what happened was totally unexpected!" He swallowed and shook his head. "I haven't had a whole lot of experience in formal counseling," he admitted. "But I see now that even so, I was foolish." He thought a second. "Naïve, I guess you'd say."

He hesitated, gathering his thoughts, then continued by telling the elders that he could see now, looking back, that he should have spoken to his superior at once. He made it clear that Dr. Martin was always available, if humanly possible, to see anyone on staff. It was Jason's fault alone that the two of them didn't get together about the matter. He admitted that it was his pride that had held him back. He didn't want Pastor Martin to see that he had made a mistake.

"Of course hindsight is always 20/20, but the thing is, I should have swallowed my pride, but I didn't. And then there were consequences. Now, I know that you elders have a right to punish me in some way. I deserve that. Actions do have consequences, even foolish actions. And,

I'm willing to accept a punishment. But," he stopped here and looked from face to face, "I honestly don't think I deserve to lose my pastorate over this.

"I've learned a very hard lesson. Obviously, I will do my utmost to make sure nothing like this happens again. I know Pastor Martin will help me. He's told me as much. Mentor me, you know. And I'm asking you to take this into consideration. What happened was very unfortunate, but what I've learned will stand me in good stead in the future. In fact, with Dr. Martin's help and the help of all of you, I know I can grow and improve and eventually be the pastor you expect me to be. And I'll work at it 150%. You can count on that. Well…I guess that's all." He sat down and breathed deeply.

Howard and Martin seemed well satisfied, but Richard and Mike, predictably, had several points to make, some of them quite blunt. Mike began by saying that Jason might be tempted to think that because he thought he had done nothing actually wrong, he should not be penalized by losing his job. However, the term nothing wrong was open to debate, and it didn't take anybody with a degree in rocket science to figure out that you shouldn't take a woman in your arms who isn't your wife! Whether anybody can see or not. "It just is not done! Because there are consequences!" He shrugged as if to say, *any idiot can see that.*

Richard spoke up and delivered a diatribe against using youth or inexperience as an excuse for bad behavior. "It is true," he said, winding down, " as you have admitted yourself, Mr. Price, that you didn't have a great deal of formal training in counseling when you were hired to do a job that required experience in that area. And that is regrettable. Actually, I'll be honest with you here, that is the church's fault." And here he glared at Jefferson Martin.

"Because, if we had followed policy, the Elder Board would have reviewed your application before you were hired. There is a reason that the Elder Board has always had the final say in ministerial appointments in the past. We look at other things besides good grades," he said pointedly. "We look at the maturity of the person."

"Which is why we never hire a pastor under the age of fifty," Howard groaned to himself, but said nothing.

At last, after allowing Mike and Richard to blow off a bit more steam, Pastor Martin stood up. "Well, if that's all," he said, "Jason and I will wait in the hall. Thank you for listening to both of us." He left and Jason followed him out.

"Before we vote," Mike said to those who were left, "I still want to make it clear that I believe a fair alternative has been offered to Price. The demotion doesn't need to last long. After counseling and re-training, he is welcome, as has been stated before, to candidate for upcoming positions."

"It's not like we're kicking him out," Richard said. "We are simply taking a decisive action so that the entire community will know where we stand on this sort of thing. "

"No tolerance!" Ernest said, jerking his eyes from face to face.

Elliot nodded to Richard and Mike. "So let's vote."

A written ballot, prepared by Richard Ko, was handed around. The men reached for the pens that had been set out for them. Ernest and Raymond put on their glasses, and a great silence fell over the room.

It took only a few minutes for everyone to cast his vote. Howard collected them and, as a courtesy, handed them to Raymond Sato, the eldest man present. Raymond looked at them for a moment as though he didn't quite know what to do with them, but then he gathered them in his gnarled fingers and looked around. "Is there a clerk here?" he asked in a quavering voice.

Don Webber stood up. "Here," he said.

"Okay," Raymond said. "I guess you need to record this." Then, carefully reading each document in turn, Raymond stated Yea or Nay revealing a vote for or against each of the two motions before the board. Even to Clayton, it seemed to take forever.

In the end, Raymond voiced what they all knew. He read, "The motion to remove Jason Price from the pastorate at Aloha Community Church for reasons of impropriety, and place him in another position, has been defeated by a vote of four to three."

"Furthermore," he continued, "the second clause about placing a letter of censure in his file has also been defeated. Now, does anyone want to say anything?" he looked around the table.

Howard spoke up. "One thing that hasn't been decided. Does the letter of allegation remain in the file?"

"Well, I would think so," Richard thundered. "Although it's a poor substitute for the letter of censure which should be placed there.

Remember, the letter of allegation simply states that charges were brought against him. The letter of censure would have stated that he had been found guilty of the impropriety even if there didn't seem to be any penalty."

"Which doesn't seem right to me. There has to be some penalty," Mike Dunn interjected angrily.

"I think there has been!" Howard protested. "The whole church knows that this young man came before the Elder Board today, and many of them know why. I think that is quite enough."

"Well I don't," Ko said stubbornly.

A heated discussion ensued for nearly twenty minutes during which time Mike Dunn demanded that *some* sort of penalty be given, and suggested that a fine could be considered, at the very least, or even reducing Price's salary during the time he was suspended. This just served to exasperate Howard who said that the letter in Price's file *was* the penalty, plus the embarrassment he faced by appearing before the board. But Mike waved him away demanding more.

Mr. Kam then spoke up. He admitted that additional punitive measures could be put forward if somebody really insisted on it, but then he stated flat out, "Honestly, Mike. I don't think you'll find the votes here to push the matter through." And that ended that.

"Now here's what I think," Elliot summarized. "The letter stays in Price's file as is, showing the allegations that were brought against him with an addendum as to how the board voted on the matter. I think that is sufficient." He looked at every face, his lips clamped shut as if to defy anyone to disagree with him.

But Mike Dunn could not take this dictum without protest. "That's how the vote turned out, but it's not unanimous by any means, " he complained.

"Then change the rules," Elliot shot back. "In the meantime, the vote stands."

"Very well," Richard said after a tense moment. He had done some quick thinking and decided that pressing forward on the matter was accomplishing nothing except alienating Kam who was becoming stubbornly defensive. So he took a deep, calming breath, and made a decision to salvage what he could.

"There do not seem to be enough votes to sustain measures that some of us think appropriate," he said carefully. "So, the letter stands, but I want one stipulation. That letter must be forwarded, with other pertinent information, to every prospective employer Price contacts in the future and who comes to us for references."

Elliot looked from face to face. Howard, Clayton and Raymond nodded in the affirmative They had expected something like this from Ko and were prepared for it, but Mike was still not through.

"So, in effect, after putting us through all of this, after causing who knows how much grief throughout the congregation, Price is going to get a slap on the wrist?"

"The letter in his file is the penalty," Howard repeated stubbornly, "and the fact that he was brought before this board!"

Mike was not happy, but after exchanging a look with Richard, he shrugged, admitting defeat and the official proceedings ended. Howard left to inform Jason and Martin of the verdict. The others stood up, preparing to leave. Just then, Clayton Kobata spoke up. "Just a minute," he said. "I have something I want to say." He turned to the Elliot and Raymond. "I need to talk to these guys for just a second. Something kind of private. Do you mind?"

Both Raymond and Elliot were anxious to get over to the missions conference anyway. They waved goodbye to everyone and walked out. Clayton turned to the others. "I'm going to ask Pastor Martin and Jason Price to come back in and I'd appreciate it if you'd just wait a minute."

"Is this necessary?" Mike looked around.

"Absolutely," Clayton assured him. "Just a sec'." He went into the hall.   A moment later he came back with Howard, Martin, and Jason who looked a little confused.

"Mr. Kobata!" Richard Ko thundered, not for the first time, "I have an important meeting, and I have to leave immediately!"

"I am only asking for a few minutes."

"Sorry, I don't have even…"

"I'll make you this guarantee," Clayton said in a solemn voice. "I'm going to show you something right now and if you look at it and tell me it is unimportant, then by all means, go ahead and walk out the door. Agreed?"

"No." Ko began gathering his things.

"Let's give him two minutes by the clock," Howard said. "I think we can all spare that."

Pastor Martin sat down and so did Howard. Ernest sat as well. He sensed something brewing and didn't want to miss out on it. Mike and Richard exchanged an exasperated look, but remained standing.

"Clayton, you're on the clock. Two minutes. We've had a long morning," Howard warned.

This will only take a second," Clayton said, "but it's highly confidential and very important."

Howard was surprised. What could be so extremely important? Especially now that the matter with Jason Price had been taken care of.

Clayton looked from face to face. "I really hate to do this," he said. "But I want you to know, I have no choice. Clayton reached inside a large manila envelope and carefully removed a few a few items. His fingers trembled slightly and his eyes were dark. He walked over to each man and handed him a sheet of paper, face down. "All of these photographs are the same," he said.

Jason turned his over, took one look at the picture, and felt his stomach go into a sudden spasm so intense he thought for a second he was going to be sick. He stared at the photo as if he were looking at the end of the world. After a second, he tore his eyes away and looked up at Clayton as if to say, "Is this some kind of joke?" but the young man refused to meet his gaze.

Howard and Martin exchanged worried glances. Even Mike frowned deeper than usual and Richard looked up from his copy of the photo with eyes blazing.

Jason returned his unwilling eyes to the picture in his shaking hands, still unwilling to believe what was laid out before him. There he was, froggie glasses, lime shirt, red suspenders and all, looking with absolute adoration at a young lady. In fact, his arms were outstretched as though he was about to embrace her. The lady, although seen from the back, was easily recognizable by her height, her billowy blond hair and distinctive black and white purse. The two were standing in the lobby of a second rate hotel clearly identified by a sign to one side.

"What does this mean?" he turned to Pastor Martin in horror.

"You tell us!" Ernest demanded.

Chapter Thirty-five

"The thing about this photograph that you'll want to notice is the date at the lower left hand side," Clayton instructed. He looked over at Jason, but avoided his eyes. "Pastor J, I don't know any other way to do this. I'm really sorry, but I'm going to have to ask you this question: Were you at this place on this date?"

"I—I—" Jason stuttered. "I don't even know what day of the week this is!"

"Let me help you," the young elder said, with a deep regret. "Because I think we will all agree that this date is important. This day is the second day you were suspended. And we all know for a fact that you were not at church. As far as anyone knows, you weren't meeting with anybody from the church. So, where were you?"

"Well, I guess I was home," Jason said in wonder.

"Were you home the entire day?"

"To be really honest, I don't really remember what I did that day. I may have gone out for a walk. Wait a minute, I went to the store. I remember now. I bought milk."

"Anybody see you there?"

"I-I don't know." Jason stopped. Except for the brief trip to the store on one day, he had been home alone each of the days of his suspension. The store had been crowded. No one, to his knowledge, would remember seeing him there.

"So, you are saying that you can't tell us anything about where you were or what you did that entire day?" Clayton continued relentlessly. Howard was about to interrupt when Jason turned blazing eyes on the young elder.

"I was home!" Jason said angrily. "I wasn't exactly in the best frame of mind that week, okay? I wasn't exactly anxious to meet people who would ask questions I didn't want to answer. So, I stayed home. I went to the store at some point, but I can't tell you the exact day."

"So…on the day this picture was taken, you could have been… anywhere…?"

"Just a minute!" Martin spoke up. "This makes so sense. Why would Jason be seen in a hotel of all places with Miss Townsend *after* all the trouble started?"

"Pictures, don't lie," Richard said. Hardly believing his eyes, he absently pulled out a chair and sat down.

Howard looked closely at the photo. The evidence was damning, that was for sure. An unsubstantiated rumor was one thing, but here was evidence in living color. He looked at Jason and shook his head. "I don't believe it," he said.

"I'm awfully sorry," Clayton continued. "But it's right here before your eyes. And…I checked the dates myself."

Mike Dunn ran his fingers through his military haircut. He scrutinized the photo closely but said nothing. It was clear that he didn't know what to say.

Ernest was beside himself. "I told you where there's smoke there's fire," he gloated, under his breath.

Martin looked up. "I agree with Howard," he said determinedly. "I just don't believe it."

There was an embarrassed silence as one man looked at the other.

"Did you send these pictures to anyone else?" Martin demanded.

"Only the people in this room," Clayton said, deliberately remaining calm.

Richard cleared his throat. "I think this throws a new light on everything," he said, although a little reluctantly. "I think we need to…"

"We need to do nothing. It's a hoax!" Howard cried. He turned to Clayton, "And where did you get…"

But Mike interrupted, still looking very closely at the photo. "I

don't think so," he said thoughtfully. "I've seen composites before. "
He looked up. "This seems genuine."

"That's Hazel Townsend, that's for sure," Ernest said excitedly.
"Even from the back you can tell. That purse!"

"Well I'm not convinced." Howard would not be swayed.

"Neither am I," Martin agreed.

"Well I am," Ernest said. "Look at it!"

"Okay," Clayton looked from Howard to Martin. "I thought
perhaps that might be enough, but I see that it isn't."

"You mean there's more?" Ernest's mouth dropped open.

Clayton shook his head. "I wish I could say no. Believe me, this
is really painful, but I have to do it. So…" He reached in the envelope
and pulled out more papers. "I guess I'll have to give you these." Once
again, He handed one paper to each man personally. The papers were
printed copies of an e-mail from Jason to Helen Townsend. Everything
was perfectly in order, the addresses, the date, everything. The e-mail
read,

"Darling Hazel.
Can't wait until we meet again. Love your kisses and want
much much more.
Your frustrated lover,
Jason

Jason looked as though he were about to burst into tears. There was
absolute silence in the room.

"I saw the original of this e-mail myself," Clayton said. "and if you
want me to, I can pull it up on the church's computer."

"That won't be necessary," Howard said, staring in shock at the
printed words in his hands.

A minute passed as the men digested this new information. On
each face several emotions passed: disbelief, anger, certainty, indecision,
resignation. Even Mike seemed puzzled and clueless.

Then, Pastor Martin got up from his seat, and walked slowly over
to Clayton. He pulled out a chair, turned it backwards, and sat facing
the younger man. "Okay," he said with a twinkle in his eye, "How did
you do it?"

"Do what?" Clayton tried to look innocent.

"The photos, the e-mail."

"I don't know what you mean," Clayton protested.

"The game is up. Confess."

"Shoots! I knew the e-mail would be a little over the top," Clayton grinned.

"A little. And you'd better explain before poor Jason passes out," Martin said.

"Explain! Well I should think he'd better explain!" Mike sputtered.

"Of all the…" Richard Ko could hardly find the words to articulate his displeasure.

"Okay, okay," Clayton paused and threw up one hand as if to deflect the unspoken anger directed against him. "Here's the deal. I have a friend who's a computer pro. He has access to all the latest equipment. He put together the composite in, like, no time. Look closely, you can't spot a flaw."

"I told you," Mike said defensively. "It looks genuine."

"But why," Howard asked. "Why on earth did you…"

"And if you traced the date back, in the left hand corner, you would find that it does really correspond to one of the days Pastor Jason was suspended. I heard, from several people, that he just stayed home and refused to see anybody. But of course, that couldn't be proved…in a court of law," he turned to Mike.

"But Clayton," Jason said, color returning to his face, "Am I really looking at Hazel Townsend… like this?" He held up his copy of the picture.

Clayton grinned a little wider. "Actually, that was taken at the Christmas banquet. Miss Elsie came over to you with a present. You were reaching for it." Miss Elsie, at ninety-two, was one of the oldest and most beloved members of the church.

Jason shook his head. His mind was still reeling.

"So it was easy to take that and add a picture of Hazel I found in the candids our church photographer, Millie, regularly keeps on file. It shows Hazel outside the sanctuary."

"But the light. The shadows. They're perfect," Mike was annoyed, but intrigued.

"I told you my friend was good. By the way, Pastor Jason, sorry for the scare."

"Are you kidding?" Howard said, "Heart attacks have been induced with less provocation!"

"I'm really sorry, Mr. Nakata," Clayton was sincere. "But I didn't know any other way to..."

Ernest interrupted. "You played a joke on us? *The elders of the church!*" he squeaked "Why?"

"Because," Clayton patiently explained. "Digital photographs are easy to fix. And, if you want to know the truth, if I had tried, I could have made sure that the e-mail from Jason to Hazel really did originate in the computer at his home! And that's without even going to a whole lot of trouble! Hey, it's a whole new world," he said. "Information can be manipulated. So, who ya gonna believe when a picture or an e-mail goes around about one of *you* guys?"

"You wouldn't dare!" Richard walked over, his face turned purple. He did everything but shake his fist at the young man.

"Nah, not me. I wouldn't do anything like that. But think about it, you tick anybody off, and they could. And evidence does hold up."

"Well I for one am fed up with this entire business," Richard said in a venomous voice, sitting back down like a king on this throne. "Falsifying documents! Handing around incendiary material." He looked at Mike for support. Mike threw up his hands and turned away. Ko turned to Clayton. "Now you listen here, Mister Kobata, it is my personal opinion, and I'm sure others will agree, that you do not possess the maturity to be an elder! I am going to institute proceedings..."

"See," Clayton sat up straight. "That's it! That's just why I did it. Look, I don't care. Being an elder isn't what it's cracked up to be by a long shot. If you want me out, I'm gone Dr. Ko, I know that. But before I go, here's what I'm going to say. From what I can see that's what you guys always do, you always want to blame somebody, punish somebody, haul out the rule book and hit people over the head with it."

"Ridiculous!" Richard spat.

"I've been raised up in this church; I've heard about that kind of thing my whole life. Yet, when Mr. Nakata asked me to be an elder, I thought why not. I'll see for myself, although my grandmother was dead set against it. And after two years, this is what I see. I see that we're divided on just about everything, we're angry with each other, and some people always want to get their own way." He held up one hand again. "Not naming names here. But here's the question I ask myself. How can we hear from God like that?"

"Well," Richard said sarcastically. "What would you, in your infinite youthful wisdom, have us do? Ignore the just rules of the church altogether?"

Clayton looked from one man to the other, searching each face, and then he said, "Well, for one thing, how about if we learned to trust each other?"

As Richard and Mike stormed out of the room, and Pastor Martin headed off to another appointment, Howard looked with affection at the young man who had just spoken: so young, so full of passion and idealism. Unfortunately, it wasn't quite as simple as that, he thought ruefully. True, some of the hasty rulings that had been pushed through the board in the past were regrettable. That he knew only too well. However, there had been other occasions, when Bible boundaries had been crossed, and decisive action had to be taken. Still, he had to admit, Clayton had a viable point, and they would be very foolish to ignore it.

But then, they'd often been foolish.

Clayton apologized to Jason once again for putting him through the ringer. But Jason just shook his head, "It's a good thing I have a strong heart," he laughed. "Man, you really had me going!"

The two young men left together, talking animatedly. Howard turned off the lights and locked the door behind them.

Chapter Thirty-six

Friday, June 4th, 7:00 pm

The small group members, Chris, Marge, Yumi and Pua, stood in the driveway, refreshments in hand. Yumi said she had e-mailed everybody, but Norman was the only one who hadn't answered. Marge wondered if maybe he had gotten confused about the change of location.

" No way," Yumi assured them. "I sent a voice message to his work and his home and earlier today I even text messaged his cell. Maybe he'll turn up later. Oh look, there's Rhoda. Let's go."

Rhoda was standing in the doorway of her Kailua home; beside her was a tall man everyone assumed was Ed. They had invited everyone to their house tonight so that they could see the "big reveal," the redecorating miracle the family had created in the living room while Rhoda had been sent off to spend last weekend with her sister.

"I guess we're also going to have a regular group meeting tonight, because when I talked with Pastor Jason on the phone, he said he had some things he wanted to tell us," Yumi said, turning up the winding path that led to the front steps.

"Not bad news, I hope!" Marge said. Although Pastor Jason had returned to work, whatever had transpired in the elder's meeting was evidently top secret because not a single word had leaked out, and the group members were concerned.

"He seemed cheerful enough when I saw him at church on Tuesday," Yumi said, over her shoulder. "Oh hi, Rhoda!"

"Come in, come in!" Rhoda smiled happily as the group walked through the door and kicked off their footwear in the foyer. "Oh, this is Ed." She turned to the tall man dressed in cargo shorts and a red and white striped polo shirt who towered behind her. Everyone said hi to Ed.

"Well," he grinned a little nervously, "here come the judges."

"Oh no, not at all!" Marge protested. "I'm sure it will be just fine." And then the four gazed over at the room straight ahead, and a big smile formed on each face.

"Oh, this is nice!" Yumi exclaimed. "Really nice!" Tonight she wore shorts and a soft blue patterned top. The stern business look was gone.

Everyone agreed, the room was magnificent.

"Come on in," Ed said, "Here, let me take those. I set out ice in the cooler." He grabbed the six packs of soda that Chris had brought and charged into the room.

"No, wait a minute. Don't you folks go in," Rhoda said. "Kristen wants to play TV host and take you through the makeover step by step. Let me take the food. Oh, thanks Marge. The two of them carried the food to a table in the back of the room, then Rhoda rushed back to answer the front door bell. Pastor Jason and Nancy stood there with two large brown paper bags of food.

Rhoda took the bags, hugged her guests, and everyone introduced themselves. Then, Kristen, age 8, and Travis, age 10, ran in. "I'm going to be like Candice Olsen on the TV show," Kristen said proudly. "'cause I want to be a decorator when I grow up." She resembled her mother a great deal: dark hair, olive complexion, huge smile, and huge personality.

"Go for it," Ed encouraged.

"Okay!" Kristen beamed. She walked on the tips of her toes to the center of the room, and turned around gracefully to face the guests. "First, to the right" she said with a sweep of one small arm," I want to show you this really lovely sofa. It has great colored stripes like green and blue. What's the green called, Mom?"

"Chartreuse."

"Right," Kristen grinned. "Shartrooz, and the yellow pillows? They call them accents," she added.

Travis, tall and fair like his dad, spoke up. "She picked the sofa out, and then the lady at the store said we had to get everything to go with it! I wanted green and brown but…"

"But that was really boring!" Kristen glared at her brother. "So," she turned brightly to the guests once again. "We had the sofa and then the lady said we should get these nice blue chairs." She walked around the room and pointed to them. "And the really nice yellow cushions, and this cool TV thingy…"

"Etagere," Rhoda said, pointing to a unit in gleaming maple wood.

"Right. And the lamps and all, and if you look up, you can see the other lamp thingy."

"Chandelier," Ed said. To his guests he added, "Cut glass. Don't even ask how much."

"And then, over here, we have Dad's place," she gestured left.

"Ed's R and R station, " Ed said proudly, pointing to the Laz-E-Boy rocker that now sported a fresh yellow pillow flanked by a green floor lamp.

"And now, back here…" Kristen said.

Travis interrupted. "Wait a minute, you need to talk about the walls. I picked out the color and painted them all by myself." His dad coughed discreetly. "Well, just about!"

The walls were beige. And everyone agreed they were beautiful. Evidently the white curtains at the windows were Ed's idea and he took credit for those. "I don't suppose anybody's noticed the floor," he said. "Talk about costing a bundle. But…" he shrugged. "The guy at the store said hard wood really does pay for itself in the long run." Everyone agreed that it probably did.

The next part of the tour took them to the back of the room where a rectangular table, under a second chandelier, could, as Rhoda explained (Kristen had tired of being host by now and danced off to the kitchen to get the cupcakes) be used for any number of things. Bible study, scrapbooking, bridge, you name it. The wide assortment of accessories in the room was eclectic (purple flowers, purple table lamps, white and blue bookshelves that held a great assortment of objects, besides books, that looked very much like the collection of school and church crafts most parents collect over the years).

Everyone agreed; the whole room looked like something right out of a magazine.

"You did a great job, Ed," Marge said. "Put those floors in yourself?"

"No way. I'm not that handy. But if I could have, it would have brought the cost way down. You have any idea what those guys charge for installation?" he whistled under his breath. "Let me tell you, I'm in the wrong line of work."

"So, now that it's over, was it worth all the trouble?" Jason wanted to know.

Ed said that, all things considered, it probably was. He looked over at a beaming Rhoda and it was easy to see why he felt that way. Then he and Travis headed off to the garage to bring in extra chairs. After that Ed said if no one minded, he'd watch TV upstairs, and he and his son went out.

As she was handing out glasses with ice, Rhoda explained that the whole thing had turned out surprisingly well. Ed still had his chair. Kristen could have her gerbil zoo in her room on a new, bigger table, and Travis was allowed to set up his drums in the garage.

"Of course, adding insulation so that the neighbors don't complain about the noise and putting in window fans so that Travis doesn't suffocate cost a fortune," Rhoda laughed, "and we can't park our cars there anymore, but…" she looked around. "I think it was a fair trade off."

"So, there was no pink after all?" Pua said, looking for something in her favorite color.

"There was nearly pink," Rhoda said wide-eyed. "On something called an accent wall—Ed saw that on TV. But, praise God, Kristen refused to paint it, and Travis (always practical, just like his dad) decided that he had to use up all of his beige paint. So, catastrophe was avoided. Oh, Krissy, put those cupcakes right here. I saved a space for them."

Conversation flowed easily after that. Nancy was pleasantly surprised to find out how easy Marge was to talk with. They discovered, among other things, that they had a dislike of exercise in common although both of them admitted they needed to drop a few pounds. While Chris talked to Rhoda about French class, which he was barely passing, Kristen showed Yumi a page from a magazine, now soiled with jam and juice spills, that she had originally wanted to use as a model for the living room. But Yumi said that for a great room her dad was probably right. Blue, green and beige was probably a better universal choice than red, yellow and white. Did Kristen ever think that maybe she could redecorate her own room in those other colors? Kristen said she hadn't but the idea was totally awesome.

The refreshments were delicious. Kristen's homemade cupcakes were lavishly praised. Then, after an hour or so, a circle was formed, and Jason started everything off with prayer. Then he said, "So, I'm sure you're all bursting with questions about my meeting with the elders last week, and I'd like to tell you what I can."

"We know some of it is confidential," Marge began, "but can you tell us if it turned out all right?"

"Could you tell us what it was actually about?" Chris asked. "I heard a few conflicting stories." He looked around. "I mean, is that okay to ask?"

"Yeah, 'cause we were worried. We been praying real hard," Pua added.

"I know you have," Jason smiled. "It got your note, by the way, and I appreciated your prayers. Okay," he thought a second. "You all know about the allegations that were brought against me. That's no secret. I told you about that myself, but the thing is, whenever that happens to anyone in leadership, the elders have to follow a process. They have to consider everything very seriously and try to get to the truth. And that's exactly what our elders did. They examined everything carefully to see what was fact and what was hearsay, and in the end they decided that the rumors were unfounded."

"Unfounded?" Pua looked around, puzzled.

"Untrue."

"Oh, that's good," she said, relieved. "'cause we all knew that already!" Everyone smiled.

"But, was it true that you could have lost your job even if the rumors were not true?" Chris asked.

Following a suggestion from Pastor Martin, who had anticipated that Jason might have to answer that question, Jason simply said that it was a non-issue as the rumors were found to be false. He said that everyone in a Christian body of believers had to be held accountable, and wouldn't everyone want that, really? It would do no good to let accusations go unaddressed. As a matter of fact, that was the worst thing that could happen, because then no one would know the truth and they'd get themselves all upset trying to guess. "So really, despite the fact that it was uncomfortable for me, to say the least, it was much better that the questions got addressed head on."

"But I still don't get why they had to suspend you." Chris said. "I mean, that seemed a little...I dunno, hard."

"They simply wanted to sidestep an awkward situation by getting me out of the way for a bit," Jason said. "I think that's just the way this church handles things, and really, that's fine. Listen, in a large group of people like a church, there are bound to be misunderstandings. You've got to expect that; wherever there are people, there are human problems. In fact, if you go way back to the early church you'll find that they had all *kinds* of problems. There were factions back then as well, and slanderous accusations that caused heartache and bitterness. There was out and out heresy, and men with a lust for power misused Christianity for their own purposes. Still, through it all, the church not only survived, it flourished. The Word went forth and took root and now, the gospel of Truth has been preached to nearly the entire world." He paused a second, then said. "I think it's important for us to consider that the church is not now, nor has it ever been perfect, but it is a place where the Spirit of God does His work, and..." He threw up his hands, "Oh look at me preaching a sermon! Don't get me started. We'll be here all night." Everyone smiled. "Well, anyway. I'm back to work, and things are back to normal. So...any other questions before we get to our lesson?"

"Is it true that a neighbor of Miss Lottie's is the one who threw the blood on her step? It was animal blood, right?" Chris wanted to know the facts; he'd heard enough rumors.

"It was animal blood mixed with some other ingredients," Jason said. "The police have a good idea who it was, but no charges have been filed."

"So, Miss Lottie moved back home?" Pua asked.

"I'm not sure where she's living now," Jason said. "But no further vandalism has been reported. So…" He looked from one face to the other, "any more questions?"

They all looked at each other. Each of them still had a question or two, that was clear by their expressions, but they were greatly relieved to see Pastor J back with them, smiling, and his wife Nancy right there beside him, and that was enough.

"Now, anything to share tonight?" He looked at Nancy. "We usually spend a little time at the beginning of our meetings talking about what's been happening in our lives." Jason turned back to the group, waiting for someone to start.

"Oh, try wait!" Pua turned to Nancy. "New people have to answer the four questions, right?"

Everyone laughed and turned to Nancy. "Questions?" she asked.

"Where you were born, occupation, something about your family, and how long you've been attending ACC," Yumi explained.

Nancy smiled and thought a second. "Okay, I'm Nancy, Jason's wife, and I was born and raised in Cedar Rapids, that's in Iowa. Um, I work at the Ocean Crest downtown and there's just Jason and me here in Oahu, though we both have family back home. What else? Oh, church. Well, I feel as though I've been at ACC a really *long* time," she laughed and everyone did the same.

"We've been looking forward to meeting you," Marge said.

"Well, I'm really glad to be here tonight. And I'll try to get off on Fridays when I can from now on. I know I've missed a lot of sessions, but Jason has been filling me in on some of the major things. For one thing, he told me all about that vision that you had, Rhoda. The man with the flashlight? And do you know what? Since I heard about it, I haven't been able to get it out of my mind." She stopped for a moment as if deciding what to say, then it was obvious she was going to be forthright.

"Look, you don't know me, but I don't believe in beating around the bush." She glanced from one face to another. "I don't want to go into all of it, but I'm sure you know that, as necessary as this process was, this has been a really hard time for Jason and me. It's been a real struggle in a lot of ways. But once I had that picture in my mind, Rhoda, I could see that the light and the truth really were working together. And the darkness was falling away, just as you described. Little by little. But enough. And that gave me a lot of comfort."

Everyone looked at her expectantly, but Nancy raised her hands, palms up, as if to say she could continue talking on the subject, but would rather not right now. Jason reached over and gave his wife's arm a squeeze.

Pua looked at Nancy. "My son's been having troubles," she said. "But everybody's been so good to pray for him. And I keep seeing that light shining, too. Right on him. He's learning. He's seeing things different now, I think. He's growing. Step by step he's climbing out of the darkness. I think it's all gonna turn out good in the end."

Next, it was Chris's turn. He said that the whole thing with the Chinaman really changed his life. One of the things that happened was that he wasn't living so randomly as before. "It's like I suddenly know I have a responsibility not to live just for myself. Not to be just thinking about my own problems. The night is coming, although we don't know when, and so I have to really think of other people and where they are. And what will happen if they don't find Jesus."

Everyone sat and thought about that for a while. Then Yumi spoke. She said that the light Rhoda talked about had become a very vivid picture to her also. "I think the light is focused on my heart," she said, "I haven't said a whole lot about my personal problems, because they're all just too complicated. But I think being in this group has changed my heart. It's made me see that, as people struggle to find answers, there is hope. I've been watching you guys during these past weeks when we have been studying about the Holy Spirit, and I can see that you are getting "illumination" I guess you would say, on your problems and it's bringing you a lot of peace and some happiness too. I'm not sure I'm there yet," she smiled. "But I have hope now that I didn't have before."

They all thought about this for a minute, then turned to Marge who, uncharacteristically, hadn't spoken up yet. "Gee," she said, "So much has happened in the past few weeks I don't know where to start. Okay, I'll start with prayer. I think that one thing I realized, through the group, is how important prayer is. I mean, we pray for each other every day—that was one of the rules of being in the group. And I know that's helped. I mean, sometimes, I can feel you guys' prayers."

"Me too," Jason said. "I've felt them lots of times in the last couple of weeks."

"And I thought, for a while, that the dreams..." she turned to Nancy. "You weren't here, but bottom line I had these dreams, about things that happened in my past life. But the endings of the dreams were not the way things really happened. The dreams ended in death, in one way or another. And I couldn't for the life of me figure out what that meant. And then in the middle of the night, not too long ago, I realized that if I was really honest with myself I would have to admit..." and here she took a long breath, " that when Danny died I did too."

She hesitated a moment, then continued. "My body kept going, but inside there was nothing. I even gave away my dog (and I really loved that dog) and bought an imitation one because I just didn't have the heart to give the real one the love and attention he needed. And then I came to this group—which I did *not* want to do, I can tell you. But looking back I can see that it was the Holy Spirit at work nudging me. So, I just had to come whether or not I wanted to.

"But I really loved you guys right from the beginning," she said, tears forming in her eyes. "This wasn't just a bunch of people sitting around reading out of a book. You guys had questions (she looked at Chris), and problems (she looked at Pua and Jason), and family stuff (she looked at Rhoda). And even you, Yumi, although you didn't say much, just by the way you asked questions during the lessons I could see that you were really searching for something."

"I still am," Yumi said.

"And then there was Norman who, beneath that act he puts on, had—what should I say-- issues?" Everybody smiled. "And whether or not I wanted to, I got involved. I got concerned. And all of this, little by little, dragged me out of my comfortable darkness. I look back now and I see it was like a grave, and I was just letting myself sink down into it. And I think that's what the dreams were telling me. They all ended in a death that wasn't real. And my wallowing in my own grave wasn't real either. In real life, whether I liked it or not, I was still alive. Does that make any sense?"

The group members nodded their heads, thinking.

"But there was another word that kept going around and around in my head, and that was the word *redemption*. It took lots of hours praying, but it finally dawned on me that God wants to redeem everything about us that isn't right, even, in some instances, our grief, if we will just let him. Because my grief was cutting me to pieces, I was drowning in it. Again, like what happened in the dreams.

"And I began to see that when we reach out to share in the sorrows of other people, that's how our own sorrow is redeemed. I've just started down that path," she shrugged, "but I am beginning to believe that's where God wants me to be, and I'm finally getting some peace through it all. And I too am so grateful for your prayers and concern through these last weeks. I think I'm making real progress."

All eyes turned on Jason. It was time for the lesson, and he took out a Bible and opened it carefully. "I've given a lot of thought to this week's lesson," he said, "which, if you will remember, began with the chapter on the gifts of the Holy Spirit in First Corinthians. In it, St. Paul gives an analogy. He talks about the fact that our own human body is made up of many parts and says that the body of Christ is composed of many parts in just the same way. And in Chapter 12, verse 26, we see that there should be no division in the body, but that its parts should have equal concern for each other. And here's the section I like best." He read, *If one part suffers, every part suffers with it, but if one part is honored,*" he looked up, "and here I think we can include the word blessed, *then every part rejoices with it.*

"A wise person at ACC told me, right in the middle of all my recent troubles, that I needed to look and see why God allowed events to unfold the way they did and what He was showing me through it all. And one of the things that came out of that introspection was God confirming to me once again the inestimable value of the local church.

"I believe with all my heart in the local church," he said earnestly, "Because, despite its flaws, it's a wonderful thing, designed by God himself. I mean, here we are," he looked around smiling, "living examples of what that means. A group of imperfect people, nudged by the Spirit of God in one way or another, to come out of ourselves and become a part of something larger, to share in each others lives, not just the good stuff, but all the uncertainty and fear and pain as well.

"We make mistakes. We get careless and do the wrong thing

sometimes, or we do nothing at all when we should act. But in Chapter 13, we see that the one redeeming factor in all of this is that through it all, if we let it, the love of God shines through us. That love changes us. It "rejoices in the Truth" within us. It protects and trusts and hopes and perseveres through all circumstances. It is God's wonderful gift to us and it's not only meant for us, but it's meant to flow through us to everyone we come in contact with.

"And that's what you've been for me," he said, gazing fondly from one face to another. At Pua Hoaeae, beaming under her cap of snowy white hair, at Marge smiling now from deep inside, at Yumi, calm and refreshed as though she had reached a decision of some kind and was at peace with it, at Chris's broad friendly face, cheeks red from the sun, and Rhoda's eager smile. "You, and many other wonderful people at ACC, and Nancy too, of course," he smiled at his wife, "have been the body of Christ for me through the last few weeks. You've stood with me through everything, never giving up, always hoping for the best, never losing faith. I wish Norman were here, because in his way, he stood with me as well. I can't tell you how much I appreciate your prayers and all the ways you showed your support. It meant a lot. It showed me that I was not alone." He hesitated, then smiled. "And that's the way it's supposed to be. We are never supposed to have struggle alone. That's what the body is for."

"Okay, I don't know how to end this," he admitted, laughing. "I guess I'll just end by saying thank you. But please believe me, I mean it from my heart. I love you very much, and I'm very grateful to you all."

"And we love you too, Pastor Jason," Pua cried, tears streaming down her face. She turned to the others, "Hey! Anybody got Kleenex?"

One Year Later

Aloha Community Church continues to prosper under **Dr. Martin's** excellent leadership. The Peacemakers Conference was a success, and during it, significant strides were taken in restoring fractured relationships in the church. Church growth is up. ACC will soon institute a third service. This one, a youth service, will be held on Saturday nights, much to Howard Nakata's satisfaction. Martin continues to work closely with the elders, including two new recruits in their thirties, and it can be confidently stated that trust is developing between the pastors and elders of the church. **Clayton** **Kobata** never misses a meeting.

However, in a move that surprised everyone, especially those who had heard him say they'd have to carry him out feet first before he'd resign from the Elder Board, **Dr. Richard Ko** did, in fact, resign. Evidently, his daughter's demands on his time, as she prepares to serve in public office, were so extensive he had no choice. The board is in good shape, however. When Howard's term as chairman expires, Elliot Kam will step in. Raymond Sato has already bought a big box of Sees Chocolates which he plans to present to his friend at the unofficial swearing in.

Jason Price served out his year at ACC, but after Christmas he and Nancy moved back to Springfield. The church gave the Prices a lavish going away party at the Ocean Crest downtown. Jason was heartened to see that many were sincerely sorry to see him go. However, as he explained to Pastor Martin, he really felt the need for more training before he tried for the pastorate again. And even though Nancy was making friends with some wonderful people here, they both missed family at home.

Back in Springfield, Jason was offered an administrative post at Our Savior which had just, (miraculously), come open. Dr. Cooper, however, is mentoring him with a view to Jason's taking a pastoral position in the future. Nancy is attending Sunday school regularly and likes it. She has also enrolled in the distance learning program at the seminary.

Marge Givens has become good friends with **Helen Chang** and is very much involved with the intercessors group. With the help of Helen, Irene Baines, and Raymond Sato, Marge formed a committee of visitors to the hospitals and the homebound. After her initial uncertainty, she was amazed to see how well that progressed.

In January, she put her house up for sale and was surprised to discover that she had a buyer in less than a month. She now lives close to her friend Linda who, among other things, makes sure Marge works out more than once a month. Marge also bought a puppy whom she named Flashlight (Flash for short). He has brought her great joy.

At the end of June, **Norman Stern** decided to go back to the east coast. Before he left, he invited Marge out for a dinner date. She said she'd love the dinner but not the date. He said in that case she could pay for her own meal. She did, and lectured him the whole time about why, when he moved, he should be sure to find a local church and attend regularly. Norman shook his head, but listened obediently.

Pua's son, Larry, is doing well in these hard economic times. He has picked up a part- time job as well as his regular one; both he and his mother are trusting that God has something really special in store for him and his family, at just the right time.

Rhoda and **Ed** now host a small group in the newly staged area of their home. Kristen has redecorated her room in all the colors she likes best, and is over the moon.

In January, **Christopher Murray** quit school and joined an international para-church missionary organization. After a three-month training course, he headed out with a team that is traveling up and down the west coast of the US. So far, over a hundred souls have been won to

Christ. He still prays for Mei Ling regularly and has written to her twice. She answered with one very polite postcard in which she wished him well in his new life. He does not know if he will write back.

Yumi Furubayashi and her husband, who were separated, have been attending counseling sessions with Dr. Lum. They sit together at the second service on Sundays now, and go out to lunch together afterwards. All of Yumi's friends have remarked about how happy she's been looking these days, and it is true.

Howard Nakata was forced to retire from the firm where he had worked for so long. However, he was eagerly snatched up by another corporation nearly at once. Although he is required to work many extra hours and nearly every holiday, Howard is content. On the rare occasions when he gets a day off, he and Clayton go fishing.

Susan Anello moved back to L.A. for a while but, predictably, it did not work out. She is back in Oahu sharing an apartment with her good friend Kristine. She has just finished Cleansing Stream at ACC and declares that it was so life changing, it was well worth the wait. She has also become good friends with Helen Chang.

Miss Lottie has rented out her house in Kalihi and has moved in with her sister in Ewa Beach, and often attends her sister's church there. She maintains that ACC has changed too much these days for her liking. She and **Lillian Nakata** are no longer close friends as Lilian never returns Miss Lottie's calls. Miss Lottie says she can't understand it. She has always been nothing but kindness itself to everyone, including Lillian.

After giving the matter careful consideration, **Hazel Townsend** decided not to return to teaching in the fall. At the moment she is deciding on her next career move. In January, to the surprise of everyone but Pastor Martin, she joined Lawrence and Carol Sizemore's small group. She says the Sizemores have turned out to be "surprisingly understanding."

Comparing notes with other small group leaders at the end of June, Lawrence was pleased to see that, except for a couple of hitches, they had all gone well. Several significant answers to prayer had been reported and that was encouraging. Pastor Martin is sending Lawrence to the mainland for further training in how to develop healthy small groups.

Ernest Cooke is furious about the "waste of church finances," and is surreptitiously sending around a petition in protest. So far, the only one to sign it has been Gladys Hirai.

Mrs. Fujihara now has an excellent small apartment for rent in Manoa. But be careful before you let your friends know about it; some people say it's haunted.